PAPA'S WIFE

The warm and inspiring novel by the author of
Mama's Way

"In these pages, one can smell the fresh pine boughs in Lapland, and sense the gaiety of the summer midnight sun which makes up so adequately for the dark winters. One can feel the confusions that arise when a family emigrates . . . A charming book."

The New York Times

"A warmth, a human and vital understanding that command the love of the reader . . . Friendly, entertaining, rich with wisdom and bright with engaging comedy."

Christian Science Monitor

"Genuine and true. Rich in wisdom and gaiety, in strength and spirit . . . A gentle, heart-lifting tale which will enliven your hours and quicken your spirit."

Boston Herald

PAPA'S WIFE
BY THYRA FERRÉ BJORN

BANTAM BOOKS
TORONTO · NEW YORK · LONDON

*This low-priced Bantam Book
has been completely reset in a type face
designed for easy reading, and was printed
from new plates. It contains the complete
text of the original hard-cover edition.*
NOT ONE WORD HAS BEEN OMITTED.

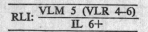

RLI: VLM 5 (VLR 4–6)
IL 6+

PAPA'S WIFE
A Bantam Book / *published by arrangement with
Holt, Rinehart and Winston, a division of CBS, Inc.*

PRINTING HISTORY
*Holt, Rinehart edition published September 1955
17 printings through February 1965*
Christian Herald Family Bookshelf edition published October 1955
Books Abridged edition published 1956
Portions of this book appeared in
MENNONITE WEEKLY REVIEW 1958
*Bantam edition / October 1966
16 printings through April 1976
17th printing .. December 1976*

ISBN 0-553-02728-X

Published simultaneously in the United States and Canada

*Bantam Books are published by Bantam Books, Inc. Its trade-
mark, consisting of the words "Bantam Books" and the por-
trayal of a bantam, is registered in the United States Patent
Office and in other countries. Marca Registrada. Bantam
Books, Inc., 666 Fifth Avenue, New York, New York 10019.*

PRINTED IN THE UNITED STATES OF AMERICA

To My Mother
Maria Wickman Ferré
This Book Is Lovingly Dedicated

ACKNOWLEDGMENT

Writing this family chronicle has been a delight, but I hope the reader will not take it too literally. PAPA'S WIFE is fiction based on fact—a happy mixture of truth and fancy—and it is hard to know where one ends and the other begins.

I should like to acknowledge with deep gratitude the editorial assistance and guidance given to me by Faustina Orner.

Longmeadow
May 24, 1955

T. F. B.

CONTENTS

THE WINE DARK SEA

"When Samson woke up and . . .

CHAPTER 1

🦁 How Mama Got Papa

Papa was an old-fashioned preacher. He preached the word of God straight from the Bible, without regard for personalities or consequences. Perhaps his method was a bit severe, but when his congregation heard his sermons of hell and its forever burning fires, they shivered in their boots. If they needed to repent, it was done right there and then, after the service. The Church, to Papa, was the House of God. He expected reverence from the oldest to the youngest.

If Mrs. Nelson whispered to Mrs. Backlund about the price of her new hat, Papa would stop in dead silence. "When you ladies are through talking," he would announce in an even voice, clipping short each word, "I will continue."

You may be sure there was no more whispering that Sunday morning. But Mama was furious. "Do you have to say a thing like that right in the middle of Job's patience? If only you had a bit of it yourself, then you might be able to teach others!"

Papa insisted that what was right was right. He certainly would not tolerate a couple of gossipers in the house of the Lord who had placed him there to preach.

He brought up his children the same way, a stick in

one hand and the Bible in the other. Still the eight of them
sinned in any way they could, just to get even with him.
Although Mama wanted her children to behave properly
and walk in the ways of the Lord, she often helped them
in harmless schemes, which was probably her way of
revenge on Papa for making her wait so long to become
Mrs. Pontus Franzon.

Mama and Papa both came from the old country. It
was Mama's greatest triumph that, in spite of arguments
and tears, Papa had finally consented to resign his pastorate in Lapland, a far northern province of Sweden,
and cross the Atlantic Ocean to take on the ministry of
a small church in New England where the Swedish language was spoken.

When the church secretary sent his letter to the Conference in Sweden, requesting Reverend Franzon to come
to Berkley Hills, he did not know there were eight children in the family, most of them of school age. He had
learned, through correspondence, only that Papa was a
gentleman of fifty-nine years, and hadn't even thought
to ask about his family. How could he have known that
Papa was forty-three when he married Mama, who was
only twenty-one, and that thereafter, about every year
and a half, there arrived either a bouncing boy or a squealing little girl?

When Papa had his blue days, he could not quite forgive Mama for coming into his peaceful life and making
him ten instead of one. But Mama was the one to get
Papa to America and, until the day he left this earth, she
tried to replant him in American soil. She never quite
succeeded.

Papa had been a bachelor, not by choice, but because
of a hopeless love for a lady who would not marry a
minister, when Mama, at the age of sixteen, had come to
work for him as a maid. To mend his broken heart, Papa
had accepted, a few years earlier, the "call" to a small
village in Lapland where the sun shone day and night

during the short summer. Here Papa had found a new challenge in life.

For a man of his standing, Papa had one fault which, strangely, often ruled his better self. He dreamed of possessing a large bank account. This could be achieved only by hoarding even the smallest coin and adhering to the most rigid frugality. So, despite Mama's exceptional qualities as a maid, Papa made it very clear that the prestige of working in a parsonage would have to make up for the very small salary which she would receive.

But Papa compensated for his "sin" by being a very handsome man, with a tongue from which eloquence flowed as rushing waters. Many a maiden's heart caught fire during his preaching. Mama's burned from the start. She felt a definite calling to become a minister's wife. How, she did not know, but her mind was made up. And when Mama made up her mind, neither heaven nor earth could stop her.

Papa did not know her determination, so he hired her, gave her a small sum of money to do the buying for the household, and at once laid down the rules. He warned her to be careful with the draft in the wood stove. He allowed absolutely no waste in any form. Mama must also keep her place. If she didn't mind, Papa suggested, she was to walk on the sidewalk across the street from him. It just did not look right for a man in his position to walk on the same sidewalk as the maid.

Mama obeyed all his rules and suggestions, but she did not forget her determination. She kept Pastor Franzon's house as well and as proudly as though it were, indeed, already her own. It was a fine house, five spacious rooms, all expensively furnished in spite of Papa's interest in a large bank account. Perhaps Papa reasoned then, as he did throughout his life, that the best was the cheapest in the long run.

Salen, which was only for company, Sundays and Christmas Eve, was a magnificent room. Here were the handsome organ which Papa loved to play after a day of work in the Lord's vineyard, and the huge upholstered gray-and-rose divan with its heavy silken tassels on each arm. In the center of the room stood a large round dining table above which hung the great crystal chandelier. On the serving table against the wall, the silver coffee service and two large candlesticks, polished to mirror brightness, stood in perfect order on a large silver tray; above it hung the gold-framed picture of the King and Queen. On the opposite wall, over the organ, hung a magnificent painting of Jesus before Pontius Pilate, a sober reminder of the sins of man.

Mama ventured into the study only in the interest of cleanliness. This was Papa's private domain. Here he would sit for hours in the high-backed upholstered chair behind the huge carved mahogany desk, pondering his sermons. Mama's task was to keep the desk shining and to see that the white-tiled fireplace was clean and its brass doors polished. A rich red hand-woven carpet covered the floor. Altogether there was an air of dignity and restful quiet in the room.

Although Papa was single when he furnished his house, he had given particular attention to his bedroom. It was an enormous room. It had to be to accommodate the massive furniture. There was a double bed with elaborately carved mahogany head- and footboards. The night table, also mahogany, held an ornate kerosene lamp, candle and matches. The washstand was very special, with a marble top on which stood the porcelain basin and pitcher, both decorated with large red roses. Underneath were two doors, one for the porcelain pail and the other for Papa's porcelain chamber.

Across the room were two massive dressers, heavily carved in the same design as the headboard. Above the dressers were two ornate mirrors reflecting the paintings on the opposite wall—*Jesus Blessing the Children* and *Jacob's Dream*. Near the window, overlooking the hills, was an overstuffed chair which in an emergency could be made into an extra bed.

But the kitchen was Mama's special pride and joy. It was a pleasant room with a wide window overlooking the valley. Geraniums bloomed on the window sill the year round. Papa had seen to it that his house, unlike most homes in Lapland, had running water, although this luxury extended only to the kitchen. The rest of the plumbing was outside. All kitchens in Sweden at that time had a large wooden sofa, and here, for the two years she acted as maid, Mama slept. It was not an ordinary sofa. The top part was loose and could be lifted off at night and the sofa made into a double bed. During the day the bedclothes were stored in the sofa-bottom. In front of the sofa were a table and two chairs. A maid did not eat with her master any more than she walked on the same side of the street with him.

Saturday was Mama's busy day, for no work was permitted in the parsonage on Sunday. When the baking was finished, Mama scoured and polished and cleaned. And there was plenty to polish. The reservoir attached to the huge wood stove was of copper, and this had to be shined to gleaming gold every Saturday. Above the stove was the *kåpa* which held the copper pans and covers. The big copper coffeepot always stood on the back of the stove, ready for chance or expected guests. Even the woodbox had a copper cover. Mama had little time on Saturdays to think about her ambitions.

By the end of the second year, Mama had done such a good job of keeping Papa's house that she graduated to the position of housekeeper. Now she did not sleep in the kitchen in the big sofa, but in the *vardags*-room, a kind of den furnished with all the odds and ends of furniture. And now, too, she was allowed the great honor of walking on the same sidewalk as her master.

"I am making headway," Mama assured herself. "But this is only the beginning. Someday I shall wear *two* rings on my finger and sleep in the same bed as the Reverend Pontus Franzon."

But two more years passed and Mama was still house-keeper.

Then one summerlike spring day, Mama was sure the moment had arrived. She was called into Papa's study for a special talk.

"Maria," he said, "you are the best housekeeper the Lord has ever made. I am humbly thankful that He gave you to me. The years we have lived under the same roof have been good years. I have come to a very important decision."

He stopped for a moment. Mama's heart was beating like a bell clapper.

"Maria," Papa said with deep emotion in his voice, "I have decided that I shall never marry and you can stay on as my housekeeper for the rest of my life."

"Thank you, Pastor Franzon," Mama finally managed, tears choking her, "thank you very much, I shall think it over." She left the study so fast that her shoes hardly touched the floor.

In her own room, between sobs, Mama faced facts. The first half of the game was played and she had not made a gain. Would Papa always remain a bachelor? Well, she had no intention of being a housekeeper the rest of her life. More than anything Mama wanted children, a whole houseful of them. In fact, she had already named most of them. All their names were picked to go with Franzon. Papa just couldn't do this to her. Mama dried her tears and started dreaming again.

She imagined herself Mrs. Maria Franzon, opening the door to the parsonage, letting people in. The caller would not turn up her nose and say, "Please tell the Reverend I am here. My appointment was for two o'clock."

No indeed! Instead, the visitor would curtsy and say, "My dear Mrs. Franzon, I am so glad to see you." Mama would call out, "Pontus dear. Mrs. So-and-So is here to see you." She might even cook coffee and serve them company cookies.

Oh, no, Mama was not licked—yet.

A plan started to take shape in Mama's mind, a web, but she must weave it very, very carefully. Men were dumb when it came to their *own* hearts. Papa might love her and never even know it himself. Somehow she must kindle the flame to life, if it existed, and she was now sure it did.

How Mama would have played her cards if she had not met Mrs. Johansson, no one knows. But she did meet her—at a church auction—and they became friends. Mrs. Johansson had a terrific problem to solve. She was planning to leave for the United States, late in the summer, to join her husband, who had gone before and secured a job as a plumber in Joliet, Illinois. Mrs. Johansson was looking for a young lady, preferably one with America fever, to assist her and her five children across the ocean. This was the opportunity Mama had been waiting for. A weapon with which to shock Papa.

Mrs. Johansson left the church with Mama's promise that she was the young lady she was looking for. But in her heart Mama expected the very next day to tell her she had changed her mind. She planned to spring the news on Papa at the breakfast the following morning. The scene was set in her imagination, and she was sure her news would hit like a snowslide. Papa would gather her up in his strong arms and beg her to stay, as his wife, forever.

So Mama laid her plans very carefully. If the way to a man's heart is through his stomach, she would prepare the most elegant breakfast. Yes, it must be Papa's favorite —fried herring and potatoes in their jackets. And the coffee—why she would even use the high-priced company coffee and put a few extra beans in the grinder. She was singing as she set the table with special care, using gleaming white linen and a bouquet of wild flowers which she had picked in the woods behind the parsonage earlier that morning.

When Papa entered the dining room, the air was filled with cheerfulness. Mama smiled demurely. Papa returned the smile. It was a happy morning, and the breakfast progressed pleasantly without comment as Mama waited for the right moment. She chose the time when Papa was buttering his third slice of *limpa* and had just swallowed the tail end of a crisp, brown herring.

"Pastor Franzon," said Mama softly, "I have important news for you this morning."

"It must be glad news, you look so happy."

"It is. I had the most amazing offer to go to America." And Mama painted Mrs. Johansson's offer in vivid colors, expecting the big moment to arrive.

But Papa was very calm about it. America was a wonderful country, he agreed. Mama was young and had her life ahead of her. If this was what she wanted, he could only wish her Godspeed—and look for another housekeeper.

Six weeks later Mama was on the Atlantic Ocean. She had almost given up the idea of becoming a minister's wife. The anticipation of the golden land in the West was gradually replacing her intense desire for Papa. Mama entered the United States of America as an immigrant.

In spite of the thrill of standing on American soil, Mama was lonely. She had never before seen people bustle about so. She felt very small and insignificant as she stood by a large trunk surrounded by the five children, while Mrs. Johansson went through customs. A rather overstuffed lady, gaily dressed, spoke to Mama in a strange tongue, pointing to the children. Mama smiled helplessly and the lady went on without receiving an answer. The tears were on the verge of breaking through, but Mama held them back. So this was New York with its skyscrapers and swift traffic. And here she was because of Papa. Her heart ached as she pictured in her mind the peaceful parsonage in faraway Sweden. She wondered if Papa was missing her—or at least her cooking. What a fool he had been to let her go! Even thinking about it made her furious. By the time Mrs. Johansson returned, Mama had banished even the thought of tears. Mrs. Johansson thanked her profusely.

"Here is where we part, my dear. You certainly have been an angel to me on that boat. My husband ought to be here any moment now and after that we will get along fine."

She explained to Mama about the Swedish-American Employment Agency and there was where she left her. Mama found herself with a dozen other "greenhorns," waiting for a fairy godmother to touch them with her magic wand and make them millionaires overnight.

Mama could speak only nine words of English; however, by mixing, pouring and stirring certain ingredients, she could create the most tempting dishes. Soon her aching heart found solace among pots, pans, and mixing bowls in an enormous kitchen on Fifth Avenue. She was now second cook for an old American family related to the Vanderbilts.

But the biggest part of her heart was still across the Atlantic in a red-and-white parsonage, and she was forever wondering about Reverend Franzon's new housekeeper. Would she try to become Mrs. Franzon, too?

After a week, Mama sat down and wrote a very formal letter to Papa, informing him that she had landed safely at her destination. She marked her address very plainly. Then she waited.

Months passed and at last there came a letter from Papa. Mama put it unopened in her apron pocket, impatiently waiting for the afternoon, when she could sit down in the wicker chair in the servants' dining room, to read it.

My dear Maria,

The fall here in Sweden has been very rainy, in fact there have been only two days of sunshine this month.

The fruit soup you cooked before you left was very good. I ate it every day for two weeks.

My health is not too good due to the fact that my housekeeper keeps the house too warm, with the result I catch cold when I go out in the cool air. It also makes a very visible hole in the woodpile.

Her cooking is not satisfactory and she is very careless with the dishes. The blue coffee cups are either without ears or nicked.

The church is progressing. Last Sunday I took in three new members, including Olga Ström, my new housekeeper.

If you would consider coming back to work for me, my offer of long ago is still good.

May God bless you!
Pontus Franzon

"I hope she breaks all his dishes!" stormed Mama through her tears. "I hope she finishes his woodpile in a month. I hope she burns all of his food and cooks it so badly he gets indigestion. His offer is still good! Well not that offer. . . . *Never*."

But Mama answered his letter promptly.

Dear Pastor Franzon,

I am sorry it is raining in Sweden all the time. Here in America the sun is shining every day. It is a wonderful country and I plan to stay here.

If I should ever decide to come back to work for you, it will never be as your housekeeper. If you have a better offer to give me, let me know.

I am feeling fine.

God bless you, too!
Maria

There now! She had told him. He could think whatever he wanted. With over three thousand miles between them, she just didn't care.

Mama did not receive any more letters from Papa. She mended her broken heart, learned some English, bought many new clothes, and almost gave up marrying Papa. A year passed.

Then one beautiful summer day in June, on her afternoon off, the second cook, Maria, took a stroll in Central Park. The sun was shining brightly on her new parasol. She felt quite like a lady, with money in her pocketbook, wearing a new white eyelet dress that reached to her ankles, but did not hide the new white leather shoes.

She tripped along gaily, aware of admiring glances. Then suddenly she stopped. There on the park bench, in a gray linen suit, sat a man so like the Reverend Franzon that Mama's heart jumped into her throat, and she stared. Then the man arose from the bench and came toward her.

"Maria!" cried Papa, extending both hands. Mama took one outstretched hand and shook it hard. Finally she found her voice.

"Pastor Franzon," she stammered. "Whatever are you doing in New York?"

"I have my vacation month," said Papa. "Crossing the ocean and seeing New York is not a bad way of spending it. I had planned to look you up tonight, but this saves me the trouble."

Fortunately Mama had the evening off. They went to a little restaurant, called "Just Like Home," for a supper of Swedish meat balls and a talk. Mama expected any moment to hear what she had been waiting five years to hear, and Papa was very talkative, but not in the way Mama hoped for.

"The ocean trip was most invigorating, Maria," he said looking past her. "The salt air certainly is a tonic for your lungs."

Well, Mama was just not too interested in Papa's lungs at that moment.

"How is everything at home in Lapland?" Mama looked dreamily out the window.

"Everything was fine." Papa stopped eating and stroked his forehead. "You know," he said, "just being in America makes you appreciate Sweden. Everything is so peaceful

over there and people don't run around like mad. I am
not at all in sympathy with all this rushing to and fro.
What in the world is their hurry?"

Oh, heavens! He is almost in a preaching mood now,
thought Mama, but out loud she said, "It's in their blood,
I guess. After a while you start running yourself and it
is sort of fun after you get used to it."

"I am sure that I would not enjoy it," snapped Papa.

Mama was sure that he wouldn't either.

Papa talked about Lapland, the church, the people and
finally ended up with the parsonage. He will tell me any
time now, thought Mama. To her disappointment, Papa
only reminded her of his offer made that spring day long
ago.

"You shall always have a home with me. Maria, please
come back," he pleaded. "My stomach is all upset from
bad cooking, my furniture is scratched. I gave my housekeeper a permanent vacation. Things have not been right
since you left."

Mama's heart sang. If that was not love, what was?
She became bold.

"Pastor Franzon," she said, without pretending, "the
only way I will go back with you to the old country, is
as your Mrs."

Papa gasped. "But I don't want to marry you or anyone
else. I need to be free! Furthermore, you are young, there
might be children. They would disturb me when I prepared my sermons."

"Poppycock," answered Mama more boldly. "Don't
you think I could keep half a dozen children quiet while
you are studying?"

"Half a dozen?" Papa was astonished. "Would there
be that many?"

"Who knows?" Mama looked mysterious. "I will give
you until tomorrow to think it over."

She really had not meant to propose, but everything
is fair in love and war. Besides, the poor man did not know
what was best for him.

In spite of her triumph so far, Mama was worried. She knew that Papa was a man of principles and that when his mind was made up it did not change very quickly.

But the next morning Papa said "yes" to Mama and arranged for the ceremony to be held the following Thursday.

Mama was dancing on clouds. Now she could put her hand on his arm and call him Pontus! He had not kissed her yet, but she was on her way to becoming a minister's wife.

But on Thursday Papa was ill. The strain had been too much for him. Poor Mama had to wait another day. Even then Papa looked pale and dejected when he appeared before the preacher with Mama beside him.

"Pontus August Franzon, do you take this woman to be your lawful, wedded wife?"

Beads of perspiration formed on Papa's forehead.

"No," he said, "I had better not, I am not sure, I only wanted her as my housekeeper."

Mama's brave heart trembled.

"Pontus," she whispered without looking at Papa, "I am warning you. I at least expected you to be a man of your word!"

The preacher refused to marry them.

"Marriage is a holy and solemn sacrament. It should never be entered into lightly." With a side glance at Papa, he said, "A minister ought to know that. I feel obliged to ask you to wait until you are both sure."

Once outside the preacher's house, Mama looked at Papa for a long while, and then, instead of crying as she wanted to do, she spoke her contempt with dignity.

"I thought of you as a new, beautiful top hat. But you are not. All you are is an old worn-down slipper! I think it is better for both of us if you don't ever see me again."

Mama turned quickly on her heel and walked down the street as proudly as any minister's wife could have done.

Papa stared after her. This was a Maria he had never

seen. Her eyes had been like two glowing coals plucked
from the fire. She had been furious and still had spoken
with dignity. Never had she been more beautiful and
desirable. His feet did not move, but his cold, hardened
bachelor's heart broke its shell and tumbled down the
street after Mama.

"Strange," he spoke out loud, "I love Maria, and I think
she is a most wonderful woman. Now I must not let her
slip through my fingers."

The next morning Papa telephoned Mama.

"Maria," he said in the same voice in which he would
deliver a sermon, "I discovered something yesterday afternoon."

"You did?" said Mama, in no mood for guessing games.
"Well wasn't that clever of you! I told you, Pastor Franzon, not to bother me any more."

But Papa continued as though he had not heard a word
Mama said.

"You have the bluest eyes I have ever seen, Maria, and
I'm in love with you."

Mama could only gasp. Pastor Franzon was not given
to flowery compliments.

Papa's voice became weak and humble. "Maria," he
said tenderly, "will you kindly inform me if you are in
love with me too?"

This was too much for Mama. What could she do but
give Papa an honest answer?

"You are the strangest and most conceited man I have
ever known, and for the life of me I can't figure it out.
But I do love you, Pontus Franzon, although I'm not sure
if I want to marry you after yesterday."

"Now," said Papa, "don't let us waste time. We must be
married as soon as it can be arranged."

That afternoon at two o'clock, Mama became Mrs.
Pontus Franzon.

Her heart was filled to the brim with happiness. The
only drawback was that she must leave her new-found

country with all its glorious opportunities for a cook like Maria.

We will be back, she promised herself, Pontus, myself and all the little Franzons-to-be.

It took sixteen years for Mama to make up Papa's mind for him. In that space of time, eight of her dreams had come true.

CHAPTER 2

☙ Papa Makes a Resolution

If Mama had grieved over the lost opportunities for
a good cook in America, she soon had other things to fill
her mind. Being a pastor's wife presented very different
duties from those of a maid of all work. She still kept the
parsonage (her own home now as she had dreamed it
would be) in perfect order and was just as vigilant about
waste or unnecessary expense. But she slept in the big
double bed upstairs, occasionally accompanied her husband on sick calls, and on Sundays walked arm in arm
with him to church. On Thursdays she received any of
the ladies of the church who wished to call, serving coffee
and fresh-baked pastries in *salen*. This was always an
especially happy time for Mama, for she loved company.

But by the end of the first year as Mrs. Pontus Franzon,
Mama knew one thing had not changed: a pastor's duty
to his church always came first. She discovered this, with
disturbing emphasis, one spring morning when Papa announced that he would attend the Church Conference
in Stockholm. This in itself was not surprising. It was an
annual event. What disturbed her was that she was expecting the first of her "dreams" almost any day, and
Pontus didn't seem to regard that as of first importance.

A tear rolled down Mama's cheek as she closed Papa's

suitcase. She had hoped against hope that even in this last minute he would change his mind.

"Pontus," she said once more, "please don't go to Stockholm to the conference. I know how important it seems to you for the good of the church. But this is our *very first* baby. What if it should come in the middle of the night? Who would get the midwife for me?"

Papa seemed so distressed Mama took a bit of hope. He placed his hand under her chin, lifting it up, and looked into her pleading blue eyes.

"Maria," he said tenderly, "do you suppose a soldier in war can go home because his wife is having a baby?"

Mama shook her head, her throat too full of tears to speak.

"God's work is even more important," Papa continued now in his ministerial voice. "You knew before our marriage that I could never let home life interfere with my duty as a pastor. Believe me, Maria, I wish with all my heart this conference were not at this time and so far away. But I hope you will go your full time, then I'll be sure to be back. Now let's consider the matter closed and let me go in peace."

Mama choked back her tears as she opened the suitcase again and packed four more handkerchiefs. It would do no harm to put them in. Sometimes things *did* happen at childbirth. It might serve Papa right if—if—no, it was a wicked thought. Nothing must happen to the baby or to her. They'd just have to get along without Papa.

"All right, Pontus," Mama agreed, tossing her head independently, "go along! If our baby should arrive before you come back, I'll just have to sort of excuse your absence. 'Don't worry, little one,' I'll say, 'you *have* a father and when he is through with his *duty* he'll gladly be back to look at you.'"

Papa smiled bleakly. "Don't be ridiculous, Maria. I shall ask Tant Renberg to stay with you while I am gone."

Mama's head went up again. "No, thank you, Pontus *lilla*. I just can't stand the way her false teeth rattle when she talks. And besides, her hands are rough. What would our baby think having Tant Renberg's rough hands touch its soft skin?"

"Maria!" Papa was losing patience. "Babies don't think or form opinions. Really, sometimes I wonder if I married a *child*."

Mama laughed, but the next minute she was crying again. "Don't mind me, Pontus. Women are queer at a time like this. After all, I still have two more weeks to go, and you'll be back before that."

But when Papa kissed her good-bye at the door, she clung to him, trying hard to keep from crying. He released himself tenderly. "I'll be back as soon as I can, Maria."

Mama watched him until he disappeared around the bend of the road, then she let her tears flow freely. But even as she wept, she knew Pontus was right. She was being ridiculous about the whole thing. Women all over the world had babies. Some of them had no assistance whatsoever. She must stop acting like a child.

She dried her tears, suddenly aware of the heavy silence. How empty the parsonage seemed without Papa. This was the first time he had left her in the ten whole months of their married life. It scarcely seemed possible ten months had passed since that morning in late July when they had boarded the Swedish-American liner in New York to return to Sweden and Papa's pastorate in Lapland. What a wonderful honeymoon it had been even if they had had to occupy quarters at opposite ends of the boat. For by the time Papa had made up his mind to marry her, there simply was no space left on the boat except an upper berth in a cabin occupied by a schoolmistress returning to Stockholm. It hadn't been easy to say goodnight at the door of her cabin to a brand-new husband, and, though he tried not to show it, Mama knew it wasn't easy for Pontus either. So they would meet for breakfast in almost the same manner they had in Lapland when she had been only his housekeeper. And sometimes Mama wasn't sure that Papa remembered she was now his wife. But she was so gloriously happy she didn't mind his absentmindedness.

I'll make him the best wife in the whole world, she promised herself. Pontus will never, never regret that he married me.

Only one thing had disturbed her. Papa disliked emotion. Even his good-night kisses were reserved, and Mama was sure if she hadn't put her arms around his neck and kissed him, he would have just tipped his hat to her and gone to his own cabin.

Never mind, she had consoled herself, watching him disappear into the shadows at the other end of the passageway, Pontus will get used to love.

And when, the next day, her arm linked in his, they walked miles around the deck, the salty spray and the wind in their faces, Mama was convinced his education had already begun and that he was as happy as she herself.

"Isn't this wonderful, Pontus?" she had cried, shouting to make herself heard above the wind.

Papa had holloed back, clasping her arm a little tighter. "It's like climbing Gellivara mountain in the wintertime."

Later, when they sat in their deck chairs, away from the wind, Papa had spoken of their homecoming. "It is going to be a shock to all the church people, Maria," he said, looking wistfully out over the white-capped waves, glistening in the sunlight. "No one had an inkling that I crossed the ocean to get married. In fact, Maria, I have to admit it is still a surprise to me."

Mama laughed gaily. But Papa continued soberly. "It will be awkward for me to tell them. They might even belittle you, Maria. You know marriage between a pastor and his housekeeper does not often take place in proud Sweden."

For a moment Mama's spirit sank. What Papa said was true, of course. A man of Papa's standing in the community did not marry a mere maid. And that is what she had been, even though he was kind enough to call her a housekeeper. But she also knew that she loved him

more than anything else in the whole world, and was
going to be the very best wife any man ever had. She
would *make* the church people like her. She had to! But
would that be enough? Her great love for Pontus must
never bring him sorrow or humiliation.

A young couple swung by, laughing happily. Mama
looked after them until they were out of sight. Then,
"Pontus," she said softly, "how do *you* feel about it?"

He had taken both her hands in his with more emotion
than he had ever shown before. "I love you, Maria," he
said gently.

"Then we will tackle them together, Pontus. And if
they don't like it, we'll just go back to America!"

Papa had not seemed as sure they were equal to the
battle alone. "We'll leave it in God's hands, Maria," he
said.

But Mama had known he was more worried than he
admitted; and, in a strange way which was difficult for
her to understand, he was a little ashamed. A man of
forty-three, and a pastor, just didn't run off and marry
his former maid who was only twenty-one. Mama was
quite aware that wasn't an easy situation to face, but,
as for herself, she could face anyone with Pontus beside
her.

They had arrived in Lapland on a Saturday night about
eleven o'clock. In the saffron twilight of the never-setting
sun, a gentle peacefulness lingered over the western mountains and the low houses with their well-kept gardens.
Mama was thankful that the road which led to the parsonage was deserted. It would be better for Pontus to
feel the good earth of his own garden beneath his feet
before he had to face the townspeople.

At the door of the parsonage, Papa stopped. "Oh, it is
good to be home, Maria," he exclaimed fervently. "Is
there a place in the world as beautiful as Lapland?"

"I think America is very beautiful, too," Mama said
simply.

"But it is dark there in the summer," argued Papa.

"Imagine, lamplight in the summertime. Why here in Sweden we can pack our lamps away until fall."

"You are forgetting the awful long winters, Pontus, with only a few hours of daylight. In America it is more evenly divided."

Papa had looked at her for a long time. "You do love America, don't you, Maria?" he said, a note of disappointment in his voice. Then as if to impress upon her that this was *really* her home, he had taken her hand in his. "Come, let us kneel in prayer right here on our doorstep before we enter our home."

Mama had knelt with him in silent prayer. She would never know what Papa had prayed for that day, but it must have been, like her own prayer, for their happiness together. For when they rose from their knees and hand in hand stepped over the high threshold, the sun broke from behind a cloud, bathing the parsonage in a stream of rosy light like a heavenly benediction.

When Mama opened her eyes early the next morning, bright sunshine flooded the bedroom. It took her a moment to remember she was back in Sweden, in the parsonage. She rubbed her eyes and looked over at Pontus sleeping heavily beside her. The quilt, rising and falling gently with his breathing, covered half his face. Mama peeked at the clock. There was still half an hour before she had to get up and start the coffee. She settled back for a few more winks. Suddenly she remembered. Why, this was *Sunday* morning and she was a married woman now! Mama almost chuckled aloud. Would Pontus remember, too, that a husband was supposed to bring his *wife* coffee on Sunday morning? For years as a housekeeper she had brought Pontus coffee *every* morning. On weekdays she had used the brightly painted wooden tray; but on Sundays she had carried the silver tray with a very special coffeepot and Papa's favorite *vienerbröd*. She would knock softly at his door, then wait for his sleepy voice to answer before she entered.

Now she glanced over at him again, sleeping so soundly.

What if he didn't wake up in time to bring *her* coffee?
Well—she better make sure that he did. Cautiously she
touched his leg with her toe. Papa slept on. She "touched"
a little harder. This time he stirred and threw back the
quilt from his face.

"Pontus," she whispered softly. "It's morning—our *first*
morning in the parsonage."

"So it is—so it is." Pontus stretched luxuriously. "And
our first *coffee*, too. It will taste good, Maria."

Mama's heart sank. He *had* forgotten. But there was
still time if only she could think what to say.

"It's Sunday, Pontus," she ventured.

"Well?"

Mama settled back against her pillow and closed her
eyes pretending to be sleepy. "Don't you remember what
husbands do on Sunday, Pontus *lilla?*"

Papa sat up suddenly and stared at her without speaking.

"This is *my* day, Pontus," Mama murmured sleepily.
"You are to bring *me* coffee this morning."

Papa pushed back the quilt reluctantly and threw his
legs over the side of the bed. "Of course, Maria, I never
thought of it," he said, and started for the kitchen.

Mama smiled as she watched him. He looked so funny
in that nightshirt, with his carpet slippers flapping. But
she loved him so much. She was glad she had made everything ready in the kitchen the night before. The *tyre-
wood* lay beside the stove, along with the exact amount
of regular wood needed to make the coffee boil. (Pontus
had always been very particular about how much wood
she used; and only enough *tyre-wood* to make sure the
regular wood caught fire quickly.) She had filled the
coffeepot last night, too, and measured out the right
amount of coffee. Even the tray had been prepared—the
big silver one, for she had completely forgotten that *she*
was the one who would be honored.

Mama snuggled into her pillow and waited. Presently
Papa pushed open the bedroom door. The coffee smelled

so good. Maria sat up brushing back her hair from her face. "You are a real husband, now, Pontus," she cried.

Silently Papa placed the tray on her lap and sat down beside her. Maria poured out two steaming cups.

"Maria," Papa said after several moments, "I've been thinking it would be best for us to go to church separately this morning."

Mama almost dropped the cup and saucer.

"I don't want them to think I have come to church with a strange woman," Papa hastened to add with a smile. "No one would know you in those stylish clothes!"

Mama smiled back, but some of the Sunday morning joy went out of her. Hadn't she dreamed for a long time of walking to church arm in arm with Papa? But when she saw how concerned he was over the situation, she tried to hide her own disappointment.

"You just come early, Maria," Papa directed, "and sit down as a stranger. I will break the news in my sermon."

The little church was filled to the doors to welcome back Pastor Franzon from his vacation. Maria had arrived early, as Papa had requested, and sat quietly as the church people filed into the pews. When Papa rose to preach, she prayed that he would be given the right words.

"My text this morning," began Papa solemnly, "is from the thirteenth chapter of First Corinthians and from the fifth verse: *Love seeketh not her own.*"

Mama's heart almost stopped. Was this Papa's way of telling her before his congregation that she shouldn't have proposed to him and that he was sorry he married her? She did not hear much of the sermon. Her heart was too full of sorrow for herself—and Papa's eloquence. Finally when the sermon was finished, Papa had not said the usual "Amen." He had paused significantly, looking out over the congregation, and smiled.

"Today I have a confession to make," he said slowly, and Maria held her breath. "I have preached a sermon against love seeking its own, yet I myself am guilty of that sin."

A rustle of surprise passed through the congregation. Questioning glances were exchanged.

"In our midst here today sits a beautiful young lady," Papa continued, a little twinkle in his eyes. "I guess you have thought her a tourist from America. Well, her lovely clothes are American, but her *heart* is Lapland. She is an old friend to all of you. Let me present the woman I love and had to go three thousand miles to tell her so—Mrs. Maria Franzon."

Mama's heart had almost burst with pride and happiness. The church people were all looking at her and smiling. Mama stood up and smiled back with her warmest, sunniest smile—and all the congregation stood up too. They couldn't cheer or applaud in God's house, but Maria knew this meant the same welcome. Deacon Lund had spoken then for all of them.

"Our warmest congratulations and God's blessing over our pastor and his bride."

Mama had taken her place beside Papa after the service and received the handshakes and curtseys as the church people filed out. At last her dream had come true. She was Mrs. Franzon for all the town to see. God had been very good to her.

As they walked back to the parsonage, arm in arm, Papa had said, "They all love you, Maria. We must be grateful for the spirit in which they received you." But there was a note of relief in his voice.

Mama had smiled up at him. "That's because God made us for each other," she said softly.

Life in the parsonage as Mrs. Franzon was even more wonderful than Mama had dreamed. Oh, there were times —when Papa had things on his mind perhaps—that he forgot she was no longer the housekeeper and started ordering her around. Then Mama had only to look at him and smile, and he melted like butter in the sunshine.

It was the week before *Lucia Day* that Mama was finally

Papa Makes a Resolution   25

ready to tell Papa about the baby. She had wanted to tell him immediately she knew about it herself, but a miracle as wonderful as this had to be told in a special way. And what day could be more appropriate to break the news than the day all Sweden honored—"*Santa Lucia*," the Queen of Light? She had always thought it the loveliest celebration of all, and this year the parsonage could have its own *Lucia* in the old tradition.

Mama was up before daybreak on December thirteenth. By the time Papa should be awakened, she had everything ready. She chose the prettiest cloth for the coffee tray, and on a special plate arranged the fat *Lucia cats* which she had baked secretly the day before. The crusts were nicely browned in butter, cinnamon and sugar, and the raisin eyes looked almost alive. "They are so real I could just hug them," Mama laughed to herself.

On the table beside the tray was the crown bearing its seven tall burning candles. Just as the first light of dawn broke over the horizon, Mama fastened the crown over her golden hair and marched ceremoniously to Papa's bedroom. Gently she pushed open the door and started to sing the funny little song which she had made up for the occasion:

> "Awake, awake my sleepyhead
> So I might know you are not dead
> I'll bring some coffee to your bed
> My darling, lazy sleepyhead!
>
> As a beautiful Lucia I come to you
> To whisper a secret so very new
> A sweet little angel with eyes so blue
> Shall soon come to live with me and you!"

Papa stirred in his sleep and turned over. Mama put the tray on the little table and knelt beside the bed, singing the song again, close to Papa's ear. He sat up then rubbing his sleepy eyes.

"Pontus *lilla*," laughed Mama, her eyes shining as brightly as the candles in her hair, "*it is Lucia*. Have you forgotten?"

Papa was wide awake now and saw the burning candles. "Maria," he cried, "how dare you put all those burning things in your hair? Remove them at once, *please!*"

Mama only laughed at his scolding. "Not until you have heard my secret," she whispered. "I have told you already in my song and you never heard a word of it."

"Told me *what?*" asked Papa.

"Pontus, the most wonderful thing in the world has happened. *You* are going to be a *papa*."

For a long breathless moment, Mama did not know whether Papa was pleased or not. Then silently he removed the burning candle-crown, and her head was against his shoulder and he was smoothing her golden hair.

With her own secret happiness, Maria fairly danced through the Christmas baking and preparations. She even refused to be disturbed that Papa seemed embarrassed about the baby and blushed each time she called him Papa. Well, she would just talk so much about the baby that Papa would *get over* his shyness before it arrived.

One evening a few weeks later, Mama decided it was time she talked to Papa about a name for the baby.

"I am sure it is going to be a boy, Pontus," Mama said, "so we got to think of a real special name for him."

Papa had looked up from the sermon he was preparing.

"I have been thinking, Maria, that Engelbrekt would be a grand name."

"Engelbrekt!" Mama gasped, then quickly controlled her disappointment. "Isn't it a rather long name for such a little fellow? What would he ever do with it?"

"He would try to live up to it," Papa answered proudly. "Engelbrekt was one of Sweden's greatest men. If it weren't for him, we might still be subjects under Denmark. Have you forgotten your history, Maria?"

Mama had not forgotten. "But that was way back in

fourteen hundred and thirty-five." She smiled, hoping she
could make him think of something else. "Pontus, I bet
you never thought I would remember!"

Papa did not answer her directly, but she knew from
the softness of his voice that he was pleased she was so
smart. "We can give him more than one name, Maria,
can't we? You find one for him."

"I think he should have one name from the Bible. How
about David? And then Pontus after you. One name for
the Bible, one for Sweden and one for his father!"

"Engelbrekt David Pontus Franzon," Papa repeated
slowly. "I think that will be very fine, Maria."

The winter had seemed longer than ever to Mama that
year. On mild days she took brisk walks up the mountainside, breaking little narrow paths in the thick fleecy white
carpet that seemed to cover the whole world. Spring was
not far away she knew, for underneath the snow she
could hear the low-voiced song of the mountain streams.
And her heart would beat a little faster, for her baby
would arrive in the springtime. Often she would talk
aloud to her baby as though he were already born. "Little
one," she would say, "your father is a very strange man.
Sometimes it is very hard to understand him. But he loves
us and we just have to love him a lot."

Maria wouldn't have admitted it to anyone, but deep
in her heart there was a yearning. A wish that Pontus
would be more romantic. Sometimes she felt she would
just burst with this love she had to keep bottled up inside
her. Love for Pontus, the baby that was soon to be theirs,
and for the whole world. As spring drew nearer, a strange
kind of restlessness possessed her. Soon young lovers
would stroll the crooked little mountain paths. The bud-
ding new world would be filled with gay songs and happy
glances, and love words whispered cheek to cheek. Sometimes Maria dreamed that Pontus was a young and ardent
lover. "My dearest darling," he would say, "in all the
world there is no one so beautiful. My love for you is
like the skylark rising high above the earth in the cloud-

less sky." And then Pontus would take her in his arms
and their lips would meet and he would hold her close,
whispering sweet love words. Oh, it was wonderful! Then
almost at once Maria would chide herself for this yearning. Wasn't Pontus the husband she wanted most in all
the world? He was just timid about love. Hadn't she
promised herself that day on the boat that she would
love him so much he would get used to love? Anyway,
how could Pontus know that at a time like this a woman
needed more affection? She would have to go on making
believe, and when the baby came Papa would love them
both so much his heart would just run over with it. . . .

Suddenly the grandfather's clock in the hall chimed
the hour. Maria came out of her dreaming with a start.
My goodness! Here she sat like a *herskaps-fru* although
there was work to be done. She hurried into the kitchen.
Tant Renberg would be coming to look after Pontus
when the baby was born, and Mama wanted to make
sure there were plenty of rusks even if Tant Renberg
didn't lift a finger. By midafternoon the baking board
was piled high with cinnamon rusks. "I've enough to feed
a whole army." Mama laughed as she packed them away
in tins. "Pontus won't starve while I am in bed, that's
sure."

From the ceiling, in a corner of the kitchen, hung the
thin-bread on a wooden pole covered with a clean white
baking sheet. Why, thought Maria, there would be almost enough to last all winter! And there was a whole
crockful of fruit soup. Mama smiled as she pictured Pontus relishing his favorite food. "This is a meal for a king,"
he would say as he broke a whole round cake of thin-
bread into his plate.

When the kitchen was cleared up and the stove polished
and shining, Mama went into the bedroom, where the
many tiny new clothes were stacked on the bed. Tenderly
she caressed the soft woolly sweaters, holding them against
her cheek. The baby stirred within her. Suddenly she was

uneasy. "What if God sends the baby before Pontus returns?" For a fleeting moment she was afraid; then almost at once her heart was so full of gratitude for this baby that God was giving to Pontus and her that she just couldn't worry about anything. By the time she blew out the lamp that night, she felt safe and happy with all fears banished.

In the darkness, Maria sat up with a start. How long had she slept? Her forehead was wet with perspiration, though the room was cold. Suddenly she grasped the sides of the bed with both hands. She hadn't imagined pain could be so sharp—a strange kind of pain that tore at her like frantic fingers. Dear God! It had come—her time— her hour and she was all alone!

"Oh, Pontus," she cried into the darkness, "how could you do this to me?"

And Mama buried her face in her pillow and sobbed with pain and fear.

All afternoon on the train Papa had been restless. Too many thoughts, crowding like swarming bees through his brain. Over and over he tried to discipline himself. He was supposed to be thinking of the speech for the conference, but he could not get Maria out of his mind. Unseeingly he stared out the window, oblivious to the majestic beauty of the rugged mountainside. He could see only the pleading in Maria's eyes as she begged him not to leave her and clung to him like a frightened child. She had been heavy in his arms. And Papa smiled, thinking how each day Mama looked more like a big round rubber ball! And how dear she was. It was not the way she looked now that bothered him; it was her melancholy mood. One moment she would be looking at him with those big eyes and they would be full of laughter; then suddenly her arms would be around his neck and she would be in tears. "Oh, Pontus," she would say, "oh, Pontus." Just that, over and over. No matter how hard he tried, he couldn't understand her. A woman's ways seemed a bigger mystery every day.

Papa stirred uneasily in his seat as the train rumbled through the early night. He was sorry he had to leave Maria when her time was so close. But this conference was very important. He couldn't seem to make her understand that. Ministers of small churches could not run the risk of letting larger ones swallow them up. He had seen this happen too often. No, a pastor's duty was to look out for his parish; to be at each conference and see and hear what was going on. A small church's vote was as important as a large one's. Why couldn't Maria see that?

But even as he argued with himself, Papa could not get the picture of her off his mind. How warm and alive she was, and what a gift from God to have her sunny disposition in the parsonage. He recalled the morning she had told him of the baby. She had almost scared him to death with all those burning candles in her beautiful hair. Why, there should be a law banning such foolishness. Quickly he had taken the crown from her head, realizing how very precious she was to him. And then she was in his arms, her arms about his neck, and her golden head on his shoulder. "Darling," she had whispered, "I'm so happy I think I am going to die. And I *will* if you don't just about eat me up this minute."

Papa squirmed uncomfortably. He loved Mama with all his heart, but he just couldn't get used to the way she acted and talked sometimes. He had tried to express his feelings to her, but the words just wouldn't come out of his mouth. Years ago he had given up emotional things for the sake of his high calling. And now, when he wanted to tell her how much he loved her, he couldn't. But when she was in his arms, her lips soft and sweet upon his, Papa found that he was a fool and a weakling like other men.

That *Lucia-Day* had been one to remember. It had snowed all night, and the village looked like a toy town made of cotton. That afternoon he and Maria had taken a long walk and stopped to visit a Lapp family where a baby had recently arrived. Mama had taken the tiny bundle in her lap and cuddled and cooed with it until Papa was red-faced with embarrassment. Especially when she had asked him to hold it. When they reached home again that evening, they had celebrated with an extra special Lapland treat—a supper of *soursmelts* and *tatemilk* with thin-bread.

"What a crazy meal this is," Papa had joked, feeling carefree and lighthearted. "The fish tastes as good as it smells *bad*—the bread is thinner than the butter—and the milk is so elastic that when you try to eat it, it snaps right back into your plate!"

Mama had bubbled over with laughter. "Maybe we could roll it into a ball like yarn, Pontus. How could it ever get this long?"

"All I care about is how good it tastes," Papa had replied, his mouth full of fish. . . .

Presently Papa was aware that the train had stopped and new passengers were boarding. Filing into the seat opposite him was a family—a rather young man with five small children and a baby in his arms. The children were clean and well behaved as they shyly cuddled close to their father.

"Nice children," Papa remarked to start the conversation. "How old is the baby?"

"She'll be three weeks old tomorrow," the man said as he pulled the pink blanket around the small head.

Papa smiled friendlily. "Quite a job handling all those little ones alone, isn't it? Where is the mother?"

The young man swallowed hard a couple of times, before he tried to speak. Too late Papa realized how he had blundered.

"I'm so very sorry," he said kindly. "I should not have asked. Forgive me, please."

The young man lifted sorrow-filled eyes. "How could *you* know? She just isn't with us any more. Somehow we shall have to get along without her. We did all we could, the midwife and I, but something went wrong, and there was no doctor within miles."

Papa could feel the tears of sympathy moistening his eyes. "And now what will you do? You can't care for this little one alone."

"I am taking them to my wife's mother for a while. After that I don't know." He sighed deeply as the baby stirred fretfully in his arms.

"May the good Lord send you strength," was all Papa could say. His heart was suddenly heavy with anxiety.

As the train clicked over the noisy rails, now it seemed to be whispering over and over, "Maria—Maria—Maria." And then he would hear her voice, "Pontus—Pontus— Pontus."

Suddenly he could stand it no longer. What a fool he had been to leave her. He would get off at the next station and go back as quickly as he could. Even then it would be hours before he could get home. He prayed to God it wouldn't be too late. Meantime he would send a telegram to Tant Renberg to go to Maria at once.

"How long will it take?" Mama asked, her voice weak from pain.

Tant Renberg's rough hand wiped the perspiration from her forehead, and Mama followed her glance over to the midwife, sitting in the big easy chair having a good nap. How *could* she sleep? Didn't she realize, thought Mama anxiously, that her baby was about to arrive?

"I had twelve," Tant Renberg was saying. "It was different with each one. But the first is the hardest. It might take hours."

Mama gave a long deep sigh. Hours of this pain—and no one seemed to care. Then instantly she regretted her thought. She was so grateful that Tant Renberg had come when she did. And so very, very happy Pontus had worried about her enough to send the telegram. If only he himself would come. But of course he couldn't. The conference was so important. She was acting like a coward, expecting him to turn back from his first duty. Then as the pain began again, Maria wondered which *was* his first duty—the Church or their first child? She glanced at the tiny clock by the bed, seeing it dimly through the pain that gripped her. Almost nine. The past hours had seemed like a million years. And Tant Renberg said it would be hours more.

Suddenly a sound reached her ears. No, it couldn't be! But it sounded so like Pontus's footsteps. He had a way of scraping his feet just before his hand touched the doorknob. Was she imagining things because of her pain? And then before she could even think the answer, Pontus was in the room tossing his coat on a chair. In another instant he was on his knees beside her bed and would have taken her hands in his had not Tant Renberg cried out a sharp command. "Keep your cold hands off her, Pastor Franzon! She has pain enough."

Never had Mama wanted so much to feel the coolness of his hand on her forehead and to throw her arms about his neck and tell him how happy she was that he had come back in time. What had happened to her voice? It seemed lost somewhere in the forest of her pain, and she was aware of the tears on her cheek.

Gently Pontus brushed them away. "Oh, Maria," he cried, "I never knew it would be like this. Never, never will I permit you to go through this again."

In spite of the pain, Maria smiled at his dear foolishness. How could she tell him that a baby—their own little baby—was worth all the pain she might have to suffer? Weakly she lifted her hand and placed it in his.

Then the midwife was bending over them. "Please," she ordered curtly, "you must go, Pastor Franzon. A man is just a nuisance at a time like this. What a woman has to suffer she will suffer. A husband can't help." Then as he rose from the bedside she added wryly, "But I'm sure if he had to have just *one*, the population wouldn't multiply so fast."

Mama watched Papa moving slowly away from her,

his head bowed in anxious prayer. "Don't mind her, *lilla* Pontus," she wanted to call after him. "All midwives are just old cross-patches!" But no sound came from her lips.

As the night deepened, the pain increased. Maria bit her lips to keep from crying out. For endless hours it seemed to her, Pontus's footsteps had been going back and forth, back and forth, outside her door. She wanted to tell him to go to sleep—not to worry. God wouldn't let anything happen to her or their wonderful baby. Soon, soon they would have a son.

Now it was morning and Tant Renberg stood at one side of the bed with a little woolly bundle in her arms, Pontus at the other. When she opened her eyes, it was like seeing the sunlight pass across his face. Mama laughed in spite of her weakness. He had looked so forlorn and worried.

"Come to your Mama, precious," she murmured. "Welcome to the Franzons'! My goodness, I never dreamed you would be such a funny-looking little fellow. But I do believe you look just a *little* bit like your handsome father."

Papa leaned down and kissed Mama tenderly. Almost fearfully he touched the baby's tiny hand. "Thank you, Maria," he said softly, "thank you for giving me a son."

All the pain of yesterday was forgotten. Such happiness as she had never known welled up in her heart. "Oh, Pontus, isn't he wonderful! Just look at him. And to think he is *all* ours." Mama pulled back the blanket from his tiny head so that his father might have a better look at him.

"Maria," Papa exploded. "He has *red* hair!"

Mama laughed gaily. "So he has, Pontus."

"But—but," Papa stammered, "I—I don't like red hair."

Even Tant Renberg laughed this time. Mama snuggled her baby closer. "I'm afraid we shall have to take little Engelbrekt the way he is," Mama said. "And Pontus, I don't think it says in the history books, but it *could be* that the great Engelbrekt had red hair. Did you ever think of that?"

It was Papa's turn to laugh aloud. "You always have an answer, don't you, Maria? I guess you are right. We'll just take little Engelbrekt as he is. And very wonderful he is, too."

Mama caressed the soft head, smoothing down the few golden hairs. "I hope we haven't hurt your feelings, little one," she whispered, "but I better tell you this right from the beginning: Your *father* is *definitely* the head of this household."

Papa smiled proudly. Outside the window the bright May sun was shining. Spring had come to Lapland, the most beautiful, glorious spring that Lapland had ever seen.

CHAPTER 3

✠ Papa Sees Red

For a week or two Papa was so busy receiving congratulations on his first-born that he forgot about his son's red hair. Gradually the baby became an accepted member of the family. But as the excitement subsided, Papa began to worry.

At first he endeavored, sternly, to push his worries aside. A minister who truly believed in God and His teachings, knew very well that superstitions were the work of the devil. He reasoned, however, that *customs* and *superstitions* were two entirely different matters. Of course he didn't believe that seeing the new moon for the first time through the trees was bad luck for the entire month; or that singing before breakfast was a sure sign of tragedy before the day was over. Such things were rank superstition and the work of the devil. But a son with red hair . . . !

Papa walked up and down the length of the study, his hands clasped behind him, his chin on his chest. He could always think better while walking, especially when he had a problem to solve. And this one was knotty indeed. There was some *reason* why his first-born son had red hair and he just had to find it. But the miles he had walked in the past hour or so had brought him no nearer the solution.

The furrow between Papa's brows deepened and he pulled thoughtfully at his mustache, trying once more to reason it all out. So far as he was concerned, no true-blooded Swede begat red-haired children. Why, as far back as he could trace the Franzon line, there had never been *one* with red hair. His own rolled back from his forehead like sun-ripened wheat rippling in the wind, and Maria's hair was bright as a summer morning. Yet here they were with a redheaded son. It was unthinkable. Perhaps, he decided sorrowfully, this was God's way of punishing him for yielding to the desires of the flesh after so many years of single devotion to his calling.

Presently Papa stopped as though a brake had been applied. It was just possible! Why hadn't he thought of that before? But how did it happen? Quickly he climbed the stairs to ask Maria about it, and, as he climbed, some of the anxiety left him. Marriage, he reflected, had its problems, but Maria certainly made up for most of them. And Engelbrekt *was* a wonderful son. If only he didn't have red hair.

Sunshine lay in a golden mantle over the bedroom. Maria sat in a high-backed rocking chair near the window, nursing little Nim (as she had already nicknamed him), and singing as she rocked. Papa paused in the doorway, caught by the picture they made. Maria looked more like a child than ever with her hair falling loosely over her shoulders, held back from her face by a blue ribbon that seemed reflected in her shining eyes.

She stopped singing as Papa came into the room, and smiled, holding little Nim closer to her breast. "Isn't he adorable, Pontus?"

Papa gazed tenderly down at them. "He is growing fast, Maria. Tomorrow he will be three weeks old and already he is a little man."

"No wonder he grows so fast," Maria laughed. "He's always hungry as a little bear. Why this morning I was sure he would gobble me up."

When Papa said nothing, Mama glanced up. The deep

frown was still between his eyes. "Pontus, darling. What-ever is the matter?" she cried.

Papa crossed to the opposite window and stood looking out for a long moment before he spoke. Then, "Maria," he said irrelevantly, "can you see Larson's old barn from this window? *I* can of course, but I'm taller than you."

Mama was puzzled. "Why, Pontus, I never even thought of Larson's old barn. It certainly is nothing to look at."

Papa began pacing the bedroom floor. "I just thought it could have been that," he finally said in a disappointed voice.

"Pontus," Maria said sharply, "will you please stop walking up and down and explain yourself? What has Larson's old barn to do with me, I'd like to know?"

Papa stopped abruptly and stared down at the baby. "Because, Maria, it is *red*, that's why—like our baby's hair!"

Mama laughed. "Oh, *lilla* Pontus, I thought you were serious."

"How can you laugh, Maria?" he asked tensely. "And how can I ever explain having a son with red hair?"

All the love of her heart was in Mama's voice as she said softly, "Darling, *please* don't fret so. You don't have to explain anything. Engelbrekt is a beautiful boy even if he does have red hair. And I just guess he is going to follow right in his father's footsteps and be a wonderful man."

Papa was a little ashamed, but not yet pacified. "But it is so ridiculous, Maria—so utterly ridiculous. How can we be sure all our children—*if* we have any more—won't have red hair too?"

"Of course we will have more children. And if they have red hair we'll love them just as much." Mama looked down at Nim sleeping quietly in her arms. "He is so wonderful I wouldn't care if he was twins. Pontus," Mama suddenly cried, her blue eyes wide, "*I bet I know*."

"What, Maria? What?"

But Mama took her time. Gently she wrapped the blanket about the sleeping baby and placed him in the cradle, pulled the window shade and motioned Papa to follow her down the stairs. Only when they were seated on the parlor sofa would she speak.

"You know, Pontus," she began excitedly, "our church janitor has two boys with *flaming red hair*. But that is not all. You know that every Sunday morning those little boys sit on the front bench."

"Well?" asked Papa eagerly.

"Don't you see what I mean, Pontus? Every Sunday while I was that way, I sat and *stared at those red heads* while you preached for a whole hour. No wonder our little Engelbrekt has red hair."

Papa gave a deep sigh of relief. "Maria," he said proudly, "you have found the answer." Then as a new thought struck him he cried, "But, Maria. What happened to *you* can also happen to others. Why, in a very few years our church will be filled with redheaded children."

"You are right, Pontus," Maria agreed in an awed whisper. "What can we do?"

Papa took a turn around the room, his head lowered thoughtfully. "I shall have a *talk* with that janitor, Maria, this very day."

It was midafternoon when Papa knocked at Lars Erickson's door. Lars himself answered the knock, delighted to see Papa.

"Welcome to our humble home, Pastor Franzon. Come in and be seated in the best room."

He ushered Papa in, talking briskly in his quaint manner. "Emma is out doing *Patron* Karlberg's washing today, so Pastorn have to kindly excuse the house. But I assure him coffee I am expert in cooking. I shall get the *coffee-petter* on right away."

Papa sat on the edge of the wooden sofa and stared for a moment at the two large pictures of King Oscar and Queen Sofia in imitation gold frames. In the center of the room stood a large table, covered with the lace cloth Maria had made them for Christmas. The small table near the window held the many flowering plants and the family Bible. It was a comfortable room and Papa relaxed a little. He could hear Lars poking about the stove, preparing the coffee.

Presently two small faces, topped by flaming red hair, peered around the doorframe. Timidly they came inside. For a moment the boys stared at Papa, then as if on signal marched to the sofa, shook hands and bowed almost to the floor.

"Good day, *Farbror Pastorn*," they said as one voice. And, as suddenly as they had come, disappeared toward the kitchen.

Papa smiled and shook his head in dismay. They certainly have red hair. No wonder it had been catching and poor Maria had been the innocent victim.

Lars came in with the *coffee-petter* and a plate of *pepparkakor*. They talked pleasantly of the repairs the church needed, until coffee had been drunk. Then Papa cleared his throat. "Erickson," he began tactfully, "I have come here today because I need your help."

Lars beamed. "This has not happened before, Pastorn— that you come to me for help. I am happy you ask."

Papa crossed the room and took up the family Bible, opening it expertly to the passage he had been thinking of this morning, then handed the open book to the janitor. "Please read the thirtieth chapter of Genesis, starting with the thirtieth verse, to the end," he said kindly.

Lars Erickson read. When he had finished Papa asked, "What do you make of it, Erickson?"

The janitor scratched his head. "Good," he said. "Very good indeed, you have to give him credit. That Jacob was a smart one."

Papa took the Bible and settled himself on the sofa again. "You miss the point, Lars." And in his best Sunday-morning voice he read:

32. I will pass through all thy flock to day, removing from thence all the speckled and spotted cattle, and all the brown cattle among the goats: and of such shall be my hire.

37. And Jacob took him rods of green poplar, and of the hazel and chestnut tree; and pilled white strakes in them, and made the white appear which was in the rods.

38. And he set the rods which he had pilled before the flocks in the gutters in the watering troughs when the flocks came to drink, that they should conceive when they came to drink.

39. And the flocks conceived before the rods, and brought forth cattle ringstraked, speckled, and spotted.

Papa closed the Bible quietly and placed it back on the table. "That all happened thousands of years ago, Lars. But it could just as well be today. Basic principles never change."

Lars stared at him as though he wondered if the Pastor suddenly had lost his wits. Papa plunged on. "This morning, for instance. Mrs. Franzon and I had a little talk about our baby having red hair. We came to the conclusion, my good man, that *you* are to blame."

Erickson almost leapt from his chair. "I beg your pardon, Pastor Franzon. I am but a poor janitor, but I am a man with honor and respect for God and man."

Papa blushed in embarrassment. "Indirectly, I mean, Lars. Please don't misunderstand me. That is why I wanted you to read that chapter. You see it even makes a difference what a woman *looks* at at such a time as Mrs. Franzon has just been through. And that is why I need your help."

"I don't understand, Pastorn."

"Well, you see, your two little redheaded boys sit in the front pew every Sunday. And Mrs. Franzon, who attended church even though she was in that condition, had to sit and look at them. Result—our baby has red hair. Now do you think you could kindly move them to the back seat for the benefit of others who might not want their children to have red hair?"

The janitor looked up helplessly. "I'll be glad to do anything you suggest, Pastor. But what puzzles me is how *my* boys got red hair. Emma had no redheads to look at."

Papa had no answer for that, but he could never let Erickson know he had stumped him. "I guess women have strange ways, my good man. Just now suppose you try to help *me*. Will you do what I asked? Or, if you prefer, you might have their hair dyed."

Erickson laughed relieved. "I'll put them in the back seat, Pastorn. You see I don't care what color their hair is if they are good kids. I guess you just don't like red."

Papa rose and warmly shook Erickson's hand. "Thank you, Lars," he said. "You are a fine man—the salt of the earth. May God bless you."

But as Papa walked home, glad that the mission was over, he pondered certain church reforms. Matters like this should be handled by the conference. It would save a lot of embarrassment. He would propose that a church law be made, forbidding people with red hair to sit in the front pews. Yes, that would take care of the situation splendidly. It would, he suddenly realized, *if* he was not minus an excellent janitor.

"Don't go so fast, Pontus," Mama called as she reached the top of the hill, puffing for breath.

But already Papa had topped the hill and was on his way down. "I can beat you to the clearing, Maria," he shouted back. "You never could ski very fast."

Mama watched him skimming gracefully and effortlessly down the hill and around the curves, gliding in and out among the trees as easily as if they had not been there. Papa was certainly an expert skier, she thought. No wonder she had a hard time keeping up.

"Wait for me at the clearing, Pontus," she shouted after him, her voice echoing across the snowy hillsides.

Papa had the thermos bottle of coffee in his knapsack. It would taste good right now, but he had said, "Let's wait for the clearing, Maria," and she hadn't wanted to tell him how tired she was or the reason for it.

Now she took her time. From this high point she could see endless miles across the glistening hills. It was so beautiful she just wanted to hug the whole world. It wasn't only the view that made her happy. Mama knew both her happiness and her tiredness were for another reason. And she wasn't sure Papa was going to like it at all. Nim was only nine months old. All summer she had been confined to the parsonage a good deal. Pontus had looked glum when she couldn't go berrypicking with him, but finally would set off by himself. On Midsummer's Day, Tant Renberg, who vowed she was too old for hill climbing, had looked after Nim. And once Papa had insisted that Nim was old enough to go picnicking, and Mama had laughed and packed him in a big basket like a lunch. Papa had carried Nim in the basket, and Mama had looked out for the lunch.

Today Tant Renberg was nursing a touch of rheumatism and was glad enough to stay by the fire and watch over the baby. He was such a good boy. Maria smiled, remembering how Papa would beam when little Nim held out his chubby arms to be taken up, squealing with joy at the sight of him. But no matter how much Papa seemed to love his son, he would still tease about his hair.

"Engelbrekt," he would say, loud enough for Mama to hear in the kitchen, "you are a fine big boy. Smart and good-looking, too. If only you didn't have that red hair!"

Mama knew he was just joking, but she couldn't help being hurt. Somehow she felt she had bungled the job with Nim; that she should have made sure God sent a golden-haired baby—not one with red hair.

Mama sighed happily and examined her skis. Well, she wouldn't have to worry about that with the new baby, now that the janitor's boys had been moved to the back

of the church. The next little Franzon would be blond,
and Papa would be so happy he wouldn't even mind how
fast it had happened.

Papa was waiting in the clearing in the woods. He had
already removed his skis and taken the thermos from
the knapsack.

"Let me help you with your skis, Maria," he said. "This
coffee is going to taste good with some of your fine
bullar."

It was wonderful to get the skis off and stretch out a
bit. They hadn't seemed heavy when she started out
earlier this afternoon. Mama sat on the tree stump and
sipped the coffee slowly, nibbling on a *bulle*. The coffee
warmed her and chased away some of her tiredness. She
looked up as she felt Pontus's eyes on her.

"You look tired, my dear," he said gently. "Are you
not feeling well?"

"I *am* tired, Pontus," she answered hesitantly, deciding
this was as good a time as any to break the news. "I guess
I have to expect to tire quickly these days."

For a long moment Papa just stared at her, and when
finally he spoke it was with sharpness in his voice. "I hope,
Maria, you are not telling me you are 'that way' again
so soon."

Mama's eyes filled with anxious tears. How could Pontus talk so about their new little one? He should be happy
as she was. Somehow she must make him—but *how* she
did not know.

Papa finished his coffee in silence. He packed the cups
in the knapsack and strapped it on his back; then he tied
the two pairs of skis together and hung them over his
shoulder.

"Come," he said kindly taking her hand in his. "We'll
have to walk all the way home. You should know better
than to go skiing in your condition."

Mama's anxiety vanished. Pontus wasn't angry. This
was just his way of showing her how much he loved her.
As she crunched over the snowy trails, her hand in his,

Mama had never felt so safe and cherished. Occasionally Papa would press her hand tightly and look down at her with a smile full of love.

It was not until supper was over and little Nim had been tucked in the cradle that Papa mentioned the new baby. They were sitting before the open fire, silently watching the sputtering flames that made an endless bright chain up the chimney.

"I am afraid it is going to be hard on you, Maria, with Nim still a little baby," he said softly.

Mama knew he was remembering the long hours of anxious waiting and the agony of her pain. She too had thought of that. But the joy of having another baby pushed the memory of pain out of her mind. Suddenly she wanted more than anything else in the world to assure Pontus—dear frightened Pontus—that everything was going to be all right.

"Oh, Pontus," she cried, "it is just going to be wonderful having a new little baby. It won't be hard at all. You know Nim is good as gold. He just coos and laughs and sleeps. I won't mind to manage two of them, not a bit."

"We'll have to make the best of it, Maria," Papa said, caressing her hair. "I guess I never expected them to come so fast."

Poor Papa looked so perplexed that Mama's heart went out to him. After all it had not been easy to adjust himself to one baby in the house—and now it would be two. Her arms went about his neck. "Pontus *lilla*," she whispered in his ear, "do you think it could be because we love each other so?"

But as her time drew near, Mama was frightened. Hard as she tried not to remember, the memory of those long painful hours before Nim's birth swept through her like a nightmare. She must not let Pontus know, she told herself, and when he looked at her anxiously, she would push away her own fears and smile. "It is nothing. Don't you worry even a little bit. It is only the first baby that makes trouble. Why having the next one will be just like a song."

And it *was* almost that easy. Tant Renberg had just stepped inside the door and the midwife hadn't even had time to take off her coat. Little Charlotta Maria arrived with a lusty cry.

Mama was all smiles when Papa came in. "Didn't I tell you it would be easy, darling? You see! It was nothing to worry about. And look, Pontus," she cried excitedly, "what we got. A beautiful little girl with *blonde* hair."

Papa kissed her tenderly, and Mama folded the covers back from the baby's tiny face. The happiness that shone in Papa's eyes more than made up for any doubts she might have had.

"Maria," he whispered with awe, "she *is* beautiful."

And because Papa's joy was overflowing and he wanted to say something very special to his little golden-haired daughter, he covered up his embarrassment by speaking in English. "You sweet little thing," he said, "that nose of yours looks just like a tiny pink button."

Mama's laughter was triumphant. "Oh, Pontus, that is exactly what we shall nickname little Charlotta. Button. Won't that be the cutest name in Swedish?"

"Nim and Button," he repeated slowly. "Maria, I think that will sound very special."

She had been right after all, Mama rejoiced silently. Papa had forgotten all about his redheaded worries.

But their joy was short lived.

Before little Button was a week old, even Papa admitted there were worse things than red hair. Button had a pair of lungs that would have made a mountain yodeler proud. And what was more, she used them day *and* night. The peacefulness of the parsonage, in one short week, had become only a memory. The lamp burned in the bedroom throughout the night while Papa and Mama took turns walking the floor with Button, so little Nim could sleep.

"Is this going to keep up, Maria?" Papa asked wearily after the third week of nightly floor walking.

"It looks like it, Pontus," yawned Mama.

"How shall I ever prepare my sermons? All night I walk the floor and all day I'm so sleepy I cannot keep my eyes open." Papa stopped walking and Button began to cry.

Mama was so tired she could not help speaking crossly. "You didn't think redheaded babies were good enough, Pontus, so the Lord sent you a beautiful blonde one that *cries* all the time."

Papa wasn't going to blame the Lord for this. "Don't let us be too hard on her, Maria," he said sleepily. "It might be she has pain and can't tell us. We will just have to give her time to adjust to this big world."

Mama waited.

Every day Button seemed to grow more beautiful—and more troublesome. She screamed during the day if you picked her up, and she screamed at night if you didn't. She would sleep all day like a little angel, and cry all night like an imp from the other world. As if that were not enough, she began cutting teeth at an early age. Mama was almost afraid to nurse her.

"You see, Maria," Papa said when the first tooth manifested itself, "she did have a pain she couldn't tell us about. Soon she will be all right."

Mama just looked at him for a long time. She put Button into the cradle and gave her a *socka* to chew on. Cutting teeth took a long time, and it would be months and months before Button would be all right. How could babies be so different? Nim had been no trouble at all after his first tooth. He would sit all day and chew on a *socka*, and if he had pains he kept them to himself like a little man.

For a few minutes now there was quiet. But only for a few minutes. Presently the sharp cries filled the room again. Mama took the baby from the cradle and walked up and down, patting her gently. Button would not be pacified.

"Believe me, Pontus," Mama exclaimed in desperation, "the next one is going to be a good baby—*red hair* or not."

It was a full minute before Papa could make himself heard above the din. "Maria!" he almost shouted, "how can you even *think* of a next one?"

Mama did not answer. Little Button had finally fallen asleep.

Winter gave way to spring. Icicles dripped and fell from the eaves of the parsonage, and the coverlets of snow vanished from the hillsides. The twilight grew longer and longer, each passing day. Silvery buds fattened on the fruit trees and shrubbery. Nim toddled happily about the house, and Button, on all fours, seemed to be everywhere at once. Usually she slept the night through now, except when a new tooth was starting. But she found other ways to disturb the peace of the parsonage. If she couldn't crawl forward, Button crawled *backward*, wriggling outside any protective barrier Maria set up. She was into everything within reach. Mama couldn't leave her alone a moment.

"Why can't you be good like your brother?" she scolded as she put Button back on the floor blanket for the tenth time that morning. Button gazed up at her with wide blue eyes, her golden curls like a halo, and Mama melted. She sat down on the blanket and cuddled the child to her. The baking and cleaning would have to take second place this morning. Papa was working on his sermon, and she wanted to keep the children quiet. Nim would amuse himself for hours with never a sound. But not Button.

"I think you will grow up to be an explorer, Button," Mama said. "You never want to stay in one place a minute."

At least she wasn't crying, Mama thought as she went back to her baking. On the window sill above the baking board, the rows of geraniums flaunted their bright red blossoms. Beyond, the greening countryside stretched invitingly. Soon, Maria thought, it will be warm enough for picnics. This year they would take both the children. What fun it would be!

Suddenly an earsplitting crash behind her brought her out of her dreams. Button, screaming loudly, sat in a pool of milk, surrounded by broken dishes and baking tins. She had caught the end of the tablecloth which hung too near the floor and had literally brought it down about her head. Papa came rushing in from the study just as Mama picked Button out of the clutter, examining her for injuries.

"What in the world!" Papa cried. There was more fright than anger in his voice.

"I just turned my back for a moment. Thank Heaven, she isn't hurt." Mama handed the baby to Papa while she mopped up the milk and gathered up the pieces and pans. "Whatever are we going to do with her, Pontus?" she asked when she had finished.

Button was quiet again. Papa was bouncing her on his knee and she loved it. "I've been thinking about that too, Maria," Papa said. "I guess you are right. Perhaps God is punishing me for asking Lars to put his fine little boys in the back seat just because they have red hair. I think I better have another talk with Lars Erickson."

When Mama arrived at church the following morning, Lars and Emma Erickson and their two little boys were sitting in the front pew. Mama couldn't help feeling proud of Pontus. It took character and courage for Papa to admit, especially to his janitor, that he had offended God. But still Mama worried. More than anything else in the world, she wanted to please Papa. And though he had said now that he didn't care if all his children had red hair, Mama knew that deep inside he did care. It was up to her to give him the kind of children he wanted. But how could she be sure with the janitor's redheaded boys in the front pew?

All the following week Mama wrestled with the problem.

It wasn't until Saturday night, when she was putting
Button to bed after a particularly trying day, that the
answer came to her. Nim had been asleep in his crib for
an hour, but Mama had to sit beside the cradle and rock
Button, until her arm was numb. Now the baby had
finally closed her eyes and Mama rose from the chair.
She moved about noiselessly, not to waken her. It was
hard to believe that this baby, who looked like a little
sleeping angel, could be so different when she was awake.

And suddenly Mama knew what she had to do.

She wanted to rush right down to tell Pontus. But he
might not approve. She had better wait. All day Sunday
Mama went about with that twinkle in her eyes that
should have told Papa she was guarding a secret. She was
sure he was thinking she was that way again, but she just
let him think. He would find out soon enough.

It took Mama almost another week to find what she
wanted. Then one evening when Papa came in from
making a call on old Mrs. Nelson who was down with
rheumatism, Mama was ready with her surprise.

"Come with me, Pontus," she said taking his hand and
pulling him up the stairs after her.

On the bedroom wall, beside the two large mirrors,
hung a large picture of a beautiful angel.

Mama stopped in front of it still holding onto Papa's
hand. "See," she cried like a child before a lighted Christmas tree.

"It *is* beautiful, Maria. But don't you think we had
enough pictures in this room?"

Mama laughed. "I guess I just got too excited to explain,
Pontus *lilla*. But you see, it worked with Nim when I
looked at the janitor's boys. And it worked with Button
too, for I never thought of anything except she must *not*
have red hair. Now I shall look at this beautiful angel with
the next one, and think of goodness, and she will be just
perfect."

It was Papa's turn to laugh. "Maria, always you are a

surprise. Is there no end to your fanciful ideas?" He put his arm around her and hugged her to him.

Mama's excitement was almost more than she could bear. "Oh, Pontus, I'm so happy you like it. With both of us looking at it, we'll just have the most wonderful children in the whole world."

CHAPTER 4

𝕰 Mama's Model

What Papa really thought of Mama's model he never revealed, but her own faith in it, he was fully aware, was steadfast.

The long Swedish winter gave way to the brief twilight which heralded the coming of spring. Gradually the twilight hours lengthened to the full brightness of day, the days themselves became increasingly longer, until by the middle of June, the sun did not set at all.

Twice, since the advent of the model, this cycle of seasons had completed itself. Summer lay on the Swedish hills like a gentle hand. Inside the parsonage on this bright morning all was peace. Nim played contentedly with the cat. Papa went about with a happy smile. Even Button was behaving these days as a good child should. It had been this way, Mama reflected, ever since she had hung the picture of the angel in the bedroom as a model of perfection for the next child. So far, the model had proven a good influence in every way—except one. The one for which it had been bought. Almost two years had passed now and still there was no sign of another child.

A little frown grew between Mama's brows. Maybe God had decided not to let her have any more children. Maybe it was punishment for not being pleased with the babies He had already sent her. It was an awful thing to think about—never to have more than two children. Silently Mama prayed for forgiveness. She hadn't really meant to be displeased with her children; she just wanted them to be good. Surely God would understand that. Surely it was not sinful for a wife to want to please her husband who was one of God's chosen.

But more weeks drifted by. Soon Button would be three years old.

It was on a midsummer day, when they climbed Gellivara mountain, that Mama knew her prayers had been answered at last. She had been almost too tired to reach the top of the mountain. But, as always, she kept her secret until she was really sure. This time even Papa seemed pleased. Maybe, thought Mama, he was getting used to love—and children. She was happier than she had ever been in her life. Eagerly she waited the day, for by now it held no terrors for her.

When the day finally arrived, everything went on schedule. The midwife was snippy as usual and sent Papa for a long walk. Since no one ever crossed midwife Eklund, Papa went. Mama watched him reluctantly put on his hat and coat and, with a backward glance at her, walk slowly out of the room. She wanted to tell him to stay, but suddenly her throat was too full of love for words.

An hour later he returned. By that time it was all over. Tant Renberg met him at the door.

"Go right in to Maria, Pastor Franzon, and take a look at your little angel."

Mama's eyes were sparkling as Papa came into the bedroom. "Oh, Pontus," she cried, "it worked. Our new little baby is the *picture* of that angel."

Papa kissed Mama and then gently pulled the quilt back from the baby's face. "I'm so happy, Maria. You really got your little angel this time. Now I just hope she will be as good and sweet as she is beautiful."

"Oh, Pontus, there is only one thing. It isn't a *she*," said Mama softly.

Papa's eyes almost popped out. "Don't tell me, Maria," he demanded needlessly, "that this angelic-looking child is a *boy?*"

"I do tell you just that, Pontus." Mama twinkled.

"Don't you see what you've done? Just tell me how will a boy with a face like an angel get along in this world? What can he *do?* If only you could be like other women, Maria. But always you have to do something no one else ever heard of. We'll get rid of that picture at once."

Mama only laughed. Nothing could dampen her spirits today. "Don't be so silly, Pontus. It won't hurt him to be beautiful, and I assure you he will grow up to be a real he-man. And why not with a handsome Papa for *his* model."

As always Mama had had the last word. But when it came to naming the baby, it was Papa who had the final say.

"Peter Gabriel Franzon," he announced the next morning, when they discussed the baby's Bible name.

"Why *Gabriel,* Pontus?" Mama had asked. "There are so many fine names in the Bible."

"That's for the angel part of him, Maria," Papa answered firmly, with a little twinkle in his eyes. "You made him *look* like an angel, didn't you?"

Mama said no more. From the first the baby was nicknamed Pelle.

The picture of the angel remained on the bedroom wall. If God had sought to punish either Mama or Papa, He must have relented, for thereafter about every year and a half the parsonage was filled with the excitement, cries and laughter caused by a new baby. And each one of them in one way or another, Mama assured Papa, resembled the angel.

Now there were seven. If Papa tired of the happy confusion, Mama would send him off to meditate in the church.

"They got to make noise and be happy, Pontus. Someday they will all grow up, and then you and I will just sit here and remember their shouting happy voices."

But Mama knew there were days when Papa wished they were grown up already. On such days it was hard to convince him that she still wanted one more. Uneven numbers were unlucky! One more and she would be satisfied.

"Well I certainly *hope* so, Maria. But it seems to me you have more than plenty of work with the seven we already have," Papa commented dryly.

"Why, Pontus. It doesn't seem like work at all to me. It is such fun to watch the children growing up like little plants needing love and sunshine."

And they were growing up. The days and weeks and years seemed to float by, so filled with love and happiness that Mama couldn't believe there was another woman in the world as happy. Of course there were times of anxiety and strain when illness struck; when the rest of them spent long hours in prayer and waiting and tender service. But always when these dark days had passed, there was even greater happiness and a deeper love. Then Mama would sing more softly as she went about her work, as if this were another way of saying, "Thank you, God!"

The house seemed to expand with the years without the addition of rooms. Sometimes after supper Papa would play the organ and everyone would sing. Even the littlest one would join in. And then everyone would laugh at the cracking notes in Nim's changing voice. These were gay and happy days, indeed.

But for Mama, Saturday nights were the best of all. This was the time she felt nearest to her children; when she could plan and think about their futures.

This was the night she shined the shoes.

It was the last task of the busiest day in the week. For Saturday was a day of preparation in the parsonage. By nightfall every room in the house was in order. The hand-woven rugs were bright splashes of color against the newly scrubbed white floors. The copper pots and pans and all the silver had been polished. White-tile fireplaces gleamed. The pantry gave off tempting odors of pre-cooked meat for Sunday dinner. Prepared vegetables stood in bowls of water. On the baking board, covered with a clean towel, were Mama's pride—coffee bread and a special dessert. No cooking ever was permitted on the Lord's Day. Even the table was set on Saturday night. It was Nim's job, just before he went to bed, to place a chair at each place.

Truly for Mama it was the end of a perfect day. From the back hall came the spicy fragrance of fresh spruce-mats, on which nine pairs of shoes were carefully wiped before daring to step on Mama's scrubbed floors.

Finally, when the children were in bed, and Papa was busy in the study, Mama would sit on a low footstool in the kitchen and shine seven pairs of shoes.

"Why don't you let Nim and Button tend to that?" Papa had asked. "Surely you have enough to do on Saturday."

But Mama only smiled dreamily. "I shall always do this, Pontus. As long as the children live at home. When they grow up and move away, one by one, most of all I think I shall miss this beautiful hour on Saturday night, shining their shoes."

Papa did not quite understand it, but he had to admit that for some mystic reason shining the children's shoes made Mama happy.

Mama always shined the shoes according to age. How like Nim was the first pair. Strong and sturdy. And a little bit slow, for Nim was never in a hurry about anything. Except his scissors! By the time he was five he managed to find the scissors wherever Mama hid them, and had tried his skill on everything from Papa's best white church shirt to a perfect barber job on the tail of Kurre, the cat. Sometimes, even when she was most exasperated, Mama couldn't help wondering tenderly what great talent was hidden for him in a pair of scissors.

But it was Papa who worried most.

"Maria," he said sternly, when Nim had chopped off half of Button's beautiful golden braids, "he will never amount to anything. The best I can figure for him is the life of a barber!"

"And what's so tragic about that? Barbers do an important job in the world."

"How can you joke about it, Maria. You know I have dedicated my first-born to be a great missionary. Why, imagine a man with a noble name like Engelbrekt being just a barber."

Mama's eyes began to twinkle. "Maybe he could be both."

"Don't be ridiculous, Maria."

"But it isn't, Pontus. With a razor in one hand ready to shave a man, he would only have to say *'My good man, are you ready to die?'* and he would have a convert for sure."

Papa had to laugh. He should have known better than to criticize one of the children to Maria. "Well, perhaps he will outgrow it," he said consolingly.

But Nim didn't. Now he was twelve years old and still cutting up everything in sight and reach. Something had to be done, but what? Mama made suggestions, but Papa was convinced that the best system was the application of his right hand to a certain bottom.

It wasn't long before Papa had a chance to test his theory.

It had happened on a Saturday when Mama had been especially busy. Not only were there the regular duties of cleaning, polishing, cooking and baking, but there was to be a special guest at Sunday dinner. Pastor Mickelson from Haparanda was passing through on his way to Stockholm and would attend Sunday morning service, saying a few words after Papa's sermon. Then he would have dinner at the parsonage.

As soon as Papa had received the news, he had set about preparing a special sermon for the occasion. His pastorate might be smaller than Pastor Mickelson's, but Papa would not be found wanting when it came to preaching the Word of God. For three days now he had been shut up in his study, scarcely coming out for meals. Maria had been asked to keep the children quiet, and she was especially careful to make as little noise as possible herself.

It was almost noon when Maria heard the study door open. Papa had just finished copying, in his clear and precise handwriting, the most powerful sermon he had ever prepared. At least so he assured Mama as he came into the kitchen where she was putting a pan of coffee bread into the oven. Nim and Button were playing quietly at the big table as Mama had commanded them to do.

"I tell you, Maria," Papa said reverently, "sometimes I think that, of all the disciples, John was the greatest. His words are as appropriate to our times as if they had been written today."

Before Mama could tell him that she thought St. John would have been pleased with the way Papa delivered his word of redemption, there was a knock at the kitchen door. Papa put his sermon on the table and went to answer it. It was Lars Erickson about the arrangements for tomorrow. Mama went on with her baking. Both had forgotten Nim and Button. When Papa came back after several minutes with Lars, Nim was proudly showing Button his handiwork.

"See, it's a deer head!" he cried excitedly.

Button had taken the cutout from his hand. "Let me see what's written under it," she said, and then read aloud, " *We shall all come short of Glory!* What a silly thing to write under a deer head."

Papa was across the room in a stride. His powerful sermon was now a pile of scrap paper.

"Come with me, young man," he said firmly, "and we shall see who will come short of glory!"

Mama tried to be a peacemaker. "Oh, Pontus, he didn't *know* it was your sermon. Please don't be too hard on him."

But Papa had already departed, with a protesting Nim, in the direction of the woodshed.

By virtue of considerable midnight oil and his remarkable memory, Papa's sermon was rewritten in time. The church was filled for Sunday-morning service, and Papa had never been more eloquent. Afterwards, Pastor Mickelson spoke for ten minutes. Nim, thoroughly chastened, sat next to Mama, as unhappy and quiet as a wounded deer. Mama's heart ached for him, remembering the severity of Papa's "laying on of hands." Perhaps a child did need a spanking once in a while, but she was sure Nim was cured of his cutting habit. Just the same she resolved to ask Pontus to deal gently with him if ever there was a next time.

It was November before Mama was confronted with a resolution of her own.

On a particularly cold day, Mrs. Lund, who daily exercised her little French Poodle, Sippan, regardless of the weather, had stopped in for a visit at the parsonage. Mama loved company. Quickly she made a fire in the open stove in *salen* and served coffee and company cookies. The time passed so pleasantly that it was late when Mrs. Lund shook hands, thanking Mama for a lovely afternoon. At the door she called, "Come, Sippan! We must be going."

Sippan came bouncing into the room—and Mrs. Lund let out a scream.

"Sippan! What has happened to you? You are naked in the middle of the winter," she cried, wringing her hands and throwing her scarf over the denuded little dog.

But Mama knew too well what had happened. When she had pacified Mrs. Lund with profuse apologies and sent her on her way home with promises that she would knit Sippan a coat, she went in search of Nim. She found him behind the sofa in the kitchen, scissors still in hand. Her resolution completely forgotten, she did not wait for Papa. Firmly she took Nim's scissors and, with

tears running down her own cheeks, sheared off every
red hair on his head.

"Now, young man," she said sternly, "perhaps you
will understand how Sippan is going to suffer without
a coat in the middle of winter."

But that night Mama was a little longer over her prayers
for Nim.

Gently Mama put Nim's shoes on the floor and picked
up the small narrow boots belonging to Button. It was
easy to see that they belonged to restless feet. Button was
eleven years old now and, while she had outgrown her
baby temperament, she had developed new tendencies
that kept Mama on the jump most of the time. In Papa's
eyes she could do no wrong. But hard as Mama tried,
there were a good many quirks she just couldn't understand. One was the child's interest in "magic."

"When I grow up," Button would announce, "I'm
going to join the circus."

Mama would look at Papa and say nothing until Button
had performed one of her disappearing acts, which she
did whenever something happened Button didn't like.
Then Mama would ask, "How in the world, Pontus, could
she ever get such an idea? Why, she has never even *seen*
a circus."

"It's beyond me," laughed Papa. "No circus would ever
lose itself in this part of the world."

Mama could only pray a little harder that the child
would forget about this silly dream, for, as the apple of
Papa's eye, Button *had* to turn out right or it would break
his heart. But Button went right on practicing magic and
disappearing, especially when there were dishes to wash,
or it was time for prayer meeting.

How long this might have continued Mama would
never know, if Button had not begun disappearing from
the supper table during grace. At such times, Papa's eyes
were closed, and, if dinner consisted of something Button
did not like, she would slide slowly from the chair under

the table and quietly disappear on hands and knees into the *vardags*-room. When Papa opened his eyes, her chair would be empty. After several such occasions, Papa resolved to say grace with his eyes open.

One night when there was *rot-mos*, turnips and potatoes mashed together, which Button particularly disliked, she waited her chance. Papa bowed his head, but Button failed to note that his eyes were not closed. Slowly she began to slide under the table. Papa's prayer, to the amazement of the rest of the family, had a very strange ending:

"Crawl back, my sweet. It won't work. The devil may tempt, but just now I have caught him by the tail. . . . May this food be blessed and our hearts made grateful. Amen."

Mama smiled now as she put Button's shoes, brightly polished, into the line and picked up Pelle's. How completely he lived up to his real name, Gabriel. Five of her children had had the angel as a model and all of them were wonderful children. But Pelle was goodness itself. As a baby, he had given her no trouble at any time. Later, when the other children quarreled over who would be served first, or would get the biggest piece of *appel-kaka* Pelle would stand aside, with wide clear blue eyes looking up at her. "I'll wait, Mama." It was, Maria reflected, this big heart that had got him into the only situations he had ever created in the family.

From the time Pelle was old enough to read, he had been fascinated by the Bible. At first Papa had read the stories to all the children, and Pelle would sit in the little circle which they had formed at Papa's feet, his eyes wide and his mouth a small "O." But when the others had tired, or gone off to bed, it was Pelle who asked for more. Then Papa would take him on his lap and Pelle would trace the lines with his tiny finger as Papa read. As soon as he could read them himself, he did more than read; he began to live what he read. This, Mama and Papa agreed, was wonderful, until a certain winter day when Pelle had come home blue with cold. He had given his

warm coat to a little Lapp child who had been scantily
dressed. Later, when spring had loosened the ice on the
streams, Nim had rescued Pelle from the swift-flowing
waters and tried to explain that not everyone could walk
on the water like Jesus.

It was not until Pelle had suggested, as a remedy for
Nim's cutting and Button's acting, that "the Bible says
to cut off the hand and foot that leads into mischief,"
that Papa knew something had to be done. He forbade
Pelle to read the Bible alone. But Pelle only listened more
intently to Papa's sermons.

Then had come a special night. Mama chuckled now
remembering it, but at the time it hadn't seemed funny
at all.

She had been fixing *råraker* for supper. The whole
family loved these raw potato pancakes, and she had just
finished grating a large bowlful. Pelle came rushing in
from outside, happy and excited.

"I better grate a whole lot more potatoes for you,
Mama," he panted, taking off his cap. "We will have lots
of company for supper. I did just what Papa preached
last Sunday."

Mama's heart sank right into her shoes. Frantically she
tried to remember what Papa had preached, but she
couldn't.

"Pelle," she finally asked slowly, "what *did* Papa preach
last Sunday?"

He was surprised. "You don't remember, Mama? He
asked if any one of us, when we gave a dinner, ever invited the poor and the lame and the blind. And if we did,
God's blessing would smile down on us."

Mama trembled as she realized what he was saying.

"Oh, Pelle," she whispered while her heart stopped,
"you didn't!"

Pelle had just looked at Mama with eyes as clear and
deep as a mountain lake. "Yes, Mama, I did. Only five,
though. One lame, two poor and one crippled. And do

you think one with a glass eye is just as good as a really blind man, Mama?"

In her heart Mama cried, Oh, Pelle, Pelle, what shall we do with you? But aloud she only said, "Well, you better start grating lots and lots of potatoes."

When the "party" was over that night, and the last of Pelle's guests had gone, Papa had considerable explaining to do to his second son. Something to the effect that even *his* preaching shouldn't always be carried out *too* literally.

Vickey's shoes were long and narrow. Aristocratic, thought Mama, like the child herself. She was only six, but already quite tall and, according to Papa, the perfect result of the angel model. Indeed, Mama had to admit that, much as she loved all her children, Vickey was certainly the most beautiful. She had been named for two queens, Victoria Sofia, and, as though she had understood the significance, the child had seemed to live up to her queenly namesakes almost from the day she opened her deep blue eyes upon the world. Now, young as she was, her lashes were long dark fringes accenting the depth of her eyes and the petal-like skin of her slender oval face. She walked like a little princess and never showed confusion or excitement. Sometimes Mama thought Vickey was almost too kind, too quiet, too restrained. It wasn't always good for a child to suffer so intensely in silence.

Mama's heart still ached when she thought of what had happened at the Christmas "robbing" party last year.

Christmas in Lapland, as in homes over most of the world, was the most festive season of the year. From December twenty-fourth to January thirteenth there were parties and celebrations. Every home, however modest, had its Christmas tree party. While everyone took part in the games, only the children were allowed to "rob" the tree. Then there would be coffee and many kinds of cookies for the grownups, and finally, to the gay accompaniment of folk tunes and laughter, the Christmas tree was "danced" out. This was the gayest ceremony of all. Papa would take the top of the tree, Mama the trunk. Everyone else at the party would hang onto the branches, scrambling happily for the best position, and "dance" the tree into the back yard.

It had been an especially happy Christmas last year. Mama as always had spent weeks getting ready. In the center of the floor in *salen* stood the tree, loaded with good things to eat. There were candies wrapped in all colors of fancy paper, and unwrapped candies shaped like Santas, bells, hearts, angels, and stars. And most important of all—*julbocker* and gingerbread men, that belonged only to Christmas. Under every candle hung a red shiny apple. On the big table, which had been pushed aside to make room for the tree, was a pile of white paper bags.

When the time for the robbing ceremony arrived, everyone formed a circle and danced around and around the tree. Even Papa completely forgot his dignity and joined in the games, dancing and laughing with the children. Then suddenly the grownups dropped out and the children pounced upon the tree, robbing it of its goodies and piling them in a great heap on the table. When the tree had been picked clean, Mama gave each child one of the paper bags, counting the number of children aloud as they circled the table. There were sixteen, so the big heap of candies and cakes were quickly divided into sixteen little heaps, and on top of each was placed a red apple.

When Mama gave the signal, each child began filling his or her paper bag with one little heap of goodies. Suddenly Mama noticed that Anna-Lisa Lund, who was next to Vickey and a year older, was taking Vickey's goodies as well as her own, popping them all into her paper bag. But Vickey was making no protest at all. Instead she was quietly putting into her own bag the few candies and cookies that remained, and the red apple. Then she slipped away into the *vardags*-room.

Mama started to follow her, but the line around the refreshment table was forming. Mama poured the coffee and Button handed each guest a plate for the many kinds of cookies Mama had made. Gay voices and laughter filled the room.

"No one makes *spritz* like Maria," Mrs. Lund exclaimed.

"Or *mandelformar*," cried Mrs. Nelson.

"One day I shall start a bakery," laughed Mama, "then we will *see* how good I bake." But Mama's mind was not on the gaiety.

When the plates were filled and the coffee poured, she went in search of Vickey. She found her curled up in a corner of the sofa in the *vardags*-room, crying bitterly. Mama picked her up and held her close.

"Darling," she comforted, "you mustn't cry so. I saw Anna-Lisa take your goodies. Why didn't you ask her for them? She would have given them back."

"She—she—wouldn't, Mama," Vickey sobbed, "she doesn't like me."

"Of course she likes you, darling. You're a fine little girl."

Slowly Vickey dried her tears. "Papa says we must love our enemies, Mama. I couldn't tell on Anna-Lisa. She would get a spanking and then all our fun would be spoiled."

For a moment Mama's throat was full of tears. Vickey adored Papa, and to her whatever he said was next to the voice of God. She had preferred to suffer in silence rather than bring punishment even to one who was guilty.

"Papa is right, darling," Mama agreed. "God does want us to love our enemies and forgive them."

Vickey threw her arms around Mama's neck. "I feel better now since the tears came out. I have forgiven Anna-Lisa, and God will give me a new bag of goodies when I get to Heaven."

Yes, thought Mama now as she put the shoes aside, that was little Vickey, too kind for her own own good, but willing to wait a whole lifetime for Christmas goodies, rather than to hurt others. And all because Papa said it was right!

Greta's shoes were short and stubby. Greta was the nickname for Margareta Kristina—names which Mama had picked from the royal family in Stockholm. But there was certainly nothing regal about Greta. She was small and round, with twinkling eyes and quick easy movements. She was always happy about something—and hungry.

"Can I lick the cake pan, Mama? Please, Mama, make me a special little cake." This was Greta's song every Saturday when the baking started.

When Mama passed over the cake pans from which most of the batter had been scraped, Greta would get three or four spoons and head for the back porch steps. In a moment, as if by signal, she would be surrounded by her playmates, all dipping in for a "taste."

Mama, watching through the open door, would smile with special fondness.

"Greta is always the little mother," Mama remarked proudly to Papa one morning.

As usual Papa laughed with his eyes before he spoke. "Just you wait, Maria. Greta will grow up and get married and have as many children as her Mama."

"Won't that be wonderful, Pontus? What could be nicer than just loads and loads of grandchildren?"

Papa didn't seem to agree. "Maria," he chuckled, "Greta is only four and already you are counting *her* children."

But Mama had wondered if Papa might not be right, the day she had left Greta to "help" Tant Renberg look after her two baby brothers, while Mama took Vickey to buy new shoes. She had thought this would teach Greta a sense of responsibility, to "help" Tant Renberg. But as it turned out, Greta had had her own ideas about the meaning of the word. When Mama and Vickey returned, the parsonage was in a turmoil.

In the forbidden *salen*, four-year-old Greta presided over a very fancy tea table. Mama's best silver and her finest lace cloth had been spread, and Greta was serving lump sugar and cream and company cookies to four wide-eyed little girls. Tant Renberg was not in sight, but she most certainly could be heard. From the direction of the bedroom came loud cries and pounding.

At the sight of Mama and Vickey, four frightened little girls scurried out, leaving Greta to face the music alone.

But Mama released Tant Renberg first and learned what had happened. Greta had brought in four of her little playmates and asked her "to make a party" for them. Tant had told her she was too busy and left the kitchen to look after the two babies. Greta had followed and turned the key in the door, and all Tant's pounding and screaming had done no good.

"How could you do such a thing to Tant Renberg," scolded Mama. Greta hung her little golden head, but kept silent. "You know sugar costs very much money and you have used the cream for Papa's board meeting tonight. What do you think Papa is going to do about that?"

Still no answer. Mama brought the switch from the kitchen *kåpa*, but she used it as sparingly as she dared and still hope to teach the child a lesson. Only when the spanking was over and her tears had been dried would Greta talk.

"It was the black angel, Mama. It whispered it would be fun to lock Tant Renberg in." And then to Mama's amazement Greta began to laugh. "And it was fun. Tant Renberg screamed, 'Open the door or the black angel will take you.' And all the time it was the black angel doing it."

In the front hall the big clock struck nine resounding chimes. Only two more pairs of shoes—busy little baby shoes—and this most loved of all Mama's tasks would be finished for another week. Calle was a year old and Torkel two. Almost twins, Mama thought as she watched them trotting unsteadily about the house, following Greta

wherever she went. And Greta never seemed to tire
of mothering them.

Tenderly Mama placed the four little shoes in her lap,
caressing each one before she started polishing it. Soon
there would be no baby shoes in the row on Saturday
night. Soon—much too soon—the children's shoes would
be carrying them into the world, leaving the parsonage
hushed and empty. Mama sighed deeply. Suddenly she
couldn't bear to think of the house without a dimpling
little baby to care for. And she knew Pontus loved them
as much as she did. He just didn't say it so often. Mama's
heart swelled with happiness and love, thinking of what
a wonderful Papa Pontus was.

Now seven pairs of shiny shoes stood in a row on the
kitchen floor. Mama knelt reverently, folded her hands
and bowed her head. Aloud she prayed a little prayer
that she had made up once while shining the shoes—a
special prayer for a special night.

> "God bless the step each foot will take
> Of each dear child a staunch soul make
> Help them to grow to do thy will
> And with Thy love my children fill.
> Amen."

Mama arose, tiptoed to the study door and knocked
softly. "May I see you just for a moment, Pontus?" she
asked.

When Papa opened the door she whispered, "Come,
darling, I want you to see how many children we have."

Papa looked annoyed. "I think, Maria," he said sternly,
"I have reason to know how many children we have."

Mama only laughed and led him into the kitchen. "If
we count all their feet, it makes fourteen."

"And if we count all their hands too it will make twen-
ty-eight. And how about their fingers and toes?"

Even Papa was laughing now with Mama. "Oh, Pontus,"
she cried, "I think we are just the luckiest Papa and Mama
on the whole of God's earth!"

CHAPTER 5

✻ Mama Stands in Papa's Shoes

Papa had very strict ideas about most things. He was particularly definite about the place God had allotted in this life to men and women. He permitted Mama to run the parsonage as she thought best and proper, so long as she gave due consideration to his bank account. But when it came to matters of the Church, they were entirely within his domain.

At least so Papa thought until he awoke one spring morning with a headache and a fever.

Papa let his head fall back onto the pillow and pulled the quilt up over his shoulders. It was no use. He was really sick. And what was worse—it was Sunday.

Outside the brightness of the day mocked him. The past three Sundays it had rained. Now when the late spring sun was high and warm in a cloudless sky and he had prepared a fine sermon, he had to be flat on his back with a fever.

"Please, Pontus," Maria pleaded, "stay in bed and be sick in peace. And don't fret, dear. I have a thing or two to tell that congregation and I might as well do it this Sunday morning."

Papa sat up again horrified. "Maria! You can't do that!" he shouted hoarsely.

Mama only pushed him gently back onto the pillow and tucked him in. Papa submitted weakly; he was too sick to argue. Anyway, he might just as well try to stop the midnight sun as to argue with Mama. She always managed to get her own way. As a preacher he could soften the most rebellious hearts, make men confess their hidden sins and women weep over erring lives. But when it came to handling Mama, Papa knew he was lost. If he blocked her in one place, she would loophole through another. If he thought he had her cornered, she would miraculously squeeze by his all-seeing eye.

Now he stared gloomily out the window, only too well aware that if Mama had made up her mind to preach, she would preach, one way or another. Desperately he wracked his brain. If only he could get in touch with Deacon Lund. But Mama had refused to call him—just kept repeating that ridiculous command, "Stay in bed and be sick in peace." Surely there was some way to make her listen to reason. But even as he hoped, Papa knew he was helpless. Maria had a way of twisting him to her wishes no matter what he said or did. Oh, why had the Lord ever created Eve in the first place? She was a thorn in Adam's flesh, a chain around his neck—a weight on his foot.

For the hundredth time since his marriage Papa asked himself why he had been such a fool to get married. He might now be serving one of the large churches if it were not for a wife and seven children. It was a bit odd—and Papa admitted that he himself did not understand it—that the larger churches objected to calling as their pastor a man who had obeyed the Lord's command to propagate the earth. So he had to be content with a small church and the small salary that went with it.

Suddenly he was ashamed of himself. Maria had never complained. She *was* hard to handle, but that was only part of Mama. Most of her, he thought warmly, was bighearted, loving and beautiful—and she was only half his age. Without wanting to, he remembered that morning on the boat so many years ago, when he had spoken of his fears that the congregation would not welcome her easily. "We'll just tackle them together, Pontus," she had said, her eyes shining like a child's.

Papa sighed. Of course he loved his children and he loved Mama with all his heart. But if Mama insisted upon preaching this morning, he would lose even this small church and its small income. His heart pounded with fear; his head and body ached. If only he *could* be "sick in peace." But there was about as much chance of that as jumping over Gellivara mountain.

Mama came in with a glass of water and a small white powder-envelope. "You'd better take this before I leave, Pontus. It will take away your headache."

Papa sat up obediently and took the medicine. "Maria," he barked, "don't you know that to be able to preach you have to have a text?"

Mama smiled and showed her dimples. "Don't get so excited, darling," she soothed. "I have had a text for years. It is about those fishermen that fished all night and caught nothing. Of course I might change it just a *little bit* and make it 'His Twelve Lean Years.'"

Papa gasped and sank back on the pillow. "You can't do that, Maria," he wailed. "You'll preach me right out of a church."

"Pontus," Mama said firmly, "our bank account is leaner than a rabbit's front tooth, and I intend to do something about it. Just you wait and see."

Mama set about dressing with special care in her finest black dress with white trimmings. Her blonde hair was piled high on her head and held in perfect order with two simple combs.

"How do I look, Pontus *lilla?*" she asked when she was ready.

Papa did not answer. He turned his face to the wall and closed his eyes, but it had no effect on Mama.

"Now I'll put Torkel and baby Calle to bed for their morning nap. The other children can go to church with me. You see, Pontus, there isn't a thing to worry about."

Nothing except ruin, thought Papa, as he heard the front door close.

Beads of perspiration formed on Papa's forehead. It was lucky for him that his occupation was not an engineer on a fast passenger train. Mama, being Mama, would have taken over that job just as confidently.

After a while Papa turned over again. Through the window, he could see the white church down the street. It was a homey church, friendly and inviting. The doors were wide open. Up in front was the pulpit he had occupied all these years. Today Mama would be standing there, slim and blonde—*and preach him right out of a job.*

Papa watched the family procession until it reached the church. Mama and Greta were in front, then Vickey and Pelle, and finally Nim and Button. All in their Sunday best. Any other time Papa would have been proud, but he was not in a mood this morning. Now Mama was smiling a greeting to everyone as she guided the children ahead of her into church.

Papa sighed and closed his eyes. What a stubborn woman! She would never know how to handle that congregation. They were a touchy bunch of people, especially about money. Hadn't he hinted for a raise for the past three years? And hadn't they completely ignored the hint? Such a thing as a raise for their underpaid shepherd had never even been taken up at a board meeting. Now what would happen when Mama suddenly appeared in *his* pulpit and preached about "His Twelve Lean Years?" Gooseflesh covered him at the very thought.

Papa tried to pray. He tried to sleep. He succeeded only in counting the minutes until Mama would return to the parsonage. Never had an hour seemed so long. His body felt old and his soul discouraged.

At last he heard Mama's laughter in the kitchen, and the eager chatter of the children. Mama was telling them stories as she prepared their dinner. Why didn't she come into the bedroom? Didn't she know he wanted to know what had happened? Even if the roof of the church had fallen in, Maria would only smile and find some good reason for the catastrophe. Today Papa was just tired of being Mama's husband. She was too young for him anyway, and too full of tricks—and stubborn.

By the time Mama opened the bedroom door, carrying the bowl of hot broth, Papa had worked himself into such a rage that his temperature was soaring.

"If I were a well man, Maria, I would turn you over my knee," he said grimly. "You know you have completely gone against my wishes."

"Drink this broth while it is hot," Mama commanded, ignoring his remark. "As for preaching—Pontus, I wouldn't undo that for a barrel of gold."

This was too much. "Preaching," he almost shouted. "What do you know about preaching?"

"I know this," said Mama sweetly. "*I simply love it.* And if it weren't for the children I think I would go into the business."

Papa was completely paralyzed with anger. He tried to speak, but only managed to sputter inarticulately. Mama patted him on the cheek, utterly oblivious to the destructive effect of her words. "You should be very proud of me, Pontus." There was a twinkle in her eyes that could only mean more mischief. What more had she done to destroy his career? She is keeping something from me, thought Papa. She always looks like that when she has a secret. Well, he decided as he finished gulping down the broth, she could keep her secret. He'd never give her the satisfaction of asking her about it.

And for the rest of the day Papa lay with his face to the wall, sulking. Several times he heard the door open softly and knew that Mama was peeking in to see how he was getting along, but he pretended to be sleeping.

It was late afternoon when Papa heard the doorbell. After a few moments his door opened.

"You have a visitor, Pontus," Mama whispered as she touched his shoulder gently.

Papa turned over to find Deacon Lund standing beside
the bed. When Mama had gone out and quietly closed
the door, Lund said sympathetically, "You don't look so
well, Pastor Franzon." And he eyed Papa critically.

"This is the first time I have missed a Sunday in *twelve*
years," Papa almost snapped, "except of course for my
vacation Sundays."

"Sorry. I didn't mean to offend."

The deacon sat down on the chair next to the bed,
tapping his foot up and down on the floor. Papa's nerves
were jumping and his head ached, but he forced himself
to speak more kindly.

"I'm sorry I was unable to preach this morning," he
said, watching the effect upon Lund.

"Of course," the deacon hastened to say, "I understand."

Papa was getting nervous. Obviously this wasn't just
a social call. Deacon Lund had something on his mind.
Something he was finding very difficult to say. Inwardly
Papa groaned. It would be hard to leave the church and
Lapland; they had made up the happiest years of his life.

"When a man is sick, Deacon Lund," Papa ventured
after several minutes of unbearable silence, "sometimes
things happen over which he has no control."

To Papa's utter surprise the deacon smiled sympathetically. "Indeed they do, Pastor Franzon. I know I speak
for the entire congregation when I say we are very sorry
you are ill. But we made out just fine this morning. Mrs.
Franzon did a splendid job." He chuckled to himself.
"She has a most engaging way of putting things over,
you know. In fact she made us remember certain responsibilities which I'm afraid we have overlooked."

Papa couldn't believe his ears. Was it possible that
Deacon Lund was *praising* Maria's outrageous behavior?
Or was he merely trying to ease Papa's embarrassment?
If that were the case, thought Papa, he had better let him
know where he stood on the matter.

"A woman's place is in the home. I assure you, Deacon

Lund, it was not by my choice that Mrs. Franzon preached this morning."

"Well, that is beside the point. Mrs. Franzon is a very gifted lady—very gifted indeed. We feel you are a lucky man, Pastor. And the church is mighty lucky too to have two preachers."

Papa stuttered, "T-*two* preachers!"

The deacon cleared his throat before he continued. "I am here to bring you good news, Pastor. We were so impressed by Mrs. Franzon's sermon this morning that we called a meeting of the board right after the services. The vote was unanimous to raise your salary twenty *kronor* a month."

Long after Deacon Lund had departed, Papa lay very still and stared at the ceiling. Somehow he could not rejoice over that longed-for and much-needed raise. Mama had done it again as she had said she would. He would never hear the last of it. He could just see her strutting about the parsonage like a crowing rooster. No, if he was to have any peace in his own house, he must never let Mama know how that raise came to be. Why, she might even think it her duty to do half the preaching. And, being Mama, she would gradually take over the ministry. Papa could almost picture himself in a pink gingham apron cleaning house, tending the babies, and washing diapers, while Mama sat in his study and wrote sermons.

The horror of such a thing caused Papa to exclaim aloud, "That must never happen—never."

Too late he realized how loudly he had spoken. Mama rushed into the room. "Did you call me, Pontus?" she asked anxiously.

"No," snapped Papa, angry with himself, "I did *not* call you."

"That is strange. I was sure I heard you calling." Mama sat down on the side of the bed. "Are you sure you are all right, Pontus?"

"Of course I'm not all right, Maria. I am a sick man."

"Did Deacon Lund upset you, darling? You look so flushed."

Mama's eyes were big and very blue. Papa wished she would stop looking at him that way—like a child who had been scolded. As always, he melted as though he were on a hot stove.

"The Deacon was very kind, Maria," he said gently. "He just paid me a friendly visit, that's all. Nothing about that to upset me, is there?"

Mama moved a bit closer. "Pontus," she said leaning over him, "could you stand to hear some news? I mean if you are well enough and won't get too excited."

There was that secretive twinkle in her eyes again. Could she have already heard about the raise?

"Well or not," he said warily, "if you have news I better hear it."

Mama tilted her head a little to one side and smiled her sunniest smile. "Pontus, darling," she whispered, "we are going to have an increase."

Papa was speechless. She did know. Somehow she always outwitted him.

"I saw midwife Eklund yesterday and had a little talk with her," Mama continued. "I didn't want to tell you until I was sure, Pontus *lilla*."

It was several seconds before the full truth of what she had said hit him. Then Papa almost exploded. As if seven children were not enough for a poor preacher to bring up. How much good would the raise do him now?

He stared at Mama knowing he had to say something. Suddenly a thought struck him. A broad smile quickly erased the gloom of a moment ago. What better luck could have happened? For now, with another baby on the way, Mama would not be able to preach. She would have to step right out of *his* shoes and back into her own—and just be a wife.

All his ill temper vanished, and miraculously he felt almost well again. "Maria," he said softly taking her hand in his, "I think that is fine news—very fine indeed. Now I shall immediately *demand* a raise from that Church Board."

With Maria's arms about his neck, Papa felt a bit guilty because of the fib. But a husband *must* prove himself important before his wife. Even the Lord, he was sure, would understand that there were certain things a Papa could not tell a Mama.

CHAPTER 6

🦁 Mama Makes Up Papa's Mind

They were a happy family. If Papa was too strict at times, Mama softened his severity with gentle humor and warm understanding. The boys, especially Nim and Pelle, planned what they would be when they grew up, changing their ambitions with the whim of children, which they still were. But none of them worried much about education. Especially the girls. In Sweden, at that time, it was not considered important to educate girls. They were supposed to marry, bear children and make fine homes for their husbands and families. What need had they for higher education?

But just as Mama had dreamed, while a preacher's maid, of the time when she would marry the handsome minister and have a large family, so now she moved on to her next dream. Education. She had not forgotten her promise, sixteen years before, to return to America, although she had been too busy during the years to talk about it or give it much special planning. With eight children and the parsonage to care for, and her many church duties, Papa believed Mama was as happy and contented as he was.

Then one winter morning, when his oldest son was about fifteen, Papa learned just how long a woman's memory can be—especially Mama's.

Papa leaned back comfortably against the pillowed headboard, munching a piece of *bulle* and sipping his morning coffee. Between bites and sips, he watched Maria vigorously brushing her hair. It fell like a golden veil below her waist, shimmering in the lamplight with a million refracted rays. And for the millionth time, Papa silently thanked God for the wonder of her.

"Just think, Pontus," she said, peeking bright-eyed through the veil, "the Lord in all His goodness has given us *eight* beautiful children. Healthy—and *smart*, too. It is up to us to see they get a chance at education. And where can they get a chance, but in America?"

Papa did not answer. Irritation swept all the loving thoughts of a moment ago from his mind. Mama had talked of nothing else but America for months. How could a man hold his tongue against this ceaseless pounding of words? Wasn't it a father's right to think about the welfare of his family and do what he thought best for them, with the help of God?

"Nim will be fifteen years old in May," Mama went on, not even noticing that he hadn't answered her first question. "He is almost too old now to go back to the first grade in America to learn English. Education just can't wait forever, Pontus."

Papa set the tray on the side table, threw back the quilt and stepped out of his warm bed. Still he did not speak, but walked past her to the washstand and poured cold water into the basin. Suddenly he felt embarrassed standing there in his short nightshirt. He waited for Maria's usual giggle and her remark about how "unpreacherlike" he looked, but it did not come. She is so full of America, Papa fumed inwardly, that she can't even see how funny I look in my nightshirt! Well, he'd have to settle this America talk one way or the other soon, but he did wish Maria would let him handle it his way for once.

Cautiously he glanced over his shoulder at Mama. She had stopped brushing and now twirled the golden veil into a mass on top of her head, securing it with large yellow pins. Papa dressed hurriedly, picked up the coffee tray and started toward the stairs.

"I shall go for a walk before breakfast, Maria," he announced before she could continue her speech. "I am getting nowhere with that sermon about Daniel for Sunday morning, and I can always think better on an empty stomach."

Mama's laughter stopped him. "Empty," she cried. "Oh, Pontus! What happened to the three *bullar* you ate with your coffee?"

Papa continued in silence down the stairs. He put the tray on the kitchen table, then slipped into his heavy fur coat and pulled the fur laps on his cap down over his ears. "Good-bye, Maria," he called from the front door.

The morning was clear and very cold. It was past nine, and the first rays of the sun were lifting rosy fingers into the bright sky. Snow-covered bushes bordering the garden gleamed like jewel-coated guards. Under Papa's overshoes the frozen path sang a morning song. After a while all irritation left him. The crisp high air gave his steps wings.

Desperately Papa tried to meditate on the Prophet Daniel. But all he could think of was America and Mama's urgent pleadings. A hundred times during the past few months he had been tempted to tell her about his letter to the Conference, but always caution stopped him. It would be too great a disappointment to her if the American pastorate, which he had requested, was not given to him. Lately he had become more than a little concerned. It was now almost three months since he had written and no reply. What could he tell Mama? Suppose there was no pastorate available, or that an American-born pastor was preferred? Would she give up her pleadings to go to America and be content in Lapland? There were many days when Papa sincerely hoped so. The thought of leaving the land he loved, and the little white church that had been like a gift from God when his very soul seemed lost, was almost more than he could accept.

Papa paused and looked back over the path he had come. His throat filled with emotion. The tiny steeple of the church seemed very tall this morning and the parsonage across the way especially dear. For there he had first met Maria, and there she had given him eight wonderful children. At the thought of her, his heart pounded like a young man in love for the first time. Yet she had not been his first love. Was it possible that there had been a girl named Alvida who had broken his young heart and caused him to vow that he was forever through with love and women? How had life *been* before Maria?

Truly, thought Papa, God moves in mysterious ways.

It had been Papa's first year at the University in Upsala. He was young and very much in love. For who could help being in love with the beautiful Alvida? Tall and stately as a queen, she walked with regal grace. Her hands were lily-white and her voice like the mellow tones of the organ she played so perfectly. Her father was very rich and much pleased with the engagement of his daughter to a "rising young lawyer," though that young lawyer-to-be had very little money.

"Don't ever worry about money, dear," Alvida had whispered one evening shortly after they had become engaged. "Father will lend you as much as you need to finish at the University."

"I do not like borrowing money, Alvida," he had told her, more worried about finances than he dared let her know.

"But my dear, you can repay him when you are prospering as a practicing attorney-at-law." She did not speak banteringly, but rather with a fleeting note of annoyance that he would allow anything to disturb her smooth and perfect way of living.

Papa had not known how to answer her, but even now he recalled the strange tumult within him. He needed the loan very much, but somehow he could not let himself accept it. Perhaps later, if there were no other way, he would have to consider the loan, but first he had to try to earn it himself. They had come close to quarreling over the matter.

Nevertheless, when the term ended, he had taken a job as a farmhand on a friend's farm near Gnesta in the beautiful Södermanland. He had missed Alvida terribly. But gradually, as his health improved and he gained physical strength from the hard farm labor and long sweating hours under the summer sun, he found himself thinking less and less frequently of her. Often when the day's work was done, he would walk slowly back across the fields, golden with God-given harvest, and a peacefulness would pervade his heart such as he could find no words to express. And suddenly he had felt himself a part of earth and sky—and God. And it was good.

And so the summer had passed and he had come finally to the last night on the farm. He would not have believed leaving could be so difficult. It was almost as though he were leaving a big part of himself here, so that never again could he be a complete and a whole man. Slowly he had packed his few belongings while conflict swirled within him. Then to still the turmoil, he had set out along the narrow path beside the small lake, walking briskly. It was a night white with moonlight, and an almost unearthly stillness surrounded him. After a while he had paused, gazing out across the silvery expanse of water and the silent fields beyond; then upward into the misty blue-white of the heavens. And suddenly it was as though he were alone in the universe. For a seemingly endless time he stood motionless, knowing not fear, but a sense of utter quiet. Then a voice that was not a voice, but rather the gentle stirring of the night wind seemed to speak to him, and in that moment he knew what God wanted him to do. He had dropped to his knees, his face lifted to the heavens, and signed his contract with God.

Papa had returned to the city, eager to tell Alvida of the wonderful call he had received. But she had not thought it wonderful at all. She had stared at him with contempt in her beautiful eyes.

"Pontus," she had said in that perfectly controlled voice which betrayed no emotion, "are you telling me you are not going to be a lawyer? That you intend to become a *preacher?*"

Desperately he had tried to explain what a great honor it was to be called to the Lord's work; that her position as a minister's wife would be even more important. Alvida had listened quietly, and for a moment he felt he had won her understanding. Then she had *laughed.* And the next moment stripped his ring from her finger and handed it to him. Automatically Papa had taken off the ring she had given him and held it out to her. The fingers that touched his were cold. Then she had walked away from him, tall and straight, and unbelievably graceful, without a backward glance. For weeks he had been numb with pain, for she had been the other half of his life. But it had never occurred to him to change his mind. If it was God's will, she would come back to him; if not, he would devote his life to a higher calling—service to his God.

By the time he had completed his work at the theological seminary in Stockholm and received his first pastorate, he expected Alvida would be married. But she wasn't. With hope still in his heart, he furnished the parsonage with the finest of everything, though it took most of his savings. But when three more years had passed and still there was no word from her, he knew that his long and cherished hope was dead.

Now a bitter restlessness possessed him, one which his most fervent prayers failed to dispel. Surely God was testing him. Somehow he must meet the test. As the months passed into years and his wisdom increased, he began to feel that at last he had won the battle with himself and that God was pleased. Then had come the "call" to a small village in Lapland, in the ore-mining country of the rugged northern part of Sweden. Once more he would be close to the earth where he might draw strength from the everlasting hills. A tremendous sense of thanksgiving filled him.

It had been an arduous undertaking, moving his fine furniture so great a distance. But once there, the neighbors had helped and soon he was comfortably settled in the parsonage. Slowly, with God's help, he found peace and contentment. . . .

Papa had been so absorbed in remembrance he hadn't realized how far he had walked until suddenly he found himself on the mountainside. It had been a long and bitterly cold winter. Hunger had driven the wolves close to the village—closer this winter than he ever remembered their venturing. Only a few nights ago he had been awakened by their howling. For a long time he had listened to their eerie wail, hoping Maria would not be awakened by it. But she had awakened.

"Pontus, the wolves," she had whispered as though they might hear her. "It must be a whole pack from the noise— and they are so near."

"Yes, Maria, it sounds like a pack, but they won't come any nearer. They must be very hungry to come this close."

Mama had clung to him. "Oh, Pontus," she cried, "let us move away from here. Let us go to America. There at least all the wolves are in the zoo."

It was difficult not to tell her then about the letter to the Conference. But he had resisted the temptation and, pulling the quilt up around her ears to shut out the howls, had told her to try to go back to sleep and not worry.

"Promise you won't go on the mountain road, Pontus, until spring. Promise me, please." And he had promised.

Quickly now he turned back along the path he had come, glancing up from time to time cautiously. Even now in the morning sunlight, these mountain roads were dangerous. After a few minutes he was back in the village and beginning to be hungry from his long walk. He hadn't meant to walk so far. Mama would be worried about him.

How good God had been to send Maria to him. Again

he wondered how he had lived without her. From the moment he had looked up from the sermon he was preparing, that long ago summer morning, and saw her coming up the road to the parsonage, his life had taken on a brighter glow—a richness he had never dreamed possible.

It had been one of the first really warm days of that summer. Maria was wearing a blue dress, which later he noticed matched her eyes perfectly. At the little bend in the road she had stopped and surveyed the parsonage and its garden and the little white church as proudly as a traveler returning home. Then she had smiled, and it was as if suddenly she stood in reflected light. Presently she took from her pocket a white handkerchief and wiped the dust from her high-button shoes, then squared her shoulders and marched straight to his front door. In a moment the knocker sounded three sharp raps.

"I am Maria Skogberg," she announced as he opened the door and stood facing her. The smile was still in her eyes, but there was a firm almost determined set to her mouth, which in an older person would have been offensive, but which, in one so young as she apparently was, was rather amusing. "I have heard through *Patron* Karlberg that you are looking for a maid."

"So I am," Papa had answered with proper dignity. "Step right in and be seated while I interview you."

Strangely enough it had not occurred to him at all to show her into the kitchen where a maid properly should be interviewed. Instead he had led the way to *salen*. Timidly she had seated herself on the rose-colored divan and twirled the large silk tassel on the arm until he feared it would fall off in her hand. But he had said nothing, sensing her embarrassment; only sat opposite her on the organ chair and questioned her as directly as he could. Even then, there was something about her that disturbed him and caused him to feel more like the one being interviewed.

"Have you ever worked in a household before?" he began. "You seem rather young."

"I was sixteen last March, Pastor Franzon. My mother, God bless her soul, died when I was seven. Since then I have taken care of my father's household. Until last spring." She stopped and her lips quivered. "You see, Father was killed by a train last spring."

"I am truly sorry, Maria," he said gently.

"Thank you, Pastorn. You are very kind." She brushed away the tears that were about to overflow. "Mrs. Karlberg has permitted me to help with her children for my keep, until I could find a place."

Papa was aware that he was becoming too concerned about the girl's welfare. This would not do if she were to work as a maid and keep her place in his household as befitted a minister's servant. So he had cleared his throat and made sure that his next words carried dignity.

"Well, you seem like a capable girl and I might consider you for the position. But first I want you to know that the salary is very small, and working in a parsonage will mean that you must be especially careful to live a godly life, avoiding frivolities."

"Oh, yes, *Pastorn.* I do understand how important that is. I will try my very best."

For a moment Papa was apprehensive. Being godly should not be an effort for a girl so young. But when he had looked into Maria's honest blue eyes, it was as though he were looking into her heart, and he knew that this girl could never be anything else but kind and godly.

To change the subject he cleared his throat again. "My household, you understand, must be run with great economy. I permit absolutely no waste. You must watch the draft in the wood stove. It must be kept at a minimum and still maintain enough fire to throw plenty of heat. Can you light a fire in the morning noiselessly, using only three sticks of *tyre-wood?*"

Maria had moved to the edge of the divan and now stared at him as though he had accused her of a serious crime. But there was no fear in her voice when she spoke.

"Pastor Franzon," she said firmly, "my father was not

a skinny man and we lived on only seven *kronor* a month, for that is all he earned at the railroad. He was a strong man and his job was to shovel coal all day long. He did not believe that heat should go up the chimney either, but he liked his house to be always warm and cozy. We never had *tyre-wood*. I lit the fire with bark."

It was Papa's turn to stare. Why the girl was a little wonder! He had almost stammered his next question. "Did you dry the bark in the oven first?" He realized too late that he had released a torrent.

"Only if it was sour. And, Pastor Franzon, I know how to split a match in two. I can make soup from an almost meatless bone. If you like *råraker* I can make them light as a feather, without egg, and crispy brown with almost no butter." She paused and tilted her head knowingly, "You see it is the egg that makes *råraker* heavy. I save the egg for mashed potato cakes; it makes *them* light."

Already she had him dreaming of delicious food that he had never had a chance to taste in his household. Tant Renberg had her own large family to take care of. He could only expect the simplest food or cleaning service from her. He pulled himself back to the interview and carefully explained to Maria that it was most important for a bachelor pastor to avoid all suggestion of gossip. Therefore she must walk on the opposite side of the street from him in public and conduct herself with utmost dignity at all times.

She had laughed then, and there was a touch of sarcasm in her voice when she spoke, unbecoming to one of her age.

"I understand, *Pastorn*. It is right to *live* in the same house with a bachelor pastor, for goodness knows a man needs a woman to look after him. But it is wrong to walk on the same sidewalk in public."

Color flooded his cheeks. "Well," he had stammered, "not wrong really. Just looks wrong to some people." Then almost before he realized what he was saying he had blurted out, "I think you may consider yourself hired,

Maria. Can you start tomorrow morning? I shall ask Tant Renberg to show you your duties."

She had beamed with happiness, and then come up with another surprise. "It is going to be wonderful working for a minister."

"And why is that more wonderful than working for Mrs. Karlberg?"

She had raised shining eyes to his, with an expression akin to awe. "Because that is almost like working for the Lord God," she said sweetly.

And the wonderful thing about it, thought Papa now as he turned into that same road leading to the parsonage, she had meant it. All through their years together, even when there were arguments and she had had the last word, there was still that little note of respect and sometimes awe which she had expressed that first day.

Well, now he must try to be patient and understanding with her. It was not much wonder that Mama pestered him about America after the winter she had had. First baby Kerstin had the whooping cough; then Nim had come down with the mumps and of course Greta and Torkel had caught them. And before they were out of bed, Vickey and Button caught the chicken pox. And all through it, not a word of complaint from Mama—just tenderness and hours of prayer with never a doubt but that God was looking out for all of them and would not fail her trust. Just watching her had made Papa a little ashamed of himself for much as he tried, he had never quite achieved that perfect faith which, with Maria, truly moved mountains.

Now as he reached the front step, the delightful aroma of fried herring reached out to draw him into the warmth of the kitchen. Breakfast would taste good after his long walk—particularly the way Mama fried herring to a crunchy brown.

But before he could open the door, Calle and Torkel came racing around the house. Seeing him, both stopped abruptly and bowed a polite good morning.

"What are you playing so early in the morning?" he asked.

"It is a new game Mama taught us," Torkel replied courteously. "It is called 'Going to America.'"

"It is fun, Papa," explained Calle. "You just run around the house seven times without stopping and the one that does it fastest gets a cooky from the Statue of Liberty."

Papa glanced around him. "But I don't see the Statue of Liberty."

The boys laughed. "Oh, she is in the kitchen," declared Calle.

"She is just Mama," confided Torkel.

Papa went into the kitchen, his appetite of a moment ago somehow not so hearty. What would Maria think of next?

Papa was to learn the answer later that evening.

All day he found it difficult to concentrate on the preparation of his sermon. He kept wondering if there might be a letter at the post office now, deciding his—and his family's—future. He consoled himself with the promise that after supper he would walk down to the post office. Postmaster Olauson lived in the back rooms and would be glad to get the letter for him if it had arrived. But when he had gone into the *vardags*-room to tell Mama that he was going out for a while, he had found all of them sitting on the warm brown carpet in front of the cozy fire, playing with matches! At first he couldn't believe he was seeing properly. Then Mama had looked up.

"Oh, Pontus. Come play the game with us. It is so much fun."

He started to excuse himself, but the pleading look in Mama's blue eyes melted him as always. Presently he was sitting with them on the floor before the fire, feeling most undignified.

"Where did you learn this game, Mama?" Nim asked as he dumped a box of matches onto the carpet.

"In America, of course, darling. Now listen carefully

while I explain how the game is played. First I will divide the box of matches equally. Then each of us must build a house of matches. When all are finished, each of us blows softly on the house. The secret is to see whose house will stand the longest. The one whose house stands the longest gets a wish, which is sure to come true."

"Really come true, Mama?" asked Calle.

Mama winked at Papa. "Well, I remember playing this game one night in New York City with a little Swedish maid. *I* won and *my* wish came true."

"What did you wish, Mama?" asked Vickey.

Mama's eyes filled with dancing lights. "I wished that a tall handsome blond man would come from across the ocean and take me back to Sweden, and he did!"

Greta jumped up and down with glee. "I know who the pretty man was. It was Papa!"

"I shan't give away any secrets," laughed Mama. "Come on, let's start the game."

Papa wouldn't have believed the game could prove so exciting. In a moment he had forgotten about the post office and the hoped for letter from the Conference. With much laughter and squeals of delight, one by one the match houses were finished, and a sudden quiet settled over the room. Only the whispering sounds of soft blowing pervaded the room.

Papa had tried to blow softly, but his house was the first to fall; then Nim's and Vickey's. Next Mama's. By this time everyone was laughing so hard it was impossible for anyone to blow softly. The rest of the houses fell in rapid succession. Finally only Kerstin's house stood.

"Kerstin wins!" Papa thought the shout would lift the roof.

Button protested, "Baby shouldn't count. She hasn't any wind to blow with anyway."

"Be fair, Button," Papa said firmly. "Kerstin's house stands and that was the point of the game. Now let us hear her wish."

"Yes, little one, tell us your wish," urged Mama.

Kerstin pulled at her hair in excitement, then looked at Mama with her big blue angel-eyes. "Oh," she said, as if repeating a lesson, "I wanna go 'Merica on big boat."

Papa pulled Kerstin up on his knees. "And who told you to say that?" he whispered.

Kerstin pointed her chubby finger at Mama. "You did, didn't you, Mama?"

Early the next afternoon Papa set out to make his weekly calls on the sick. But first he would inquire about the letter. It had been too late last night when the games were finished to call on Postmaster Olauson. Papa had intended to go early this morning, but there was his sermon. It wasn't going well and already it was Thursday. Sternly he told himself that if a man could not discipline himself, what right had he to feel he could guide others— or, indeed, serve the Lord at all?

Now as he hurried along the snowy path toward the post office, he gave full rein to his eagerness. And as if to reward him for self-discipline, the letter was there. For a moment he held it unopened, keenly aware that its contents, whatever they were, would greatly affect the rest of his life. It was, he thought fleetingly, like opening a strange door not knowing whether light or darkness waited on the other side. Finally with clumsy fingers, he tore open the envelope:

Dear Brother Franzon:

We are happy to inform you that word has reached us from the Swedish-American Conference in Saint Paul, Minnesota, that a small church in New England is seeking a pastor from their native land. As the immigration is at a high point, there would be great opportunity there for a man of your qualifications.

Berkley Hills is an ideal location for a man with a family. It has an excellent high school and a small

college. The church is without a pastor at present.
Therefore, we earnestly request that you advise us
immediately of your decision. If you accept, we trust
you would be able to begin service in Berkley Hills
by the first Sunday in May.

We shall, of course, regret losing so excellent and
zealous a preacher as yourself from the Lord's work
here in Sweden but the education of your children,
the reason for your request, is of great importance
and, I am sure, a worthy one in the sight of God.

Yours in the Master's service,

Harald A. Backlund
CONFERENCE SECRETARY

After a long moment in which he seemed unable to
think or feel, Papa slowly folded the letter and put it into
his pocket. And then suddenly excitement possessed him.
He wanted to rush back to Maria with the glad news.
He wanted to see her eyes open wide with surprise and
then melt into a thousand dancing lights when she finally
realized her dream had come true. But again the stern
hand of discipline held him. His duty must come first.
He remembered that Mrs. Nelson was very ill with lum-
bago; that Farmer Larson, a godly man, had a broken
leg, and dear Miss Asp, the schoolteacher, was suffering
from an infected ear. Why, he wondered, did so many
saintly people have so much sickness and the sinners stay
so well? Truly, "Whom the Lord loveth He chastiseth"!
He must remember to preach a sermon on this very soon.
Papa's calls took longer than usual. Mrs. Nelson had
asked him to read two chapters from the book of Job,
and Mrs. Larson insisted he must have a cup of hot coffee
and some of her newly baked coffee bread before going
out into the cold again.
It was after six and many hours past darkness when Papa

arrived back at the parsonage. Reflections from the open fire in *salen* threw purple shadows on the snow beneath the window. Papa stopped, surprised. Why should there be a fire in the best room in the house on an ordinary week night? Important unexpected company must have arrived. His wonderful news forgotten for the moment, Papa hurried through the door. Inside all was strangely silent. By the door, motionless as a statue, stood Button in her best dress. Wordlessly she took his coat, hung it on the coatrack, then with sweeping dignity, ushered him into *salen*.

Papa gasped. The whole family dressed in their best was seated about the big table which glowed with "company" silver and linens. But there was no company.

"Sit down, Pontus *lilla*," said Mama, her eyes laughing at his surprise, "this is a very special night."

Papa sat down.

"The children and I have planned this night to tell you why we want to move to America," continued Mama. "We call it America Night. See, Pontus, even our food is American hamburgers, scalloped potatoes and Harvard beets. *And* the biggest surprise of all—American apple pie. I made it from dry apples and it smells just like America! After dinner we shall have a program."

Papa was too overwhelmed for speech. Now the silence which had greeted him was transformed. The familiar family noises restored a little of his usual poise. He realized that he was very hungry. Even an American dinner would taste good.

When the last crumb of the apple pie had been devoured, Mama signaled for quiet. "Now we are ready for the program, Pontus," she said, settling back comfortably in her chair. "Each of us will tell you why we want to go to America."

Papa started to speak—to tell them there was no need for this. They were *going* to America. It was all arranged. Then, as he looked about him seeing as if for the first time tonight the shining, eager faces of his children and the proud affection with which Maria met his gaze, he was silent.

"Come, Nim. You are the eldest. You may speak first," said Mama.

Nim arose. Awkwardly he smoothed his unruly red hair. He was tall for his fourteen years and, as Papa watched him wavering, as it were, on the threshold of manhood, he could not help seeing a mischievous little boy cutting up everything in sight with his wicked scissors.

"I have a special wish to go to America," Nim began, looking straight at Papa. "You see, last summer I suddenly knew what I want to be when I grow up. I had been down by the brook and found a dead frog and I cut it up with my scissors. Not in pieces—just one big cut. Then I knew I wanted to be a doctor—a surgeon who would help people by cutting out the sickness." Nim blushed in embarrassment and sat down quickly.

Of course, thought Papa meeting Mama's eyes for a moment, that was it. A doctor was what he was meant to be. Papa almost laughed aloud, remembering that he had thought him destined only to be a barber.

Now Button was on her feet, her eyes sparkling with mischief. "With your permission, Papa, I shall read you a poem I have written telling you why I want to go to America." She cleared her throat and read:

> "America is a country where we will go some day
> That is—I am sure we will—if Mama has her way
> They have no King or Queen or such
> You just get rich by a magic touch
> They have more fruit than you ever know
> You eat yourself sick if you don't go slow
> You are free and happy and gay of heart
> And *I* am asking Papa—when do we start?"

Everyone was laughing now. Button sat down triumphantly.

"Oh, Button," cried Mama, "that was perfectly wonderful! Just think, Pontus, so far we have a doctor and a poet in the family."

Now it was Pelle's turn. He stood up, his angel-face beaming with excitement. "I want to go to America because I can go to school and read a lot of books, but if Papa doesn't think we should go I know that is best and I shall just stay in Lapland and read only a few books."

"Thank you, Pelle," whispered Papa. The lump in his throat too big to permit him to say more.

There was no embarrassment in Vickey's manner. She stood as poised and regal as a little princess beside her chair and spoke in a low, vibrant voice. "The streets in America are very wide and there are many store windows filled with pretty clothes. I want to grow up and be very beautiful and marry the President."

The burst of laughter that followed did not disturb her at all. Even Papa tried to suppress a chuckle and think of the proper thing to say. This was not the time for reprimand. "You don't want very much, do you, little Vickey? But to me you are beautiful now, and I guess I wouldn't mind having a daughter in the White House."

Greta was giggling so hard by this time she could scarcely make her speech. "In America I can have all the cream puffs and ice cream I want and when I grow up I shall marry a baker so I can lick all the bowls in the bakery."

The merriment was in full swing now and, as always, Greta was a good target. "You'll get so fat," teased Button, "that nobody will want to marry you. Certainly not the baker. You'd eat up all his cakes."

"And how can you wear pretty clothes if you are fat?" chimed in Vickey.

"Too many cakes are bad for your health," put in Nim, the doctor-to-be.

"Come, come, children," laughed Mama. "It is time for Torkel's speech."

Torkel seemed to have forgotten whatever speech he

had prepared. He stood for a moment twisting the corner of his coat into a roll and finally the room was quiet as a church.

"I think," he finally said in a high, singsong voice, "that in America there are lots and lots of trains. Some of them run under the ground and some in the air. Most of all, I want Papa to take Calle and me on the train under the ground." He wriggled back onto his chair and sat looking down at his plate as though expecting jeering laughter.

"I'd like that, too!" cried Calle who always followed in Torkel's footsteps.

The smile that suddenly flooded Torkel's small face, thought Papa, was like a light turned on inside.

At last it was little Kerstin's turn. She stood up in her chair and curtsied daintily to Papa. "Go—go! 'Merica on big boat," she said. At the laughter which followed, Kerstin jumped up and down, clapping her tiny hands.

Then as if by unspoken command, sudden silence settled over the festive room. Mama stood up and for a moment her eyes rested lovingly on each of her children and finally on Papa. "Pontus lilla," she said softly, "now you know how much we all want to go to America. We hope we have convinced you America is the right place for us. But if you still think we should stay in Lapland, we shall stay and be very happy, for we all love you very much."

Mama paused. Her eyes held the brightness of tears. "And now," she continued, "a speech from the most prominent speaker in all Lapland, Papa Franzon!"

The family applauded as Papa got to his feet. For a quick moment he remembered his excitement this afternoon when he had wanted to rush home with the letter to break the news to Maria and the children. How grateful he was now that he had not done so. Why, at that very moment the children probably were busy with their speeches and Maria joyously planning this special evening. He wanted very much to tell them he hadn't been blind to their wishes, that their happiness would always be first in his heart; that he had wanted only to be sure of his

surprise for them. But to tell them this now would destroy
the triumph which shone with radiant eagerness from
the dear faces around the table. He would just let them
think *they* had convinced *him*. What did it matter whose
idea it was, so long as they were always as happy as now?

"Dear family," he began, including them all in his smile,
"let me thank you for a most enjoyable evening and for
all your very fine speeches. I think you will all grow up
to be orators, for you have *completely* convinced me
that we should go to America. I shall write a letter to
the Conference this very night. Now I would like to ask
Mama a question. How soon can you get ready?"

For a moment there was utter silence. Mama's blue eyes
were as big as cookies, staring unbelievingly at Papa.
Then everyone started talking at once. Papa sat down,
amply rewarded for the sacrifice of his own simple
triumph.

Suddenly Maria's arms were around his neck. "Oh,
Pontus, thank you, thank you."

Jubilantly the children formed a circle and began
marching around the table singing "America" in high-
pitched voices. So, thought Papa, Mama had been very
sure of herself, using that song as a climax to this special
evening.

Later, when the children were in bed and Maria was
busy with her mending, Papa went to the study to write
his letter of acceptance to the Conference. Finally he
sealed the envelope and stamped it ready for mailing at
the railroad station in the morning. Then he leaned back
in his big chair and closed his eyes, giving himself over
completely for the first time today to the turbulent emotions within him. Soon spring would touch with flowering
hand the Swedish hillsides. The silvery birches beside the
little white church would sway gently in the soft wind.
A new pastor would be standing in his pulpit. In the
garden across the way, the cherry and plum trees would
be lavish with bright blossoms. Other hands would

smooth the paths of his sand-yard and tend his cherished strawberry plants. Other childish voices would echo in the red-and-white parsonage and other happy feet would climb Gellivara mountain on Midsummer Day. Their eyes would mirror the excitement of roaring waterfalls, salmon jumping, the wonder of huge logs floating downstream and finally the miracle of a flame-tinted June sky in which the sun did not set at all.

For a moment Papa felt it was more than he could relinquish. His roots were deep in Swedish soil. How could he tear them up and hope to replant them in a strange new country? Suddenly another picture imposed itself—the circle of happy faces around the table tonight when he had told them they would all go to America. There was no longer room in his heart for selfish desire.

He got up and crossed the study to the wide window which overlooked the hills, now snow-garmented and sparkling like silver in the starlit night. And suddenly it was as though God's hand, reassuringly, was on his shoulder.

The clock in the front hall sounded ten long strokes. As Papa came back into the *vardags*-room Mama put aside her mending. "Oh, Pontus darling," she cried, her arms around him, "I'm just one big heap of happiness."

And two large tears rolled down her cheeks to prove it.

CHAPTER 7

✲ Lost—One Preacher

The next few months were busy ones for the whole family. They lived in a state of breathless excitement. For each of the children the big journey to America carried an individual significance. Parting with small but to them very important possessions was a major problem. Leaving forever their friends and the places which were especially dear to them—a woodland path, the ski run on the snowy hillside, the river where in summer they boated or picnicked on the grassy banks—all required the courage of sacrifice. How many times they sorted their toys and books, selecting an increasing number which they simply *must* take. And just as often Mama reasoned gently with them, until at last they were happy to leave most of them behind, as presents to their best friends.

As the months sped by, Mama was quite sure that the children had begun to regret the decision. Education just wasn't that important. They were happy and doing very well, they thought, without it. Button had always had a gift for light verse and rhymes, and a few of them actually had been published in a small church magazine. She doubted that America—or education—could offer greater happiness. So it was Button who sowed tiny seeds of rebellion, which Mama carefully dug up before they had a chance to take root.

Early in April the new pastor arrived and Papa arranged to sell him all the furniture. Departure now became an inescapable reality. Up to this time Mama had kept her own emotions carefully veiled behind a cheerful smile for the benefit of the family. Of course she loved Sweden; but education was *important*, and important things required sacrifice. But parting with her home was not easy. Her eyes lingered lovingly on each separate piece of furniture as she followed Papa and the new pastor from room to room. When she came to the picture of the angel which had served as a model for the virtues she hoped her children would acquire, she touched it gently and for a moment her eyes filled with tears.

But when the day of departure finally arrived, Mama was determined that no note of sadness should creep into their final farewells, whatever emotions tugged at their hearts. All must eagerly look toward the future—and education.

Even Mama might have lost some of her eagerness for education had she known then the severity of their first "lesson" in the new world.

The whole Franzon family waited on deck of the big Swedish-American liner, peering through hand-shaded eager eyes toward the famous skyline. It was early morning. Mist, like a rose-gray veil dropped from Heaven, hung over the choppy waters, and, far beyond, the first faint flame-tints of sunrise touched the horizon. Soon they would land in a magic new world.

"And those mountains way in the distance," Mama whispered excitedly, "are not mountains at all. They are just tall buildings in New York City."

There had been little sleep last night. Everyone had eaten too much at the sumptuous "Captain's Dinner," and the dancing and games had continued until long after midnight. Not even Kerstin had been put to bed early. Now, wide-eyed at Mama's remark, the children stood in a quiet little group apart from the other sleepy passengers on deck, awaiting with awe and suppressed excitement the first glimpse of this unbelievable land.

"Are they really as big as mountains, Papa?" asked Torkel.

"Well, not exactly," answered Papa winking at Mama. "They just seem that big when Mama talks about them."

Mama laughed softly. She was so happy she wanted to tell all the people on deck how her wonderful dream had come true. Tense with inner excitement, she kept her arm about Vickey and held on to Kerstin's warm little hand. Nim and Button were leaning on the rail now, quiet but so eager she had to watch that they didn't lose their balance and fall overboard.

"I bet it would take a lot of faith to move them, wouldn't it?" asked Pelle solemnly.

"Move what, dear?" asked Mama who had been busy with her own thoughts.

"Why, the houses big as mountains," Pelle replied.

Everyone laughed, as much at his earnest big eyes as at the question.

But Papa put his hand on Pelle's shoulder and swallowed hard before he could speak. "It would indeed, Pelle," he said softly. "But just remember, nothing is *too* big for faith to move."

The mist began to lift now. Slowly, thought Maria, as though the hand of God was raising the curtain of night to reveal, especially for them, this wonderful new world. In the distance the famous skyline gradually emerged, at first like a faded etching, then clearer and clearer until at last the tall towers stood sharply engraved against the bright spring-morning sky.

Mama was awed to silence at the wonder of it. Then she placed her hand gently on Papa's arm. "Oh, Pontus," she whispered, "isn't it beautiful? I think we should all say a little prayer of thanks for our safe journey."

"Of course, Maria," agreed Papa, his voice husky with emotion. "Come children, let us form our family circle and all say 'Thank you, God, for a safe journey.'"

For a moment all eyes were closed and heads bowed. Then Mama linked her arm in Papa's. "Thank you too, Papa *lilla*," she said quietly. "Now we are ready to enter our Promised Land."

Papa smiled down at her and she saw the brightness of tears in his eyes. For a second she wondered if it was because he was happy too, or was he already homesick for the little white church and the red-and-white parsonage in Lapland? It was not going to be easy for him, she knew. But she loved him even more for sacrificing his own desires, so that she might have her dream and the children a chance at education.

Landing was even more thrilling than the first time, decided Mama, as she watched the eager excited faces of the children and listened to the gay laughter of the other passengers now crowding the deck.

Papa lined up the children in pairs. "Now hold on to each other's hands," he directed when the big gangplank was down and everyone began trying to reach it at once. "And stay close to the pair ahead of you so we won't get separated. I shall walk ahead of the line and Mama will follow with Kerstin so the other passengers will not crowd between us. Nim will end the procession. It would not be good to get lost in the crowd."

Finally they were safely on the pier, waiting in line again for customs inspection. Mama could not help remembering that first time she had stood here with Mrs. Johansson's five children. How long ago it seemed! Now there were eight children around her and—even more wonderful—they belonged to Pontus and her. God had heard her prayers and indeed had showered her with His blessings. And now they were all in *America*. Mama's eyes were dripping tears, but her heart pounded with happiness.

At last the inspector reached their pile of trunks and suitcases. He frowned heavily at the huge stack. If only she could assure him, thought Mama, that there was nothing in all those trunks and bags but a few household items and their clothing, most of which she had made herself. But it was his job to look, so she better not interfere. Then, as though he had heard her wish, he looked her way. Mama smiled. She couldn't bear for anyone to be unhappy this day, especially because of them. Maybe, thought Mama, he had come from another country, too, and now was remembering how he had felt when he arrived.

An hour later they were in taxicabs on the way to Grand Central Station where they would get the train for their new home. One cab was not enough so Papa and Nim rode in one with the luggage, and Mama and the other children followed in a second cab.

"Wait for us in front of the station, Pontus," called Mama as the first cab pulled away. "We just might get separated."

All the way uptown the children chattered and gasped at the incredible sights and sounds. "How will we ever find Papa in all these crowds, Mama?" worried Calle.

Kerstin took up the cry. "Papa's lost! Papa's lost!"

"Papa and Nim are right there ahead of us. See," assured Mama. But they weren't listening.

"Oh, Mama, look. The man is all *black*," cried Calle.

"Yes, darling," whispered Mama, realizing that the children had never seen a Negro or even a dark-skinned person before. "There are lots of people in America with dark skin. Some brown and some black skins as well as white. And they are all God's children."

"If I touched him would it come off, Mama?" asked Torkel.

"Of course not, silly!" said Vickey disgustedly.

Mama smiled, trying to remember *her* impression the first time she had seen a dark-skinned person.

There was so much to see, no one thing held their interest very long. From the taxi they could not see the tops of many of the buildings.

"Are all the houses in America that tall, Mama?" asked Calle.

"Will our house be that high?" wondered Torkel.

"No, yes, no." Mama couldn't answer the questions fast enough. Only Pelle was awed to silence and little Kerstin snuggled close in Mama's arms, frightened by the ceaseless noise and confusion.

But it was *good* to be here in America.

At the station Papa learned that it would be several hours before the next train to Berkley Hills. "I better send a telegram to Mr. Olson to let him know we have arrived safely." Mr. Olson was head deacon of his new church.

When Papa came back from the telegraph office, although it was not yet eleven o'clock, he took all of them into the big station restaurant.

"What funny long names they have for food, Mama," laughed Button as Papa gave the order in English to the waiter.

"But it will taste just like our ham and eggs in Lapland," smiled Mama.

After lunch Mama found a long, unoccupied bench in the station and settled the girls about her to wait until train time. Papa had taken the boys to the washroom. Kerstin slept in Mama's arms. Greta leaned against her on one side and Vickey on the other. Beside her Button sat erect and wide-eyed, not missing a thing.

"Mama," said Vickey suddenly for no apparent reason, "is the Statue of Liberty alive?"

Mama laughed so gaily that people in the waiting room turned to look at her. "Whatever made you ask that, Vickey?" she asked.

"Well I heard you *talking* to her when we passed her this morning."

Mama hesitated a while before answering. "The Statue of Liberty, darling, is not alive, but it is very real. So real it is easy to *think* of it as alive. I call her Lady Liberty, and we have been friends for years."

"Aw, how could you, Mama, if she isn't alive?" scoffed Greta.

"You see, darlings," Mama said softly, "a long time ago I asked God please to send Papa and me a lot of wonderful children. I knew He would, for God always answers our prayers if we *really* want what we ask. So when Papa and I left America, I told Lady Liberty some day I would come back and show her all my 'dreams.' That is what I called all of you in my heart. And today I kept my promise to her."

Greta still was not satisfied. "Papa says the Statue of Liberty is just a hunk of steel—and things."

Mama slipped her arm about Greta and hugged her closer before answering. "Little one, that is true if you look at the outside. But inside that steel lady I think there is a very big heart—big enough to love all the thousands and thousands of children that come from all over the world to this beautiful country."

"Nim says he wants to shake hands with Lady Success," said Button.

"And I'll bet he will, too," said Mama. Then she added softly, "But if you want to meet Lady Success, you must first place your hand in God's. And that is just what we all did this morning when we thanked Him for a safe journey."

Papa and the boys had returned now, so Lady Liberty was momentarily forgotten.

"Maria," asked Papa, "what would you think about my taking the boys for that subway ride they wanted? It is still almost three hours before our train leaves, so there is plenty of time."

"Oh, Pontus, I think that would be fine."

"I'd better stay here and take care of Mama," said Nim importantly.

"I want to stay too," cried Pelle. "I don't want to go under the earth. Nim says the trains go right under the buildings and everything."

"They do, indeed." Papa smiled. "All right, son, you and Nim stay here and help Mama. Come, Torkel and Calle! We better get started."

Mama watched them cross the high-ceilinged station. How American the boys looked in their short blue pants and sweaters, thought Mama proudly. At the subway entrance they turned and waved before disappearing into the dark cavern.

After a while the younger children began to get sleepy and curled up on the seat for a nap. Mama let her own head rest against the back of the seat and closed her eyes. She wasn't sleepy; she was far too happy for that. But she still found it hard to believe they were in America at last. Maybe for the rest of their lives.

At that thought Mama sat up quickly. Somehow it hadn't occurred to her before that they might never see Lapland again.

I guess I didn't have time to think about that, she thought, seeing dear old Tant Renberg's wrinkled face again as she handed her her most precious possession—a small alabaster statue of the three graces. Tant had wept unashamed. It had been hard for Mama not to cry, for she knew how much Tant Renberg loved that statue. She had given it into Pelle's care for the journey, promising the old woman it would have a cherished spot in their home. How could she ever have managed all the years without Tant? Her hands were rough and her voice often sharp, but her heart was always big and full of love for everyone.

It had seemed the whole town had come to the station to say good-bye. Even Kurre the cat, who now belonged to the Ericksons, and Sippan, Mrs. Lund's poodle. Mama smiled, remembering how Kurre, at the sight of Sippan, had tried to make himself as big as a lion and as ferocious. But Pelle, who had been saying good-bye to the cat for the hundredth time, stroking its sleek sides, had quickly scooped him up in his arms and held him. Sippan, a haughty, well-bred little dog, had marched stiffly past them as if to say, "Don't you know better than to start a *fight* at a farewell party?"

Everyone had brought some kind of special food for

the long train ride. Three dozen hard-boiled eggs, new-baked coffee bread and thermos cans of hot coffee. There were big bags of cookies for the children and dozens of cheese and ham sandwiches.

But the flowers were the most wonderful surprise of all. Mama had not expected anyone to observe the Swedish custom of giving flower wreaths to America-goers. It was too early for garden flowers and the greenhouse flowers were much too costly. But that hadn't made any difference. It seemed they had emptied all the greenhouses in Lapland!

Mrs. Lund placed a lovely wreath about Mama's neck; then a more dignified one around Papa's. Deacon Lund called for quiet.

"Anna-Lisa wants to say a few words to the children," he explained.

Anna-Lisa Lund, as spokesman for the young people, came forward carrying a pretty braided basket filled with small flower-wreaths. Solemnly she placed one about the neck of each of the children, even little Kerstin. Then she curtseyed and spoke her piece.

"We shall miss you all very much. God's blessing on you in your new home across the ocean."

"Thank you, thank you," chorused the children. The boys bowed properly and the girls curtsied as Mama had taught them to do.

It seemed no time at all after that until they were on board and the train was pulling away from the station. Mama's last sight of all their friends and neighbors was a sea of white handkerchiefs waving good-bye, the beautiful melody of their song, "God Be With You 'Til We Meet Again," slowly fading in the distance.

"Oh, Pontus," sobbed Mama, "if only we could take them all with us."

"Heaven forbid, Maria," Papa had said soberly. "I am glad they will all stay in Lapland where they belong."

There was so much sadness in his voice that Mama knew his heart must be very heavy. She had begun talking rapidly to the children about the two days they were to spend in Stockholm, seeing all the wonder of Skansen Park with its fine zoo, and the old, old houses with grass growing on their rooftops. And the fun of watching the folk dancing on the green lawn with every province represented in its own costume. Soon Papa was smiling again and joining in the fun and anticipation, and she knew, at least for the present, he had put aside his heartache. . . .

Button's hand on Mama's knee awakened her from her daydreaming. "Nim and I would like to go and look around in the station. Is it all right, Mama?"

"Of course, dear. I'll be right here keeping an eye on you. Don't go out of sight."

Vickey and Pelle were getting restless too. "May we get a drink of water from the fountain, please, Mama?" Mama nodded, and they pattered off across the stone floor, holding on to each other's hand. As proudly as if they were going out to conquer the world, thought Mama. Well now that they were in America they would soon be doing just that.

When they returned Mama glanced at the clock. Almost two o'clock. Papa and the boys should be back soon. Then they would be on their way to their new home. What would it be like? Mama wondered. She hoped the church would be white, with a steeple, and there would be a big garden where Papa could grow strawberries and lots of flowers; maybe then he wouldn't be too homesick for Sweden. After a while, she was sure he would be so happy in America, he would be glad she and the children had made up his mind to come to this wonderful country.

Papa was trying very hard to get into the spirit of adventure as he crossed the huge vaulted station. The two boys held onto him excitedly as they descended the subway stairs. Perhaps, he thought, if he could just regard this arrival in America as a vacation like the other time, it wouldn't seem so *final*. Then he might be able to swallow the lump in his throat, which had been there ever since the train had left the small village in Lapland, and really enjoy the subway ride with the boys. So far he hadn't been able to pretend very well, but the boys hadn't noticed; they were too busy trying to see everything at once and asking a million questions.

Suddenly Torkel grabbed his arm and pulled him to one side. "Papa," he almost shouted to make himself heard above the roar of the trains, "are those people kidnapers?"

"Why of course not, Torkel. Whatever made you think such a thing?"

"Well, Nim told us in America every hundredth person you met would be a crook. We must have passed a hundred people by now, and a kidnaper is the meanest crook of all, so I just thought . . ."

Papa wanted to laugh. Instead he said sternly, "Nim should not have said such a thing, in the first place. There are bad people in America as there are in every country. But why would any bad man want to harm you or me? Now let's get that subway ride before it is too late."

"Nobody can kidnap us while Papa is around," boasted Calle.

Both boys clung to a hand and said nothing more until they were down another flight of stairs. Then: "Papa, if a kidnaper tried to take all your money, would you let him have it?" asked Torkel.

This time Papa did laugh. "Are you still worried about kidnapers?"

"Well, if he took all your money, how could you buy furniture for the new parsonage?" put in Calle.

Papa stopped again. "We better settle this right now. First of all, a kidnaper steals the *person* and then tries to get money for returning him. I don't look like a rich man, do I? So how could they get a lot of money for returning me? Now do you see how foolish this kidnaping idea is?"

"I'd pay a—a *hundred* dollars to get you back, Papa. Honest I would," promised Torkel who could just count to a hundred.

"Me too, Papa, honest," echoed Calle as usual.

Papa didn't think it wise to ask where they would get the hundred dollars, so he changed the subject. "Come now, boys. One more flight of stairs down under the buildings and we'll find the subway train."

Papa had forgotten how crowded a subway platform could be at midday. He cautioned the boys to stay close to him as they edged their way through the packed masses. The deafening roar of incoming trains made conversation difficult. It was impossible after a while even to walk side by side, so Papa pushed the two boys ahead of him as they neared the yawning mouth of the train. Like a hungry giant, it gobbled up the crowd in one big bite.

Torkel and Calle were part of the bite, but not Papa.

Just as the door was about to close, a huge workman had forced himself in between Papa and the two boys. By the time Papa realized he couldn't act like a gentleman in the subways of New York, the train was halfway down the platform on its way to Brooklyn.

Papa had always considered himself a brave man. But now he was scared. Scared and helpless. He tried to think as the hurrying crowds pushed him about like a piece of paper in the wind. Faces, faces, faces. Everywhere strange faces. People too busy with their own affairs to tell him what to do or even to listen to his questions. Anxiously he looked about for a policeman, but there was none.

"Dear God, help me," he whispered, almost too frightened to pray.

Panic left him. Of course. The boys would get off the train at the next stop when they missed him. If he hadn't been so filled with fear he would have thought of that sooner. Now he hoped it wasn't too late. Poor little chaps! They must be frightened half to death alone on a subway and—the thought almost paralyzed him—unable to speak a word of English. Papa didn't stop to be courteous this time. He pushed his way into the first train that came along.

But the platform at the next stop was just as crowded. Anxiously, hopefully, Papa worked his way from one end of the platform to the other. No Torkel or Calle. He tried the next station and the next, with the same result. For hours he rode the subway and prayed. At each station he got off and searched the crowd, then on to the next station. But it seemed now even God had deserted him.

By five o'clock Papa had reached the end of the line in Brooklyn. Still there was no clue to finding his lost boys. Several times he had considered returning to Grand Central Station. Mama always had good suggestions. She would know what to do. But how could he go back and tell her that he, a grown man who had been in America before, couldn't even take two small boys for a subway ride without losing them? No, he *had* to find them himself! So he had continued the search. Now his stubborn pride wilted. Pride! That was why God hadn't answered his many prayers this afternoon. Didn't the Bible teach that "Pride goeth before a fall"?

Papa staggered a little with relief at the thought. Humility, deeply sincere, swept through him. "Forgive me, Lord," he whispered half aloud over the lump in his throat. Just let him find his children unharmed and he wouldn't care if Mama reminded him of his carelessness the rest of his life.

He started across the platform to get the first train back to Grand Central Station. Suddenly a headline, in bold black type, stared up at him from the newstand. MINISTER FEARED KIDNAPED.

For one awful moment Papa just stared at the newspaper, then he snatched it up and started toward the subway.

"You savin' yer money, Bub?" shouted a heavy voice.

Papa stopped, realizing what he had done. "I'm sorry, sir. I wasn't thinking. How much is it?"

He put down the pennies requested, stuffed the paper

into his pocket and pushed into the train just as the door
was closing. Jammed in with the evening rush crowd, it
was impossible to get at the paper in his pocket. But the
headline had told him two things: *He* was supposed to be
kidnaped; but his boys were safe; where else but from
Torkel and Calle could the paper get such a ridiculous
story?

Papa squirmed in the unyielding crowd. Why Mama
must be frantic with worry! He only hoped she hadn't
seen the paper.

Then suddenly the gravity of his own situation struck
him full force. He could never go to Berkley Hills now.
He would be the laughing stock of the whole town. Deacon Olson must have been worried when they were not
on the train they were supposed to be on, and by this
time, with news traveling so fast in America, no doubt
he had read the story. He'd better send him another telegram as soon as he could get out of this sardine can. Why
hadn't they all remained in Sweden where they belonged,
where people were content to travel slowly, not on underground lightning, with crowds acting like madmen?

For two endless hours Mama had watched the enormous clock in the center of the station ticking off the
minutes. And with each vanishing minute her anxiety
grew.

"What has happened to Papa and the boys, Mama?"
questioned Nim, and Mama knew he was worried too.

"It takes longer to get places in New York," she said
consolingly. "They will be along any minute now."

"But, Mama," put in Greta, "Papa said the subway
goes like lightning."

"It does, dear, once you get on it. It is getting *to* it that
takes so much time. See how big the crowd is in the
station now? Well, that is the way it is almost everywhere
in New York City." Mama smiled reassuringly though
she did not feel like it.

Three o'clock came. Still no sign of Papa and the boys.

Now they had missed the train to Berkley Hills. With one corner of her mind Mama remembered that Deacon Olson was to meet that train, but she was too troubled by this time to give much thought to the Deacon or the good church people of Berkley Hills. What if something had happened to Papa and the boys? No, she must not think that. God wouldn't *let* anything happen to them. They were good and God was good. But she couldn't help wondering just a little what she would do with six children and not a penny for food and shelter. In New York you had to pay for such things. There were no kindly neighbors to help you when in trouble. Mama prayed silently.

The hands of the big clock moved like the arms of an evil giant waiting to destroy them. Half-past three. The children were restless and hungry. Nim and Button's faces were white with anxiety. Mama could stand it no longer.

"Here, Button," she said quietly, "you hold Kerstin for a while."

Button took the sleeping child without question. Mama hoped she would think she was just going to the rest room, as they were called here in America, so she wouldn't have to explain. But she prayed there would be a telephone somewhere beyond that protecting wall. Inside the big anteroom a woman in white uniform sat at a small table. Mama approached her and in her best English explained the situation. The woman picked up the telephone. "Please give me the Police Department," she said importantly.

Mama was speechless. Was it a crime to let one's children and husband get lost in New York? She had been away from America a long time. Maybe things had changed since she had lived here.

"Please, Miss . . ." she began. But someone on the other end of the line was answering the woman in white.

"Give me the Missing Persons Bureau," commanded the woman. "Sergeant Malm."

Relief swept through Mama, but her knees felt weak.

She had forgotten about special places like that in New York. Why in a way, New York *did* have good neighbors to help you. But there must be so many people to be helped, they had to do it like a business.

The woman was speaking to her. "What's the name, Madam?" Mama spelled it out for her. "Sergeant Malm? Mary Mullen at Grand Central. A little Swedish woman with eight children seems to have lost her husband and two of the children. Name's Franzon. Reverend Pontus Franzon. Kids' names, Torkel and Calle. Got anything on it?"

She waited. So did Mama, breathlessly.

A little frown appeared between Miss Mullen's eyes. "Well, be on the lookout, won't you. What's that, Sergeant? Okay?"

She hung up. "Sergeant Malm—he's Swedish too, you know—says to send you and the children down to the Bureau."

"Do they—have they—found them?" gulped Mama.

"Not yet, but they will. Now don't you worry. Meantime, you'll be better off there than sitting in the station all night."

"All night!" exclaimed Mama, terrified at the thought. "Oh, I'm sorry. I didn't mean to be discourteous. You are so kind. But suppose my husband and the boys come back to the station and we aren't here? Then he will have to look for *us*."

"Well, that could happen. But the sergeant said to send you down there, and I guess I better obey him."

Mama did not want to break any laws, but she just couldn't take a chance that Papa and the boys would return and find them gone and not know where they were. Anxiety gave her courage. "Would it be all right to leave the children in the station with Nim and Button, and I will go talk to the police officer myself? They are big children and very reliable. They will take good care of their sisters and brothers."

Miss Mullen hesitated. "I guess that would be okay.

I'll keep an eye on them for you too. Now where are they?" She followed Mama back to the bench where the six children waited.

As they walked the short distance, Mama tried to think what she would tell them. If she expected Nim and Button to be big enough to look after the younger children, they were big enough to know the truth, she decided.

"This is Miss Mullen, children," she said in Swedish. "She will stay with you until I come back. I have to take care of something." Then she took Nim and Button aside and explained, assuring them she wouldn't be gone very long. Miss Mullen would know how to get her if Papa and the boys came back before she returned.

Mama got out of the taxicab before an imposing-looking building and paid the driver with the money Miss Mullen had given her. Inside the lights were very bright, and many men in blue uniforms stood about, talking and laughing together. One young officer separated himself from the others and came toward her. "And what might I be doing for you, young lady?" he asked cheerfully.

Mama smiled in spite of her worries. He was so friendly, and he had called her "young lady." What would he say when she told him she had eight children and a lost husband?

"I'm Mrs. Franzon—Maria Franzon. Sergeant Malm is going to help me find my husband and missing children."

"Glory be to God, now," exclaimed the young officer. "Imagine a husband running away from a pretty little thing the likes of you. And kidnaping the kids, too."

Mama did not know whether he was taking God's name in vain or not. Some Americans, she thought, had a funny way of talking. But she certainly didn't like him accusing Papa of running away from her and stealing his own children.

She started to tell him so, but stopped in time. It would only make matters worse. Maybe he just meant to be kind, anyway. In New York some husbands *did* run away from their wives and children. How could the officer know how much she and Pontus loved each other and their children?

"Please take me to Sergeant Malm, officer," she said with dignity; then smiled again.

He jumped to attention. "Right this way, young lady." Mama was sure he winked as he smiled back at her, then led the way down a brightly lighted hall.

He knocked on the door. When the voice inside said, "Come in," he swung the door open and stepped back for Mama to enter. "Sergeant Malm," Mama began, but got no further. Two flying arrows came at her faster than she could think.

"Mama, Mama, Mama," cried Torkel and Calle throwing themselves into her arms. "Oh, Mama, we thought we would never see you again."

When Mama could get her breath she looked around for Papa. He was not there. "Where is Papa?"

At that the boys began sobbing so hard they could not speak. Mama's heart almost stopped. "Torkel, Calle," she commanded in Swedish, "where is Papa?" She hated being severe with them, but it was the only way to stop their tears.

Sergeant Malm, who had had no chance to speak before, came forward. He spoke to Mama in Swedish. "The children were found by Officer Murphy on the subway in Brooklyn an hour or so ago," he explained. "He could not speak Swedish and they could not speak English. He *could* understand they were lost. So he brought them here. Luckily Miss Mullen had just telephoned me a few minutes before. I hoped they would be your children. They insist their father has been kidnaped by a big hoodlum. That is all I have been able to get out of them."

Mama sat down on the straight-backed chair and pulled the boys to her, an arm about each of them. "Please, boys. You must stop crying and tell Mama everything that happened. Don't you know God wouldn't let anything happen to Papa? He just got misplaced, that's all. Now tell me right from the beginning."

Torkel got control of his tears first. "The big train came roaring in, Mama, and millions of people got on and the door shut fast. When I looked around for Papa he wasn't there. Then I knew that big man kidnaped him! He *did*, Mama. I just know he did!"

"What big man, Torkel?"

"The one that we saw on the way to the subway. I saw him first, and I tried to warn Papa, but Papa said nobody would want to kidnap him. He said kidnapers only wanted money to bring you back."

Mama held onto her patience. So far none of it made any sense. Poor little chaps. They were so upset their imagination was playing tricks. Gradually, with much patient questioning while Sergeant Malm listened, Mama got the story.

When the boys had realized that Papa was not with them they were very frightened. Calle had tried to ask a man standing next to him if he had seen Papa, but the man only shrugged and looked at him and said something in a strange language. Suddenly they realized that no one could understand them either.

By this time the train was traveling through the underground tunnel with the speed of an angry dragon.

"Do you think we might ride on and on for years, Torkel?" Calle had asked.

"Of course not," Torkel had answered, trying to be brave enough for both of them. "It has to stop sometime."

"Maybe we'll be in—China—or—or India by then," speculated Calle.

"Of course not," repeated Torkel. "Trains can't run under the ocean."

Frightened and trainsick, the boys had huddled together for comfort and stayed on the train. After what seemed like a long time to them the train stopped and a lot of passengers got off and more got on. Eagerly they had looked for Papa. One passenger had a round collar and looked very kind. He had smiled at them and Calle had wanted to ask him if he had seen Papa, but he remembered in time that he could not speak English.

Again the train rushed on, jolting and rocking in its speed. More stops and more people. None even looked like Papa. Finally almost all the people left the train.

"Do you think we should get off too?" asked Calle.

"No, we better stay on," Torkel said hesitatingly. "I've been thinking, Calle. Papa says the world is round so maybe in a year or two we'll come right back to New York station and find Mama and Papa."

Calle settled back in his seat. "Won't we be awfully hungry?"

Torkel had not thought of that.

The train rumbled on, stopping and starting at intervals. Hundreds of people coming and going, but none of them Papa. Again the train was almost empty.

"Torkel," whispered Calle, "my stomach feels awful funny."

Torkel looked at his brother. He was white as milk. "Calle, please! You can't be sick here."

Calle only rolled his eyes back and forth.

"And the next moment, Mama," Torkel related, "Calle's sickness was running down the aisle."

Two men at the other end of the waiting train, attracted by Calle's groans and what had happened, tried to help them.

"But we couldn't understand them, Mama, and they couldn't understand us."

The train had started again.

At the next stop one of the men took them off the train. "I thought we were being kidnaped like Papa," explained Torkel, "but I hoped the kidnaper would take us where they kept Papa and then we could fight the kidnaper and get away and come back to you."

But presently the man had stopped beside a policeman and after a lot of words which they did not understand, the policeman had taken both of them by the hand and led them away.

"He's taking us to jail," Calle had sobbed. "We'll never see Mama again."

Torkel had not been sure he wasn't right, but he had to be brave and look after his younger brother.

After a while they emerged from the cavern of the subway and presently found themselves in a brightly lighted room with many policemen. Several of them tried to talk to the boys without success.

"Finally one policeman led us to a bench and then went away. When he came back Mr. Malm was with him and he could talk to us," finished Torkel.

"That was about half an hour ago, Mrs. Franzon," explained Sergeant Malm. "They were too frightened, I guess, to tell me very much except that their father was kidnaped. I was sure then they were the children Miss Mullen had telephoned about."

"But where is my husband?" asked Mama in English, fears crowding in despite her prayers. "Could the boys be right? Do things like that happen in New York City now in broad daylight, Sergeant Malm?"

"Lots of unfortunate things happen in New York City, even in broad daylight, I am sorry to say, Mrs. Franzon," said Sergeant Malm.

Mama's eyes filled with tears, but she managed a faint smile. "I must go back to my other children now. How grateful I am that you found my boys. I am sure my husband will come back, soon, too. It might be he is at the station now."

But Papa was not at the station.

The children sat close together on the waiting room bench, trying not to cry. They were hungry and too concerned about Papa to talk about the subway adventure. Sergeant Malm had instructed Miss Mullen to telephone him if Reverend Franzon had not shown up.

Mama watched the big clock, praying silently as the minutes ticked off an hour—then two. She knew Sergeant Malm was trying to find Papa. She must not worry.

"Mama, I hope Papa will give the kidnaper the money

so he can come back soon," Pelle said and Mama's heart wept because of the ache in his voice.

"Darling, please don't worry so. God will take care of Papa and bring him back safely to us."

"We never should have let go of Papa's hand," Torkel regretted with half-stifled sobs.

Mama put her arm around him and pulled him close to her. Torkel's anxiety was reflected in the faces of all the others. "Everything is going to be all right, children. Remember, trouble is just *luck* turned inside out. It will turn back again very soon now. Just you wait and see."

Mama tried to feel as cheerful as her words. She would just wait and pray and have faith so the children would not be so frightened and worried. How patient they were. Not a word of complaint, though she knew they were hungry. Now Pelle was praying a little too loudly and people were looking his way.

"Tell him not to pray so loud, Mama, please," Nim protested. "After all, God is not deaf."

Mama smiled. "Indeed He isn't, Nim." And immediately she felt better. *Out of the mouths of children,* thought Mama. She *had* been acting as though she believed God were deaf—not hearing her prayers. She had wanted to have faith, but deep down she had been doubting. Now Nim's innocent words of criticism of his brother had made her realize the truth. Mama closed her eyes. "Lord, forgive me my unbelief," she whispered fervently under her breath.

It was as though God had been waiting for her humility.

"It's Papa! It's Papa!" shouted Calle.

Mama opened her eyes quickly and there was Papa almost running across the station waiting room. Mama didn't care if it *was* Grand Central Station. In a moment her arms were around Papa's neck and, for the second time that day, tears of happiness were on her cheeks.

"Oh, darling, darling," she cried, "I don't care if they stole all your money. You're safe—you're safe!"

Papa squirmed uncomfortably. "Maria, people are staring at us." He loosened her arms from about his neck and wiped the tears from her face with his best pocket handkerchief. "Of course I'm all right, Maria. I'm so glad the boys are safe." Mama noticed there were tears in his eyes too.

The children were all trying to talk at once and hang on to Papa. All but Torkel and Calle, who stood back a little and seemed to be waiting for Papa to scold them for letting him get lost.

Papa pulled them both to him. Instantly their arms were around his neck like little ropes. "Oh, Papa, Papa! We didn't mean to let you get kidnaped," they cried.

For the first time in hours Papa laughed. "How would you boys like to go for a subway ride?" he asked, winking at Mama.

"No, no. Let's go home," both agreed at once.

"We're hungry," said Greta. "Did the kidnapers leave you any money?"

Papa assured them again that he had not been kidnaped, and that his money was safe. With full stomachs, life seemed right once more. The children were eagerly listening to Torkel and Calle's adventure. At last Papa could talk to Mama without being overheard.

"I'll never live this down, Maria," he sighed. "It is bad enough having my name smeared all over the front page like a common thief——"

"Pontus," exclaimed Mama, "what are you saying?"

Only then Papa remembered the paper still crammed in his coat pocket. He hadn't intended to mention it if Mama hadn't seen it. Now he took out the paper and unfolded it, displaying the headline.

"Story on page 6," directed the small print under the black headline.

Papa turned the pages reluctantly.

"Here it is," said Mama. Then she started to laugh.

"I don't think it is amusing, Maria," snapped Papa.

"Oh, Pontus. It's not *you* at all: it's a minister in some-place called Kokomo."

Papa seized the paper and read. By the time he had finished, his face was almost as red as Vickey's hair ribbon. He had *assumed* the headline referred to him, apparently because of Calle's ridiculous remarks earlier, and he had been too upset by it to take time to read the facts. He had had only one thought—to get back to Grand Central—and of course there had been no chance to read on the subway. Mama certainly would never let him forget *this*.

Quickly he changed the subject. "That still doesn't excuse us for not notifying Deacon Olson in time about our delay. He's probably waiting for us right now at the Berkley Hills station." And suddenly Papa realized he had forgotten to send the second telegram.

"Pontus," Mama began thoughtfully, "maybe Deacon Olson wasn't expecting us."

Papa stared at her. "Why of course he was. I sent him a telegram as soon as we arrived. Don't you remember?"

"I mean maybe he won't be expecting so *many* of us."

Papa opened his mouth to ask "why," then stopped. Good Heavens! Mama was right. He had neglected to mention that there were eight little and not-so-little Franzons. Now he realized that the matter of the children had never been mentioned by the Church secretary either. Apparently they *assumed*, knowing his age, there would be just himself and wife.

"I'm afraid you are right, Maria," Papa admitted finally. "Well, probably we will soon be on our way back to Sweden—where we should have stayed in the first place," he finished sharply.

Mama patted his hand. Poor Pontus. He had had a very tiresome day, and she couldn't blame him for being cross and depressed.

"You'll feel better after a good night's sleep," she said gently.

"You mean what's left of the night by the time we get

there," answered Papa, glancing at the big clock. "And we had better not miss *this* train."

While Mama assembled the children and the baggage, Papa hurried across the station to the telegraph office. He hoped Deacon Olson was a God-fearing man and wouldn't mind meeting a train in the middle of the night to welcome a lost preacher and his family.

CHAPTER 8

✻ Button Goes Wild

The adjustments to be made in a new country were excitement enough for all the Franzon family during the next few years. How they struggled with the language and the seemingly unreasonable and strange customs! Even Mama, who had lived in America before and now spoke the language quite well, had to learn many American ways all over again.

She was thinking of this as she surveyed the dozen white sheets on the long line in the parsonage garden, blowing softly in the May morning breeze. How easy washday was in America. Here, every Monday was washday. *Every* week, instead of twice a year as it was in Lapland. Of course, in Lapland she had not done all the work herself on those twice-a-year washings which consumed an entire week. Tant Renberg and Emma Erickson had helped. All the white clothes were boiled in *lut* and pounded vigorously with a *klappträ* on a board in the brook, until they were white as the mountain snow. Twelve dozen sheets and several times as many towels and pillowcases. Now she had only two dozen of each.

Mama laughed softly thinking how shocked dear Tant Renberg would be to know that. Why, in Sweden, no girl would have thought of getting married until she had twelve dozen sheets, pillowcases and towels, all marked in lovely embroidery with her own first initial and the second initial of her husband-to-be. But even more important were the bride-sheets. The bride-to-be worked almost a year on them. Every stitch by hand and delicately embroidered. With these she herself prepared the bridal bed.

American girls missed a lot of fun, thought Mama. Then suddenly she realized that she had too. *She* had had no bride-sheets. She had slept alone on ordinary sheets, in a bed made by a stranger on a ship. And even when they reached Lapland, there had been only sheets made by Tant Renberg, who had no idea that a bride was to sleep in the big hand-carved parsonage bed.

Mama grunted apologetically. What was a girl to do when the man she wanted to marry could not make up his mind until two days before the wedding?

Mama gathered up the clothesbasket and bag of clothespins and went inside. Never again would they have a home as lovely as the parsonage in Lapland, even if she had not had bride-sheets. She loved being in America, but sometimes she had to admit that she missed the parsonage almost as much as Papa did.

"Maria," he had said one evening, walking up and down the living room, "it was indeed kind of the church members to furnish the parsonage before we arrived, but sometimes my heart aches for our beautiful home in Lapland—our own furniture instead of this weird mixture of everybody's leftovers."

Mama had forced herself to answer cheerfully. "Don't worry, Pontus. Some of the furniture is too old to last very long. And maybe the owners will want it back when we have worn out our newness. Besides, we must never forget how thankful we were that first night, when we arrived at two o'clock in the morning, to come to a home instead of an empty house. Why, Pontus, this furniture is really 'love' furniture, and anyway in a few years it will be just memories like Button's curtains."

Button had looked up from the English paper she was working on, and laughed. "Curtains!" she said disparagingly. "Why they were straight from Mrs. Lindström's ragbag. Every time the wind blew on them they developed a new hole until they looked like a spider web."

"But now you have beautiful ruffled curtains, dear," Mama reminded her. "And some day we'll have those fluffy-ruffle curtains at every window. You'll see!"

Button had gone back to her English paper, but Mama stood looking out the window, a dreamy smile curving her lips. "Just like a bride . . ." she murmured to herself.

Papa had quickly changed the subject. "Anyway Button is a lucky girl to have a new maple bedroom set in her room."

Button giggled. "You mean lucky for me that the Widow Beck fell in love at the age of sixty-five and was the first to ask for her furniture back!"

"That was Papa's first marriage ceremony," exclaimed Mama, for in Sweden only the State-Pastors could perform wedding ceremonies.

Papa chuckled softly. "If I only had a chance to perform one for Miss Lilja so she would ask for her desk back. Can you imagine how difficult it is, Maria, to write *sermons* on an old-maid schoolteacher's desk?"

Mama put the clothesbasket away, smiling over her happy memories. What a funny and dear parsonage this was. Even if the house was a bit on the tumble-down side, it was big and the rooms were large and spacious. To be sure, the furniture was odd, a conglomeration of strange pieces, most of which had seen far better days. But it had been a source of much merriment in the new parsonage.

"Please don't lean too hard on the Anderson table, boys. The leg might fall off again," Papa would warn.

Or it was the Almgren chair, or the Hanson rug, or the Frilen stove.

All these had been given under a keep-it-as-long-as-you-need-it policy, and Mama would remind them, before the merriment reached a point of ridicule, that these things had been given in a kindly generosity and they must never forget it. But even as she spoke, she could not help remembering longingly all the lovely things she had left in Lapland.

But if the furnishing of the parsonage left much to be desired, the garden made up for it. Loving hands had designed the garden and planted the flowers which bloomed lavishly every year for each pastor and his family that lived in this old house.

Mama tidied the kitchen, now, removing all traces of washday. When lunch was over and the children had gone back to school and Papa set out for his afternoon calls, she went into the sunny garden with her sewing and mending. The red and yellow tulips, bright against the picket fence, were dropping their lovely petals, making a gay patchwork quilt of the dark soil beneath. Soon lily of the valley and bright purple iris would take their place. Near the house, the lilac bushes were in full glorious bloom, shedding their nostalgic fragrance over the whole garden.

Mama buried her face in the lavender blossoms. "Oh, you sweet beautiful things," she whispered to them. "You're almost as beautiful as our white lilacs in Lapland."

Indeed, she thought, as she sat down on the rustic garden bench beneath the big elm tree at the far end of the garden, life had been more than wonderful this first year in Berkley Hills, in spite of the longing they all felt for the good life in Lapland. Even Papa, who, Mama was sure, had not really wanted to come to America, now seemed reconciled and happy. But this had not happened easily. At first he had seemed to live entirely in the past, and it had taken a good deal of planning to keep him too busy to think about it more than was good for him. All those first months Mama had gone with him on his sick calls, so he wouldn't have too much time alone to think about the past.

Until last October, when her strategy had almost brought about a tragedy.

Miss Temple, the schoolteacher, had given Torkel and Calle each a small jack-o'-lantern for their first Hallowe'en in America.

"You must wait until dark, and then light the little candles in the lanterns and place them in the windows," she had directed.

The boys had run all the way home, too excited to talk coherently. Mama had not had time to listen, for she and Papa were ready to leave on a sick call. Vickey, Greta and Kerstin had gone to a party, and Nim, Button and Pelle had little afterschool jobs. Torkel and Calle would have to stay home alone.

"Now be good little boys," Mama admonished as she kissed them good-bye, "and look after the house like little men. Papa and I will be back soon."

Torkel and Calle, as Mama learned later, had sat down dutifully at first, waiting impatiently for darkness. In each small lap rested a bright orange jack-o'-lantern with its single candle waiting to be lighted.

"I wish the dark would hurry," said Calle, when half an hour had passed.

Torkel glanced at the window. Outside the soft rosy light of Indian summer lingered. "It will be a long time, I'm afraid," he sighed.

"If only we could *make* it dark," said Calle hopefully. "Do you think if we pulled the shades it would be like night?"

"Let's try." They had pulled all the shades, but it still was not dark enough to please them.

"Perhaps we can find a dark corner," suggested Torkel. "It won't be as good as night, but when night really comes we can put our lanterns in the window too."

It was Calle who finally cried, "I've found one! Under the Ekdahl sofa." The boys got down on their knees and peered speculatively underneath.

"It sure is dark under there," agreed Torkel.

They had scrambled up and run to the kitchen for matches. Soon two small candles glowed from the lanterns. Trembling with excitement, they pushed the lanterns under the sofa, then sat back admiring the flickering light from the funny faces of the jack-o'-lanterns.

"Look, Torkel," shouted Calle after a moment, "my lantern shines a lot brighter than yours."

Torkel looked. "Calle!" he exclaimed, "I think your whole lantern is burning."

Calle's eyes filled with tears. "Save it, Torkel! Save it!"

"I can't." Torkel's face was ghostly white. "The Ekdahl sofa is smoking, too. I am afraid it is getting burnt."

Calle got to his feet. "I'll get some water."

"No, Calle. Go for the fire engine. I'll get the water," said Torkel taking command.

Calle had been only too eager to agree. "I might get a ride on the fire engine," he yelled, starting for the door.

"Wait, Calle, I'll go with you," decided Torkel. "I want to ride on the engine too."

And the next moment they were racing down the street, leaving the Ekdahl sofa to its fate.

Mama and Papa had arrived home a split second ahead of the fire engine.

When the fire was out and the fire engine was gone, Papa had taken the boys into his study, and a few minutes later two very unhappy little boys, lanternless and with very sore seats, had gone to bed without their supper. Mama had examined the furniture for damages. The Ekdahl sofa was badly burned, and there was a great brown hole in the Hanson rug. But she was thankful that was all that had burned, and she was sure the boys had learned a valuable lesson in patience. . . .

Mama dismissed the memory and picked up a pair of Nim's socks that needed mending. Not just Nim's socks, but a whole basketful of socks and stockings. Well, it took a lot of mending to keep up with a large family. Mama chuckled softly. No wonder the welcoming committee that had met them at the station, in spite of the late hour, the night they had arrived in Berkley Hills, had been openmouthed in surprise!

Deacon Olson had found his voice first. Red-faced he had stammered, "Are—all—these—children yours, Pastor Franzon?"

Papa had stared bleakly at him for a moment, then answered, a note of irritation in his voice. "I should hope I would not bring eight children that did not belong to me, all the way from Sweden!"

"I'm—I'm sorry, Pastor Franzon," stuttered the Deacon, "you see we were under the impression you were an older couple past the age to have so many children." Then apparently realizing he was only making matters worse, he lapsed into flustered silence.

Mama had extended her hand to him, feeling sorry that the poor man was so embarrassed. "It was thoughtless of us, Deacon Olson, not to write you about our children. But it won't be long before you know us all. We're really a very nice family."

"Of course. Of course." The Deacon beamed. "We are happy to welcome you to Berkley Hills, Pastor Franzon —and family!"

"We are happy to be here," said Papa, a little more gently. "And it was most kind of you to meet us at this unearthly hour. Now would you please show us where we are to live. The children have had a very tiring day, I'm afraid."

The next morning, Pontus had been able to laugh with her over the shocked faces of the committee.

"And Deacon Olson will never forgive us for making him forget his speech," laughed Papa. "Well, tomorrow the whole church will have a chance to look us over, Maria."

"They will like us, Pontus. You'll see!"

Mama went back to her mending. Six pair of socks for Nim and three for Pelle. It was the same almost every week. Such busy feet, thought Mama, but her heart was full of pride for the way those boys worked. Nim had a paper route, and Pelle searched for odd jobs which they both worked at when the papers had been delivered. Now they had regular window-washing and floor-scrubbing jobs on Wednesdays after school, and on Saturdays. And the money they both earned went into the big tin box on Nim's bureau. Mama knew that Nim was saving up to become a doctor, but that didn't explain Pelle's contributions.

"Don't you want to save for something special, too, darling?" she had asked Pelle one evening when he had emptied his pockets of his day's earnings, into Nim's tin box.

"I'll wait, Mama. It's awful important for Nim to hurry up to be a doctor, don't you think?"

Unselfish as always, thought Mama, hugging him. "It is, indeed, Pelle. Papa and I are very proud of you both."

"Just think, Mama," he boasted. "Sometimes we earn as much as *four dollars* a week. It won't be long now 'til Nim can start."

But even a fortune like four dollars a week hadn't been fast enough for Pelle and Nim. A few days later, when she was finishing the supper preparations, Pelle had come bursting in, too excited to remember his manners and almost too excited to talk.

"I got it, Mama! I got it! We'll earn *three dollars* just there. We'll be rich pretty quick now."

"Well, that's fine, Pelle. But suppose you catch your breath and tell me what is going to bring about this miracle of riches."

"It's Doctor Davis, Mama. I got a job for Nim to wash windows in his office and scrub the waiting room two nights every week."

"Why, Pelle, that's just wonderful."

"But that's not all, Mama. I told Doctor Davis all about Nim and I spoke very good English. I know he understood every word I said. I told him how Nim is going to be a great doctor, too, some day, and he promised to let Nim help on Saturdays when he has lots of sick people."

Mama smiled and patted his eager little face, her own heart ready to burst with pride. "Does Nim know about this?"

"Oh, yes, Mama. I ran all the way to Mr. Ekdahl's where he was washing windows, to tell him. He says maybe Doctor Davis will let him peek into his black bag to see how much tools he will need to save up for."

"That's just fine, dear. Now get washed up for supper. Papa will be coming in soon and you can tell him all about it."

It had been Papa's idea to let the children work at odd jobs. Mama had thought it might not be looked upon as proper for a minister's children, but Papa had insisted. "Best way for them to learn English, mingling with people who speak nothing else." And Mama knew he was right.

Nim and Pelle loved it, and Mama had to admit they were learning the language very rapidly. But with Button it was a different story.

Sometimes Mama was sure that Button just naturally rebelled—against *what* made little difference so long as she stirred things up. Even as a baby, Papa often reminded her, she had rebelled against order, keeping him up half the night walking the floor to quiet her yells.

Papa had arranged for her to help the Rogers family, who lived a few blocks down the street, an hour or two each evening after school. There were only Mr. and Mrs. Rogers, so the work wasn't heavy, and it gave Button an excellent opportunity to learn English and American housekeeping methods. Button hated it. And after several months, Mama realized Button wasn't learning English. Several times she determined to speak sharply to Button, but one look at her confused face, when she came home from her afterschool work, melted Mama's heart, and, instead of scolding, she would try to make the child smile again.

Papa conducted classes for the younger children three evenings each week, and they were making remarkable progress. After a while Button was so far behind the others, she refused to speak English at all unless forced to do so. Mama was worried. This might prove harmful to Button in more ways than one. Button had always been high-spirited, gay and happy. But lately she seldom smiled and no longer made up the little songs which she used to sing at the top of her voice.

"We must do something, Pontus. I just know inside her heart is heavy. She is so ashamed she can't speak English as well as the others, she just refuses to talk at all —even in Swedish."

Papa hadn't said very much at the time, but a few days later, when the family was gathered for breakfast, he had made an announcement.

"Starting tomorrow morning, all of us will speak English during mealtime. Anyone speaking Swedish during meals will not be recognized," he said solemnly, including all of them with a sweeping glance. "And by tomorrow morning I trust you will make sure you are prepared."

It had proved a wonderful plan for all the children— except Button. Mama was deeply concerned now and again mentioned her concern to Papa. But this time he only frowned. "I'm afraid, Maria, she will just have to adjust herself to America, like the rest of the children," he said calmly and went back to his reading.

How, thought Mama, could she make Pontus understand that some people just couldn't learn *some* things as fast as others? Why Button was a perfect housekeeper and a wonderful cook. It was just English that was hard for her.

The mending was done and Mama walked slowly across the soft green grass, her thoughts still on Button. Must there always be an ache in my heart for that child, she was thinking, and is America the wrong place for her? She would have to pray a little harder that Button would be happy like the rest of them.

One evening, a week or so later, when Mama had just finished the supper dishes, Button came into the kitchen, her eyes bright with tears.

"Button *lilla*," exclaimed Mama, "whatever is wrong?"

Button ran into her arms sobbing. "Oh, please, Mama, help me to make Papa see how wrong it is to make me work for the Rogers. They laugh at me, Mama. It's awful. I wish—I wish we were back in Lapland."

Mama held her close to her heart. "Please, Button, don't cry. Just tell me all about it if you want to."

"It's awful, Mama. I won't go back."

"Now, now, dear. Dry your tears and come upstairs with me and tell me what happened."

Mama closed the door softly to Button's room. Button sat down on the bed and for several minutes just stared at the floor, fighting her tears.

"Well," she finally began between sobs, "this afternoon Mrs. Rogers was showing me how to iron a shirt."

"Why, Button, you know how to iron a shirt."

"Oh, no I don't, Mama. Not according to Mrs. Rogers. She doesn't want anything done the Swedish way."

Mama smiled. She was beginning to think Button's problem wasn't serious after all.

"We were in the laundry in the basement. Suddenly I looked up and right in front of me, on the wall, was a spider web with a little spider in the center."

"Button! Don't tell me you were afraid of the spider."

"Of course not, Mama. But Mrs. Rogers pointed to it and said, 'That is a *spider*, Button.' I guess she wanted to help me with my English. So I said it over and over, ten times, so I would be sure to remember the word."

"I think that was kind of Mrs. Rogers, darling."

"I know. But that is not all. Later when I was getting

supper, she called to me from the dining room, 'Please put the spider on the stove. I'll be in in a minute.' I didn't know why she wanted to cook the poor spider, Mama, but they do funny things in America. So I went down in the basement hoping the little spider would still be there and it was. I caught it in a towel and put it in a pan of water on the stove."

Mama wanted to laugh, but this was serious to Button, so she kept silent.

"Oh, Mama," Button sobbed, "when Mrs. Rogers came into the kitchen she looked in the pan and asked me what that was. I was so proud I had remembered, and I told her. Then she laughed so hard she cried. And she called Mr. Rogers and they laughed some more. Then she picked up the frying pan and tried to tell me *that* was a spider. Oh, Mama, I'll never go back. Tell me I don't have to!"

Mama put her arms around Button. She didn't blame Mrs. Rogers for laughing, and someday she knew Button would laugh about it too. But right now she was heartbroken. She had to do something to make her see the whole incident in a different light. Suddenly she remembered some of her own experiences when she had come to America the first time. In a few moments they were both laughing together over the stories.

"See, dear," explained Mama, "it is funny when it happens to someone else. That is the way you must feel when people laugh at your mistakes. They don't mean to be unkind. And anyway, don't you think it is wonderful to make people laugh, even if it is because of your funny English?"

"Well, I didn't think about it that way before," said Button. "I guess I am just hurt because I am so stupid, Mama."

"Of course you're not stupid, Button. Why, look at all the things you do very well—better than most people. English is not easy to learn."

For the next week, Button was more like herself, even

humming her little songs as she helped with the late evening chores at home. Truly, thought Mama, God moved in mysterious ways.

But just how mysteriously, Mama did not understand until later.

Button came bursting into the house, one evening, ready to explode with excitement. "The circus is in town. And look! Mrs. Rogers gave me two tickets. Oh, Mama, isn't it just wonderful? At last I'm going to see a real live circus!"

Long before Mama had begun to insist upon education and had transplanted her family to American soil, Button had had a burning desire to join the circus. What put the idea into her head in the first place was a mystery. She had never even seen a circus. At the time, Mama dismissed it as merely the normal desire of any child for color, gay music and excitement, which the circus stood for, or perhaps a natural rebellion against the restrictions which surrounded girls in Sweden, especially if they happened to be part of a minister's family.

Now, as she regarded Button's joyous excitement, she wanted to agree that seeing the circus would be wonderful, but she wasn't at all sure Papa would permit her to use the tickets. But she didn't voice her doubts, and Button was too jubilant to notice her silence.

"There's a beautiful dancer, too, Mama. Princess Mitzi in her fire dance. I saw a big picture of her on the signboard. Oh, she is so beautiful, Mama."

For the rest of the evening Button floated about on dreamy clouds. Fortunately Papa was attending a church meeting and did not return until after Button had gone to bed. He went directly to his study to work on his sermon.

Mama waited an hour, then knocked on the study door.

Inside, Mama hesitated. Now that she was here she wasn't sure how to begin. She waited a moment for inspiration.

"Don't you think it is wonderful how American the

children are, Pontus?" she began. "Even Button is working very hard on her English."

"Maria, did you interrupt my sermon just to tell me how remarkable our children are?"

"I've been thinking, darling, it would be nice to give the children a little reward for working so hard to be good Americans. Maybe do something specially American —like the hamburger supper we had the night the children convinced you to come to America."

Papa cleared his throat, a puzzled frown between his brows. "Maria, you have never consulted me before about the kind of meals to serve. I'm sure if you think a hamburger supper would please them, I shall enjoy American food."

"Oh, I don't mean food this time, Pontus. I was thinking of something even more American—like—like the circus, maybe."

Papa jumped up from his desk and stared at her.

"Maria! I can't believe my ears. Surely you're not suggesting we take *our* children to a *circus*."

"I don't know why not, Pontus *lilla*. It's just *animals*. It would be educational for the children and do us all good. We could make it a family party."

Papa was walking rapidly up and down the study. His frown had grown into a very big scowl. "I am surprised at you, Maria. In Lapland we had no such temptations. America is full of cheap entertainment. I trust you have not suggested this to the children. Besides costing a great deal of money which we cannot afford, what do you think the church board would say about their pastor and his family attending a *circus?*"

Mama laughed. "Oh, Pontus! I bet Deacon Olson—and well, just everybody will go. Besides, it won't cost much. Mrs. Rogers gave Button *two* tickets."

Papa strode across the room and back, then stopped in front of Mama. "We shall not attend the circus, Maria," he said quietly as if he were announcing his Sunday morning sermon. And Mama knew the subject was closed.

"Very well, Pontus," she said softly and went out, closing the door behind her.

If Mama expected Button to receive the verdict with tears of defeat, she learned how wrong she was the next morning. There were tears—but they were tears of rebellion, not sorrow. Button stamped her feet and stormed.

"I don't care what anyone says or does. *I* am going to that circus."

Mama said nothing.

"Papa is just an old-fashioned preacher! Everything that's fun is wrong," she raged. " 'Don't, don't, don't'— that's all he ever says. 'Don't talk so loud—don't wear make-up—don't go to the movies. Remember, you must be an example for others.' Well I don't want to be an example. I want to live like other girls."

"Of course you do, dear," Mama said softly.

Button stopped pacing the floor and stared. "Aren't you going to scold me for acting like a heathen?"

"No, darling. This is no time to scold you when your heart is breaking with disappointment."

Button threw herself into Mama's arms and wept stormily. Mama let her cry until the tears diminished to controlled sobs. "Now dry your eyes, little one. I shall talk to Papa again. Perhaps he will go *with you* to the circus."

"Oh, Mama, please try! I'll be the happiest girl in the world, and I won't ever complain again about working for Mrs. Rogers."

"Now run along, dear. You'll be late for school."

But when she was gone, Mama wasn't at all sure that the miracle of getting Papa to change his mind could be accomplished. Perhaps she was wrong, as Pontus had suggested, in encouraging the child to want to go. Well, she would ask God's guidance, and everything would turn out right.

It was Friday, the day before the circus, that she got the inspiration.

Mama waited until the children had left for school. Papa was getting ready to go to town. "I've been promising Nils I'd come in and inspect the seats for the Sunday School room the first chance I had," he remarked, as he took his hat from the rack in the front hall.

"I'd like to talk with you a minute before you go," Mama said.

Papa came back into the living room and sat down, his hat in his lap. Mama sat down on the sofa beside him.

"Isn't it wonderful, Pontus, how God sets an example for us in just everything?"

Papa stared questioningly at her, then spoke sternly, "I think we are all aware of the goodness of God. But I fail to see why it is so important to remind me of it at this particular moment."

"I've been thinking, Papa *lilla*. Do you realize it was God Himself who started the first circus?"

"What a ridiculous thing to say, Maria."

"It's true, Pontus. God commanded Noah to bring all kinds of animals into the ark. Not just one, but two of every kind."

Papa got up and started toward the door. Then he turned, and Mama could see a tiny smile nibbling at the corners of his mouth. "You do think of the queerest things, Maria. Long ago I should have learned that when you make up your mind, an earthquake couldn't shake it."

"Oh, Pontus, it isn't *bad*. I know it isn't. And the children will have so much fun. Seeing all kinds of strange animals—and the clowns—and horses. . . ."

"And the naked dancing girls like the advertising?"

"Of course not, darling. Besides, that's just advertising. If there are dancers, they will wear beautiful costumes."

However difficult it had been to change Papa's mind, it was worth it, Mama decided that evening when she broke the news to Button. The child was simply transformed.

Saturday afternoon was declared a holiday for the whole family. Nim and Pelle hurried through their window-washing jobs, and Doctor Davis assured Nim nobody could be very sick with the circus in town, so he wouldn't need him that afternoon. Mrs. Rogers gave Button the afternoon off. When finally they were on their way to the big circus grounds, Papa seemed almost as excited as the children. Mama and Button used the two tickets from Mrs. Rogers, and Papa took his place in the long line to buy tickets for the rest of them. Then they all entered the big tent together.

It was cool and shadowy inside, and the blare of bands made it almost impossible to talk. But the children were too excited to talk anyway. The dancing clowns, the elephants, the prancing horses, and the colored streamers and balloons everywhere kept their eyes so busy Papa had difficulty getting them into their seats. When they were lined up at last on the long benches, Mama glanced at Button, next to her, to see how she was taking all this. She was sitting like a stone image, on the edge of her seat; only her eyes moved, trying to see everything at once.

Suddenly there was a blare of trumpets. The circus began.

First the parade of animals, followed by the clowns, playing pranks and turning somersaults every few minutes. Papa was laughing with the rest of them as each act appeared. He had just opened a big bag of popcorn and was passing it among the children, when the trumpets let out a mighty blast, the drums rolled, and the spotlight flashed in the center of the circus ring onto a color-draped elevated stage.

Button clutched Mama's arm. A chariot entered, drawn by prancing white horses, bearing, according to the announcer: "That greatest of all dancers—the most daring— the most beautiful—the magnificent *Princess Mitzi!*"

Button sat transfixed. As Princess Mitzi swept into the opening measures of her dance, Button exclaimed, "Oh, Papa, isn't she just divine?"

"You mean that girl jumping about like a wild woman? Button, don't let me ever hear you call a human being divine. Only God is divine."

But Button wasn't listening, for now the sensational part of the dance had begun. Suddenly a circle of leaping flames appeared in the center of the stage. The music rose to a throbbing, intoxicating rhythm. Twice Princess Mitzi whirled on her toes around the outer circle of flames. Then with a wild cry, she leapt into the fire. Through the encircling wall of flames, the audience could see the frenzied dance of death, until, apparently overcome by the fire, the dancer sank like a dying bird into a motionless heap.

The lights went out, leaving the little stage in semi-darkness, and the big spotlight swung to the trapeze act which was just beginning.

It was during the intermission that Mama leaned across Button to whisper to Papa, "Look, Pontus. There's Deacon Olson, just two rows ahead of us. You see. Everyone is on a spree today."

"And *Mrs.* Olson," said Papa. "She was too sick to attend prayer meeting this week. But she seems to have recovered remarkably. We must go down and shake hands with them."

"Oh, Pontus. She could have been really sick on Wednesday and still be well enough to be here today. Now don't spoil her good time by mentioning her health." She turned to Nim. "Please look after the children, darling, while Papa and I speak to the Olsons."

When they returned to their seats, Button was not there.

"Nim, where is Button?"

"Oh, she just went for a drink of water, I think."

The lights went down and the second part of the show began. But Button had not returned.

"I'm worried, Pontus. Maybe she is having trouble finding her way back. I think you better look for her."

Several minutes later, Papa returned, looking worried. "There is no trace of her, Maria."

"Oh, Pontus. What shall I do? Something awful could

have happened to her in all this crowd." And Mama began
to pray.

"We had better send the other children home, and you
and I will start looking for her," Papa decided.

"Nim will take care of the others, Pontus. No use to
alarm them. I'm sure we'll find Button without trouble."
But she did not feel as confident as she hoped she sounded.

Papa went back and spoke to Deacon Olson, making
an excuse that would not excite him, and the Deacon
agreed to see that the children got home safely when the
circus was over. Then Mama left the tent with him. Outside, Papa asked, "How do we know where to start looking? Perhaps she got sick from the excitement and is in
the rest room. You look there and I'll go back to the
fountain. If she isn't either place, we'll meet at the door
and decide what to do."

Button was not in either place. Mama found a worried
Papa when they met again at the door. Then suddenly
she remembered Button's enthusiasm for the dancer.

"I bet I know, Pontus. That dancer! What's her name?
Princess something. Let's go find her tent."

"But surely, Maria, Button would have more sense
than to go there."

"It isn't a matter of sense, dear. Button is young and
young people sometimes get strange ideas. I think we
better hurry."

It took Mama some time to locate the dressing-room
tent of the star performer. Papa was about to pull back
the tent flap, when Mama stopped him. Loud angry voices
came from inside. "You dirty devil," screamed a woman's
voice, "I told you not to come back here. Get out and
leave me alone."

Mama's heart almost stopped. Did the woman mean
Button?

Papa tore aside the curtain. On the dirty tent floor lay
Button. And across the room a frowsy woman and a
drunken man faced each other in anger.

Quickly Papa gathered Button into his arms. "What have you done to her?" he demanded.

"So she's your kid, eh?" growled the man. "Well, get her out of here. We didn't ask her to come. And we didn't do nothing to her. She fainted."

Neither Papa nor Mama waited to learn more. With Button in his arms, Papa hurried through the crowd to their car.

Hours later, with Button in her own bed, conscious, though still shaken by the experience, Mama sat beside her, changing the cold wet towels on her head. Papa was downstairs with the other children.

"Oh, Mama," sobbed Button. "I didn't mean to spoil everything. Honest I didn't. I just wanted to see Princess Mitzi and ask her to let me join the circus with her."

"Everything is all right now, darling," comforted Mama. "Try not to think about it."

"It can't ever be right again, Mama. Poor Princess Mitzi! She was so afraid of her husband and I know he will kill her. Can't we do something to save her?"

Mama had not realized until now that a good deal must have gone on in that tent before Button fainted. She had to erase it from the child's mind, but she could only do that if she knew all that had happened.

"Button, darling. Would you feel like telling me everything from the beginning? Sometimes it helps to talk about it."

Button just looked at her with vacant eyes for a long time. Then she shut them tightly and a big tear rolled down each cheek. "All right, Mama."

It had been during the fire dance that she had made up her mind to see Princess Mitzi in person. But the problem was getting away without Papa seeing her. When he and Mama had decided to greet Deacon and Mrs. Olson, she knew her chance had come. She waited until Nim was

busy watching the clowns, then she had slid out of her
seat and stolen from the tent. There were so many little
tents she hadn't known which direction to go, so she just
wandered around looking at everything. It was almost
as much fun outside as inside the tent. So many exciting
things happening. Finally she had met a boy with two
pails of water.

"I'm Princess Mitzi's cousin," she had said politely in
her best English. "Would she kindly direct me to her
tent?"

The boy stared at her for a minute then pointed to a
large ornate tent. Above the entrance hung a huge silver
star. "Right over there. But you better be careful. She's
pretty nasty after a performance."

Button had tossed her head and laughed confidently.
"Oh, she won't be nasty with me!" She set off in the direction of the tent.

She knew it was wrong to lie and run away from Mama
and Papa, but they would forgive her when she was
famous. She would beg Mitzi to let her work with her,
take care of her; and maybe Mitzi would teach her the
fire dance, so she could do it when Mitzi was tired or
wanted a holiday.

Outside the tent she stopped. It did not look so beautiful
close up. But she stepped inside, trembling with excitement.

Mitzi's back was toward her. She was taking off her
beautiful costume, and her golden hair fell over her bare
shoulders almost to her waist, like the pictures of the fairy
queen Button had seen in books. Mitzi had not noticed
her yet. She had flung her costume onto the cot and sat
down at a small table, littered with dishes, glasses and
bottles. To Button's horror, she saw her idol pour half
a glass of what looked like whiskey and drink it at one gulp.

Button took a step toward her. Mitzi turned quickly at
the sound.

"Hey, kid," she snapped in a scratchy voice, "what the
hell you doing in my tent? How'd you get here?"

She was staring with cold, hard eyes at Button. Button's knees began to tremble. She tried to speak, but no sound came. Mitzi was getting up now and moving toward her. Suddenly Button saw the long hair fall to the tent floor, revealing straggly strands of gray. Mitzi's face, which had seemed so divinely beautiful as she danced, Button now saw was deeply lined and scowling. She wanted to turn and run, but she couldn't. Mitzi was standing before her now. Button had to find her voice.

"I—I—only wanted to tell you how beautiful you are."

Mitzi glared at her for a second, then let out a loud harsh laugh.

But having found her voice, and for the first time forgetting her difficulty with English, a torrent of words burst from Button's mouth. "I want to work for you. I'll do anything you tell me. I'll take care of you, wait on you. Oh, please let me stay! I want to learn to dance like you."

Mitzi sobered. "Well, I must say that's a new line." Then her face twisted into a rage. "What did you steal? Tell me before I call a cop!"

Button was stunned. "I—I didn't steal anything, honest!" And suddenly she was afraid. She began to cry. "How could you think I came here to steal? I just wanted to see you."

But her tears and compliments had no softening effect upon Mitzi. "Don't you move an inch," she snarled, "until I've checked my money and trinkets."

Button obeyed, wondering how she could ever have thought Mitzi was divine. Mitzi went to the battered trunk standing next to the entrance and clawed through her belongings. Then she came back and faced Button.

"I guess you are right, kid," she said more kindly. "You didn't steal anything. So you want to work for me, eh?"

Button wasn't so sure now. She didn't know what to say. She just wanted to get out of there and die.

Mitzi dropped down on the cot. "It's no good, kid. You better run home to your folks if you have any. This racket ain't for a sweet kid like you. I *was* beautiful once, and I was a great dancer. But not any more. You better go."

Suddenly Button was sorry for Mitzi. She wanted to tell her she was sorry, but her throat was like cotton. Then she saw the man crawling under the side of the tent. Mitzi must have heard him, for she jumped to her feet and yelled, "Get out of here! Get out before I call a cop."

The dark evil-looking man stood up and looked at her and laughed. "Not even the law will stop a man from seeing his dear wife."

"Wife," sneered Mitzi. "That ain't what you came for. You know I got paid yesterday. Well, you're not getting a dollar, do you hear!"

"Don't be so sure about that," he said and started toward her.

Button had been standing in the shadows near the entrance. The man apparently had not seen her until now. He stopped. "Who is she?" he snapped suspiciously.

Mitzi smiled calmly. "An admirer. Believe it or not, I still have them."

"Get her out of here."

"The kid stays, Max." Even though Mitzi's voice was calm, Button knew she was afraid. She wanted to do something, but her legs were like jelly, and she couldn't make a sound. Her head began to swim.

Then she saw the man coming toward her, his eyes bloodshot and angry. She tried to run, but her knees crumpled under her. She could hear Mitzi yelling, "You dirty devil! I . . ." Then nothing.

Mama did not speak for several minutes. She was thinking, and praying. Praying for the right words to help mend her confused little girl's heart and make her glad again.

Presently she realized Button was crying bitterly, "Oh, Mama, I wish I could die. Everything I thought was so beautiful is just ugly and awful."

"No, darling. Life hasn't changed. Everything is still

beautiful. Sometimes God has to let us get hurt because we refuse to listen to Him. You are very young, and I am sure God has wonderful and beautiful work for you to do. Something much nicer than being a dancer. Trust Him, darling, and He will show you the way."

Button stopped crying. Mama kissed her tenderly and turned off the light.

"Now go to sleep, darling. Tomorrow is a new day; a brand-new day God has given us to be glad in."

CHAPTER 9

⚞ Any Woman's Privilege

Whatever else could be said for youth, thought Papa, one of its virtues was flexibility. For his children, America, after three years, was still a place of adventure, though even they admitted at times that many of the customs were strange indeed. To Mama, however, it always had been the land of opportunity, and she seemed daily more determined that the children realize that.

But Papa was not finding transplanting so easy. Although he spoke the language with very little trace of accent and was proud of the progress his children were making in education, there were some things he simply couldn't understand.

In Sweden, every man was master of his own home. If he was a minister, he was also the leader of his "flock." Children were polite to their elders, and a wife respected her husband's wishes. But in America, Papa stormed inwardly, it was difficult to tell where a man's authority and responsibility began or ended. America, it appeared, belonged to women. There had been a time when *his* wishes were a law to his family. But no longer—not in America! Here even his *opinions* counted for little.

"Someday I am going to change the marriage vow. I swear I will."

Papa talked aloud to himself in the study. "Do you, So and So, solemnly promise that as a married man you relinquish your own opinion and do and think only as your wife desires?"

He straightened his black bow tie, gave his tailcoat a couple of jerks, then placed the notes for his Sunday sermon on the large family Bible and noiselessly opened the study door. Through the long narrow hall he could see Mama at the table by the window of the sunny kitchen, preparing coffee bread for baking. The sunbeams played in her blonde hair, but there was a deep frown on her forehead.

Papa walked with slow, even steps to the kitchen. She is still boiling mad, he thought. She hasn't even cooled down since our last discussion. But he could try anyway. Even if she was this earth's most determined woman, she looked like an angel and the coffee bread she made was out of this world.

Mama's blue eyes had a glint of steel in them as she went about her work. Papa walked the length of the kitchen floor twice before he stopped and spoke.

"Maria," he said, putting some ministerial authority into his voice, "when you are through baking, we shall take the children for a ride. I want you all to have a look at that farm."

Papa waited in vain for an answer. Mama was chopping nuts and raisins. She did not even stop that, forcing Papa to raise his voice on his next words.

"Didn't you hear what I said?"

"I heard," answered Mama softly.

"Well doesn't a question call for an answer?" thundered Papa.

Still Mama did not raise her voice. "That was not a question. It was a demand."

The fragrance of cardamon and cinnamon found its way to Papa's nose. It softened his heart a bit. He changed his tone almost to pleading.

"My nerves need a rest, Maria. I am preached out. A few

years on a farm would make a new and better minister of me. If you could only grasp how good this farm idea is for all of us."

Mama placed her hands on her hips and faced Papa.

"Pontus. *I* know what's happened to you. You have developed an evil eye. The Good Book teaches us to pluck it out before it is too late. Just think of it. You want to give up your noble calling as a pastor to become a *farmer*."

Papa's head ached from too much thinking. He knew Mama was an exceptional woman. Few wives could cook, bake, keep a parsonage immaculate, besides tending eight children and accompanying her husband on pastoral calls. Papa was convinced there was not another woman in the world that could be compared with Mama. But as efficiently as she ran her home and children, she tried to run him and that had to be stopped.

"Evil eye," he mumbled. "As if giving up preaching for a time could connect me with evil."

Mama brushed her hair from her forehead, leaving a streak of flour across her eyebrows.

"I married a minister not a farmer, Pontus. And I don't want to become a farmer's wife. Not even a gentleman farmer's wife, or whatever you name it."

Papa was desperate. If only there were some way to talk reason into Maria. She was braiding the coffee rings now, her body moving gracefully back and forth. Carefully she dipped the pastry brush in the beaten egg yolk and penciled the top of the rings. Papa wondered as he watched her if she were through bearing children? Nim was eighteen and Kerstin five. Having babies had seemed such a pleasant, natural process to Mama as though she enjoyed going on increasing the earth. It seemed to Papa that Mama would fit perfectly in the large, spacious farm kitchen with more than ample room for the children to run around. He looked dreamily into space, thinking aloud.

"There is a lake below the farm where I could do a lot of fishing."

But Mama found the words to pull him back on the straight and narrow road.

"Pontus! I think the kind of fishing the Lord wants you to do is not done with hooks and sinkers."

Papa tried once more to convince her.

"Look how much fun the children could have on a place like that, Maria," he said eagerly. "How healthy it would be for them away from city life, with plenty of fresh air and sunshine."

"Yes," said Mama sarcastically, "and look how much fun *I* would have. I can just picture myself as a farmer's wife with a milk pail hanging on my arm. A pair of old shoes with worn-down heels that would smell far from perfume. Oh, yes, I can feel the flies buzzing around my face as I am milking. And I suppose the cow will give me a slap across the mouth with her smelly sharp tail every so often. For of course *I* will have to do the milking. I can't visualize you on a three-legged stool under a cow."

Mama went to the sink and washed her hands energetically under the faucet. Papa heaved a deep sigh. There was not a thing he could say or do to convince Maria. He put on his hat and went for a walk.

Mama stood by the kitchen window and her eyes followed Papa as slowly, with heavy steps, he walked down the street. His head was bent a little forward and his hands were locked behind his back, as always when in deep thought. Mama wanted to be fair, and just now her heart ached for him. She knew how deeply hurt and disappointed he was. She wanted to follow her impulse and rush after him, calling, "Papa *lilla*, come back. I didn't mean a word I said."

If she only could have told him that she had been thinking a lot about the farm idea herself. It must be a beautiful place and it could be such fun. She understood too well how tired he must be of a demanding congregation. She, too, was tired of all the little pinpricks she had to endure as a minister's wife. She would have loved to agree with Papa, but all she could do was to stand there and watch him wander off lonely and dejected.

Poor Pontus, she thought as a flood of love welled up in her heart. But after tomorrow he would know her reason and that had to be her consolation. He would understand then why she could not be a farmer's wife—why she could not leave the city. Mama was running for President of the Woman's Club.

In Papa's estimation a woman's duty was at home with her children. Mama loved her home, her children, her husband but she also loved to "climb the social ladder." To be President of the Woman's Club had been Mama's dream for years. It would give her influence. She would "sit in the council with the wise." She would be respected and honored and invited to every function of importance. Tomorrow the newspaper would carry the story. It might even make the headlines. Mama could already see them in her mind: MRS. PONTUS FRANZON ELECTED PRESIDENT OF THE WOMAN'S CLUB. And then what could Papa do but be proud that he had married a woman who was capable of such honor. He would drop the thought of the farm at least until Mama had served her two years.

Only it was important how Papa received the news. It must come as a pleasant surprise and not as a shock. Mama would arise early the following morning. She must be the first one to put her hand on that paper so she could bring it to Papa when she served him his before-breakfast coffee. Mama still served Papa coffee in bed. It was one habit from Sweden that he had refused to give up.

It was with purpose Mama had baked Papa's favorite coffee bread this morning. (It was not often that she made coffee bread in the middle of the week.) But tomorrow morning it must be extra special with lots of butter and sugar and cardamon. She would also wear her blue dotted

Swiss dress which was his favorite, and she would smile very sweetly as she came with the tray. When Papa was on his third *Kringla*-bread and had asked her to pour his second cup of coffee, she would slip him the paper. And there from the front page her picture would smile at him. The rest she would have to leave in God's hand.

When the coffee bread was in the oven, Mama went into the study to be near the telephone. The nominating committee meeting would be over any time now. She sat down in Papa's favorite chair to wait for Miss Thompson to call and to dream about the future. At first she had refused to run for such a high position because of her Swedish accent. But Miss Thompson, the chairman of the nominating committee, had assured Mama that her accent only added to her charm.

"In our democratic country," Miss Thompson had explained, "we disregard such things. If a woman is willing and capable of leadership, we clubwomen are proud to have her serve regardless of foreign birth. And you, Mrs. Franzon, are a born leader!"

Mama had felt better about it after Miss Thompson's remark and had decided to run. If she only could have told Papa and he could have shared her happiness. Still she would handle him when it was all over. First she would point out that the church membership would be sure to increase through her election. It might even double in two years. What an honor for Papa to take a leave of absence and go farming at the height of his career.

The clang of the telephone broke in on her dreams.

"The election is over," Miss Thompson said in a toneless voice.

"Oh," answered Mama with a pounding heart, "how sweet of you to call."

"My dear Mrs. Franzon," Miss Thompson continued, "I am brokenhearted to bring you such bad news. It is my duty to inform you that you lost to Mrs. Rodney. I am terribly, terribly sorry."

Something broke inside Mama. Her whole beautiful

world tumbled down. For a moment she was speechless. If she could only think of something to say to Miss Thompson—something to save her face. She must pass it off lightly, no one must ever say she was licked. But what? Then the idea clicked.

"Miss Thompson," she heard herself saying easily, "don't feel badly, please. I am really relieved. You see, Miss Thompson, Mr. Franzon is leaving the pulpit for a rest, and we are buying a beautiful old estate in the country. If I had won, I would have had to resign at our first meeting. But thank you so much for calling, and good luck to Mrs. Rodney from me."

Mama hung up and sadly stared at the telephone, her "wonderful friends" were just a bunch of cats.

Papa had walked past the city limits out toward the open country. It was springtime and a bright sun shone from a clear blue sky. Somehow, at this season of the year, Papa was always especially homesick for Sweden. Today even his soul seemed sick with longing for the small white church which he had left back there in dear, beautiful Lapland. In spring the little mountain streams, chained by icy fetters during the long Swedish winter months, regained their freedom. Then they would rush from the mountainsides down the deep ravines and race with lightning speed toward the river. Along the riverbanks the tiny dwarf birches would be thrusting forth their furry buds and tender green leaves. Papa longed to fill his lungs with clear, cool mountain air, and once again to feel the "peace that abideth" among the snow-covered hills of Sweden.

Why had he listened to Mama and left his native land? He had known he could never be replanted in happy-go-lucky America, with all its noise and bustle. Even here on the highway far from the city, the noise of traffic never ceased. How could Mama be so perfectly contented in this screaming world? If only he could make her understand that it was peace he needed and that the farm by the lake far from the highway could give it to him. How well it could have worked out. That farm was one in a thousand!

Papa sighed and walked on. After a while he left the highway and followed a narrow path through the woodland. At least this would take him away from the stench of gasoline-smelling cars that seemed to enjoy making his life more miserable by blowing their trumpetlike horns as they passed him.

The path led to a little brook gurgling happily through the forest. Papa seated himself on a large rock and gazed down at the water. A fish caught his eye. It must be a brook trout! If only he had his fish line along. Then sadly he remembered Mama's words of the morning, reminding him that his work was to be "a fisher of men." He was supposed to look neither to the right nor to the left; only straight ahead at the road he had chosen. Papa sighed again. Life was hard. Perhaps getting married had been a mistake. A married man could not call his soul his own. He might as well admit that he was licked. Not just licked about the farm, but about everything else in life. Since he had become the father of eight children and had brought them across the ocean, his once quite sizable bank account had become very slim and undernourished. It was all Mama's fault. *She* had made him leave Sweden. For sixteen years she had kept at him and, like the slow dripping of water on a hard stone, gradually had worn him down. He remembered that summer morning, now so long ago, when Mama had *won* her first point. They were having coffee under the white lilacs.

Suddenly Mama had asked, "How do you ever plan to educate our eight children here in Sweden? In America, high school is free. They don't even have to pay for the books. And over there they could all work themselves through college."

Papa knew Mama was right. For education, America

was the promised land. But Papa loved Sweden; and besides he could not let Mama win *every* time.

"I never wanted eight children in the first place, Maria," he protested. "Three would have been ideal. And I think I could have managed to educate three, *even here* in Sweden."

Mama had been horrified. "Why, Pontuš. You ought to bow your head in the dust. You just take a good look at the five you never wanted and tell me if you would really have the heart to deny them their rightful place here on earth. It is wrong, Pontus—very, very wrong. You are playing at high stakes with the devil."

Papa had felt guilty and very ashamed of his hasty words, and he had told Mama so. "Of course I love all the children, Maria. But it isn't good to spread love so *thin*. Don't you agree that eight children are enough, Maria?"

Mama had just looked at him for a long time and, under her steady gaze, Papa had felt very evil. So, to change the subject, he had promised to give America some thought.

But summer in Sweden was especially wonderful that year and Papa hadn't had much time to think of America. It seemed to him that the red-and-white parsonage outshone all the other homes in the village. This, Papa was sure, was because of the garden—his own creation. With God's help of course. He kept the sand-yard neatly raked and the paths where the children were allowed to walk were as smooth and straight as a godly life. Grass bordered the sand-yard like a thick green carpet, and on the outer rim the currant and gooseberry bushes grew in lush profusion. At one end of the garden, three cherry trees and two plum trees blossomed in all their pink-velvet glory.

"They are like a bright fringe on a green shawl, Pontus," Maria had said one morning in early summer. Later, when the bushes were heavily laden with black, red and yellow berries, Maria had called them "old women kneeling in prayers of gratitude for a rich harvest." Papa had agreed, squirming uncomfortably as he always did when Mama got poetic or emotional.

But the strawberries were Papa's pride. Every day during the dry season he had faithfully carried five dippers of water from the nearby well, to each thirsty plant. Even Mama agreed that the fruit was the largest and the reddest and the sweetest in all Sweden.

By the middle of the summer, when it was daylight the clock around, tourists poured into the village from all over the world to see the wonders of the Midnight Sun, and they often stopped at Papa's little white church to pray. He was sure that life had never been so full, so rich in God's bounty and blessings. Maria, he decided, must think so too, for she hadn't mentioned America again.

On Midsummer Day (the twenty-fourth of June), all Sweden celebrated. That afternoon, late, Maria and he had left the children with Tant Renberg and begun their long journey up Gellivara mountain. At midnight they had stood on its highest peak, breathlessly watching the sun descend to the horizon, linger a moment, then swiftly turn and rise again in majestic glory into a cloudless blue sky. They had knelt in a silent prayer before this vision of everlasting peace that, one day in God's good time, would spread throughout the whole world.

Short as summer was, that last one in Sweden had been especially filled with happy times. Picnics under the tall straight pines beside mountain lakes; long peaceful hours of fishing while Mama and the children scrambled into the little rowboat and went adventuring downstream. America was just a name on a map to all of them, if, indeed, Maria ever thought of that faraway country.

By early September the strong winds had begun to blow their chilly breath over Lapland. The birches put on gay autumn colors, for a time flaunting their brilliance before the spruce trees in somber green. Then the rains, day after day, poured down the mountainsides. Inside the parsonage there were warmth and happy voices and a thousand spicy odors. Gallons of lingonberries simmered in huge pots on the back of the stove. Papa had picked most of them himself, relishing the rich red sauce, which Mama served over mashed potatoes as a substitute for expensive meat.

Presently the cellar was filled with wonderful things to eat. Great barrels of potatoes; and boxes of apples, round and red, to be hung under each candle on the Christmas tree; eggs in water glass, and tubs of brine in which lay hams, sausages and pigs' feet. From the rafter hung great quantities of dry fish, which later would be soaked in strong *lut*-brine for the traditional Christmas *lutfisk*. Papa could almost taste it now, white and fluffy on the Christmas Eve supper table. Why, it wouldn't have been Christmas in Sweden without it!

So summer and autumn had passed all too quickly, and before Papa realized it winter had wrapped a heavy white coat about the world. Still Mama had said nothing more about America, and Papa was sure even she had now completely forgotten that foolishness. He could settle down and live out his life peacefully in dear Lapland.

Then one winter morning, when the snow almost reached the window sills, and Mama had been busily baking *julbockar*, their favorite Christmas cookies, Papa had glanced up from the sermon he was preparing, to find Mama standing in his study door. Her shining childlike eyes looked past him over the endless white snowland.

"Pontus," she said excitedly, "I was just thinking about all the fruit in America."

Papa's heart skipped a beat. So! She hadn't forgotten America. She had only waited until she thought *he* had. Papa was annoyed. "And what has that to do with us?"

Mama had gone right on talking as though she hadn't heard him. "How *cheap* it is, Pontus. Why it costs hardly anything. I could even buy a whole big bag of bananas and give the children two each. And a big orange for each of them, too. And for you, dear, a heaping plate of grapes."

Papa knew he had to say something, but what? While he was trying to decide, Mama turned, and as abruptly as she had arrived, went back to her work, humming a little English folk song. Papa had been so upset, he hadn't been able to finish his sermon. All the rest of the day he was dreaming of fruit in the middle of winter. Mama was certainly clever. She knew his weakness for fruit and that there wouldn't be any in Lapland until summer; even then it would be very hard on his pocketbook. . . .

A branch from a nearby tree fell into the little mountain stream, reminding Papa that this was America not Sweden, and that his dream of a farm was farther away than ever. Mama always found a way to make him give in to her. If one method didn't succeed, she had another. Both were very familiar to Papa. One, Mama would go around the house with tears dripping down her cheeks, her eyes filled with reproach. That always made him feel so mean that he would do and say almost anything just to see her smile again.

But even worse than that was the other method. Mama would go about with lips tightly pressed together, never saying a word. The house became a tomb. Meals were eaten in silence. If the children spoke, they were hushed up quickly. Any attempt at conversation ended with "yes" or "no." Papa was certain Mama was going into this stage now.

"Well," Papa said aloud, as he arose from the rock, "this time I will surprise her. I will *give up* the farm all by myself. Then life can go on as peaceful as before."

Yes, he would preach until his time was up, then go to receive his reward—*if* Mama did not snatch *that* from him too. Papa was not at all sure how a Higher Power would handle Mama, but then the responsibility would be out of his hands. A preacher's life was not as glorious as some people, especially a preacher's wife, seemed to think.

Reluctantly Papa followed the woodland path back to the main highway. At the intersection, he turned for a last look at the peaceful scene. Early afternoon shadows

lay now across the path, and the birds' chorus had become
a symphony. Busily they twittered from twig to twig,
building their nests, accepting God's promise of a new
earth and all things added thereto, with a kind of faith
that suddenly made Papa more than a little ashamed of
his own doubts. Here he was complaining about Maria
and their wonderful children, when he should have been
grateful to God for entrusting so many precious lives to
his care. Papa was so contrite that he felt like kneeling
right there in the dusty highway and asking forgiveness.
But he couldn't do that. The cars were thick on the road
now, and he would have to keep to the path along the
highway to avoid being hit.

Well, one thing he *could* do. He'd hurry back to the
parsonage and tell Mama that he was sorry, just as he had
done that long-ago day in Sweden, and that he loved all
of them, even if they did complicate his life, especially
his bank balance. He'd give up the farm so cheerfully she
would know that he wasn't just giving in to her. He'd
be a "fisher of men" if that was what God—and Mama—
wanted him to be.

It was long past lunchtime when Papa reached the parsonage. Before opening the door, he stood for a moment
outside, listening to the noise of the children, Mama's
laughter and Greta's giggle. This morning they would
have annoyed him. Now he could feel only humble gratitude. Gently he opened the door. The homey fragrance
of newly baked bread greeted him. On the baking-board,
the coffee rings were lined up on a clean towel. Mama's
cheeks were bright roses, and she wore his favorite dotted
Swiss dress.

She looked up from tying Kerstin's hat ribbons and
greeted Papa with a big smile. "We are all ready now,
Pontus."

Papa couldn't believe his eyes and ears. He just stared.
"Ready for what?" he finally managed in a weak voice.

"Why, to go for a ride to look at the farm, of course,"
said Mama sweetly.

Papa gasped, "But I thought you——"

"Never mind what you thought. We have to hurry if you want to see it in daylight."

Papa sat down for a minute and took a long breath. *One thing he had completely overlooked in his planning—a woman's privilege of changing her mind.*

CHAPTER 10

❦ The Sunny Years

Mama exercised her prerogative to change her mind on more things than buying the farm. By the end of March, when they were ready to move to the country, she was, if anything, even more enthusiastic about the farm than Papa was.

To the children, the farm meant only escape from the rigidly proper behavior which was expected of them as "the preacher's children" and the stern scrutiny of everything they said or did. They had been "the preacher's children" all their lives. To suddenly become "Farmer Franzon's children" was like acquiring a new personality, and for a whole month they planned accordingly. "When we get to the farm . . ." became a common expression among them, a to-be-desired state of existence which compensated for any self-discipline they still had to endure.

Life on the farm wasn't, of course, the perfect state they had envisioned. Few things ever do measure up exactly to dream specifications. Still, seeing how much they could "get away with" was a challenge to all of them (with the possible exception of Pelle, who came as close to being a saint as a human being could), and they made the most of every opportunity. Fortunately there was work to be done, which kept them out of too much mischief, and Papa saw to it that personal discipline was

162

quite as exacting for a farmer's children as for those of a minister. Nevertheless, the farm was a new kind of freedom for all of them. Good behavior somehow seemed easier. The chores were fun, and they loved the animals and all growing things.

Even Mama, who had wanted so desperately to be President of the Woman's Club, now seemed just as happy being a farmer's wife, actually enjoying the very chores she had earlier ridiculed.

Mama walked jauntily down the path toward the big red barn, a milk pail swinging on each arm. The sun, a big coal of fire, peered cautiously over the horizon, promising a hot day. But at this early hour the green and golden fields of grain beyond the barn rippled, fresh and cool, in the morning breeze. Birds twittered and sang, flitting happily from tree to tree. Busy with their morning chores, too, thought Mama. What a wonderful new day!

Suddenly Mama found herself listening for the low mellow voice of the cuckoo. Then she laughed softly. At least in this part of America there were no cuckoo birds to foretell the future. In Sweden everyone waited eagerly for the return of the cuckoo in the spring, for you could tell what the future had in store by the direction from which the call first came. Like that spring morning in Lapland so long ago, when she had walked up the road to the parsonage to apply for a job as Papa's maid. She had heard the cuckoo then for the first time that year, and her heart had stood still at the sound. She had stopped and listened, scarcely breathing until she realized that the call came from the west. Then she had known she would have the best year of her life.

With the cuckoo on my side, she had thought joyously, I can't fail.

And as she neared the parsonage, she realized how lucky she had been that the sound had not come from another direction. For had it come from the east, it would have meant she would need to be comforted before the year was up; or from the north, a heartbreaking disappointment. And the south meant death!

Well, it was a good thing there were no cuckoo birds around the farm. In spite of its wooing call, it was ugly and a heartless false charmer, a disgrace to the bird family. The mother cuckoo was so busy all day just cooing "cuckoo" that she had no time to raise her family. And besides, she was a robber and a murderer. First she would steal into another bird's nest, destroy its eggs, then lay her own eggs and fly away, leaving her helpless babies for some other mama bird to take care of.

Just thinking about it made Mama angry, and she walked faster.

It was over a year now since they had bought the farm. And Mama was sure it had been the happiest time for all of them. It was good to be free. Especially good for Pontus. She wondered if church people realized how demanding they were of their pastor and his family. How wearing it was never to have a moment that really belonged to you. Why Papa was like a new man since they came to the farm. Just watching him as he went about the heavy work, laughing even when he was tired, made her wonder if maybe this was not Papa's real calling after all. Perhaps she had been wrong to insist that he remain a preacher as long as he had.

"A man needs to be close to the soil, Maria," he had said one spring night as they had walked together across the freshly plowed fields. "It makes him feel very close to God. Sometimes I wonder if it is not even a closer walk than preaching. Seeing the miracle of creation in nature makes a man stand in awe before the power of the Creator."

A little thread of fear ran through her. "You mean, Pontus," she had asked, "that you might not go back to preaching?"

"No, Maria. I only said I was wondering, that's all."

They had walked for a while in silence, and Mama was sure Papa was remembering, as she was, the offer the

church people had made at the farewell banquet the week
before they had left for the farm.

"Pastor Franzon," the moderator had said that night,
"as a church we have voted not to give you up completely.
We realize that working in the Lord's vineyard for so
many years and the adjustment to your new country have
been very tiring. We know you need a rest. But we want
you to come back to us. The minister we have selected
to preach during your absence was about to retire, but
he has agreed to postpone his retirement for two years.
We hope that will be long enough for you to think the
matter over carefully, and we hope you will decide to
return to us. The pulpit in Berkley Hills will be waiting
for you, Pastor Franzon."

Papa, deeply moved by their affection, had promised
to think it over and let them know his decision before the
two years had passed.

And for more than a year now, Papa had relaxed on
the farm, happy and carefree. The farm had prospered
remarkably. Already they had been able to pay off the
loan from the bank, and now the profits went regularly
to nourish Papa's bank account. . . .

Suddenly Mama stopped and almost dropped the milk
pails.

The stillness of the morning was broken by the sound
of Papa's rich, strong voice coming from inside the barn.
It was not the voice of Farmer Franzon, but that of
Reverend Franzon, in his best ministerial tones.

"And I say to you, that to hear with your ears and
see with your eyes is not enough in the sight of the Lord.
The fires of hell may still await you at the end of your
days . . ."

Mama could not believe her ears. Something had happened to Papa's mind. No sane man would preach a
sermon on hell at six in the morning to five uninterested
cows.

Frantically she pushed open the barn door. "Pontus!
What in the world are you doing?"

Papa's voice stopped abruptly. His face was red with embarrassment, and he stared at Mama as though she were a creature from the lower world. Finally he walked slowly toward her.

"No, Maria," he said calmly, "I am not crazy as you perhaps think. I was just practicing. I can't afford to lose the quality of my voice."

Mama drew a sigh of relief. If she had been wondering what decision Papa would make next spring, she no longer needed to wonder. The knowledge brought both happiness and regret. Much as she loved the farm and knew Papa loved it, she had not been able to convince herself that this was his rightful place, that his call to God's work had not been for all his life.

But seeing Papa's embarrassment over having been discovered at his strange preaching, Mama laughed outright.

"Oh, Pontus *lilla*," she said, "for a moment I thought you really expected the cows to repent. But let me ask you: do you always preach to them about hell? Of course I can see the connection. They have the horns and tails and you the pitchfork."

This was too much for Papa. "I don't think it is funny, Maria," he grunted gloomily. He dropped the pitchfork, seized the big broom standing by the door and began sweeping the barn floor vigorously.

Mama was still giggling as she sat down on the three-legged stool beside big, good-natured Albertina and started to milk. Albertina was a very special cow. In fact, all the Franzon cows were special, Mama thought, listening to the soft music the little streams of milk made against the tin pail. And they were lucky too. Papa insisted that Sweden was way ahead of America when it came to farming. He thought it was disgraceful the way American farmers allowed their cows to run about, using up the energy that should have gone into making them good milkers. The Franzon cows were not permitted to remain outside the barns at night, even in summertime. Days, they were allowed to roam the grassy pastures, but at night they were brought back to the barn.

"Cows are not unlike people, Maria," he had said that first day at the farm as the whole family eagerly surveyed their new possessions. "They like attention and they appreciate it."

"Of course, Papa," exclaimed Button, "and instead of saying 'thank you, sir,' they give a couple of extra quarts of milk."

Everyone laughed. Laughter was so easy when there was so much happiness in your heart.

Both Button and Papa had been right. In a few days the children had named the cows, Swedish names which carried special affection, and the cows responded with brimming pails of milk. . . .

The pail was almost full now. Albertina turned her head and looked at Mama gratefully. Just as if she wanted to say "thank you," thought Mama. She patted the cow gently. "Thank you, too, Albertina, for the good fresh milk," she whispered, and picking up the pail and the stool, moved past the next stall—Rosa's stall.

Rosa would bear her first calf in a few months and now was having special care. Mama turned back for a moment and patted her proudly, feeling the satiny sleekness of her bulging sides, and receiving a patient "moo-oo" in response. Rosa was always patient, and Mama thought how right the children had been to name her Rosa, a name which seemed to mean gentleness and goodness. Beside Albertina and Rosa, there were Stjärna Hjärtros and Lilja.

"Just like their dispositions," Calle had explained to Papa.

And it was true, thought Mama. Albertina was fat and easy-going, and Rosa was patient and gentle. Hjärtros was a snippy little animal. Once she had kicked Mama right off the stool and made her spill a whole pailful of milk. But that was before Mama had learned how to

handle her. Now she always patted Hjärtros first and
talked to her before she started milking. Stjärna was the
hardest. She had a habit of switching her tail which, if
Mama did not duck in time, would leave a red mark on
her cheek for days. Lilja was the gentlest of all. She would
stand as still as a candle while Mama milked her, chewing
her cud contentedly. Perhaps it was because Mama always
sang as she milked Lilja. Or did she sing because Lilja
was so good? Mama wondered.

She put the full pail on the low shelf by the door and
took down the second pail. Lilja stood motionless as
Mama placed the stool in the right position. Then to the
music of the milk in the pail, Mama sang:

> "Morgon mellan fjällen
> Klara bäck ock flood
> Sorlande på hällen
> Sjungen Gud är god
> Gud är god."

By the time she had finished the milking, Papa had
apparently given up trying to convert the cows to God-
fearing creatures and had gone to the fields with Pelle.
Last summer Nim and Papa had worked side by side,
planting and tending the crops, so that by fall the harvest
had been very good. But this summer Nim was helping
Mr. Jones, a neighboring farmer, with the morning chores,
and adding his earnings to the pile of coins in the tin box
for his medical education. So it was Pelle who now went
proudly every morning to the fields with Papa.

With brimming milk pails, Mama started back to the
house. Farm life was indeed a good life. It was good not
to have to worry about what other people thought or
said. Especially where the children were concerned. Here
there was no Mrs. Olson to complain that Button was too
young to wear face powder and to insist that she should
be called Charlotta instead of a crazy name like Button.
Or a Mrs. Svenson to contend that here in America a girl

as old as Button *should* wear a little make-up. And Mr. Skoglund thought it was downright selfish of Papa to allow Nim, a growing boy, to work so hard; while Mr. Benson complained that all the children old enough to work should contribute to the family budget. Even Papa had come in for criticism. One member thought he did too much house-calling; another thought he should call on every member at least once every month. A minister was supposed to please everyone but himself!

Well, thought Mama, here on the farm the children could work as they wanted to, Button could wear make-up or not as she chose, and, when she and Papa went calling or received callers, it was because they enjoyed them.

Mama chuckled out loud, remembering the first time farmer Jones had called, and the way Kerstin had embarrassed Papa. They had been sitting on the front porch, drinking coffee and enjoying some of Mama's freshly baked *bullar*, when Kerstin had rushed up the steps exclaiming, "Oh, Papa, Papa! Come quick! Rosa is walking in the flower garden."

Papa and Mr. Jones got up and followed her.

"I was under the impression, Franzon, that you had only eight children. I thought I had met them all, but I don't remember meeting Rosa. How old is she?"

Kerstin did not wait for Papa to reply. "Oh," she said quickly, "there are four more."

"Well well, thirteen children. That's a mighty big family these days."

"I'm afraid, Jones," said Papa somewhat sharply, "you are mixing up our children with our cows. We happen to have *five cows* and one of them is trampling down Maria's flowers. We had better hurry."

Later that evening, Papa had laid down a firm rule about the cows. If the children insisted upon calling them by human names, at least they should be sure to make clear that they *were* cows. Thirteen children, indeed! And with a final grunt, Papa had decided to go for a walk.

Mama had to admit that this habit of naming the animals could be confusing. If you added the names of all the animals on the farm to those of the family, Papa would really have some explaining to do. Two horses, two dozen or more chickens, and two pigs. The horses were named Bläsan and Brunte; the pigs Napoleon and Josefina. So far the children hadn't been able to think up enough names for the chickens.

Mama sang as she went about her work in the sunny kitchen. She strained the milk into three huge stone jars. Later she would skim the cream from one jar and put it into small containers for delivery to her customers. Another jar would be divided into quart pails for the same purpose, and the third jar was kept for family use. Two large baskets of eggs, which Vickey and Greta had brought in last night, waited for sorting into dozens— some for market and some for home use. This task held special interest for Mama, for the egg money belonged to her. How surprised and delighted she had been that morning when Papa had announced this decision. She had thanked him properly, but she had not told him the idea that began to take shape at once in her mind. But the chickens received extra special care from that moment, and they rewarded her kindness. The amount in her bank account was evidence of that. And every market day added to it.

The only trouble, Mama thought now, as she counted the eggs into the containers, was that Papa took the milk, cream and eggs to market because she could not drive. How could she keep the surprise she was planning for Papa a secret when he knew exactly how much money she had in the bank?

She had just finished sorting the eggs when the bold idea hit her. She would learn to drive the car herself. She knew this remarkable feat would have to be accomplished in secret—perhaps while Pontus was working at the far end of the fields. It wasn't that she wanted to do anything dishonest. It was just that she knew already Pontus's attitude on the subject. He had made that very clear the first day on the farm. Mama had innocently suggested that he teach her to drive so she could take over the marketing.

"God made woman to cook and have children and care for a home and love her husband, Maria. He did not intend her to risk her life and every other life on the highway by driving a car."

"Oh, Pontus! I bet I'd be the best driver on the road. Do you think I'd risk breaking the eggs and spilling the milk and cream?"

But for once Papa could not be cajoled into agreeing. "Absolutely no, Maria. The subject is closed." And Mama knew it was. For the time being.

But, she thought now, if she could *prove* to him how wrong he was—well, then he couldn't forbid her to drive. She just had to prove it.

For several days Mama's conscience bothered her. Maybe it was wrong to go against Pontus's decision. But, she reasoned, didn't the end justify the means in this case? She only wanted to make a big happy surprise for Pontus, and somehow Mama felt God would approve of that. A week later, she was sure God had sent her a sign.

They had just finished the morning chores and Papa was about to set off for the south field, when a car drove up. It was Deacon Olson.

"I was hoping I'd get here before you got into your day's work, Pastor Franzon," he said, when he had greeted them warmly. "Old Mr. Stenström passed away yesterday, and it was his last wish that you conduct the funeral service. Mrs. Stenström would like to see you to talk about the arrangements."

Papa did not hesitate. He was especially fond of the old gentleman, and he was pleased by this final expression of regard. He changed into suitable dark clothes, and in a few moments Mama watched the Olson car disappear down the road. Papa's car, for want of a garage on the farm, was parked near the lake under a large oak tree

whose foliage was almost like a roof. Mama's eyes fell
upon it as she started back into the house to continue her
work. Surely this was a sign from God! *This was her day*.

She hurried with her housework, and by noontime the
house was spotless. The boys went to the fields, and Button and the younger children set off for Ellen Jones's
birthday party. Mama had the farm to herself.

She climbed into the car and settled herself importantly
behind the steering wheel. She had sat often enough beside
Pontus, watching what he did to start the car, how he
shifted the gears three times until finally the car was
humming contentedly along the highway. It was very
simple. Papa was foolish to think a woman could not
handle a car as well as a man.

First, she must turn this little switch, then step gently
on the big button on the floor. The car leaped into action.
Mama was so surprised that for the life of her she couldn't
remember what to do next. Then as she looked up, she
realized with horror that she was headed straight for
the lake. Frantically she tried to think what Papa did to
stop the car. Too late, she realized *that* was one thing she
had forgotten to notice. By the time the car stood in two
feet of water, reason had returned. She flicked off the
switch she had turned to start the car, and grabbed the
brake. The car stopped as abruptly as it had started.

Mama sat there shaking with fright. The sign she had
thought came from God surely had come from the devil.
She had almost drowned the family car, and Papa's wife,
too. And instead of proving *her* point, she had only
proved how right Papa was. Now he would never let her
learn to drive.

At a time like this, Mama would ordinarily have prayed.
But she was so ashamed of letting the devil fool her into
thinking he was God, she just couldn't pray. There were
real tears of contrition in her eyes as she removed her
shoes and stockings, climbed out of the car and waded
to shore.

How could she ever explain to Pontus what she had

done? She had to think of something so he would not be so angry. Maybe God would forgive her if she told him how truly sorry she was for listening to the devil.

By the time she had reached the house, she had an idea.

When Papa and Deacon Olson drove up half an hour later, Mama, barefooted, and with her dress pinned up to her knees, was scrubbing away on the family car as though it was one of the children in the bathtub.

Papa was out of the Olson car in one jump. "Maria," he called angrily, "what in the world are you doing with my car in the lake?"

Mama, all smiles, called back, "Isn't this a wonderful way to wash the car, Pontus? It seemed silly to carry all that water when it was so much easier to drive the car into the lake."

Papa stared, horrified. But Mr. Olson roared with laughter.

"Leave it to a woman, Pastor Franzon. They will always find a short cut."

But Papa did not think it was funny. Something else was bothering him. "Maria," he said sharply, "did you say *you drove* the car into the lake?"

"Of course, Pontus. It was easy," Mama announced proudly.

Papa, too surprised to speak, pulled thoughtfully at his mustache, then scratched his head. Finally he glanced at Deacon Olson who was still chuckling over the incident. Mama could not believe her ears when Papa spoke.

"You did very well for a beginner, Maria," he said with dignity, "but I have come to the conclusion that the highway is a much better place to drive. Tomorrow I shall see how well you can drive on the road."

Mama waded back to the shore as fast as she could, and, ignoring Deacon Olson, threw her arms around Papa's neck. "Oh, Pontus! I think that's just wonderful."

Papa cleared his throat in embarrassment. "Very well, Maria. But just promise me one thing. That in the future you will allow *me* to wash the car the old-fashioned way."

By midsummer, even Papa admitted Mama could drive the car as well as anyone, and Mama was quite sure he was glad she *had* learned, for he was too busy in the fields to make the trips to market. And Mama loved it. It was such fun spinning along the highway in the early morning before the sun got too hot, thinking about how much she would add to her bank account that day. Wouldn't Pontus be surprised when she told him she had saved enough money to let him go back to Sweden for a visit? But still, it was going to be a long time before she had saved enough and could tell him. Meantime she had to think of some way to thank him for teaching her to drive and for not getting angry when she almost drowned the car.

Then one morning, as June turned into July, and Mama tore a leaf off the big picture-calendar in the kitchen, she knew what to do.

Pontus had a birthday on the twelfth. Birthdays in the Franzon household were always special occasions, for that was the one day of the year that was completely "your day." And this year Pontus's birthday was going to be extra special.

For the next week there was much whispering and planning with the children, everyone making sure Papa was not around to overhear the plans. The presents had to be selected very carefully, and of course there must be a present from everyone. By the end of the week everyone had decided except Pelle.

"I haven't thought of anything good enough yet, Mama," he would say each time Mama asked him about it.

"Well, you better decide, darling, or you won't have time to get it."

But it was not until two days before the big celebration that his decision was made. Actually it was made for him. And Pelle was sure God had a hand in it.

Mama had asked him to bring in the milk pails from the back porch. When he returned, instead of the milk pails, he was carrying a large black cat.

"Pelle," exclaimed Mama. "Where did that come from?"

"From God, Mama. God sent him for Papa's birthday."

Mama wasn't so sure about God's part in the gift, for she knew too well how Papa felt about cats. But she hadn't the heart to dampen Pelle's excitement.

"It is not going to be easy to hide this present, son."

"But I will. I'll keep him in the cellar, Mama, and take good care of him."

Button helped him prepare the big wooden box, which would be the cat's home for the next two days. Then they set about making a cardboard box for the presentation. It was covered with blue-and-white wallpaper and was to be tied gaily with red ribbon. Two round air holes were cut in one side.

"Oh, I hope Papa will like my present, Mama," said Pelle as he started for the cellar. Mama said nothing, secretly worried about the situation.

"I know how we can make him like it," chimed Button. Pelle stopped. "How?"

"Oh, just call him Lapland. That will do it."

"Why, Button, that's a wonderful idea," cried Mama, relieved. Papa just couldn't help liking anything which reminded him of his beloved Sweden.

Papa's birthday celebration started at five o'clock in the morning, with coffee in bed. The coffee was carefully boiled to just the right golden brown, and the big silver tray—one of Mama's treasures from Sweden—was laden with special cakes and coffee bread. Most important was the *tårta*. It was filled with applesauce and on top, in large pastry letters, Mama had written "sixty-three," surrounded by a huge circle of whipped cream.

When the tray was ready, Mama lighted the two tall candles on the tray. Then the procession started. Mama carried the tray and the children carried the presents. Only Pelle was empty-handed. His present now stood on the kitchen table.

"You better wait, darling," said Mama, "until Papa has had his coffee and opened the other presents. Your present will be the biggest surprise of all, so I think it should come last, don't you?"

Pelle reluctantly agreed, casting anxious glances back at the box as he followed at the end of the procession.

Outside Papa's bedroom door, Mama waited a moment, then signaled for the singing to begin as she opened the door. It was a special song she had made up for this special occasion:

> "Happy birthday, Papa dear,
> So sweet and happy and free from fear
> We love you more than the birds in the tree
> Or the stars in the sky—or the bumblebee
> For Papa—our Papa—so fine and tall
> Is the very best Papa of them all!"

Papa sat up and rubbed the sleep from his eyes. Then he stared for a moment at all the smiling faces and the festive tray.

"Well, well! The whole family up so early, and look at all the good things to eat! My birthday. Sixty-three years old! Do you have to remind me of that, Maria?" But he was smiling and Mama knew he was very proud.

One by one the children placed their gaily wrapped gifts on the foot of the bed. Mama poured the coffee and Papa cut the *tårta*. When the tray was empty, Papa started opening the gifts. Socks, overalls, handkerchiefs, shirts, books—Papa exclaimed happily over each present. As he started opening the last package, Pelle slipped away and a moment later returned with a big box. His eyes were shining as he placed it in Papa's lap.

"What in the world is this, Pelle?"

"M-e-o-w!" said the box.

"Hush, Lapland," warned Pelle. "Are you going to stop being a surprise?"

Papa opened the lid and was almost knocked out of bed by the big black cat. He glared at the family.

"Is this a joke you are all playing on my birthday? I am sure you know my feelings about cats."

Mama's heart sank. But before she could say anything, Pelle spoke excitedly, "Oh, no, Papa. This is a very special cat God sent for your birthday. His name is Lapland. See how dignified he looks. I am sure he knows he has been sent to serve a minister."

"But . . . but . . ." stammered Papa, "we have two cats already."

"Maja and Kurre are just *barn* cats," put in Vickey. "And barn cats live in the barn and catch rats. Lapland is a *herskaps*-cat. He will be your very special escort."

But it was Lapland himself who saved the day. He jumped up on the bed and curled up on Papa's lap, purring like a motorboat. Papa stroked his glossy black fur, which only made Lapland purr the louder. "So you are Lapland," he said slowly. "I wonder how you happen to have a name like that?" And he winked at Mama.

Within a week, it was plain to see that Papa was as attached to Lapland as the big black cat was to him. The cat followed him everywhere during the day and at night slept in the big cushioned chair by Papa's bed.

One afternoon, about two weeks after Lapland had joined the family, Papa set out for the Jones farm, to help with the repair of a piece of machinery which Nim reported had broken down the day before. Nim and Mr. Jones had tried to fix it but, as Mr. Jones admitted, he never had been much of a hand with machinery. As Papa started down the front steps, Lapland appeared from nowhere and trailed after him. Papa did not discover this until he reached the Jones farm, and then only when he became aware of something white streaking across the Joneses' lawn, followed by a black streak. The white streak was Bunny-Betty, Ellen Jones's pet white rabbit, and the black streak was Lapland, in hot pursuit. Papa stood paralyzed, then caught a thankful breath as Bunny-Betty disappeared through a crack in the barn, too small for Lapland's big body.

In a moment Lapland was back, rubbing himself against Papa's leg. Papa picked him up and carried him to the

machine shed where Nim and Mr. Jones were already
working on the tractor. He found a wooden box in a
corner of the shed and, to Lapland's surprise, put him
on the floor and turned the box over him. And here Lapland had to remain until Papa and Nim were ready to go
home. That night, at supper, Papa told the story and
issued an order that Lapland was never to be allowed
on the Joneses' farm. As Lapland was usually with Papa,
this order did not seem a difficult one to carry out.

Life went on placidly about the farm for several weeks.
Then one Saturday afternoon, while Mama was busy with
the week-end baking, the telephone rang. It was Mrs.
Jones, inviting the Franzons to Sunday dinner. Mama
accepted graciously. As she hung up, she wondered why
Mrs. Jones had not extended the invitation earlier in the
week. It was all very well for the Joneses who did not
have a big family to plan for, but she had already done
most of the cooking in preparation for Sunday. Well,
thanks to the big icebox, her own food would keep for
another day.

When they arrived at the Jones farmhouse on Sunday
after church, they found a big picnic table, loaded with
food, under a large elm tree on the back lawn.

"A picnic," cried Greta, always interested in food.
"Look, Papa, at all the good things!"

Mama began to understand why Mrs. Jones could
entertain on such short notice. There was indeed an array
of good things. A heaping platter of fried chicken, big
bowls of potato salad, coleslaw and pickled beets. Fresh
bread and butter and two large apple pies for dessert.

"And ice cream, too, Mama! Ellen said so," boasted
Greta.

"Have you forgotten your manners, Greta?" said Papa
sharply.

But nothing could dampen their festive spirits today.
It was cool here on the big lawn under the elm tree, and
the food was delicious. Everyone passed his plate for
second helpings. Only Ellen seemed unusually quiet and

ate very little. Well, thought Mama, excitement did that to some children. But it certainly hadn't affected her children's appetites.

Mama and Button helped Mrs. Jones and Ellen clear the table after dinner. The other children were too full of apple pie and ice cream to do more than stretch out on the grass in the shade. Papa and Mr. Jones sat by, talking of crops and farm problems.

Mama was stacking empty plates for Button to carry into the house when Papa said, "You must let me in on your secret, Jones."

Mr. Jones looked quickly at Papa. "What secret?"

Papa chuckled. "How to raise chickens. I've never seen such large meaty chicken legs as your wife served today."

Mama had been wondering about that too, so she stopped to listen.

Farmer Jones dropped his eyes, then swallowed a couple of times before answering. "Oh, that," he finally said, "that wasn't chicken you ate today." Then he sat up straight and faced Papa. "Yesterday afternoon a murder was committed on our farm. Your Lapland made an end to our Bunny-Betty. We decided it was proper to invite you folks to the *funeral*."

Papa was horrified. "You don't mean that—that—chicken was—Bunny-Betty?"

"That's just what I mean!" snapped farmer Jones.

Even the boys were sitting up now, and staring at Mr. Jones.

Pelle's eyes got bigger and bigger. Torkel turned white as the tablecloth. And Nim was not smiling. The good food suddenly wasn't happy in Mama's stomach.

Papa's face was a thundercloud as he gathered his family together and stalked silently down the dusty road toward home. Mama almost had to run to keep up with him.

"I must say," said Mama when they were once more in their own kitchen, "that was an awful way to punish us for Lapland's sin."

"We could invite them back next Sunday and roast Lapland," Button suggested sarcastically. "Anyway, how do we know Lapland ki—did it?"

"That's right," said Nim. "Lapland was with Papa all the time."

All eyes went to Papa, slumped morosely on a kitchen chair.

"Wasn't he, Papa?" pleaded Pelle.

Papa did not answer at once. Heavy silence hung over the sunny kitchen.

Finally, "I'm afraid Lapland does not have an alibi," he said sadly. "He hasn't been with me in the field for several days. I just thought it was too hot for him. Thought he was sleeping in some cool spot."

"Maybe he was, Papa," said Pelle. "Just because Bunny-Betty got dead doesn't prove Lapland did it."

Papa put his arm around Pelle and hugged him. "That's right, son, but I'm afraid the circumstantial evidence is pretty strong. Farmer Jones would not tell a lie about a thing like that. But we must not blame Lapland too much. He cannot help it that he was born with cat instincts. We shall just have to forgive Lapland—and Mr. Jones."

Mama almost dropped the pitcher of lemonade she had prepared, she was so surprised that Papa wasn't angry at Lapland or the Joneses. That meant that Papa really loved Lapland, just as Pelle had hoped he would.

That evening, after the children were in bed, Mama sat with Papa on the big front porch, listening to the peaceful sounds of the night—the chirping of the crickets, the low-voiced song of the frogs, and the gentle whisper of the wind in the leaves. God found so many ways to show His love for His children, thought Mama, her heart too full of happiness and thankfulness for words. Out of what might have been the evil of neighbor set against neighbor had come love and forgiveness and better understanding.

"I think I'll take Mrs. Jones one of those extra-special

coffee rings, tomorrow, darling. Don't you think she would like that?"

"I'm sure she would, Maria," answered Papa, and there was a softness in his voice that told Mama more than his words.

But if Mama and Papa had expected the Joneses to accept forgiveness for the "fried chicken" dinner and forgive the death of their pet, they found out soon enough that it takes two to make forgiveness.

Early the next morning the telephone rang. Nim answered. It was Mr. Jones, brusquely informing Nim that he would not need his help on the farm. Mama wanted to cry when she saw the hurt in Nim's eyes as he hung up the receiver and told them what had happened. And her heart was still heavy as she watched them leave for the fields. She just had to do something. She would bake that special coffee ring and go and have a good talk with Mrs. Jones.

After lunch Mama wrapped the still-warm coffee ring in waxed paper and set out for the Jones farm. It was cooler today, and the light breeze ruffled the ripened wheat in the fields beyond. Mama's spirit rose as she walked. Mrs. Jones was a fine, sensible woman. Together they would be able to bring harmony once more between the two families. Nim would be back to work on the Joneses' farm tomorrow, the hurt look gone from his eyes. The girls and Ellen would be friends again.

Mama climbed the four wide steps of the front porch and knocked. The front door was closed, which was strange on a summer day. She waited, then knocked sharply again. Still no answer. She was about to decide they were all in the fields, or had gone to town, when she saw the lace curtains at the front window cautiously pulled aside for a second, then dropped. The window was closed, so the movement couldn't have been the wind. Mama's heart pounded anxiously. She just couldn't believe Mrs. Jones would refuse to see her. But when she had

knocked again and again, and still no answer, she had to
accept the unhappy truth.

It was Pelle who took the matter the hardest. After all,
he told Mama, he had found Lapland and Lapland's sins
were his fault too. Mama tried to reason with him, but
nothing she could say brought that happy light back into
his eyes. Mama worried, and took her worries to God in
prayer. But for once God did not seem ready to answer
her prayers. The Joneses ceased to be good neighbors.

With the approaching harvest, everyone was too busy
on the farm to give much thought to the problem. Maja
became the proud mother of five black-and-white kittens.
And a week later Rosa had her first calf.

Papa had kept Rosa tied up in the barn for several days,
watching her closely. One night, just before bedtime, he
and Nim had gone back to the barn to size up the situation. They were gone so long, Mama decided something
was wrong and went to the barn to investigate. Papa and
Nim were with Rosa, and beside her was the most perfect
little baby calf. The proud mama stretched out her long
tongue to lick her baby.

"Oh, Rosa," cried Mama, "what a nice little baby you
have. I'm so proud of you!"

But at that moment Papa and Nim took the calf away
from Rosa and locked it in a stall at the other end of the
barn. Rosa bawled in protest.

"Pontus! What are you doing? Why do you take the
baby away from her mother? Can't you hear poor Rosa
crying. Bring it back, please."

Papa stormed. "Maria! Nim and I are bosses here, and
we know what we are doing. I don't have time now to
explain farm laws to you. Please go back to the house and
leave this to us."

Mama went, but all the way back to the house she
could hear Rosa's sorrowful cries. Maybe Papa did know
best about farm laws, but he wasn't a mama and he
couldn't know how terrible it was to lose your baby.

Mama went to bed, and when Papa came in an hour

later she pretended to be asleep, for she had a plan. She waited until Papa was snoring soundly, then crept out of bed and tiptoed to Button's room.

"Wake up, darling," she whispered. "Rosa has had her calf."

Button sat up, wide awake instantly. "Oh, Mama . . ."

Mama put her finger to her mouth. "Hush, dear. Don't wake the others. Get dressed quickly and come with me. I need your help."

On the way to the barn, Mama told Button the story.

"Papa just doesn't understand, darling. You and I must undo the wrong he and Nim have done."

But it did not prove easy to get the wobbly calf back to its mother. Its long shaky legs kept crumpling under the weight of its body, so that Mama and Button were forced almost to carry it the length of the barn. But it was worth it, thought Mama, to see that little baby calf snuggle up to its mother and enjoy its first good meal.

Papa, however, had other ideas the next morning. He stormed and threatened. Mama would leave the farm decisions to him or he'd just sell the farm right now and take them all back to Lapland, where they should have stayed in the first place. Mama had never known him to be so angry.

"Oh, Pontus, you wouldn't be so angry if you had seen how happy that mama-cow was to have her baby. And besides, just once couldn't hurt. I think Rosa will understand now if you take her baby away."

Papa said no more. A few minutes later he stalked silently back to the barn.

Mama was preparing supper one evening about a week later, when the doorbell rang. She dried her hands and took off her apron, and hurried to the door.

Mrs. Jones stood there, all smiles.

"Good afternoon, Mrs. Franzon. May I come in?"

"Why of course," said Mama, recovering sufficiently from her surprise to unfasten the screen door.

Mrs. Jones sat down in Papa's big rocking chair, and for a few moments there was a strained silence.

"I'm afraid we owe you an apology, Mrs. Franzon," Mrs. Jones began.

"Oh?" said Mama, still more or less speechless over the turn of events.

"Yes. You see Ellen was pretty broken up over losing Bunny-Betty, and I guess my husband and I acted kinda mean about it. Not Christian-like at all. But I guess Ellen is even fonder of Luke now than she was of Bunny-Betty."

"Luke?" echoed Mama.

"The kitten. The one Pelle brought us. Oh, I know I should have thanked you long before this. It was so kind of him to want to make up for your cat's crime. I declare, I never saw a boy so concerned. Why, I think his heart would just have broken if Ellen hadn't liked Luke."

So that was it! Pelle had returned good for evil.

"That's all right, Mrs. Jones. You don't need to apologize. But how did Ellen happen to name the cat Luke?"

"She didn't. Pelle named him." And Mrs. Jones chuckled. "It was the oddest thing for a boy his age. He said we should call the kitten Luke after one of the Gospels because he was sure a cat with a name like that would never even think of killing a rabbit."

Mama and Mrs. Jones laughed together over the story.

"And do you know, Mrs. Franzon, not a single one of my cabbages has been nibbled since we lost Bunny-Betty. I just wonder if she was as good as we thought she was."

"Well," said Mama, laughing, "maybe Bunny-Betty just had rabbit instincts like Lapland had cat instincts."

And when Papa and the boys came in from the fields, Mama and Mrs. Jones were chatting happily over coffee and some of Mama's new-baked coffee bread.

With harmony restored, Nim went back to helping Mr. Jones with the morning and evening chores, and Ellen came to the Franzon farm almost every afternoon to go swimming with the girls. The families visited each other on Sundays and holidays, but no one mentioned picnics. Summer sped. Happy days filled with toil and play. Another leaf was torn from the big calendar in the kitchen. July had passed into history, and soon August was racing to catch up.

And then it was harvest time.

It was wonderful, thought Mama, how the farmers helped each other. One day at one farm and the next at another. And presently the crops were all in, and they were better neighbors for having shared their labors.

Almost before they could realize it, there was a tang of autumn in the air. Papa came in one evening in an unusually happy mood. After supper, Mama learned why.

"Jones is going to help me with the butchering next week," Papa announced. "He thinks Joe Ryan may be able to help too. We'd like to make a day of it. It will mean extra cooking, Maria, and hot coffee all day long."

"Why of course, Pontus," Mama agreed.

"That way, we can get it all done in one day. Nim and I could probably do most of it ourselves, but I'm not sure we could handle Napoleon alone. He's a mighty big hog."

Mama gasped. "Pontus! You don't mean to tell me you are going to make meat out of Napoleon?"

"That's just what I mean. Why do you think we raise pigs?"

A sickness raced through her, and a bitter taste filled her mouth.

"I—I—just thought . . . Well, I just thought it went with farming!"

"And so it does, Maria. Steers and pigs and chickens and turkeys, to have good meat summer and winter."

A new and more horrible realization struck Mama. Did Papa mean that not only was Napoleon and maybe Josefina to be turned into meat, but Hero, Rosa's boy-calf, too? Oh, that was too much! Button and Pelle would be as heartbroken as she was. Somehow she had never thought about where meat came from before. She wished Papa would sell the farm right now and—yes—go back to Sweden where he didn't have to kill helpless animals, especially animals you had taught to trust you. Maybe it wasn't right for a preacher to be a farmer too.

Mama sat very still for several minutes, trying to think. Papa was reading the *Church Quarterly*. Surely, thought Mama, if he thought it was right to raise animals for food, no matter how fond you became of them, then it must be right in the sight of the Lord.

But on butchering day Mama stayed close to the house, and Button and Pelle received a sudden invitation to visit Mrs. Jones.

The first snow fell early that year. The evergreens bordering the farm were stately in their white coats, and the lake was an endless sheet of white paper. The snowy hills beyond might have been the Swedish hills that rose in cold grandeur outside the parsonage windows. Even Mama felt a pang of homesickness for Lapland. But presently she was too busy with Christmas preparations to think of anything else.

An atmosphere of "work well done" pervaded the farmhouse. The harvest was in. The potatoes had been dug and stored in great bags in the hayloft where they were safe from freezing, along with bushels of turnips, cabbage and onions. In the cellar stood the barrels of pigs' feet, sausages and dill pickles, and from the rafters hung Napoleon's hams, smoked and wrapped in burlap, ready to be made into Christmas delicacies. Papa had been able to buy *lutfisk* from the Swedish store in town, and herrings for pickling, and real Swedish *Bond-ost*. The apple trees on the farm had yielded several barrels of apples—more than enough, thought Mama gratefully, for the traditional Christmas apples. She herself had made *sylta* and *korv*, forgetting entirely that these were part of her dear Napoleon.

By the week before Christmas, the farmhouse gleamed and exciting odors of cakes and cookies and spicy deli-

cacies filled the air. Papa and Nim came in from the hills
one evening, carrying a big Christmas tree which they had
cut from the forest beyond the lake. After supper the tree
was set up in the center of the big living room and the fun
of decorating began. Even Kerstin was allowed to stay up
late that night to help deck the tree. Mama had promised
there would be a Christmas tree robbing, just like in
Sweden, and some of their friends had been invited to
share in the festivities.

And finally it was Christmas Eve.

The children had taken care of Christmas for all the
animals. The cows and chickens had had special feed. The
horses had been given an extra measure of oats and some
sugar lumps. Lapland had a bowl of cream. And two
sheaves of wheat had been placed outside the kitchen door
for the birds. Soon the guests would begin to arrive.

Mama stirred the rice, which had cooked all day, and
poured in a little more milk to make the *jul-gröt* especially
good. Greta sat on the high kitchen chair watching.

"Will there be enough rice for *Tomte-Nisse*, Mama?"
she asked, her anxious eyes following Mama's stirring.

Mama put down her spoon and gathered the child into
her arms. All the children but Greta had accepted Santa
Claus as the American symbol of Christmas. In Sweden
it had been Greta who always remembered to set out the
bowl of rice on Christmas Eve, so that *Tomte-Nisse* would
not be hungry as he went about the world, distributing
Christmas joy.

"Here in America, darling," Mama explained, "there is
no *Tomte-Nisse*. He belongs to Sweden. Here there is
Santa Claus, who comes in a big beautiful sleigh drawn
by eight prancing reindeer. Don't you remember? Why,
just last night Button taught you the names of the reindeer
—Donner and Prancer and Blitzen——"

"I remember, Mama," Greta broke in, her eyes shining.
"And the sleigh is just filled with toys and everything,
and we hang up our stockings and on Christmas morning
every stocking is filled with just what we wanted."

"That's right, darling. Now isn't that just as nice as *Tomte-Nisse?*"

Greta didn't answer. She squirmed uncomfortably in Mama's arms and stared at the floor.

"It will be a wonderful Christmas, honey. Just you wait and see!"

Greta twisted around and looked up at Mama, her eyes wide with doubt and a little hint of fear. "But just suppose, Mama, *Tomte-Nisse* didn't know we came to America and got lost looking for us. Wouldn't he get awful hungry? Maybe I could set out just a *little* bowl of rice—in case."

Mama laughed, but her heart was warmed by Greta's deep concern.

"Why, Greta, I never thought of that," she exclaimed. "I think we better put out a *big* bowl of rice. It's a long way from Sweden to America."

Greta threw her arms around Mama's waist and hugged her tight. "Oh, Mama! Thank you. Thank you." Then she ran to the cupboard and came back with a large bright-red porcelain pan. "Is this big enough, do you think?"

"I'm sure it is, darling," chuckled Mama. "Even if *Tomte-Nisse* brings a lot of little helpers with him." And she poured the pan half-full of rice.

Later, when the family were all gathered at the table, and Papa opened the big Swedish Bible to read the Christmas Story as he always did, Mama could not help being glad that here on their wonderful American farm, *Tomte-Nisse*, the Swedish Spirit of Christmas, had not been forgotten.

CHAPTER 11

✾ Papa Learns a Lesson

Being one chosen by God to preach His gospel was, to Papa, a heavy responsibility, and he accepted it with great seriousness. He had an unswerving devotion to Biblical truth, believing that the laws of God were unchanging dictates which, if ignored, brought pain and suffering, but which, if obeyed, could result only in peace and happiness.

Outwardly he was more severe than Mama in handling his children, for he was convinced that discipline was quite as important as education, and he desired above all that his children walk in the ways of the Lord always. He endeavored to set a good example, though there were times when he admittedly found life confusing and decisions difficult. On such occasions, he would sternly search his own soul, confess his faults and shortcomings to God, and, with His help, rise above them.

One of these occasions—which was to have a profound effect upon his entire life—he faced on a spring morning toward the end of the second year on the farm.

Papa cut across the freshly plowed garden patch just beyond the house and took the narrow path toward the woods. Over one shoulder dangled a fishing rod, and in the other hand he carried a packet of sandwiches and

189

hard-boiled eggs. It was Saturday and a glorious spring day. Almost too warm for March, he thought. In the far field Nim and Pelle were plowing. He felt a pang of guilt taking a holiday, going fishing when there was work to do. But Maria and the boys had insisted.

Presently the path plunged into the woods, and Papa forgot his guilt in thinking of the fine perch he would bring home for supper. Farmer Jones had told him about the little pool in the woods, and, when he described the size of the fish he caught there, Papa was skeptical, but anxious to find out for himself.

Well, it couldn't be very far, he thought, filling his lungs with the tangy spring-scented air. It was good to be alive on such a day. The trees were faintly green against the silver-blue sky, and along the path wood violets lifted their delicate heads. Birds twittered a hymn of joy that winter had passed. Everywhere there was a clean sparkling freshness, as though the world had been washed and spread out in the spring sunshine to dry—and grow to new life.

He came upon it abruptly—a small, quiet pool so clear that he could see the rocky bottom, mossy-green and red-gold. Beyond the tracery of soft shadows near the shore, the sunlight made a diadem of the gently rippling water. Papa dropped his fishing rod onto the grassy bank, tucked the packet of lunch into his pocket and sat down on the rock which jutted out over the water. This was, indeed, a perfect spot for fishing. Now if the fish were biting well as Jones said, he'd soon have that mess of perch he'd promised Maria for supper. He was especially fond of perch with parsley sauce, the way Mama had made it in Sweden.

"Do you still remember how to make that parsley sauce you made for perch in Sweden?" he had asked this morning as she fixed the lunch for him.

"Of course I remember, Pontus," she laughed. "You just bring home the perch and I'll fix it fit for a king."

Mischief had danced in her eyes as she waved him good-bye. "And don't strain yourself carrying them home."

Papa stared down through the clear water at the big fish darting merrily among the rocks. Well, Maria was going to be surprised at the catch he brought home tonight! He slid off the jutting rock, onto the grassy bank and stretched out, watching the float bobbing up and down. Any minute now it would disappear and he'd have his first perch. But when half an hour had passed and still no bite, Papa began to be disturbed. The fish, he saw, were still there, playing tag with his bait, but not biting. If this kept up, Mama would have the laugh on him for sure. He just had to get at least one big fish. Otherwise there would be *plättar* for supper. It wasn't that he didn't like *plättar*. They were all very fond of the little Swedish pancakes. It was just that Maria always substituted them for uncaught fish, and the whole family knew he had been fishing and caught nothing.

Papa lay back on the grass. He couldn't *make* the fish bite. He'd simply have to be patient. Even if he caught nothing, just being here was a tonic to his soul. It was good to lie close to God's earth, to feel the warmth of the sun and listen to the rustle of swaying branches above him in the spring wind. The pungent fragrance of pine made him drowsy. He was glad he had decided to remain a farmer. Tomorrow he would notify the Church Board of his decision.

But even as the thought went through his mind, he was vaguely disturbed. He couldn't explain the disturbance. What was wrong about a man his age stepping out of the ministry when hundreds of young men were waiting for an opportunity to begin their life's service in God's work? Surely he had a right to be a farmer if he felt that was best for his family and himself.

They were all so happy on the farm. Hard as the work was at times, no one complained. It was always a happy tiredness, the kind that comes from the satisfaction of work well done. A wholesome atmosphere in which the children could grow up, close to nature and God's abundant creation. In the fall, Nim would be starting to college. The fund in the tin box had increased steadily, and Papa would add to it if needed; Nim was pretty independent about that. He was proud of his achievement, and Maria beamed every time the subject of college was mentioned.

She wasn't so happy about Button. For Button had firmly refused even to consider college. She would finish high school in the spring and she had made her own plans.

"I am through with lessons and teachers," Button had announced one evening during Christmas vacation. "When I graduate from high school in the spring, I'm going to *live*."

Maria had looked up from her mending in shocked surprise. "But, Button, college education *is* living, darling."

Button shook her head and smiled. "Not for me, Mama."

But Maria did not give up easily. "Oh, Button, you will love it when you get started. There will be so much fun besides the lessons. And if you don't take the opportunity when it comes, you might be very sorry later on."

"I have my own plans about my life, Mama," Button insisted.

And that was that. Papa had no doubt about Button's meaning it. But he was not worried. Button was growing into a beautiful woman, and a woman's first duty was to get married and make a real home for her husband and give him fine children. Maria would just have to learn that not even in her wonderful America could she sell education to *all* the children.

Papa sat up and examined the line. Still no fish. He stretched out again and let his thoughts return to the good life on the farm. Presently he chuckled, remembering what Jones had said when he told him that the abundant yield of his land had been due to his prayers.

"Well, for goodness' sake, Franzon! Don't hoard all the blessings for yourself. Come over and pray for *my* potatoes."

One of the best parts of farm life, thought Papa, was the security it offered. He would not have to accept charity from the ministers' fund when he grew too old to preach. The farm would take care of Maria and himself even when the children were grown and married and living lives of their own. And they would bring their children on holidays and summer vacations. It gave him a strange happy feeling just to think of himself as a grandfather.

Suddenly Papa jumped and sat up. His line had tightened and the float had completely disappeared. Here was that fish for supper at last! He got ready for the quick pull at the right moment. But he didn't have a chance.

A sharp voice spoke directly behind him. "Don't move, Mister. Unless you want to land on those rocks at the bottom of the lake. Do exactly as I tell you."

Papa remained motionless. Vaguely he realized that the fishing line had slackened and the float was again bobbing on the surface of the water. The big fish had got away. The voice behind him was speaking again, "Don't turn around. Just take that watch out of your pocket and drop it gently on the ground behind you."

Papa couldn't believe this was actually happening to him. Not here in the peaceful forest. Then he almost laughed out loud. It was Mr. Jones playing a joke on him. Of course! Only Jones and the family knew he had come here to fish. Well, he'd play out the game with him, then they'd have a good laugh over it. Slowly he started removing the watch, pretending fear. Then a terrible thought struck him. Suppose that wasn't Jones behind him? Suppose this wasn't a joke, but the real thing—a holdup? It didn't sound like Jones's voice, but then that could be disguised. His watch was a gift which the good people of Lapland had given him as a farewell expression of their regard. He couldn't bear to think of it in the hands of a hoodlum, ending up in a pawnshop for a few dollars.

"Hurry it up, Mister," commanded the voice, "and don't try any tricks."

Papa's fingers were shaking as he unfastened the thick gold chain, then placed the watch gently on the ground behind him. He knew now this was not a joke; that the man behind him was not Jones. He'd read about crimes like this, and he knew that often they killed the victim after robbing him. The thought so shocked him that before he realized the danger, he had whirled around and grabbed the man as he stooped to pick up the watch.

Taken by surprise, the man tried to recover his advantage, but Papa was stronger, and after a moment's struggle had him on his back, his hands pinned under him. Only then did he see his face. He was young, not over twenty-five, he guessed, but his face was so dirty and sullen it was hard to tell. He stared up at Papa, anger and defeat in his eyes.

"Now, young man," said Papa, a little winded by the struggle, "what is the meaning of this?"

He didn't answer, but his gaze shifted, and the anger went out of his face. Only a sullen, defeated look remained. Papa wasn't quite sure what to do next. Then he remembered such characters carried a gun. He went through his pockets with one hand, the other on the boy's chest to make sure his hands couldn't get free. But there was no gun.

"What did you do with your gun?" Papa barked.

He reacted to that. But not in the way Papa expected. He laughed. A contemptuous laugh.

"I haven't got a gun. That's what makes it so funny. I got your watch without a gun."

Papa was relieved. But the young man's speech had told him something else. He was educated, obviously not a professional crook. Papa stood up.

"Very well, in that case, you may get off the ground."

The boy jumped quickly to his feet, spitting dirt and leaves. But he made no further move to violence.

"I suppose you know what happens to people who go

around stealing other people's possessions and threatening them?" Papa asked.

"What is this? A Sunday School class?"

Papa laughed in spite of the grave situation. "It could be at that. I happen to be a minister."

The hatred returned to the boy's eyes. "That won't stop you from turning me in," he snapped sarcastically.

"What do *you* think I should do with you?" asked Papa.

Obviously this was not what the boy expected. He stared at Papa in disbelief. Papa ignored him and began calmly to retrieve his rod and line, which had barely escaped a watery grave in the excitement. "I guess this is the end of the fishing for today," he finally remarked casually.

Still silence from his "prisoner."

It was when he started to put the tackle into his pocket that Papa discovered the package of lunch. He drew it out and sat down on the big rock and opened it.

"Now, young man, why don't you sit down and share my lunch with me, while we talk this thing over," Papa suggested calmly. "Then you're coming back to the farm with me and we'll decide what to do next."

"I thought you were a minister?"

"A minister *and* farmer," Papa corrected. "Not a bad combination."

A couple of minutes of silence. Papa unwrapped the lunch and spread the paper wrapping on the rock beside him, careful that the eggs didn't roll into the water. His "prisoner" moved slowly toward him. But this time Papa was sure it was because of hunger, not from the desire to harm him. He handed Papa the watch, then squatted on the grass. He took the sandwich which Papa offered, then picked up an egg and started peeling off the shell.

They ate in silence. Occasionally Papa stole a glance at him. Why, he was no more than a boy, a hungry, confused boy at that, and quite handsome in spite of the dirt. He wondered what he could say to get him to unburden his soul. If he could just make the boy understand that he wanted to help, not hurt him.

"What's your name, son?" Papa asked after a while. "Mine's Franzon."

The boy hesitated a moment then in a low voice, said, "Steve."

"All right, Steve. Now do you want to tell me what this is all about? You don't look like a thief. You didn't even have a gun."

"If I tell you, you'll still turn me over to the police."

"That depends. I want to help you, but if you don't tell me what made you do this—this holdup, I won't have any choice."

Steve stared at the ground. He picked up a small stick, snapping it in two with suppressed anger. "You don't know what it's like to need money desperately," he exploded.

"Not so desperately I'd commit a crime for it, no. Crime doesn't solve anything."

"It was the only way, I tell you. I didn't want to hurt *you*. I was—well, I was practicing," he blurted.

"Practicing? For what?"

His eyes were still on the ground. "So I could join up with a gang in New York."

Papa was a little shocked. But he still hadn't got to the bottom of this thing. "Why don't you start at the beginning? Why did you want to join a gang?"

"To get money for Terry and the baby," he said defiantly.

So that was it! The boy had a family. This was more serious than he had thought. But he was more convinced than ever that the man was not a criminal. Nevertheless, he *had* tried to hold him up, and that was a crime. If the boy wouldn't talk, he'd have no choice but to turn him over to the police.

"That still doesn't tell me why you decided to resort to crime, Steve," Papa said kindly.

A deep sigh escaped the boy. A sigh of resignation.

"All right. I'll tell you everything. Then you can take me to the police. It doesn't matter any more. I'm a failure at crime like everything else."

It was not a pleasant story, nor a new one. Papa's heart ached for the boy as he told it, speaking in a low voice— a story of heartbreak, defeat and desperation.

Steve had been employed on a farm near Lakewood. He had studied agriculture in college and he liked farming. Then he had met Terry Sanders, the owner's daughter, and they had fallen in love. But Mr. Sanders didn't think he was good enough for his daughter. He and Terry had eloped and kept their marriage a secret. Steve continued to work on the farm, living with the help as before, and seeing Terry only when they could meet secretly. But when they knew a baby was on the way, they could keep the secret no longer. Terry's parents were furious, threatened to have the marriage annulled. But Terry was of age and they could not do that without her consent. And Terry wouldn't give her consent. After that, Terry was not allowed to see him at all. When the baby came they refused to let him see the child—a boy. He tried to get work on other farms, but Mr. Sanders stopped that. Everywhere he received the same answer: "Don't need any help now."

Steve was frantic. To have a wife he was not permitted to see, and a son he had never seen, was too much. It was then he had decided on desperate measures. There was only one way he knew to get money fast. He'd find a gang in New York that would let him work for them. He could drive a car. That would keep him from actually committing the crimes himself. As soon as he had enough money, he'd clear out and come back for Terry and the baby. He'd slept in the woods last night and was headed for the main road to town when he saw a man fishing, the gold watch chain flashing in the sunlight.

"I know it all sounds crazy now, Reverend Franzon. But . . . I failed even in that. Terry's parents were right; I'm not good enough for her. Terry and the boy will be better off without me. I don't want them to suffer for what I've done."

For a full minute Papa's throat was too tight for words. He wondered what he would have done under the same circumstance. It wasn't an easy question to answer, for as a young man in Sweden he had had no such temptations. It was different in America. The papers were full of crimes, robberies, swindles—all seeming to offer an easy way to get rich in a hurry. Not even the threat of prison or the danger of death prevented young men, every day, from trying to outwit the police. Doing right had to come from a desire for good in a man's heart. Then, with God's help, he would not be tempted beyond his strength to easy riches.

"I don't suppose you ever asked God to help you, Steve," Papa said quietly.

Apathy vanished from Steve's face. He jumped to his feet. Anger glittered darkly in his eyes. "*God*," he shouted. "If there was a God, would he let a man's wife and baby be taken from him by a selfish father? Don't give me that Sunday School stuff! Take me to jail if you want to, but don't start preaching."

Papa said nothing. He got up, picked up his fishing rod and began unreeling the line.

"What are you going to do?" Steve asked, a hint of alarm in his tone.

"Steve, my boy," said Papa briskly, "you've just taught me a lesson about failure. I promised my wife I'd bring home a mess of perch for dinner and I'm going to do it. I was about to give up when you came along."

Papa cast. Out of the corner of his eye he watched Steve. He was just sitting there staring, as though he thought this phony minister had lost his mind.

Presently Steve sat down again on the grassy bank. Only the lapping of the water against the rocks broke the stillness. But Papa was praying. Silently. He needed those perch now for more reason than food. He had to show Steve there was a God—a God who cared what happened to His children. But this was not a time to do it by preaching. The boy was deeply hurt, too bitter against circumstances and his fellow man.

Suddenly the line tightened. Papa waited half a second, then jerked. A big perch lay squirming at his feet.

Steve was so surprised he forgot his anger. "Say, that's a big one," he exclaimed. Then added wryly, "I don't know how good a preacher you are, Mister, but you sure know how to fish."

Papa looked proudly at his catch. God had answered his prayer but he couldn't tell Steve that—yet. "I don't know about that, son. Guess it was just a matter of waiting for the fish to get hungry," he said lightly.

For the first time that afternoon Steve laughed pleasantly.

"The next one is yours," said Papa, handing him the rod. "Look at that big one down there."

Steve hesitated. "With my luck, he'll grab the bait and be gone before I can move." But he took the rod, and Papa noticed how deftly he cast.

And again Papa prayed, "Dear God, Thou knowest how important this catch is."

A few minutes later Papa was realizing once again how much better God looks out for His children than even their fondest desires. A perch, larger than his own catch, flapped on the grass beside Steve.

They took turns after that, and the fish were indeed hungry. It seemed to Papa that the bait scarcely had time to reach the water before the float disappeared, the line tightened, and presently another big fish lay at their feet on the grass. An hour passed. Papa and Steve proudly surveyed the day's catch.

" '. . . full measure, pressed down and running over,' " quoted Papa half aloud.

"What did you say, sir?"

"It's from the Bible, son. I was just thinking how abundantly God answers prayer. Do you remember the story of Simon, the fisherman? Simon had been fishing all night and caught nothing. He was about to give up, but as he turned his boat toward the shore, he saw a Man standing there. And the Man called to him, telling him to cast his nets on the other side of the boat. And Simon did as he was told, and behold the nets were filled with fishes, so many that he could scarcely lift the catch into his boat."

"Sure, I remember the story. But what's that got to do with us?"

"A great deal, Steve. Would you believe me if I told you God sent you here today?"

"Are you trying to tell me *God wanted* me to steal your watch? Not even a preacher could make me believe that."

"I didn't say that, Steve. I said God *sent* you here. He sent you to help me."

"To *help* you?" Steve echoed. "Look, Reverend Franzon, all I did was try to steal your watch, and I failed. God certainly didn't have a hand in that."

"He moves in mysterious ways, Steve. A preacher has his problems too. Yes, I'm sure God sent you to me this afternoon." Papa was speaking more to himself now than to Steve. For he was remembering a decision he had made earlier—to give up the ministry. He had told himself he had a right to be a farmer if he wanted to. Now he wasn't so sure he did have that right. Conflicting emotions surged through him. He got up slowly and collected the fish.

Steve still sat on the fishing rock, saying nothing.

"Well, I guess we'd better get started home," said Papa. "We've certainly got enough fish for supper. No one cooks fish like Maria—my wife." Then he laughed. "She's going to be mighty surprised. You see she's not used to my catching anything when I go fishing."

Steve chuckled. "I see what you mean. The laugh will be on her today."

"But it wouldn't have been without your help, Steve," said Papa.

"I still don't see . . ."

"Never mind that now. Let's go. I'm getting hungry."

The sun was low over the distant hills as they left the

woodland pool and took the path toward home, single file with Steve in front. Papa noticed some of the droop had gone from his shoulders. There was new hope in his step. But when they reached the end of the path and started across the plowed field to the house, Steve stopped.

"What will your wife say to your bringing a thief home to supper?"

"What thief? I'm sure my wife will be pleased to have a fellow fisherman as our guest. And besides, don't forget that if it hadn't been for you there wouldn't be any fish. We'd have *plättar*."

"What's that?"

"Oh, it's very good. But it is what my wife always makes for supper when I come home with no fish."

Steve laughed, but he still hesitated.

"That other incident," said Papa casually, "shall we just keep it between us for the present? And by the way, you'd better tell me the rest of your name."

"Hill. Steve Hill. You're very kind, Reverend Franzon," he said softly. But Papa noticed his eyes were suddenly bright.

Maria opened the kitchen door as they approached. "Oh, Pontus! You did get them. What wonderful fish."

"No *plättar* for supper tonight, Maria. Thanks to my young friend here. Maria, this is Steve Hill. Steve, my wife."

"Come in, Steve. You certainly are a good fisherman."

"I'm afraid your husband gives more credit than I deserve, Mrs. Franzon. He's a mighty good fisherman himself."

"Well, it doesn't matter who caught them. Now you sit down here and have some coffee. You must both be tired."

The kitchen was fragrant with Saturday baking. Mama poured two cups of coffee and set a big plate of *bullar* on the table.

"Well, I have some chores to do, Steve," said Papa, finishing off his third *bulle* and second cup of coffee.

"Would you like to come along?" He wasn't ready to leave Steve to Maria's questioning.

"I sure would, Reverend Franzon. That is if I can *move* after eating so many of those delicious rolls. They were wonderful, Mrs. Franzon, and the coffee the best I ever tasted."

"Would you like another cup?" offered Mama.

Steve laughed. "I'm afraid not. Any more and I wouldn't have room for that perch. Your husband told me what a good cook you are. Already I agree with him."

Papa was pleased that Steve was talkative. It meant the tension—and the fear—had left him. Later he would tell Maria the whole story and they would decide what to do about this young man.

Button and Greta came in from feeding the chickens. Papa introduced Steve, then he took the milk pails and they left for the barn. He realized at once that Steve was very much at home around a farm. They milked the cows, and Papa told him how the children had given each cow a name according to its disposition. Steve laughed heartily over the idea.

"I never realized that cows had dispositions, but I guess they do at that."

The pigs grunted hungrily as they neared the pen. Napoleon, who was now hams and sausage in the cellar, had been replaced by Oscar. Soon there would be a new litter of squealing little pigs. Steve helped Papa mix the feed and pour it into the long troughs.

When the chores were finished, they walked slowly back to the house, each with a brimming milk pail. Dusk was falling. A short distance away, Nim and Pelle were returning from the field. The younger children played under the big elm tree by the lake, their laughter echoing against the purple hills. In the gathering shadows the farm suddenly seemed to Papa like a giant bud, ready to burst into life, then to full-flowering as the spring winds gentled and gave way to summer. Now there were fields to plow, seeds to be planted, fences and barns to be mended and painted.

Outside the kitchen door Papa paused and placed a hand on Steve's shoulder. "I've been thinking, Steve. There's a lot of work on a farm in the spring. We could use another hand. The job's yours if you want it."

Steve didn't answer at once. Finally, "You mean you'd let me work for you after—after what I did?"

Papa sat the pail of milk on the step. "I told you before, Steve, God sent you to me today. Sent you to *help* me. I mean it."

"I'd be so grateful, Reverend Franzon. I'd be proud to work for you." Steve's voice choked with emotion.

"That's fine. I'll speak to my wife about it first. I'm sure she can arrange a room for you. *Now* I think we can do justice to that fine supper of perch and mashed potatoes, which she has waiting for us."

Supper (not at the big kitchen table as usual on Saturday nights, but in the dining room) was a gay occasion. Having a young and handsome guest added a note of festivity. Papa noticed Vickey was wearing her new dress —a birthday present. Kerstin, who usually had to be reminded to brush her hair, had every curl in place, with a pink bow on top. Even Maria was wearing her best blue home dress.

Papa was very proud of his family.

Everyone praised Papa and Steve for being such good fishermen, and they all passed their plates for second helpings. Papa assured Mama that never had she prepared such delicious parsley sauce.

After supper, while Button and Vickey helped Mama clear the table, the rest of the family gathered in the big living room. Nim and Steve and Papa discussed spring planting, the values of crop rotation and Swedish farming compared with American ways. Pelle and Torkel listened attentively. Presently Kerstin, who had been very quiet until now, interrupted.

"Mr. Steve, would you like to see my baby chickens?"

"I certainly would, young lady. My, that's a pretty hair ribbon. Did you tie the bow yourself?"

Kerstin tossed her curls proudly. "My Mama did. But I bet I could if I tried."

"I don't doubt it a bit," chuckled Steve and obligingly followed her to the back porch where the box of chicks had been placed for the night.

Papa went to the kitchen and was pleased to find Mama alone.

"When you have finished, Maria, I'd like to have a word with you in private."

Mama turned from the cupboard, alarm in her eyes. "What is it, Pontus? What's wrong?"

"Nothing at all, Maria. I want to talk with you about Steve."

Mama finished putting the dishes away, then followed him upstairs to their bedroom and closed the door. Papa told her all that had happened that afternoon.

"I think Steve needs a friend more than he needs punishment, Maria," he concluded. "I can use him on the farm if it is all right with you."

"Oh, Pontus! Of course it is all right. The poor boy! Just to think of having a baby he's never seen. And being separated from his wife, I just don't see how anyone can be that cruel."

"We'll try to do something about that soon. Right now he needs work and understanding."

"Of course. I'll fix up that big room I've been using for storage. It will be quite comfortable. Oh, Pontus, there's plenty of room. Couldn't we let him bring his wife and baby too?"

Papa hesitated. He hadn't counted on adopting a whole family just to get a farm hand. But he should have known Maria would realize it took more than work and money to make a family man content. Steve would do a better job having his family with him.

"I hadn't thought of that, Maria. But I see no reason why not."

"Oh, darling, just think. Won't it be wonderful having a little baby in the house?"

"Well, I'm not sure how wonderful it will be. I just hope he's a good baby. Steve won't be much use on the farm if he has to walk the floor all night with a fretful child."

Mama laughed. "You still haven't forgotten those nights with Button, have you?"

Papa started to open the door. "By the way, Maria, I think Steve's past should be between us and him, don't you?"

"I certainly do, Pontus. We'll be just one big family."

Papa agreed it might very well be that, when he reached the living room and found the children gathered around Steve, all trying to claim his attention. It was strange, he thought. This morning a would-be gangster; tonight, a friend. Surely that was the way God intended it to be.

When finally the children had been sent to bed, and Mama had prepared the guest room for Steve, Papa came into the kitchen where Mama was fixing the coffee tray for morning.

"I think I'll go for a short walk, Maria. Don't wait up for me. You must be tired."

Mama put her arms around him and kissed him. "Whatever you decide, Pontus *lilla*, will be all right with me."

Papa wondered, as he went out into the crisp spring night, if Maria was referring to Steve, or did she sense, as she seemed always to do, that something else was troubling him.

He stood for a moment looking up into the limitless heavens, where stars twinkled faintly, so far away they were like tiny fireflies in the night. Then unbidden, he took the path to the big lake, now a great shadowy mirror, reflecting only the deeper shadows of the leafless trees along the banks.

His doubts had begun even before Steve came. Vague, disquieting thoughts about his decision to give up the ministry and remain a farmer. He had told Steve God had sent him. At the time it had been a half-formed conviction, but now he knew with certainty that it was true. It was God's way of showing him his work as a minister was not finished. But even as he acknowledged this truth, the conflict within him began anew.

He tried to reconcile his convictions with his desires. Was he not serving the Lord as a farmer, tilling the soil, tending the crops, bringing forth the good harvest from the land? Was not the farm also the Lord's vineyard? But as he questioned, Steve's face came into his thoughts—defiant, angry, crying out against a domineering God who made his way difficult. How many such young men were there in the world, tempted to evil, seeking an answer to the mysterious, confusing thing called life? Seeking and, without guidance, never finding. Taking the easy solution which led only to more confusion and deeper sin.

As he looked out across the dark lake, faintly restless under the gentle night winds, he found himself thinking, "And the Spirit of God moved upon the face of the waters. And God said let there be light; and there was light."

Light! God called his ministers to carry that light to all the world. To the seeking, troubled souls who walked in darkness. He, Pontus Franzon, had been one of those ministers.

He remembered another night, long ago, beside another lake. He had signed a contract with God that night, not for a few years, but for *always*.

Papa covered his face with his hands. "Not my will, oh, Lord, but thine," he sobbed, and knew an inner peace which he had not known for a long time.

And suddenly it was as though the floodgates of wisdom were opened to him. The questions which had gone up from his soul earlier were now answered. He knew that his desire to remain a farmer had come not alone from love of the fruitful earth, but from the sense of security which it offered. It was selling the farm that he had resisted. He had not had sufficient faith in God to trust Him to provide so long as he did the work God had called him to do.

Shamed and contrite, he now understood why God had sent Steve to him. Not only to show him the work he must do, but because *he* needed Steve. Steve was part of God's plan for him. An intricate, mysterious, wondrous plan! It was as clear now as though a book had been opened before him.

God did not mean him to sell the farm.

In sending Steve to him, he had provided the way for keeping the farm and reuniting Steve and Terry and their child. In the fall, when the crops were in, he could go back to his pulpit in Berkley Hills, and be a better minister because of the two years close to the soil. The boys could help Steve on Saturdays during the winter, and summers the whole family would return to the farm, and he would spend his vacation there.

Papa felt like a new man. A young man with a purpose.

Tomorrow he would tell the Board of his decision to return in the fall. By that time Steve would be able to run the farm very well alone. And tomorrow, too, he was going to make his very first call as a minister under his renewed contract with God. He would have a talk with Mr. Sanders who needed a few things set straight for his own sake.

The house was dark when Papa returned, except for a light in the front bedroom. Maria must be waiting for him after all. He was very glad. He took the stairs two at a time.

Maria was sitting up in bed, her bright hair loose over her shoulders. The soft glow of the night lamp shed a radiance about her, which to Papa now seemed celestial.

"Maria," he said softly, on his knees beside her bed, "I'm going back. I'm going back to my calling."

Mama's hands were gentle on his bowed shoulders. She drew him into her arms, and kissed him tenderly as she would a child. "I thought you would, Papa *lilla.* And oh, Pontus, I'm glad—so very glad."

CHAPTER 12

❦ Man Does Not Live
by Bread Alone

Papa was sure he loved his wife and children as devotedly as any husband and father, but there had been times since that day twenty-two years ago when he had married Mama that he had questioned the wisdom of his action.

And never had he questioned it so seriously as on a particular May morning the following year, when he reluctantly faced a shocking revelation: *He was no longer wanted in his own home.*

Papa had scarcely finished breakfast when Mama, smiling, and a little too eager, presented him with a list of sick calls which she insisted must be made that day.

"It certainly is a long list, Maria. Sometimes I think the church people lean too heavily upon a pastor and his wife for prayers. But I suppose when the body is ill, one's faith needs replenishing." Papa sighed, wondering what they thought the minister did when *his* faith weakened or his body was too tired to want to be leaned upon.

He drank the last of his third cup of coffee and pushed back his chair. "I guess we'd better get an early start, Maria. I'll be ready when you are."

Mama's eyes widened. "But, Pontus, I can't go with you to make the calls. I have *so* much to do today. I'm sorry, dear. Some other time."

It was Papa's turn to look surprised. "I don't understand, Maria. I just don't understand why you are suddenly so busy. Besides, Mrs. Anderson's name is on this list, and you know it's *your* prayers and smiles she wants, not mine."

Mama chuckled. "You know, Pontus, I think Mrs. Anderson just gets sick so her handsome pastor will call on her and hold her hand. Now run along and make her happy."

Ridiculous as Maria's remark was, Papa knew there was no use trying to outtalk her, so meekly he took his hat from the hall rack and left the house.

If it had been the first time Mama had refused to accompany him lately, he wouldn't have been so surprised. But this had been going on for weeks. At first he had accepted her excuse of having too much to do, but now he knew for certain there was another reason. Strange and mysterious things had been happening of late. There was an air of secrecy in the parsonage. Quickly exchanged glances between Mama and Button or Greta or Vickey when they thought he wasn't looking. Whispered conferences he wasn't supposed to hear. And now, suddenly, the number of house calls had increased alarmingly. It all added up to one thing: *His own family wanted to get rid of him.*

Somehow he got through the list of calls and hoped he had said the right comforting word, although he wasn't sure God approved of his half-interested prayers. It wasn't that they weren't sincere; he just couldn't keep his mind on them. It kept returning to the strange behavior in the parsonage.

It was almost one thirty when Papa climbed the steps to the parsonage again. He was tired and hungry, and the delicious cooking odors which greeted him only whetted his appetite. But when he reached the kitchen, he found only a cold luncheon set out for him, and a note propped against the sugar bowl.

"Pontus *lilla*," the note read, "Sorry I couldn't wait and

eat lunch with you. Had some errands to do. There is a new list of house calls on your study desk. Some of them seemed urgent, so I assured them you would call *this afternoon*."

Papa's hunger vanished in annoyance. Mama was too busy to accompany *him*, but not too busy to run errands. What errands? What in the world was going on in his own house right under his very nose?

He stalked into the study and almost snatched up the list. Why it would take all afternoon to see all these people, even if he did little more than say "hello" and "good-bye." As he glanced up from the list, he caught a reflection of his scowling face in the mirror on the opposite wall. He was really shocked—and ashamed. He certainly wasn't acting like one of God's chosen. Contrite, he sank into a chair and covered his face with his hands. Silently he prayed for wisdom and strength and understanding; and as he prayed, the tension and anger went out of him. He got up slowly and returned to the kitchen. Half an hour later he set out once more on house calls.

As he closed the door on the last name on the list, he knew God had indeed guided him; for some of the cases had been urgent, and for several hours he had forgotten his own problems in prayers for the really ill and troubled members of his congregation.

It was getting dark when he reached the parsonage. Just as he started up the walk, a car pulled to the curb and stopped.

"Pardon me, sir," a woman's voice called, "can you tell me if this is the Swedish Home Bakery?"

Papa stopped. "It isn't," he said politely. "This is the Swedish parsonage."

"Are you sure?" the woman persisted. "I am certain this is where Mrs. Appleton bought those *delicious* cookies."

"I'm quite sure, madam," Papa snapped, his patience wearing thin. "And I ought to know. I happen to be the minister who lives here."

The woman left in a burst of speed which plainly said she thought he was lying. Papa stood there a moment in the shadows, trying to get control of his temper. But before he could sort out his thoughts, Greta came hurrying down the front walk, her arms full of boxes and packages, and bumped right into him.

"For goodness' sake, Papa," she gasped. "I didn't see you. I hope I didn't break any!"

"Break any what, Greta? Bones?" Papa laughed.

"No. The orders, of course."

"Orders? What orders?"

To his astonishment, Greta began to cry. "Oh, Papa," she sobbed, "you made me tell!"

Papa put his arm around her shoulders. "Made you tell what, Greta? Are you sure you are all right?"

But Greta only pulled away from him and ran down the street as fast as she could with her arms full of packages. Papa watched her, puzzled. And suddenly he knew! The woman who had just driven away was right after all. Mama *was* baking cookies and selling them behind his back. She had turned the parsonage into a *bakery*.

The very idea made Papa sick. His head whirled, and his stomach felt queasy. He had an impulse to rush into the house and demand that this ridiculous business be stopped at once. But his knees were suddenly weak—so weak he couldn't have run had the house burst into flames. He sank down on the grass in the shadows, momentarily overcome with chagrin and self-pity. Why was Maria doing this terrible thing? Wasn't he a good husband and father? And didn't he try to be a minister of God, worthy in His sight? How could his own Maria—his *wife*—do this to him?

As he questioned, his questions took on the quality of prayer, and he realized he had been jumping to conclusions. Who better than he knew the bigness of Maria's heart? Of course she was baking cookies. But only for charity—not just to make money. Maria would never do that. Suddenly he was very much ashamed of himself for thinking such a thing. He decided to let her have her little secret; she probably thought he would object to her spending the money. In a few days she would tell him why she had given away so many cookies.

Comforted, Papa got up quickly and hurried up the steps. When he reached the kitchen, he saw no cookies—only something bubbling appetizingly on the stove. Maria was all smiles, her eyes as innocent of guilt as a child, when he kissed her.

"Supper will be ready in a moment, Pontus. You must be tired and hungry after all those house calls."

"I am, Maria. But I'm glad I went, especially to old Mrs. Aronson. She is a dear old soul, and I'm afraid she isn't going to be with us long. She was so disappointed you were not with me."

"Oh, Pontus! Is she really that sick? I'm sorry I couldn't go."

"Were your errands more important than sick calls, Maria?" Papa asked gently, chuckling inwardly at the way her cheeks were suddenly flushed.

"They were *very* important, darling. But I'll go see Mrs. Aronson tomorrow without fail," she promised. Then added, "Even if my work has to wait."

Papa started upstairs to freshen up before supper. Mama called after him. "Pontus, I forgot! Deacon Olson wants you to call him right away."

As Papa finished talking with Olson, he wondered if there was any way in the world Mama could have had a hand in *this*. For the matter which had suddenly become urgent was not urgent at all. Mr. Stenström who had passed away the previous spring had made provisions in his will for new aisle carpets for the church. The Church Board had decided to wait until the many conferences of the winter and spring were over, then one of the board members would go to Boston to select the carpeting. Now, suddenly, with a great deal of illness among the church people, and a number of important decisions regarding the coming year to be made, the Board had decided it was only proper that Pastor Franzon himself should have the privilege of selecting the carpeting and that it should be done immediately.

Well, no doubt it was merely coincidence, but coming at this time it certainly looked suspicious. And later, when Papa broke the news to the family over supper, he was sure he detected a note of relief in their exclamations, which had nothing to do with the refurbishing of the church.

The selection of the carpeting was accomplished more quickly than Papa had anticipated. He had thought it would be necessary to spend several days visiting various wholesale carpet companies and comparing prices, but on the second morning he found exactly what he wanted in both quality and price and was able to catch an afternoon train back to Berkley Hills. He arrived at the parsonage just before suppertime and hurried into the kitchen, eager to tell Maria about the beautiful green carpets he had ordered. But the sight that greeted him froze his words in his throat.

Mama was sitting at the kitchen table, and before her lay a pile of money—nickels, dimes, quarters, and a large stack of bills.

"Maria," he exclaimed, incredulous, "where in the world did you get all that money?"

Mama started. Then with mischief dancing in her eyes, she quickly scooped the money into her apron. "Just pennies from Heaven, darling." She laughed and brushed past him on her way upstairs.

Papa was too overwhelmed to protest or insist upon an explanation. He went into his study and closed the door. He had been wrong about Maria. She *was* turning the parsonage into a bakery, and for money. It was hard to believe, but in the face of what he had just seen, he could no longer deny it. He paced up and down the study, trying to make sense out of the whole business. He realized now with a heavy heart that he had *assumed* the baking was for charity.

It seemed a reasonable assumption, for this was the time of the year when all the church groups were doubling their efforts to complete their pledges before the summer vacations began. But if that were true, why did Maria have the money? And even if she were merely keeping it for the church, why was she being so mysterious about it?

Well, whatever the reason, he had to put a stop to using the parsonage in such a manner. Why it was sacrilege. Almost as bad as the money-changers Christ had found in the Temple. Christ had driven them from the Temple, and he, as a minister of God, must now act with firmness.

He squared his shoulders and went back to the kitchen. Maria was there, preparing supper as if nothing unusual had or was happening.

"Maria," Papa began sternly, "I think it is about time you told me what is going on in this house."

"Going on, Pontus?" asked Mama innocently.

"And don't try to look innocent. I happen to know that you are making cookies for *money*. And from the amount of money I just saw, they seem to be paying you very well."

"Oh, they do, Pontus. I get forty cents a dozen for them."

"Maria. Do my ears deceive me?" Papa almost shouted. "You boldly admit you are turning the parsonage into a *bakery*?"

"Oh Pontus, it isn't that bad."

"Bad! It is sacrilege. Maria, don't you realize this parsonage is as much a part of God's house as the church? I am paid a salary for my services, to support my family. And you, my wife, are neglecting your church duties to earn *money* for yourself. What do you think Deacon Olson would say if he heard of this?"

"Mr. Olson doesn't object, darling," said Mama eagerly. "I asked him."

Papa sputtered. "You—you asked Deacon Olson if you could sell cookies? Maria, what in the world has happened to you?"

Mama came over to him and put her hands on his shoulders. "Don't be so upset, Papa *lilla*. It's just for fun."

"Fun? I don't see anything funny about a minister's wife falling in love with money. And besides, since when does Deacon Olson decide what's right or wrong in my house?"

"Now, now, Pontus. You just got through saying it is God's house. And you won't be able to preach on Sunday if you break a blood vessel. Now calm yourself while I finish supper."

But Papa would not be pacified. He bounced out of his chair.

"This baking has got to stop, Maria. This very minute. I am still head of my own family—even in America."

Mama didn't answer. Calmly she returned to the stove and went on preparing supper. This was the last straw. If he didn't get some air he *would* burst a blood vessel.

"Never mind about supper," he snapped from the doorway. "I'll eat at a restaurant."

Papa sat dejectedly at an oilclothed table in a downtown lunchroom and tried to swallow the beef stew. The meat was tough and the vegetables were soaked with grease. He began to regret his hasty action. Then he started feeling sorry for himself. Maria had done this to him. Why? For money! Money, the root of all evil—a tool of the devil. Something had to be done.

By the time he had paid for the uneaten meal and left the place, he had made up his mind what that something was. He would go right now and have a talk with Deacon Olson. Mama would listen to *him* even if she wouldn't listen to her husband.

Mr. Olson greeted Papa warmly and invited him into the living room. "I'm so glad you stopped by, Pastor Franzon. Did you get the new carpeting for the church?"

But Papa was in no mood for conversation about carpets. He came right to the point. "Deacon Olson, I want you to tell me all you know about my wife's bakery.

I understand you gave your *approval* to this sacrilegious action. I am very much surprised and shocked."

Deacon Olson laughed. "Don't take it that way, Pastor Franzon. I think your wife is a mighty plucky little woman. I see nothing wrong with her earning a few extra dollars if she wants to."

"Well, I do," snapped Papa. "It's the work of the devil, and I want it stopped. The very idea of turning a parsonage into a bakery! It's . . . it's . . ." Papa was too upset to go on.

Deacon Olson took time to adjust his necktie. "I am sorry, Pastor Franzon," he said with kindly dignity, "but I am afraid it is too late for me to be of any help to you. I've already given my consent, and so have the other deacons. We agreed that so long as Mrs. Franzon didn't hang out a sign on the parsonage, or do anything that would reflect upon the church, we could see no reason why she shouldn't bake cookies and sell them."

"And you think *that* doesn't reflect on the church?"

"I don't see that it does."

Papa started to speak, then changed his mind. It was no use. Mama had them all on her side as usual. All she had to do was smile, and they forgot the difference between right and wrong. Well, *he* knew the difference. And he intended to see that right was done.

He got up, mumbled a curt "good night" and left.

Outside the cool night wind cleared his brain. He walked slowly, aimlessly, trying to think. Was it possible that he was wrong in his attitude? Why had all the deacons of his church given their approval to Maria's ungodly actions? He had as much respect as anyone for money, rightly earned and rightly spent. But surely it was not right to turn a parsonage into a cookie store. And besides, it was humiliating—made it appear he didn't provide for his family.

"God in Heaven," he prayed unconsciously, "what shall I do?"

He walked on, his shoulders slumped. Suddenly he

stopped. Suppose Mama was just playing a joke on him? She hadn't taken him seriously when he threatened to eat in a restaurant. If she had, she would have stopped him. Now she was undoubtedly frantic with worry. Crying. Women always cried when they were worried. The moment he stepped inside the door, she would throw her arms around him and beg his forgiveness. Then she would explain the money, and she would promise to stop using the parsonage as a bakery. Peace would be restored to his home.

Papa hurried. He hadn't realized he had walked so far. But he was happy once more. He felt fine. Maria was a fine wife. His children were fine. Life was fine.

It was ten o'clock when Papa opened the parsonage door. The house was dark except for a light in the kitchen. Maria *was* waiting for his return, worried, just as he had thought.

"Maria," he called softly, "I'm home."

But there was no answer, only the ticking of the kitchen clock. He stood at the kitchen door and stared at the empty room. On the table was a note.

> Pontus, dear—I got tired waiting up for you. I hope you had a good dinner. But if you are still hungry there are meat balls in the oven.
>
> > Good night, darling.

Papa's happiness oozed out of him like air from a toy balloon. Mama hadn't worried about him one bit. Meat balls, indeed! Did she think he could *eat* when his home was tumbling down about his head? Savagely he switched off the kitchen light and climbed the stairs to his room. In the soft light from the hall, he could see Mama sleeping as innocently as a baby. He turned off the upstairs light, undressed in the dark, and crept into bed.

Mama awakened on the stroke of five the following morning. Pontus still slept heavily and there was a troubled frown between his brows. Poor dear! It was too bad he had to find out about the baking business before she was ready. She hated to have him worry, and think all the wrong things she knew he was thinking. But soon she would tell him all about it. Until then he would just have to suffer.

The fragrance of fresh coffee greeted her when she entered the kitchen. Button was there ahead of her and had a batch of cookies ready for rolling and cutting.

"Ummmm, that coffee smells good." Mama sniffed. "Thank you, Button." She poured a cup and sat down at the kitchen table. "You're a wonderful helper, dear. I'd never be able to keep up with all this work if you children weren't so willing to help."

"We're just as anxious as you, Mama, to get this finished. Then we can start living again. I don't like the way Papa looks—as if no one in the whole world loves him."

"I know what you mean, Button. Let's just pray he can hold out until we get the five hundred."

Button poured herself a cup of coffee and sat down. "How much more, Mama?"

Mama sighed. "That's the trouble. I don't know. Yesterday when I was counting Papa came in and caught me."

"Oh, Mama, how terrible! What did he say?"

"I'm afraid he is more upset than is good for him. But I can't tell him yet, Button. It would spoil the surprise. He's just got to wait and suffer, I guess."

"Poor Papa. He must be very worried. We will have to hurry, now, before he has a stroke. But he will forgive us when he knows. Haven't you any idea how much you have, Mama?"

"Well, let's see. There's a little over two hundred from the egg money last summer, twenty dollars I have saved from my housekeeping money, and we've made about a hundred and sixty dollars from the cookie sale. How much is that?"

Button added silently. "About three hundred and eighty

dollars. A hundred and twenty to go. How long do you think it will take?"

"Well, maybe two weeks, the way the orders are coming in. If we can just keep Papa out of the house that long."

"And if *we last* that long," sighed Button. "I'm so tired by night I'm not even interested in a date."

"I know, dear. But John will understand. He'll wait for you."

Button laughed. "Why John especially? What about Eric and Norman?"

"You know John is my favorite. He's a fine boy, Button."

"They are all wonderful kids, Mama. But I don't like one any better than the other. I can't very well marry all three of them."

"I should say not," chuckled Mama. "One husband is enough to handle—especially if you start a bakery!"

Mama got up and put the coffee cups in the sink.

Button rolled and cut the cookies while Mama mixed new batches. As they worked side by side, Mama was thinking what a good wife Button would make John. John Lambert was a student pastor in one of the local churches, and she hoped very much that soon Button would become serious about him and marry him. She had been so disappointed when Button refused to go to college, but being a pastor's wife would make up for that. There just wasn't anything in the world quite as wonderful as being the wife of a minister. Button was twenty now, and soon she would get tired of working as a nursemaid to other people's children and want a family of her own. Mama felt a warm glow just from thinking about having a minister for a son-in-law. But that started her thinking of Pontus again and how unhappy he looked even in his sleep. She glanced at the clock. Soon it would be time to take Papa's before-breakfast coffee to him.

"Hi, you early birds!" called Vickey, coming into the kitchen. Greta trailed after her, rubbing her sleepy eyes.

"We planned on a whole hour before we have to leave for school. Where shall we start, Mama?"

"With some coffee as an eye opener. Then one of you can watch the oven and the other can take cookies off the baking sheets."

"Just like a real bakery," laughed Greta. "But I don't think Papa is happy about the mystery."

"It's no longer a mystery," explained Button. "At least Papa knows something is up. He caught Mama counting the money yesterday."

"Did you tell him, Mama?" asked Vickey.

"Not yet, darling. Papa will just have to wait—maybe two more weeks."

Mama watched Greta as she loosened each cookie from the baking sheet and placed it carefully in the basket. The bakery really had been Greta's idea. Mama had discussed her plans with the children one evening when Papa was at a board meeting, realizing that the egg money she had saved from the farm was not nearly enough for a trip to Sweden. She had tried saving something from her housekeeping money, but that was too slow. Then Greta had suggested baking cookies, and Mama knew that was the solution. Pelle agreed to take orders, the girls would help with the baking, and Calle and Torkel would deliver the orders. Lately there had been so many orders, Greta had had to help with the deliveries after school.

At first it had been easy to keep their secret. Papa was very busy with meetings and other church duties which kept him out of the house most of the day. It was when Mama had to refuse to accompany him on sick calls that he had begun to get suspicious. Then he had found her counting money and she had had to tell him about the bakery. But she still hoped she wouldn't be forced to tell him why until she was ready.

When the kitchen clock struck seven, Mama took the tray of coffee and *bullar* upstairs. Papa sat up and accepted the coffee with a gruff "Good morning" and "Thank you." Beyond that he did not seem to want to talk, for which Mama was grateful. She hurried back to her baking.

An hour later, when he came into the kitchen, he still said nothing about the baking, although the aroma filled the room, and big baskets of cookies stood on the baking board. He ate little, and in silence, then went to his study. The children left for school and Button for her nursemaid job. Toward midmorning Papa stopped at the kitchen door.

"I think I'll go out to the farm for a few days," he announced grimly.

Mama knew Papa was hoping she would protest; that she would explain her strange behavior or suggest going with him. But she couldn't. This was the reprieve she needed.

"I think that will be good for you, Pontus. You do look a little tired. Greet Steve and Terry and the baby for me. They have certainly done well with the farm."

Later, as she watched him walk slowly toward the garage, Mama was tempted to call him back and tell him everything. He looked so terribly downhearted. He will get over it as soon as he knows, she decided, and let him go.

Papa sat on a big stone by the lake and tossed pebbles idly into the water, watching the rings widen on the sunlit surface. He felt very old and lonely. For two days he had thought of nothing but Maria and her bakery. He couldn't even concentrate on his Sunday sermon. Still he hadn't been able to figure out what had happened to his happy home and especially to his wife. Reluctantly he now concluded that he had lost her to the devil—and money. How had it started? Bleakly he remembered the day he had told her the egg money was her own, to do with as she pleased. That had been the mistake. A woman should never be allowed to have much money; it went to her head. God intended a woman to be dependent upon her husband.

A crow cawed raucously from the tree overhead. Papa stood up and threw a stone at it, then watched it fly off to the other side of the lake, its black wings glistening in the sunlight. The incident depressed him further. Like an evil omen. To clear his mind, he forced himself to think of his sermon. Already it was Wednesday and he had thought of nothing to preach about—except cookies, all shapes and sizes.

And why not? he suddenly thought. "Man does not live by bread alone," he quoted, and the words carried a new meaning for him. His spirit lifted. He'd preach a sermon like no sermon he had ever preached. Maria would hear and cease her sacrilegious behavior; and his deacons who had approved her selling cookies would know their pastor had been right. Maria would ask his forgiveness and he would be gentle with her and understanding. She would never again wander from the right path. Peace would be restored.

Perhaps God had had a hand in this after all, thought Papa. Sometimes He permitted His children to err, so that they were more conscious of the devil's evil ways and of God's mercy and forgiveness.

Papa returned to the farmhouse with lighter step.

For the next two days he worked diligently on his sermon. He was pleased with the way the words seemed to flow from his pen. Surely God was guiding his hand and thoughts. Now that he was sure his sermon would right the wrongs that had beset his household and the church, he was in no hurry to return to the parsonage. He could work better here, and besides it would do no harm for Maria to have time to realize she had driven him from his own home and family.

He enjoyed the evenings with Steve and Terry and the baby. Steve was doing very well on the farm. He was not only making expenses, but was beginning to bank a little each week from the butter and eggs; and in the fall when the crops were harvested, there might be a small profit to divide. Just thinking of the possibility gave Papa a warm, comfortable feeling. It would be only right and proper, he decided, to sell Steve the farm someday, when his own children were grown and married and in homes of their own. He certainly wouldn't want anyone else to have the farm after he was gone from this earth.

Driving back to Berkley Hills on Saturday afternoon, Papa practiced his sermon aloud. The relaxation on the farm had been good for him. and his voice had never been more vibrant and forceful. Truly God was with him.

The spicy aroma of cookies reached out to him as he climbed the steps to the parsonage. Momentarily resentment gripped him. Then he smiled. After tomorrow there would be no more cookies. Not even for home use. He would never be able to eat another cookie as long as he lived.

He expected the house to be in a fury of activity. But only Mama and Greta were in the kitchen. Mama looked up as he reached the door.

"Oh, Pontus, you're home!" She put aside a box of cookies and came over and kissed him. "Did you have a good rest on the farm? You look wonderful."

"I feel fine. Steve and Terry send their love," said Papa, taking in at a glance the many boxes of cookies on the table. The bakery business seemed to have flourished during his absence. he reflected morosely.

"Well. looks like you're pretty busy," he said, suddenly embarrassed.

"Oh, I am. Pontus. Everyone in Berkley Hills seems to want my cookies." She was back at the table. counting cookies into boxes. "But I'll start supper right away."

Papa withdrew to the study and consoled himself thinking of his sermon and the surprise *he* would have for all of them tomorrow morning.

Sunday was everything a spring day should be. Papa hummed contentedly as he dressed for church. On a day like this he could be sure of full attendance. Which was fine. It wasn't every Sunday he had such a powerful sermon. And after today, he'd have a normal home too.

As he had hoped, the church was filled. And when Papa rose to begin the sermon, his eyes were fixed on

Maria and the children. This sermon was especially for them. But after the first few words he forgot that his sermon had an ulterior purpose. He felt as though God stood beside him, spoke through his voice, lending it His power and eloquence. It was only when he had finished that he remembered to look at Maria. Her eyes, gazing up at him, were bright with tears.

"Thank you, God," he whispered under his breath. For now he was sure God had heard his prayer and despite his unworthiness, had shown him His mercy.

He stood in the church vestibule and received, humbly, the warmhearted praise of his congregation as he took their hands.

"One of your finest sermons, Pastor Franzon," Deacon Olson commented heartily. Papa was especially pleased.

Sunday was a day to remember—peaceful and *normal*. But Papa awakened on Monday morning to the unmistakable odor of cookies baking. The exhilaration he had enjoyed for a few days drained from him. His wonderful sermon had failed. But no, it couldn't have failed. Perhaps Maria was baking coffee bread. She didn't usually bake on Monday morning, but she might be fixing a surprise for him—a penitent gesture. Papa sat up in pleasant anticipation. Presently Maria pushed open the bedroom door, carrying a well-filled tray. There was no new-baked coffee bread, and her words told him there might not be for a long time.

"Darling, I hope you don't mind, but I've brought you your complete breakfast this morning. The kitchen is too full of cookies and the children want to help as much as they can before school."

"Maria. Do you mean to tell me you are going to continue this crazy bakery business? Even after my sermon yesterday?"

"Of course, Pontus. Why not? Your text was about *bread*, not cookies." Mama's eyes were twinkling.

For a moment Papa was too angry to speak. Then anger

slowly melted into black and hopeless disappointment. "Very well, Maria."

Long after the door had closed behind her, Papa lay there staring blankly at the wall. But the wall, to him, wasn't blank. Instead of the usual flower-strewn wallpaper, he saw only a huge red-and-white sign: MRS. FRANZON'S HOME BAKERY. Judging by the boxes of cookies he had seen on Saturday, it wouldn't be long until Maria's baking business outgrew the parsonage kitchen. And once a woman began to put money-making ahead of her home and family, there was no stopping her. And Maria, as he well knew, was the world's most stubborn woman.

Papa had never felt so alone in his life. Even the children were on Mama's side—including Button. He thought at least *she* would remain loyal to him. But the devil had wily ways, and it was obvious that his entire family was under an evil influence.

It was late morning before Papa dared to go downstairs. Even then he avoided the kitchen, going directly to his study. And toward noon he took his hat and left the house without explanations. For the rest of the day he kept busy with various church duties, but the activity did not alleviate his depression. Even God seemed to have deserted him.

The saffron haze of the warm spring twilight cast smoky shadows across the church lawn as Papa started home for supper. He stood a moment gazing up at the slender steeple, now an awe-inspiring finger against a darkening sky. The finger of God. Suddenly Papa was overcome with remorse for his lack of faith. He had prayed, yes, but his prayers had been selfish petitions to the throne of God.

Slowly he turned and re-entered the church and knelt at the altar in complete humility. It was an hour of spiritual communion such as he had known few times in his life. As he left the church, he knew God had heard his prayer. For over and over, like a chorus of responses, his mind kept repeating: *"Resist not evil, but overcome evil with good."*

He *had* been trying to fight the devil with force. He had tried to force Maria to give up the bakery. Now he would reason with her—show her the evil in what she was doing. Maria would listen to reason. He must act now as her pastor as well as her husband. Give her another chance.

Full darkness had fallen when he reached the parsonage.

After supper, Papa lingered in the living room, scanning the paper and waiting for Mama to finish the last of her baking for the day. He had noticed at supper how tired she looked, and it occurred to him perhaps she would be glad to give up the bakery for her health's sake. As the evening latened, one by one the children came to say good night. And finally Maria, smiling a tired smile.

"Good night, Pontus *lilla*," she said wearily. "If you want to read a while, don't mind me. I'm dead tired."

Papa put the paper aside. "I'd like to talk with you a moment, Maria," he said calmly.

Mama's smile vanished. "Oh, Pontus, please, not again. I don't want you to tell me for the hundredth time to stop my business. I just can't stop now."

Papa got up and stood facing her. "Maria, if you won't sit down, I'll *stand* and talk to you. But I must talk to you now."

"Very well, Pontus." Mama sank onto the davenport. "But please talk fast. I'm really too tired to listen."

Papa talked. He reasoned with her. He pleaded. But Mama sat silent. Papa began to get angry.

"Have you nothing to say, Maria?"

"No, Pontus. I told you I just can't stop my business now. But please don't worry." Mama pulled herself up from the davenport. "I must go to bed. There is so much to do tomorrow."

Papa sat motionless, watching her climb the stairs. He had failed. It was absolutely no use. He felt numb with despair.

The house was eerily quiet. Only the sharp ticking of the kitchen clock, like inexorable doom, broke the stillness. He would have given almost anything in the world to be able to turn back that clock—erase the past few weeks from his life. He thought of all the years Maria had been as close to him as his own heart. Together they had given the Word of God to the people; they had stood beside sickbeds; they had comforted the bereaved. Now all that was over. He had lost his wife to the devil—and money. And what was life without Maria?

Presently, as he sank deeper into the blackness of his despair, a plan began to shape in his mind. A drastic, irrevocable plan. If Maria wanted a bakery more than she wanted to be a minister's wife, then he'd just resign his pastorate in Berkley Hills and go back to Sweden. Maria and the children could remain in America and run a bakery. Perhaps he could get back his old church in Lapland and find peace in his work until God called him.

Unbearably saddened, he went to bed.

The next morning, immediately after breakfast in a cookie-filled kitchen, Papa left for the farm. Before he had slept last night, he had finally decided to really stop resisting evil, and the only good he could think of to do where Maria was concerned was to leave her alone with her bakery. In the peacefulness of the farmhouse, he'd prepare his Sunday sermon and return in time to make his house calls on Saturday. Perhaps by then Maria would have given serious consideration to his wishes. Perhaps he wouldn't be required to carry out his drastic plan.

But nothing had changed when he reached the parsonage Friday afternoon. Boxes, dozens of them, stood on the kitchen table. Mama was giving instructions about deliveries to Torkel and Calle, while Vickey and Greta packed more boxes from the heaping trays of *spritz*, *peppar-kakor* and *finska-bröd*. They looked so good Papa almost forgot his resentment against cookies. Then the full significance of the scene hit him. *Maria had no intention of giving up the bakery.* His last hope was swept away. When he returned from his house calls on Monday afternoon, he'd tell her of his final and drastic decision.

It was late afternoon by the time the house calls were finished. Papa hadn't felt at all like cheering the sick and comforting the troubled. He needed some comforting himself. It really didn't matter what time he reached home. He thought longingly of other days when he could look forward to a fine supper, the companionship of his family, and Maria's cheerful smile. But those joys had not been part of his life for several weeks, and now they would never be again. It wasn't going to be easy to tell Maria that he was leaving her and the children. And that, too, would be forever.

He climbed the parsonage step slowly, the weight of the future heavy upon him. Even Lapland, without Maria and the children, would be a lonely place.

Inside the parsonage he stopped. Surely his mind was failing him. All lights were on. The house was quiet. There was no odor of cookies—only the delicious fragrance of roast beef and onions. The table in the dining room was set with Maria's best dishes, gleaming in the soft candlelight.

"Is that you, Pontus?" called Mama from the kitchen.

"Yes, Maria." Even his voice sounded strange to him. Like a sleepwalker he neared the kitchen door. Slowly his eyes swept the room. Not a cookie in sight—only two flaky apple pies on the stove, and Maria taking the golden-brown roast beef from the oven.

And suddenly the house came alive with the chatter of happy voices.

"Come, Papa *lilla*," said Mama. "We are eating in the dining room tonight, and the children are waiting for you."

Still dazed, Papa followed her into the dining room and sat down at the head of the table. Reverently he bowed his head for the blessing. Often, automatically, he had spoken these words of gratitude for the food they were about to receive, but tonight they came from his very soul.

Papa lifted his eyes to the happy faces around the table. Then he started to carve the roast.

"Just a minute, Pontus," said Mama. "This special dinner tonight is in your honor."

"In my honor, Maria?" echoed Papa. "I don't understand."

"You will in a minute. First let me tell you that today I went out of the baking business."

It was a full second before Papa grasped what she had said. He just looked at her, then around the table. Was this a game they were playing with him? Finally, "Do you mean that, Maria?"

"I do, Pontus. Six years ago you did a wonderful thing for all of us when you gave up your beloved church in Lapland and brought us to America. We have never forgotten your sacrifice and now we want to show you how thankful we are."

Mama placed a large white envelope on Papa's plate. "Open it, darling."

Inside were five one-hundred-dollar bills.

"But, Maria—what is this?" stammered Papa.

They were all laughing now. "Money, Pontus! Five hundred dollars," said Mama. "It all started when you gave me the egg money on the farm. I began then to save every penny to give you that visit to Lapland. But when you decided to return to the ministry, I hadn't been able to save enough. So the children and I started selling cookies to get the rest of the money."

Papa's throat was too full for speech.

"Now you understand why I couldn't stop the bakery when you begged me to. We are all sorry we had to make you unhappy for a while."

There were tears in Papa's eyes now, and he wasn't ashamed of them. How could he have misjudged Maria and the children, when all the time they were working so hard, not just for money, but for *him*. Working to give him his dearest wish. He was unworthy of such love. He was unworthy to be a minister of God. He preached to others about faith, but failed to practice what he preached. How could God or his family ever forgive him?

Slowly he got to his feet.

"Maria—children—what can I say?" The words caught in his throat. "Forgive me for misjudging all of you. And may God forgive me too. I know now how a condemned man feels when he is granted a pardon. And for the rest of my life I shall try to be worthy of God's grace and such a family. From the bottom of my heart I thank God that you *are* my family."

He paused, momentarily overcome with emotion, and glanced around the table at the joyous faces.

"But grateful as I am for your wonderful gift—and I am deeply, humbly grateful—I can't go to Lapland."

"You can't *go!*" All voices were raised as one. "Why, why, Papa?"

For the first time in days, Papa smiled. "Why? Do you think I could enjoy Lapland without Mama?"

The sudden stillness of the room was electric.

Finally Torkel spoke. "Papa, do you want us to start another bakery for Mama's trip?"

"Heaven forbid," exclaimed Papa above the general laughter. "When Mama is ready to go with me, I will get the money for her fare."

"Oh, Pontus, it will be years before I could leave the children. You *must* go without me."

"Then we will just wait years. Meantime these nice crisp bills will be waiting too in a special 'Home-to-Lapland' bank account. And by that time, who knows, they might have grown as much as the Franzon family."

Papa sat down and picked up the carving set. "And now I think we can all do justice to this fine roast beef!"

But he couldn't help noticing his hand was not quite steady and his carving wasn't as expert as usual.

CHAPTER 13

✵ Miss Franzon Stands Bride

Mama settled herself in the big chair by the window, her mending basket in her lap. It had been a warm day for late spring, and the cool night breeze billowing the curtains felt good. It was Tuesday, and Papa had gone to a deacons' meeting. The children, except Button, were in bed.

"I'll wait up for Papa, Button, if you're sleepy," Mama said, fitting one of Pelle's socks over the darning ball.

Button, curled up in a corner of the divan with a book, looked up. "I'm in no hurry. This is a very interesting book." Then she laughed. "And I'll probably have time to finish it before Papa gets home if old man Stadling is at the meeting. That man sure likes to talk."

Mama chuckled. "I know what you mean, Button. Poor Papa. He's such a man of peace, but Mr. Stadling can always find some way to start an argument."

"I'll bet Papa will get even with him in the end," prophesied Button. "He'll have him close with prayer."

"I know," laughed Mama. "That is Papa's pet weapon. I guess every minister has to have one."

Button sighed. "Well I certainly wouldn't want to marry a minister," she said emphatically.

Mama put down her mending and stared at her oldest

daughter in startled surprise. "Why, Button! How can you say a thing like that? Being a minister's wife is just the most wonderful life in the world."

"Maybe—for some people. But *I* wouldn't be interested. Being a minister's daughter is confining enough. But a wife! No, thank you, Mama. I'm tired of being a target for everyone's criticism."

"It's different, Button, when you love him."

"Well, I'd have to love him an awful lot to put up with that kind of life."

Mama's heart dropped right down to her shoes. Where in the world would Button find another young man as fine as John Lambert? Not only was he handsome, but smart—really brilliant. Now he was being graduated from Theological School this spring, and already he had been assigned his first church. A minister needed a wife and, now that John could support one properly, Mama was sure he would soon propose to Button. But Button was making clear that when he did, her answer would be no. Children could be so difficult at times. Especially Button. Mama just couldn't understand her. No matter how well intentioned her plans were for her daughter, Button would make up her own mind, that you could depend upon.

A wave of tenderness flooded Mama's heart as she gazed at her lovely daughter. Why, sitting there curled up in the corner of the divan, the blonde soft hair curling around her temples, she looked liked an angel. How could she look like that and still turn Mama's world upside down with her stubbornness?

"I'm disappointed, Button," Mama finally said. "I thought you liked John very much."

"I do. He's a grand fellow—smart, and lots of fun to go out with. But there's Eric Björk and Norman Falk. I like them too. Men don't *have* to be ministers, Mama, to be nice."

Long after she had gone to bed, Mama lay awake listening to Pontus's heavy breathing beside her and thinking of Button's emphatic remarks. It was hard to believe

that her own daughter didn't even *want* to be a minister's
wife. Why, there was no occupation on earth quite as
important as being a minister of God. Button certainly
wasn't in love with either Eric or Norman. Marriage was
a woman's best career. Why, at Button's age, Mama recalled proudly, *she* was a minister's wife and the happiest
woman in the world.

Mama forced herself to relax. She certainly couldn't
make Button marry John. She would just leave it to God.
If it was right that Button marry him, God would see
that it happened.

She was just falling asleep when *the plan* popped into
her mind.

If she made Button's wedding dress now, it would be
so beautiful Button would just have to say "yes" to John.
Wide awake again, Mama could *see* the dress. It would be
of the finest white satin, yards and yards of it, with a
train. And of course it would be princess style with a
bodice of cut floral lace and a deep scalloped hem to match
the long lace sleeves. And a mandarin collar, edged with
seed pearls. It would take a long time to make it, especially
with the seed pearls, and she would have to make it in
secret, working on it only when Button was out of the
house or asleep.

Mama became so excited about the plan that it wasn't
until the next morning she realized she hadn't enough
money to buy the satin and pearls. All the money she had
saved from the bakery had gone into the "Home-to-
Lapland" fund, and she wasn't at all sure Papa would
think her plan a good one—good enough, that was, to
give her the money she needed. But there had to be a
way. A man, Mama reasoned, would do almost anything
for a woman if she handled him just right. And where
Papa was concerned, that meant appealing to his gentle
side. She would start by making him a special breakfast—
plättar and lingonberries.

She waited until the children had left for school or
their jobs, and Pontus was finishing the last of the little

golden-brown pancakes heaped high with lingonberries, before she ventured to speak.

"Pontus *lilla*," she said casually, "have you ever thought how much money it will cost to marry off four daughters?"

"Who's marrying off four daughters, Maria?" Papa asked, not really concerned.

"We are, Pontus."

"Maria," said Papa sternly, now greatly concerned, "please don't start planning the girls' wedding before they have even found their mates. I'm aware one of these days we'll have to arrange a fine church wedding for each of them. And when that time comes, we shall be able to take care of it. I don't see why you worry about it now."

Mama hesitated a moment before she dared try again. Then she looked at Papa pleadingly, and plunged. "Darling, Button is twenty-two years old and I need the money for her wedding dress."

Papa stared. "Maria, have you lost your mind? You know better than to start making a wedding dress before John has even proposed."

"Oh, Pontus, you said yourself John is going to get the church in Littlemont, and he will certainly want a wife, and Button——"

"Never mind. Time enough to make the dress when John has asked her."

"That's because you never made a dress, Pontus. Especially one with seed pearls."

Papa got up and started for the hall. "I'll be a little late for lunch, Maria. I have five sick calls to make this morning."

So—that meant Papa was through talking about the dress. Well, *he* might be, thought Mama, but *she* wasn't.

"Pontus!" she called after him. Then put her head in her hands and began to cry. She hadn't meant to cry, but she had remembered something which in her present state of mind made her feel very sorry for herself.

"Maria! What in the world are you crying about?"

Papa came back and put his hand on her shoulders.

"It's just . . . just . . ." she sobbed, lifting her tear-drenched face to his, "that I never *had* a wedding dress, Pontus. I even had to sleep in an upper bunk on a steamship on my wedding night, with my husband many staterooms away. All because *he* couldn't make up his mind soon enough to get a stateroom together. Oh, Pontus, I didn't even know . . ."

"Maria, don't cry," he said gently. "I can't undo what I did so many years ago. What is it you don't know?"

Mama spoke through her tears. "I—I didn't even—know if you loved me—or just married me to get a housekeeper!"

"Oh, Maria. Of course I loved you very much. I was just shy and you were . . . well, you were so demonstrative. I was afraid of you I guess. But haven't I proven to you all these years how much I love you?"

Mama threw her arms about his neck, her cheeks still wet with tears. "Of course you have, darling. I'm sorry! It's just that I want the girls to have all those little things in their weddings that I missed. They mean so much to a woman. And you know how Button is. One minute she is dead set *against* something, and the next minute she's all for it. Suppose she decides to get married quick, and I don't have time to make her dress myself? Oh, I just couldn't let that happen, Pontus!"

"Will twenty dollars be enough, Maria?"

"You mean——?"

"Yes, Maria. I can't very well marry you all over again to make up for my shortcomings twenty-four years ago. But I can see that my daughter has a wedding dress made by her mother."

"Oh, Pontus! You're wonderful—the most wonderful Papa in the whole world."

For several minutes after the front door had closed behind Pontus, Mama sat at the kitchen table, feeling ashamed of her dramatics. She had never in her life resorted to tears to handle Papa, and actually she hadn't intended to this time. She had just got carried away by her own emotions. And Button's wedding dress was *so* important. Well, it was done now. She'd hurry through her work this morning and buy the satin before Pontus had time to think about her plan and perhaps change his mind.

Saturday was Button's day off from her nursemaid position. She and Vickey were helping Mama with the housework and the baking, when the telephone rang. No one ever answered the telephone on Saturdays but Button; all the calls seemed to be for her. She was so popular. But today Mama didn't mind, for that would be John. Button had told her yesterday she had promised to go with John to look at the parsonage at Littlemont, and Mama's hopes had soared, even though Button had said she wasn't interested in marrying a minister.

But when she heard Button saying, "Oh, I'd love to, Eric," Mama's heart sank. "I'll be ready in thirty minutes," Button finished and hung up the receiver. "I've really done all the dusting, Mama. You don't mind, do you?"

Mama hesitated only a moment. She did mind, but it would do no good to tell Button that. Then she realized Button must have forgotten about her appointment with John.

"But, Button, you promised John today. Remember?"

"I know. But that can wait. He will understand. When he calls, please tell him I'll go with him next Saturday."

"Oh, Button. That isn't right and you know it. You *promised* John."

But Button was already on her way upstairs. In a few minutes she was back, looking as pretty as a picture in her light blue suit.

"I won't be home for supper, Mama. We're driving up to Mountain Lake with Sonja and Paul. We'll eat there." And she was gone.

Mama sighed and went into the kitchen where Vickey was cutting cinnamon rusks for drying. "Don't you ever do a thing like that, Vickey," Mama admonished, not referring to the rusks, but to Button's unseemly behavior.

Vickey smiled wistfully. "Don't worry, Mama. I'll never be as popular as my vivacious sister."

"And don't *you* worry, darling," said Mama. "Your time will come. And I am very thankful you *are* just as you are. Button is so thoughtless of others."

It wasn't until Mama went upstairs again that she remembered the wedding dress—the lovely white satin in her bureau drawer. She had intended to wait until Monday when the children would be out of the house to cut the dress. Now she wouldn't have to wait. She could cut out the dress today, and Monday start sewing on it.

Quickly she made the beds and tidied the upstairs. Then she took the satin from the drawer and spread it lovingly on the cutting table. It was almost too beautiful to cut, she thought, pinning the pattern in place. For one brief moment she was frightened. Suppose she made a mistake and ruined it? She closed her mind at once against the thought, knowing God would not *let* that happen.

Long before Papa returned for lunch, the dress was ready for sewing. She put the satin pieces away again and went downstairs. She had just reached the bottom step when the doorbell rang.

"Why, John," she said, opening the door. Then remembered the unhappy message she had for him. Reluctantly she told him.

"But, Mrs. Franzon, we had a date with my trustees. Button just can't do this to me."

"I'm afraid, John, Button does as she pleases—too much as she pleases sometimes. I'm very sorry. And she won't be back until late."

"Fine," John said heavily. "Very fine for me. Those trustees won't understand. They want the woman who is to live in the house to approve the repairs and select the wallpaper. And they'll never approve of me as the new minister unless I'm to be married. I thought Button understood that."

John sat down, disconsolately, on the sofa. Vickey came in from the kitchen. "My goodness, John, you don't look much like a minister with that long face," she teased.

"Oh, hello, Vickey. That flighty sister of yours is the cause of it. A minister is supposed to have a wife—at least a wife-to-be. How can I select wallpaper without a wife?"

"Is *that* all?" cried Vickey. "Cheer up, John. I'll help you select the wallpaper. Just a stand-in for my sister, you understand."

John looked at her and suddenly a wide grin spread over his face. "Say! That's a very good idea. Would you really do it, Vickey? That old broken-down parsonage has six big rooms, you know."

"I'd love to, really. And we'll take Mama along. At least you'll have a real mother-in-law to show those trustees. That should set their minds at ease. Especially such a lovely mother-in-law."

Mama chuckled. She had never seen Vickey so gay. And her eyes were like a couple of bright stars. Suddenly an appalling thought struck her. Could it be that Vickey was in love with John—had been in love with him all along, eating her little heart out over a man who had eyes only for her sister? Oh, dear! That *would* be a complication.

She had been looking forward eagerly to working on Button's wedding dress this afternoon. But now she decided it was best to go along with John and Vickey, just to make sure things didn't get out of hand.

When Vickey came downstairs ready for the meeting with John's trustees, Mama was surprised at how grown-up she looked. Her hair was swept up in a cluster of curls on top of her head, and she was wearing one of Button's black dresses. She linked her arm in John's playfully. "How does the happily-never-to-be-married couple look, Mama?"

They laughed together. "You certainly look older, Vickey."

"As old as John?"

Mama tilted her head, appraisingly. "M-m-m-m—older, I think."

"Good," cried Vickey. "That ought to please your old trustees, John."

The parsonage in Littlemont was a rambling old structure which for some reason had not been kept in repair. Possibly, Mama thought, because they hadn't had their own minister for some time. The church until recently had not been prosperous enough to support one without help from the Conference who had let them share an older minister with a church fifteen miles away. But now as the financial problem seemed to be solved, it would be a wonderful place for a new minister, just trying his wings in the service of God. Yes, and a wonderful place to raise a family, Mama decided, when she saw the rustic garden with rope-swings under the old oak trees, and a big fenced-in sandbox. Now, of course, there was much work to be done, but what fun a happy young couple could have planting a new garden, and watching the old house take on new life under their hands. Button would love this place, and now Mama was sure everything would turn out all right. With such a home to come to, after her beautiful wedding, Button would settle down and be a good wife to John, just as Mama had hoped and planned.

Mama had been so busy with her own thoughts she hadn't noticed John and Vickey until now. Vickey was just staring at the big old house and the garden, her eyes wide, and bright with tears. "Oh, John, it is simply lovely."

"Lovely," he exclaimed. "A lovely *mess*, if you ask me."

"I mean, it *can* be," Vickey added. "Just *look* at that apple tree at the end of the garden."

That was so like Vickey, thought Mama. Always seeing the beautiful side. For even she had not noticed the apple tree before—a mountain of soft pink blossoms.

"I see," said John pensively. "It is beautiful. But we had better take a look inside."

A car drove up then, and the two trustees got out, carrying a large carton.

"Good afternoon, Mr. Dexter," greeted John. "May I present Mrs. Franzon, my mother-in-law—to be, that is. And——"

"And the happy bride-to-be," exclaimed Mr. Dexter heartily, extending his hand to Vickey. "I'm delighted to meet you. And this is Mr. Ellison, our other trustee. . . ."

Mr. Ellison shook hands all around. "Now don't you worry about this old house, Miss Franzon. We aim to make it the prettiest place in Littlemont before you move in. It'll be ready by June." And he beamed knowingly at Vickey.

Mama started to correct the error, but when she saw the mischief dancing in Vickey's eyes and the sudden relief in John's manner, she kept silent. It would do no harm to let Mr. Dexter and Mr. Ellison think Vickey was the bride-to-be—just for today. After all, she *was* the bride-to-be's sister.

"Come along inside," suggested Mr. Dexter. "I've a lot of wallpaper samples in this box. It's the wife that should decide on the wallpaper, I always say."

Vickey linked her arm in John's, plainly enjoying this masquerade. And from the twinkle in John's eyes, he wasn't objecting to it either.

For an hour the two young people "ohed" and "ahed" impressively over the samples which the excited Mr. Dexter spread before them. They had made a tour of the house before assembling in the big, dusty living room to select the paper for each room. Mama had been even more delighted with the inside of the house, and its possibilities, than with the garden. She could just see this place, all furnished with soft colors and comfortable furniture, and crisp organdy curtains at the windows. A dream house, indeed! And so big. It didn't take much imagination to hear the happy voices of children ringing through these spacious rooms.

Mama was smiling happily over these thoughts, while

Vickey and John selected the wallpaper. Suddenly she was brought out of her dreaming by Vickey's raised voice.

"I should say not, John," she was saying emphatically. "I certainly don't intend to have my little *girls* growing up with boys' wallpaper!"

"And what about the boys?" argued John. "Do you think I want *them* growing up with wallpaper covered with dolls?"

"I didn't select paper with dolls in it," announced Vickey. "*This* is what I selected." And she unrolled a scroll depicting baby angels flying in a blue sky, dropping appleblossoms down on the world.

"But, Vickey! The boys will grow up to be sissies, looking at *that* all their young lives."

"And the girls will be little roughnecks, looking at *trucks and trains and boats*."

Mr. Dexter coughed and looked helplessly at Mama. Mr. Ellison had tactfully withdrawn to the window. Obviously they wanted no part in the argument between their new minister and his wife-to-be. And if Mama hadn't seen how close to laughter both John and Vickey were, she too would have believed the sharp tone in their voices was real.

Suddenly both John and Vickey could restrain their laughter no longer. Mr. Dexter and Mr. Ellison looked enormously relieved.

"We'll let Mama be the arbitrator," said John. "Okay, Vickey?"

"Okay," agreed Vickey, trying to subdue her laughter.

Mama finally selected a paper dotted with ducks, chickens and cows, and little woolly lambs. "This ought to satisfy *both* boys and girls," she laughed, beginning to enjoy this game as much as she knew they were.

"We'll take it," exclaimed John.

"I agree," said Vickey.

And they were still laughing about the masquerade when they reached the Berkley Hills parsonage.

"Won't you come in for coffee, John?" invited Mama.

John looked at his watch. "I'm sorry. I won't have time,
I'm afraid. I promised to meet my mother at five thirty,
and it is after five now. Thanks just the same. And thanks
so much for coming along today—Mama!" Then he
turned to Vickey. "I don't know how I can *ever* thank
you, Vickey. You were wonderful. To tell the truth, I
almost forgot you weren't my wife."

"It was fun, wasn't it?" said Vickey, but her tone was
not as gay as the words implied. "I just love that house and
garden, and"—mischief twinkled in her eyes again—"I *still*
prefer the paper with the angels."

The following Monday, when the housework was finished, Mama started sewing on the dress, watching the
clock against the time the children would be home from
school and their jobs. If all went well, the dress would
be ready for the seed pearls by the end of the week.
And until then she would try to keep it a secret between
Papa and herself.

Neither Vickey nor Mama had said anything to Button
about the play acting on Saturday, although they had intended to. But when Button returned, she was so full of the
good time she had had with Eric, Sonja and Paul, they
hadn't been able to get a word in edgewise. And Sunday,
after church, they had all driven out to the farm to see
Terry and Steve's new baby.

So it was late Tuesday afternoon before Button saw
John again. She was in the living room with Mama and
Vickey, waiting for John to call for her. Mama decided
it was time to speak.

"Button," she began cautiously, "is John driving you
over to see the parsonage at Littlemont?"

"Oh, it's so lovely, Button," exclaimed Vickey im-
pulsively.

Button looked at her in surprise. "And how would you
know?"

Too late Vickey realized what she had said. The whole
story came out then.

"It wouldn't have happened, Button, if you had not broken your promise to John," said Mama.

Button didn't reply for a moment. "Well, if I'm the one who has to live in it," she finally said, "I guess I'd better see it."

Then she *did* intend to marry John, exulted Mama secretly.

But when Button returned later that evening, she was anything but impressed. "I think it's a horrid old place," she exclaimed the moment John had left. "Why I'd be scared to death to stay there even *one* night alone. And it will be *years* before the church can afford to do all the repairs the place needs."

Mama's hopes flew right out the window. But now it was for John, more than Button, that her heart ached. He loved Button, and he needed her both because of that love and the glorious life he hoped to share with her as a minister of God's word. How could Button be so unconcerned? Why didn't she see that John was a very fine man, a desirable husband, could have any one of a dozen girls for his wife? And why, oh, why, did poor John have to fall in love with Button when apparently she didn't return his love?

But, Mama decided, hopefully, there was still the lovely wedding dress. And every day it became more beautiful as the satin and soft lace took shape. Just looking at it made Mama wish she were a girl again, planning her own wedding to Papa. Well, June was still a month away. If God meant Button to be John's wife, He would perform whatever miracle was needed. She would just wait and pray.

And so she did—for a full week. And between prayers and tending to the needs of her family, she sewed on the wedding dress. She was grateful that Pontus was unusually busy with church affairs and meetings, and this was the season when the young people's groups were particularly active with parties and socials.

Mama was waiting up for them as usual a few nights

later. Button was first to come in, and already it was ten o'clock.

"Any mail, Mama?" was her first question, as it had been for several days now. Mama began to wonder about it.

"Mail? Oh, yes, darling. I put it on your bureau."

"Thanks," she called, already half up the stairs.

A moment later Mama heard a frightened cry. "Oh, Mama! Come quick!"

Mama made the stairs so fast that her heart was not pounding from fear alone, and when she reached Button's room she could hardly speak. "Button . . . whatever . . ." and stopped. For Button was leaning against the wall, her hand clasped to her breast, with the most *rapturous* expression on her face.

Mama was angry. "Button. How could you fool me like that? I thought you were *dying*, the way you screamed."

"Oh, I think I am, Mama." She continued to stare into space with a strange, faraway expression, and Mama wondered if the girl had suddenly lost her mind.

She went to her and took her by both shoulders, shaking her gently. "Button! What is it? What is the matter with you?"

Whereupon Button threw her arms around Mama's neck and hugged her so tightly she almost choked. "It doesn't matter, Mama. Nothing else in the world matters," cried Button. And the tears streamed down her cheeks.

Mama was really alarmed now. Gently she led her daughter to the bed and made her sit down. "Now, Button darling. Try to tell me all about it."

Button dried her tears and turned a beaming face to Mama. "Forgive me, Mama. I'm just crying from happiness. It's my very first story . . . and I sold it!"

Mama sat down heavily as if her legs had been pulled from under her. Button bubbled on, now that she had found her voice. "To a Swedish magazine, Mama! *Kvinnan Och Hemmet*. Isn't it wonderful? And look! A check for *five dollars*. Oh, I'm so happy I could burst. Just think of it, Mama. Your daughter, a *writer!*"

Mama was still trying to adjust to the sudden turn of events, when Papa came home. Button ran downstairs to share her good news with him, leaving Mama with the unhappy realization that now she would never have John Lambert for a son-in-law. Well, God never made a mistake. And surely this was God's will. Slowly she got to her feet and went downstairs.

One by one the children came home and went to bed. All except Vickey. It was unusual for her to stay out so late, but Mama wasn't worried. The parties at the church often lasted until after eleven. And it was just about that time when Vickey came in.

"Hello, darling. Did you have a good time at the social?" Mama stifled a yawn. The excitement with Button had left her more tired than she had realized until now.

Instead of the answer Mama expected, Vickey ran to her and threw herself into her arms. "Oh, Mama! I just have to tell you!"

Now what? thought Mama. What in the world was happening to her children? Must they all reach some kind of crisis on the same day? Vickey was sobbing against Mama's shoulder and saying something which surely Mama had not heard right, for it sounded like, "I'm going to get married, Mama."

She lifted Vickey's head and looked at her tear-stained face. "What did you say, dear?"

"I'm going to get married. In June. I'm going to marry John."

"But, Vickey. . . !" began Mama, sure now that something was wrong with her hearing—or her daughter's mind.

"Oh, Mama. Don't take it like that." And her eyes were suddenly like sunlight after a rainy day. "We *love* each other. We thought you'd be happy for us."

"But, Vickey," Mama finished, "John is supposed to

marry Button. And besides you're just a little girl, barely seventeen."

Vickey sat back on the sofa looking at Mama solemnly. "I'm not a little girl, Mama. Not any longer. *And besides*," she emphasized mischievously, "you told me yourself you were only sixteen when you fell in love with Papa; and you'd have married him then if he had asked you."

"But that was different, darling . . ." began Mama again.

"Oh, Mama! All mothers say that. It isn't different. Or maybe it *is* . . . especially when you love someone as much as I love John. I do love him, Mama, and he loves me—not Button. We love the same things . . . his being a minister, that lovely ramshackle old parsonage and its run-down gardens, and that little nursery with the wallpaper we almost quarreled over, and . . ."

Mama gathered the excited girl into her arms. "My sweet. My precious little Vickey. How could I say anything but 'blessings on you both'? But we still have to ask Papa."

Vickey's eyes popped. "You don't think he'll—object?"

"Only Papa can answer that question, darling. And he's sound asleep now. And so should we be. We'll ask him in the morning."

But when Mama and Vickey confronted Papa in the study the next morning after breakfast, it wasn't as easy as Mama had hoped. He was shocked. "Have you forgotten," he said slowly, "that in any respectable Swedish family it is the *oldest* daughter who marries first?"

For one whole minute neither Mama nor Vickey spoke. They *had* forgotten that old, old Swedish tradition.

"But this is America, Papa," Vickey argued, when finally she had conquered the tears which were about to spill from her brimming eyes.

"Nevertheless," he continued emphatically, "Button must be consulted."

Papa had spoken.

The hours dragged, waiting for Button to come home that evening. And when finally she had heard the whole surprising story, she met it with an announcement equally surprising. "But I'm never going to marry *anyone*, Papa. I'm going to be a writer."

Papa insisted he couldn't see what *that* had to do with getting married. And Button contended she wasn't interested in getting married—especially to a minister—and then added belatedly, "Not *all* ministers are like you, Papa." Button knew how to get around Papa.

Mama knew there would be no more argument. And since Vickey was next to the oldest, Papa gave his consent.

"I'll be happy to see you and John in my study this afternoon," he told Vickey gently, "and give you my blessing. I know you will make him a good wife, and Mama and I will be proud to have John as a son-in-law."

Button placed her arms around Vickey. "I'm *glad* John fell in love with you, Vickey," she said slowly. "You'll make him a much better wife than I would have made him. And he *is* wonderful."

Mama had never seen a girl as happy as Vickey. She floated out of the room on a rose-tinted cloud. And only then Mama remembered the wedding dress, which had been made for *Button*.

"But the wedding dress . . ." she began, forgetting that Button knew nothing about it.

"Oh, I'll help you make it, Mama," said Button confidently. "We'll have it ready in plenty of time."

Mama told her then—of the dress that had been made for her and which now Vickey would wear. For just a moment Button looked sad. Then she brightened with an idea.

"Vickey's *almost* my size, Mama. Why, the dress will only need taking in a little here and there. You'll see! It will fit her as if it had been made for her."

And so it did.

What a lovely bride she will be, thought Mama when, the alterations completed, Vickey tried on the dress for the last time before the wedding. But as she watched the happy child, looking like a little girl playing at being a bride, a sharp pang of anxiety went through her. How young she was for the responsibilities which soon would be hers. In the three weeks that remained before the wedding, she would try to prepare Vickey, with what wisdom she possessed, to assume those responsibilities.

"It's the little things, darling," Mama counseled a few days later while Vickey was helping her with the supper dishes, "that you must learn to cope with as a minister's wife. Big problems have a way of solving themselves, but it's the little foxes, remember, that spoil the vineyard."

"What little foxes, Mama?" laughed Vickey.

"Little foxes of gossip among the church people, for one thing. You must learn to distinguish between gossip and real problems. For you will be required to listen to all kinds of problems, and in most cases from people much older than yourself. Women especially. Sometimes it is easier for a woman to open her heart to a minister's wife than to the minister himself."

"It frightens me a little sometimes," Vickey admitted. "But I do so want to help John in every way, Mama."

"You will learn quickly, darling, for you have the will to learn. That's half the battle. And part of the other half is observing little things when you visit the homes in John's parish, so you will understand the people who live there better. If women only realized how they *reveal* themselves in those little things. Like the woman who doesn't keep her kitchen stove clean . . . *she* is very apt to be careless in what she says about others."

"Mama! You're joking now. Those are just Swedish superstitions."

"Not at all, Vickey. You'll see! And there is the woman who never looks you in the eye when she is talking to you—just don't examine the corners of her house too closely."

"How about the woman who tells little white lies?" chuckled Vickey.

"She is the one who never takes time to fix a strap or

sew on a button. More likely *she* is put together with
safety pins."

Vickey laughed heartily. "I'll never, never be as wise
as you are, Mama. I hope John doesn't expect me to be."

"The way you manage your own home is important,
too. Very important. Little things again—like having the
table set when John comes home. And making the meal
the most important thing in your life at that moment.
Nothing lifts a man's spirit like the odor of fresh coffee
and meat and muffins baking in the oven. And when you
whisper 'Darling, I cooked this especially for you!' Well
—that's a big deposit in your happiness-for-life bank
account."

Mama opened her eyes to bright June sunlight flooding
the bedroom. This was Vickey's wedding day. And what
a lovely gift from the Heavenly Father it was.

She lay there a while, torn between happiness and
sadness. Happiness for Vickey, and sadness at the thought
of parting with the first of her "dreams." *This* part of
the wedding had not occurred to her when she started
making the wedding dress. She wondered if she would
have been so eager, had she known Vickey would be the
one to wear it. But she must not think such thoughts.
She must be happy so that Vickey and John would be
happy, and every moment of this day must be so wonderful they would all cherish its memory the rest of
their lives.

For days the preparations had outranked everything
else. Papa of course would perform the ceremony, and
so it would be Nim, who had now been home a week
from school, who would give the bride away. There had
been dresses to be made for Greta and Kerstin, and a
different one for Button as maid-of-honor, this time soft
golden satin. Then invitations, and all the arrangements
for the reception. And finally yesterday the decorating
of the church with banks of mountain laurel and roses,
so breathtakingly lovely that it brought a sob to Mama's
throat. It was all so different from what it would have

been in Lapland. For Vickey would not have wanted
the wedding in the big State Church, where Papa could
not perform the service, and where she would have worn
the little gold crown to held her long, sweeping veil.
No, Vickey would have wanted the wedding in the parsonage, with only a myrtle crown from Tant Renberg's
own myrtle plant. Instead of mountain laurel and roses,
the parsonage would have been decorated with newly
cut branches. And both Mama and Tant Renberg would
have baked and cooked and cleaned for weeks before
the wedding, for the celebrations would have lasted three
full days. . . .

Mama shook herself out of these homesick thoughts.
There was much to do before four o'clock. She dressed
quickly and went to Vickey's room to awaken her. But
Vickey was already awake, sitting up in bed.

"Oh, Mama," she cried. "It's here at last—my wedding
day! Just think, in a few hours I'll be *Mrs. John Lambert*."

It was impossible not to share Vickey's happiness. After
all, thought Mama, she wasn't *really* losing her. And John
would be a wonderful son-in-law—just what she had
prayed for. God had answered her prayers as He always
did—in the right way.

This feeling of deep gratitude to God was still with
her as, on Torkel's arm, Mama walked slowly down the
aisle, to organ music that was like a chorus of angel voices,
and was seated in the front pew. She glanced about her.
At John, with Pelle his best man, eagerly awaiting his
bride at the altar. And Papa handsome and dignified, in
his best black robe with the velvet trimming. Mama wondered if he was nervous. It was hard enough for her to
watch without crying. How much more difficult it must
be for Pontus! Would he break down in the middle of the
ceremony?

Mama closed her eyes for a moment and silently uttered
a fervent prayer for Papa.

Suddenly the majestic strains of the wedding march
filled the church. Kerstin floated up the aisle in a cloud

of pink tulle and lace, then Greta in soft shimmering blue, smiling as if it were *her* wedding. Mama blinked back the tears. This was no time for weeping. Now Button, tall and beautiful, looking almost like a bride herself in the soft golden satin. And finally Vickey, a million stars in her eyes, on Nim's arm—in the beautiful gown that had been made for Button. How precious they all were!

Now they were at the altar. And Papa, his voice husky but so very gentle, spoke the solemn words which, in the sight of God and man, gave Vickey and John to each other "for so long as you both shall live."

"Thank You, God," Mama breathed softly. "Thank You for John, my new son and Your servant."

And because she was truly thankful, she couldn't quite understand, as she stood in the receiving line, shaking hands, hearing the chatter of happy voices about her, and seeing all the happiness in the world reflected in the faces of the newlyweds, why she kept thinking of an old trunk in the parsonage attic which contained snapshots of Vickey from babyhood in Lapland to last summer as a grown-up young lady of sixteen. And those funny little drawings Vickey had brought home from kindergarten her first day in school.

Mother love, thought Mama, was a strange contradiction. But she was sure God understood what was in her heart.

CHAPTER 14

✄ Pelle Makes a Decision

Faith, to Mama, was as simple as the word itself. It was never a matter that had to be weighed, nor did it require spiritual ceremonies to achieve it. She merely believed, and it came to pass. If the day seemed dark and beset by problems, her faith in the goodness of God brightened dull skies and lightened the problems. Many times she had beheld, with wonder, the mysterious ways of the Lord, and so never questioned His wisdom. A miracle in the making, she had come to realize, at the time often appeared to be an insurmountable tragedy.

So it was on a particular Tuesday in February.

Outside, dull gray skies threatened snow, and there was a frosty nip in the wind, but inside the parsonage all was sunshine, warmth and cheer. Tempting smells of baking and of roasting meat pervaded the kitchen. Although it still lacked several minutes of nine o'clock, beds were made, furniture dusted and polished, and all the disorder of yesterday's living restored to neatness. Papa had retired to his study immediately after breakfast.

Mama sang softly to herself as she laid the dining room table with her best linen and silver. Today was a special occasion—a luncheon in honor of Pelle's bride-to-be. It was such a pleasure to do things for Pelle. He was always

252

so unselfish, doing for others and rarely asking anything for himself. Not even Mama had known how serious he was about Felicia Bronson until last Sunday night. She had known, of course, that Pelle seemed to prefer Felicia's company to all the other girls he knew in college. Her parents had moved to Berkley Hills two years ago and her father was one of the best doctors in town.

Sunday evening, Mama and Papa had been alone in the living room after supper, when Pelle came in quietly. It wasn't until he cleared his throat that they were aware of his presence.

"Excuse me, please," he began. "I'd like to talk with both of you if you have a minute."

Papa put down his *Church Quarterly* and looked up. "Why, of course, son."

"Is anything wrong, Pelle?" asked Mama, momentarily apprehensive because Pelle so seldom sought counsel.

His laughter quickly reassured her. "On the contrary, Mama," he answered. "Felicia and I are planning to be married right after our graduation in June."

"Married!" Papa sat up and stared at him. "But, Pelle, we haven't *met* this girl. Oh, I've no doubt she is a fine girl, but it is not like you to set the date for your wedding before presenting the girl to us."

"That's what I want to talk about. Could I bring her for luncheon on Tuesday, Mama? That is the day we finish our mid-year exams."

"Why, certainly, Pelle. Papa and I will be very happy to meet her."

Pelle had then explained why they had set the date for the wedding before she had met his parents, or he hers. Felicia's grandmother had died in January, leaving her little home, in the suburbs of Boston, to Felicia. Since Pelle intended continuing his studies at Harvard, they could be together. Later, when he had finished college, he intended to take up teaching as a life work. Until then, he would work during the summers and part-time during the fall and winter as a tutor.

"It is just perfect. Don't you agree?" cried Pelle, and Mama thought that to Pelle the whole world was always wonderful.

She laughed softly. "We do, indeed, son."

"Well," said Papa, "I just hope Felicia is as fine as you think she is, and it isn't the house and the furniture that makes her seem so perfect."

"You may depend upon that, Papa," laughed Pelle, "and after Tuesday you'll love her too."

And so Monday's regular duties had been put aside, while the house was made ready for the special occasion, and odors of cooking instead of washday filled the kitchen.

Mama glanced now at the little gold clock on the sideboard.

Only three hours before their guest would arrive, and there was still so much to do. The table looked lovely, but it needed a festive touch. If she hurried, she would have time to run over to Burke's greenhouse for a centerpiece.

When she returned, she carried a small blue bowl of pink hyacinths. It was just right on the table, and its spicy fragrance seemed to bring springtime into the whole house.

Mama had just finished placing it on the table when a strange sound reached her from the direction of the study. She listened. There it was again—a moan as from someone in pain. Quickly she ran to the study door and, without waiting to knock as usual, flung it open. There sat Papa, his head buried in his hands, moaning and groaning as if he were not long for this world.

"Pontus! What is it?"

"All hell is loose in my mouth, that's what is wrong," cried Papa.

Mama was so shocked at his use of that ugly word that she forgot about his pain. "Pontus Franzon! What an awful way to talk."

"You don't seem to understand, Maria, that I am not

responsible for what I say. I'm going crazy. Completely out of my mind. My teeth——"

"Oh, Pontus! Why didn't you tell me before? I'll get an oatmeal pack for you right away. It will ease the pain until you can see the dentist."

"I've *seen* the dentist. I saw Doctor Falk yesterday. He says all my teeth have to come out."

"Never mind that now," called Mama, already on her way for the hot oatmeal pack and a large turkish towel.

When she finished binding the pack to Papa's jaw with the towel, tying it securely in a huge knot on top of his head, she couldn't help laughing.

"All right, Maria, poke fun at me. Laugh at my suffering."

"Oh, Papa *lilla*. You know I wouldn't laugh at your pain," she soothed, "but if you could see how funny you look you'd laugh too, even if you do have a toothache."

"Well, I don't think it is funny. And I'm sure Pelle and Felicia will not laugh."

Mama caught her breath. For a moment she had completely forgotten the luncheon. "Pontus! What are we going to do? You can't meet Felicia looking like that."

"And do you think I could meet her with devils jumping in my mouth?"

Poor Pontus! He must be in terrible pain to keep talking like that. Of course he was right. It was more important that the pain be relieved than that he make an impression on Felicia. But Pelle would be so disappointed, though, being Pelle, he would probably be as concerned about Papa's suffering as Papa was himself. Of all the days in the world for Pontus to get a toothache! Papa simply couldn't appear at the table with a towel around his head. Felicia would decide she was marrying into a circus family.

"Come, dear," she said gently. "Lie down for a while and let the oatmeal pack do its work. Just before Felicia and Pelle arrive, we'll take it off and I'll give you some aspirin. You'll see. Everything is going to be fine."

From the look Papa gave her she knew he never again expected to be fine, but he followed her upstairs and lay down. Mama covered him with a blanket, pulling it up snugly over his jaw, then went back to her luncheon preparations.

If Pontus would just try to make the best of things until after lunch, Doctor Falk could remove the teeth and Papa's suffering would be over. She hated to think of him losing all his nice white teeth, but if that was the only way Pontus could be himself again, it would just have to be done.

As Mama worked, she prayed. If faith could remove mountains, it could certainly remove Pontus's toothache. She just wasn't going to worry about it. God wouldn't let anything spoil this special day for Pelle.

There would be only the four of them for luncheon. The other children took their lunch to school during the week of examinations. But they would be bubbling over with questions when they came home. "Is she pretty, Mama?" That would be Greta. "What kind of dress did she wear?" That from Kerstin whose first thoughts right now centered around clothes. And Torkel and Calle would tease Pelle when he came home about being "an old married man."

A little before twelve, Mama gave the table a last critical glance, then went upstairs to change into company dress. She was pleased to find Pontus sleeping and didn't awaken him until she had finished dressing. The pain, he admitted, was greatly eased, and when Mama removed the pack, she was delighted to find that the swelling too was almost completely gone.

"You look fine, Pontus. But you better take these aspirin anyway, so you can enjoy your lunch. And as soon as Pelle and Felicia leave, I think you should see Doctor Falk."

"Maria! Don't you realize that Doctor Falk wants to *remove all* my teeth?"

"I know, dear. And I'm sorry it is necessary. But we haven't time to talk about it now. The children will be here any moment. Just get dressed and put on your best smile."

Mama's faith, and the good work of the oatmeal pack and aspirin, truly performed miracles. Papa came downstairs smiling, and a few minutes later Pelle opened the front door. The pride in his eyes as he introduced Felicia was all that Mama needed. But added to that, she saw at once that Papa, true to Pelle's prediction, was very much taken with Felicia. Which wasn't surprising. For Felicia might well have posed for the picture of the angel which had been Mama's model for her children. Her golden curls encircled her composed and perfect little face like a halo, and, when she smiled, it seemed to light the whole room. But the twinkle in her eyes was not quite so angelic. She will be good for Pelle, Mama thought. She is full of fun and Pelle is sometimes too serious. And it was plain to see she adored him.

"Thank you, God, for giving Pelle so much happiness," Mama whispered under her breath. Then aloud she said, "Luncheon is ready, children. I know you have to hurry back to your examinations."

"Only one more exam, Mama. Felicia and I both finish up this afternoon. Then we have ten whole days to ourselves."

The luncheon was a great success. Papa was like his old self, and Mama couldn't remember when he had been so witty. The parsonage sang with their laughter. Afterwards, she served coffee in the living room, while Felicia and Pelle entertained them with stories of college life.

When the door closed behind them, Papa was first to speak. "A fine girl, Maria. She will be a good wife for Pelle."

"I'm so happy for them, Pontus. Pelle deserves the very best."

But already Papa had other things on his mind. "I've

been thinking about my teeth, Maria. I just can't let Doctor Falk take them all out. How could I ever face people? How could I *preach* without teeth?"

Mama laughed. despite the stricken look in his face. "Oh, Pontus! You wouldn't be without teeth. You'd have false ones. But of course Doctor Falk is only *one* dentist. He could be wrong. Maybe you should go to another one just to be sure."

Papa's face lit up. "You're right, Maria. Just because Doctor Falk happens to be a member of my church doesn't mean he couldn't make a mistake. I'll talk to Doctor Ruggles, that new painless dentist around the corner."

He set out immediately, and Mama started clearing away the lunch dishes.

Papa had scarcely left the house when the telephone rang. Why is it, thought Mama, a minister could be in all morning and the telephone wouldn't ring, and the moment he left the house everyone seemed to need him at the same time.

"Hello!" answered Mama. "Oh, yes, Mrs. Rydberg. . . . No, I'm sorry he isn't here. . . . No, I'm afraid he won't be back for several hours. Can I help? Well, call me if I can. I'll tell Mr. Franzon you called as soon as he returns."

She hung up and went back to the kitchen. Ten minutes later the telephone rang again. This time it was Mrs. Johnson, and she was in a state.

"Please calm yourself, Mrs. Johnson. Mr. Franzon is not at home this afternoon. . . . Well, that's no reason to be so upset. Girls of fourteen will get into mischief sometimes. No, whipping her wouldn't solve anything. . . . Well. if I can help of course I'll come over."

Of all the days for Papa to be at the dentist's office!

Mama left the dishes in the sink and departed for Mrs. Johnson's. She found the mother pacing the floor and young Sally in tears. The air was electric with the conflict between them. Mama did not know how Papa would handle a situation like this, but she talked quietly with both of them, then they all knelt in prayer, asking God's help and guidance. When an hour later Mama departed, peace had been restored to the Johnson household.

How very little people knew, thought Mama, about a minister's day. Everyone's troubles were his, and it seemed never to occur to them that he might have serious problems of his own. Like today. She wondered what Doctor Ruggles had had to say about Papa's teeth? She did hope he wouldn't have to have them all pulled. Papa was so proud of his even white teeth, and he hated falseness of any kind, even in teeth. It would be hard for him to accept them. She hoped with all her heart that Doctor Ruggles would find some other way to remedy the matter.

There was much to do when she got home. Soon the children would be home from school, and there was still all those dishes to wash. But Mama was so happy, nothing could disturb her for very long. She hummed under her breath as she worked, thinking how beautiful Felicia was, and what a wonderful couple she and Pelle would make. Both of them were natural students. Pelle just couldn't get enough knowledge, it seemed; he drank it like fresh milk and looked for more. And from her talk with Felicia today, she felt the same way about education.

Mama's humming stopped and a shadow crossed her face. Soon—too soon—the children would all be grown and she and Pontus would be left alone in the parsonage. It just didn't seem possible that Kerstin, the baby, was now thirteen. Torkel would probably be the next to go. He had been spending a lot of time the past year at the Joneses' farm, for Ellen had changed from a giggly, almost skinny child, to a slender beauty. Greta had all her dates with Gunnar Olson, and Mama was afraid there would be no college for her either. Only Calle seemed to prefer sports to girls. Nim, of course, was far too interested in medicine to let anything interfere, least of all girls.

With the dishes done and the kitchen tidied, Mama

went into the living room to relax a while before she
started supper. She had scarcely sat down before Pontus
burst into the house as if pursued.

"Pontus! What in the world?"

But Papa could not speak. He could only point to his
jaw.

"What did Doctor Ruggles say, Pontus?"

For answer, Papa took the handkerchief from his jaw
and opened his mouth. All his teeth were gone.

"Oh, Pontus *lilla!*" She was more shocked than she
dared let him know. He looked terrible—not like Papa at
all, but an old man.

Papa had found his voice, though it didn't sound much
like his. It was thick and indistinct. "That horrible man!
Before I knew what he was doing, he gave me gas, and
when I came to, he had *pulled all* of them."

Mama was the speechless one now. But as she became
aware of the full irony of the situation, she wanted to
laugh outright. Papa, hoping to save some of his teeth, had
lost all of them. And in spite of the pain she knew he must
be suffering, he looked so funny. A sudden thought
sobered her. How could Papa preach with no teeth? Already it was Tuesday. The dentist couldn't get new teeth
made and fitted by Sunday, and even if he could, Papa
would have to get used to them before he dared face a
congregation. Mama began to wish she hadn't mentioned
Doctor Ruggles; that they had listened to Doctor Falk
who would not have removed all the teeth at once. Her
regrets were swept away by another disturbing thought.

"Pontus! What will Doctor Falk say?"

Neither of them had thought of that. Falk was one of
the largest contributors to the church, and Pontus had
sought his advice, then deliberately gone to another
dentist, a newcomer and not even a member of the church.
At least that is the way it would look to Doctor Falk.

Papa forgot his pain for a moment. "But I didn't ask
Doctor Ruggles to remove my teeth, Maria. I just wanted
to be *sure* before I let Doctor Falk do it."

"I know that, Pontus. And I think Doctor Falk will understand if you just tell him the truth. And besides, *he* will have to make the false teeth for you."

"False teeth! Oh, Maria, I forgot about them. How can I preach with store teeth?"

"You just have to get used to them, Pontus *lilla*. And the sooner you see Doctor Falk, the more time he will have to make them before Sunday. Do you feel like going now? If he can't have the permanent teeth ready by Sunday, I'm sure he can fix up something temporary."

Papa set out at once. Mama hadn't mentioned the telephone calls to him. Surely this was one time a minister had the right to think of himself first. And when Papa returned an hour later, he was quite cheerful. Doctor Falk had not been hurt, he had just laughed at the forceful methods of the new Doctor Ruggles, and suggested it might be well if he acquired some of them himself. He had given Papa a sedative to ease the pain when it got severe and had promised to fit him with temporary teeth in time for Sunday's sermon. The permanent teeth would take longer to make, but he assured Papa no one would be able to tell them from his own and, when he got used to them, even Papa wouldn't know the difference.

"That's wonderful, Pontus. And no more aching teeth ever again."

Saturday morning Papa went to Doctor Falk for the temporary teeth. When he returned, Mama was surprised at how natural they looked, and Papa was so pleased he could even joke about the ordeal.

"You know, Maria, I believe Doctor Falk collects teeth as a hobby. He told me Scandinavians' teeth have the longest roots of all. I told him that was because we eat so much cinnamon rusk and——"

"And what?" asked Mama.

But Papa did not answer. He couldn't. His jaws were locked as if a clamp had been placed on them.

There was nothing to do but wait for Nim, who was arriving that afternoon from Boston. Papa was in the study when Nim arrived. Quickly Mama told him what had happened, then followed Nim into the study. To her surprise, Nim walked over to Papa and struck him under the chin. What a terrible thing for Nim to do. But she felt differently about it a moment later when Papa could talk.

"You better take it easy, Papa," cautioned Nim. "With false teeth you have to use your mouth the right way. And above all, don't get excited or tense, or it will happen again."

For the rest of the day, Papa could be heard practicing his sermon, carefully speaking each word. Each time he paused, Mama held her breath for fear his jaws were locked again; then breathed easily once more as his voice rose in measured tones.

On Sunday morning, under the circumstances, Mama did not expect Papa to serve her the customary coffee-in-bed. She was up early and prepared a special breakfast for Papa, and carried it upstairs. But Papa was full of gloom. The new teeth, despite the sedative Doctor Falk had given him, were hurting. And when he tried to tell her about it, his jaws stuck again. The blow he struck himself this time seemed to Mama a little more forceful than necessary. But his jaws unlocked. Nevertheless, he refused to eat for fear it would happen again, and only drank his coffee. He dressed, went down to the study, and presently Mama could hear him practicing his sermon. Poor Papa! He was so worried. And Mama was worried too, for as Nim had said, tension was the worst thing for Papa now.

Papa left early for the church. He needed time, Mama concluded, to compose himself. Nevertheless she was uneasy. She would be glad when this morning was over, and for the first time in her life she prayed that the attendance would be small. Which seemed likely, for the skies were heavily overcast, threatening rain or snow any moment.

As she set out for the church, Mama forgot her fears momentarily, in her happiness at having both Nim and

Pelle at home. The Franzon pew would be filled this morning, even if many of the other church members decided to remain at home.

Her hope for a small attendance was soon dashed. The church was quite filled when she and the children arrived, and people continued to come in even after the singing had started. By the time Papa rose to deliver his sermon, there wasn't an empty pew in the church.

How handsome Papa looked! So tall and stately and especially dignified now that his hair was completely white. As his eyes met hers she smiled back, encouraging him not to be afraid; that all would be well. Slowly Papa opened the big Bible and began to read from the seventy-eighth psalm, in a clear, steady voice:

> "Give ears, O my people, to my law: Incline your
> ears to the words of my mouth. I will open my
> mouth in a parable: . . ."

But Papa could no longer open his mouth.

Mama looked helplessly at Nim. Could he go up and strike Papa under the chin before his whole congregation? And what would people think if Papa suddenly struck himself? There was a stir of surprise throughout the church. Then she realized Pelle was on his feet and hurrying down the aisle to the pulpit. Was he going to strike Papa?

Instead, he smilingly motioned to Papa to sit down and, without further hesitation, opened the Bible to the third chapter of Ecclesiastes, and read:

> "To every thing there is a season, and a time
> to every purpose under the heaven: A time to
> be born, and a time to die; a time to plant,
> and a time to pluck up that which is planted. . . .
> A time to weep, and a time to laugh; a time to

mourn and a time to dance. . . .
A time to get, and a time to lose; a time to
keep, a time to cast away. . . .
A time to rend, and a time to sew; a time to
keep silence, and a time to speak. . . ."

As he closed the Bible, his voice rose clearly. "Today
is my father's time to keep silence. But in his zeal to do his
duty, his courage has exceeded his strength. With your
permission, I shall attempt, in my small way, to take my
father's place in his pulpit this morning. I freely confess
this is my first sermon. I have no notes, nor have I prepared a sermon. But I have asked God to fill my mouth
with His words."

Mama sat spellbound. And so did the congregation. For
Pelle was preaching with the same easy flow of words,
the same "silver tongue" which Papa possessed. And Papa
sat in silence, his head tilted a little to the back rest of the
high-backed straight chair, but there was a faint smile
about his lips, and Mama thought she had never seen such
a glow in his eyes. It was not difficult to follow his
thoughts. His son was preaching from *his* pulpit! At last
one of his children had received the call. No longer need
he worry about laying down his mantle when the time
came, for Pelle would take up his work—be his voice—
his mind; or, God willing, be given a greater gift than
he himself had possessed.

Presently Mama realized Pelle had stopped speaking.
For a moment a stillness lay over the congregation, almost
a holy hush. Then the rustling of hymnbooks as they
began the closing hymn.

"And now," said Pelle, when the hymn was finished,
"Pastor Franzon will speak the benediction."

Mama was stunned. Had Pelle forgotten that Papa could
not speak? She held her breath as Papa rose and stood
once more before his congregation. He raised his hand,
and the congregation stood and bowed their heads. Papa's

voice, as he spoke the familiar words, seemed to have a new strength with a deeper significance.

Later, Pelle stood beside Papa at the door to greet the members. Mama's heart was ready to burst with pride, listening to the warm praises heaped upon Pelle. And the way Papa was beaming at each member told her he was so proud of Pelle he had forgotten all about his false teeth.

The parsonage was a busy place during the next week. Nim had been able to stay the entire week end and, because he so rarely could be at home for more than a few hours at a time, the interest centered about him. Pelle and Felicia, their examinations finished, were making the most of their vacation, and plans for the "big day" in June. It was a very happy time for Mama even if there was more work than usual. It was such a joy to prepare special food for the children, things they could not get away from home, so the house was constantly filled with delicious and tempting cooking odors.

Strangely enough, after the events on Sunday morning, the temporary teeth had never locked again. It seemed to Mama that somewhere in all this the hand of the Lord was evident. Just where she didn't quite know.

Then, on Saturday evening, she had the answer.

Pelle was taking Felicia to a concert. He came downstairs after supper dressed in his best blue suit, and there was a glow about him which, at first, Mama attributed to the prospects of another evening with Felicia.

"Is Papa in the study, Mama?" he asked, and she knew there was something special on his mind.

"Yes, dear. He's working on his sermon. Why?"

"Do you think he would mind if I interrupted him? There is something I want to tell you both."

"If it's that important, I'm sure he won't mind."

Mama knocked on the study door, and in a moment Papa opened it.

"Pelle has something to tell us, Pontus," Mama explained when they were seated.

Papa looked at him apprehensively. "You and Felicia haven't changed your minds about getting married, have you?"

"Not exactly, Papa."

"That's a strange answer, Pelle," exclaimed Mama.

"Well, I guess what I have to say is so important I just don't know how to say it. And a minister shouldn't be at loss for words."

"A minister?" questioned Mama and Papa at once.

"Yes. You see ever since last Sunday, when Papa lost his voice and something inside me seemed to tell me to go and preach for him, everything has been different. I had thought my calling was teaching. I guess it is, in a sense. For now I know that the voice I heard last Sunday was not my imagination, but the voice of God, calling me to His work."

The stillness in the room, when he paused for a moment, was again that holy hush, such as had filled the church last Sunday morning.

Then Mama was out of her chair and had her arms around Pelle. "Oh, Pelle, I'm so glad—so happy!"

Papa got up and put both hands on Pelle's shoulders. "I'm proud of you, son. There is no higher calling than to the Lord's work," he said, his voice husky with emotion. "I *hoped* you would realize you had received that call. Now I am happy, indeed."

"Have you told Felicia?" asked Mama.

"Oh, of course. She thinks it is wonderful, too. It doesn't change our plans for marriage. Instead of continuing my studies at Harvard, I'll enter the Theological Seminary."

Pelle, thought Mama, had always been a joy to her, but never a more blessed joy than at this moment. Now that joy would be given to the world, through Pelle's sermons. Only once before had she been so happy, and that was the long ago morning in Lapland when Tant Renberg had placed her first-born son in her arms. And somehow she knew there was a connection between those two high moments—one that blended into almost unbearable happiness. For today a son had been born into the Kingdom of God.

Hours later, when even the house seemed to be sleeping, Mama lay awake, thinking of all that had happened to her family in a few days. Beyond the open window, the snowflakes drifted slowly to earth, spreading a fleecy blanket over the housetops and casting a white soft glow upon the world. How wondrous, she thought, were the ways of the Lord! For what had seemed a tragedy, only a few days ago, had indeed prepared the way for a miracle.

Suddenly the night seemed filled with a thousand singing angel voices.

Glory to God in the Highest, and on earth, peace and good will.

CHAPTER 15

✣ Nim Finds His Scissors

Late June sunshine flooded the parsonage kitchen. Much as she liked working in a sunny kitchen, it was a little too much for Mama this morning. It wasn't yet ten o'clock, and already it was as hot as a midsummer day. She pulled the shade halfway down and set the big mixing bowl on the table beside the flour and spices, thinking it might be better to put off the baking until Saturday after all. This hot spell couldn't last. It was too early for so much heat. But Nim just might be home this week end, and she wanted to have his favorite coffee bread and cookies ready. Sometimes she wished he would let her know when he was coming home, but Nim was like that —just walking in without warning. And Mama had to admit she liked being surprised. Besides, she guessed he was so busy finishing up the school term, he didn't have time to write, even if it occurred to him.

The quick sharp sound of the postman's whistle shrilled through the house. Mama dusted the flour from her hands and hurried to the door. The mailbox bulged, and when she pulled the mail from the box, Nim's letter fell to the porch. She tossed the rest of the mail on the hall table and sat down, opening the letter eagerly. She did hope he wasn't going to stay on for special work or something.

It was so unusual to hear from him when he was expected home.

Before she had finished the first sentence Mama's heart was pounding with excitement. Nim was arriving Friday afternoon—and he was bringing a girl!

Nim's homecoming each summer was always enough to set the parsonage buzzing, but this news made it a doubly special event. She remembered that Nim had mentioned the girl, Karin Peterson, a few times, but she hadn't paid much attention then for she knew how little time he had for romance. Now she began to piece together the bits of information she had heard, and they really added up to very little. Karin was a teacher in one of the Berkley Hills grade schools, and her family lived in Blue Falls, a small town in the foothills of the White Mountains, where the girl spent her summer vacations. She recalled that Nim had driven up to the mountains last summer, but she had thought he was visiting the Davises. Now she wondered.

Well, she finally decided, she just wasn't going to worry about it. She had enough to do before they arrived and only two days in which to do it.

She returned to the kitchen and set about her baking in spite of the heat. She was taking a pan of *kringlor* out of the oven when Torkel came in. She hadn't realized it was so late. Papa would be back soon too, and she hadn't given one thought to fixing lunch. As she spread the kitchen table, she told Torkel the news.

Torkel took a big bite of a *kringla* before he spoke. "She must be *very* special," he remarked eagerly. "It just isn't like Nim to be interested in *girls*."

"Any girl a boy's in love with is special, Torkel," laughed Mama. "You'll find that out some day."

Torkel grunted. "Not me, Mama."

"And where have I heard that remark before, I wonder?" chuckled Mama. "Seems to me Button said that too—and what happened?"

"Girls never know what they want," deprecated Torkel.

Mama didn't reply, but she was remembering how adamant Button had been two years ago about a career, until a certain spring night when she had come in from a date with Eric, the same kind of stars in her eyes Mama had seen in Vickey's the year before. And at once Mama had started work on another wedding dress which this time Button *would* wear. After that there had been no more talk of a career. Only of Eric and the wedding and the "simply adorable little cottage" Eric had built for her on a tree-shaded street a few blocks from the parsonage. Yes, love certainly changed things.

But when Papa heard the news about Nim, he was even more disturbed than Torkel.

"Marriage seems to be catching in this family," he remarked gloomily.

"Now, Pontus *lilla*," Mama laughed, "don't you go jumping at conclusions. Just because Nim is bringing a girl home with him for the week end doesn't *have* to mean he is planning to marry her."

"Anyone but Nim, no. But if Nim is interested enough in a girl to introduce her to the family, he is serious about her. How can he support a wife, Maria, and keep up his studies?"

He dropped into a chair beside the kitchen table and mopped the perspiration from his brow. The breeze billowing the kitchen curtains was hot, but it was a breeze. Mama brought a glass of iced tea and a plate of freshly baked *klenetter* before she answered.

"No sense in borrowing trouble, Pontus. We don't *know* that Nim intends to try to support a wife and continue his studies. Lots of young people have long engagements."

Papa sipped his tea in silence. Mama knew he was still disturbed. It wasn't just that so many weddings were making a big hole in his bank account; but he had wanted his first-born to be a minister and it had taken him a long time to become reconciled to Nim's being a doctor. Now the very thought of his taking on responsibility which might prevent his finishing *that* career filled Papa with alarm. Mama had to admit she was a little concerned herself. She certainly wanted Nim to finish his education and be a fine doctor, but she also wanted him to be happy. It was right for a young man to fall in love, and of course she wanted Nim to marry someday and have children. She just hoped if Nim were in love with Karin Peterson, she was the right girl; and if she was, Mama would simply have to convince Papa.

Karin Peterson was a strikingly beautiful girl, with dark curls and mischievous eyes and a manner and smile so warm and vivacious that she walked right into your heart.

"Now do you see why I am concerned, Maria?" asked Papa as soon as Karin had been shown upstairs to her room. "She is far too beautiful to be sensible. Nim is just swept off his feet by her looks."

"Oh, Pontus! The child can't help it if she is beautiful. How do you know she isn't sensible?"

But Papa insisted "lightning didn't strike twice in the same place"; and the fact that Mama had been a beautiful girl and was still beautiful as well as practical didn't mean you could expect that to happen twice in the same family. He was completely convinced that now he not only would have to dig deeper into his bank account to help Nim with his education, but to support a beautiful and frivolous wife as well.

For a few days it looked as though Papa might have a point. Mama liked Karin immediately, but the girl did seem to be almost too gay, too carefree. And whether she wore sports clothes, a housedress or her Sunday best, there was no denying it, she was a picture. It was true, Mama reflected, the devil sometimes worked best through a beautiful face and figure. She certainly didn't want Nim caught in any trap.

Despite the trepidation of the whole family, the week

end passed smoothly and happily. Already, thought Mama, as she prepared breakfast Sunday morning, Karin seemed like one of the family. That afternoon Mama packed a huge picnic basket and they all set out for the farm. Even Papa and Torkel now seemed reconciled to Karin, and Mama had never seen Nim so happy and relaxed. Every time he so much as glanced at Karin his heart was in his eyes. Mama wanted to be happy with him, but she couldn't help wondering how being in love was going to affect his studies. It would break Papa's heart if Nim decided to get married now. Then she reminded herself that he had said nothing about marriage, and she felt a little guilty. Here she was jumping at conclusions just as she had criticized Papa and Torkel for doing. There was nothing wrong with a young man's liking the company of a pretty girl. She was not being fair to Karin, or Nim. If he *was* serious about Karin, he couldn't have picked a finer girl.

When they returned to the parsonage late Sunday evening, Papa's fears about Karin seemed completely forgotten. And Karin further confirmed his new attitude about her, when Nim asked Papa for the car to drive her to Blue Falls.

"But, Nim," she protested, "you'll have the long drive back alone. That doesn't make sense. Of course I'd love being with you, but driving back at night alone wouldn't be much fun for you."

"Don't you think it would be worth it to have a few more hours with you?"

Karin wrinkled her nose at him, but remained unconvinced. "Just the same, Nim, it isn't sensible. I'll take the train—but I *will* permit you to drive me to the station."

Nim had to agree. Karin said her farewells, hugged Mama affectionately and followed Nim to the car. As they drove away Mama thought for the second time in two days that love certainly changed things.

With Karin's departure, life at the parsonage settled into its summer routine. That is, it seemed to. Pelle and Felicia drove home for a week end. Both of them were holding two jobs this summer, and for the first time Pelle had to think of his own "tin box" and years of study ahead at the seminary. Mama's heart ached a little. Pelle had always been so kind and now he was working too hard, but he was beaming with happiness. If there ever was a couple made for each other, it was Pelle and Felicia. Greta and Kerstin practically lived at the farm, and as soon as the church summer vacation began Mama and Papa drove up for week ends. Nim worked each summer as a camp councilor, but as his job wouldn't start until the second week in July, he had a little time for himself.

Mama assumed he would spend those few days catching up on his sleep and taking life easy. But she hadn't reckoned with Nim's energy. He was out of the house early every morning and didn't return until suppertime. And a few days later he announced that he wasn't taking the councilor job this summer. Doctor Davis had offered him a position as "helper."

"It will be almost like continuing my studies, Mama," Nim said enthusiastically. "Of course I can't actually tend patients until I have my degree, but I can observe and help Doctor Davis in so many ways. You know he isn't as young as he once was. I can take a big load off his shoulders."

Mama laughed. "You don't have to sell me on the idea, Nim. I think it is wonderful of Doctor Davis to hire you, and I'm sure Papa will feel the same way."

"Sure you don't mind having me under foot all summer?" teased Nim.

Mama thought how good it was to see him in such a light mood. He was always so serious. "I'll try to put up with you, young man."

It wasn't long before Mama began to see through Nim's strategy. Almost every week end he took the train or hitched a ride to Blue Falls. Or drove, if he could prevail upon Papa to lend him the car. He couldn't have been a camp councilor and still spent the week ends at Karin's home. This knowledge worried Mama a little. Already

Nim's decisions were being governed by his desire to be with Karin. He had two more years of medical school, then one year of interning, and four more after that to be on the Board of Surgeons. And only then could he set up his own practice. Would Karin—or any other girl for that matter—wait that long? *She* had waited to marry Pontus, but American girls were brought up differently. Marriage wasn't their only career. Karin had her position, and she must meet many young men who fell in love with her, beautiful and charming as she was. It all seemed to add up to possible heartbreak for Nim, and that Mama just couldn't let happen. But there was really nothing she could do, at least not until Nim confided in her. And again she chided herself for worrying. Wasn't God looking out for Nim and Karin?

Nim's smiling face every evening when he came home from his work with Doctor Davis reassured Mama. Nim's happy mood, she decided, was not entirely due to Karin; his job had a lot to do with it. And this conclusion seemed confirmed by Doctor Davis a week or so later when Mama ran into him on the street. She was especially surprised to see him, for it was midafternoon, a time most doctors were the busiest.

"It is good to see you, Doctor," Mama greeted him. "But I must say I'm surprised to see you on the street this time of day—and without your little black bag!"

"That, my dear Mrs. Franzon, is because I have the best helper a man could have." He laughed. "Most of my patients go away for the summer, but that doesn't mean a doctor can close his office. He has to be on hand, just in case."

"You mean you leave Nim in charge?"

"Not exactly. But I can get out and stretch my legs and get a breath of air. Nim takes care of things until I get back. Not that he couldn't take care of the patients themselves if he were permitted to. I'll tell you, Mrs. Franzon, that boy is a better doctor right now than I was when I hung out my first shingle."

Mama beamed proudly, but Doctor Davis went on talking.

"You and the pastor are mighty lucky people. What Mrs. Davis and I wouldn't give for just *one* child, and you have eight remarkable children. I don't mind telling you I've wished a hundred times that Nim were *our* son. Oh, I know it sounds selfish, and I don't mean I envy you two. I just don't understand why *we* couldn't have had a son like Nim to take over for me when I'm no longer able to practice."

"God's ways are often mysterious, Doctor Davis. Pontus and I are grateful for the blessings He has bestowed upon us in our children. But sometimes I do feel selfish, being so blessed, when others equally or more worthy are denied even one child." A note of sadness had come into Mama's voice, which Doctor Davis seemed to catch.

"Forgive me, Mrs. Franzon," he said. "I'm not complaining. God has been mighty good to us. I'm grateful to have Nim with me even for the summer. Now I'd better be getting along back to the office. Greet Pontus for me, and tell him those fish are still biting in the mountain lake!"

"I'll do that," laughed Mama.

What a fine man he is, she thought, as she watched him striding down the street, belying his sixty-five years. And how fortunate Nim was to have a chance to work with him.

A few nights later, Nim came home considerably later than usual. Mama was still up, with a basket of mending in her lap, and Papa was busy in his study. Mama looked up as the screen door closed and Nim came into the living room. One glance at him told her something had happened. He was so excited he looked as if he had swallowed a fuse.

"Nim! What is it?" she cried.

"The most wonderful thing, Mama! Is Papa still up? I want you both to hear about it."

"Well, he's working, but if it is that important, I guess we can interrupt him."

She knocked softly on the study door, then opened it. "Nim has something to tell us, Pontus. May we come in?"

"Of course. Of course." Then when both were seated, "Now what has happened, Nim? You look ready to burst."

"I better begin at the beginning," said Nim. "I guess you both know I'm very much in love with Karin and we want to be married as soon as possible. Until this afternoon I thought we'd have to wait years. Now we can be married at once."

"But what happened, Nim? You're not being very coherent," admonished Papa.

"Well, this afternoon after all the patients had left, Doctor Davis said he wanted to have a talk with me, and he offered me a *place with him* just as soon as I finish medical school and my year of interning."

"But I don't understand . . ." Mama began.

"Don't you see? It means Karin and I can get married right away. We don't have to wait even for me to finish school. Karin can continue teaching here in Berkley Hills and live with us in the parsonage until I finish school; then I will be interning at the hospital and we can be together, and as soon as I have finished that we can get a home of our own." He broke off, out of breath.

A heavy silence followed. Mama was as shocked and surprised by his suggestion as she knew Papa was. Young people, once married, should have a home of their own. It just never worked out right, living with the parents of either one. But, if Papa agreed she would not oppose him, and if Karin wanted to live at the parsonage she was certainly welcome.

Papa broke the silence. "I was under the impression, Nim, that you were studying to become a *surgeon*," he remarked solemnly. "You have five more years after you finish medical school. Do you expect Karin to live at the parsonage all those years?"

Nim's eyes dropped to his hands for a moment before he answered. "Well, no. You see I'm not going to be a surgeon."

When neither Mama nor Papa said anything, Nim rushed on:

"I figure good doctors are just as important as surgeons, and working with Doctor Davis I have a chance to become a really good doctor. If I do want to become a surgeon later on, I can do that after I've earned enough as a doctor to take care of Karin." He glanced anxiously from Mama to Papa as he talked.

"But Nim," interposed Mama, "you've wanted to be a surgeon since you were a little boy, cutting up everything in sight. You *can't* give it up now when you are so close to your goal."

"Close," exclaimed Nim, and Mama had never heard so much impatience in his voice. "Do you think seven years is close? It's *forever* when you've found the girl you want to marry. It just isn't fair to Karin to ask her to wait so long."

"Does Karin agree to your plans?" asked Papa quietly.

"She doesn't know them yet. How could she? Doctor Davis just told me this afternoon. But she will. I *know* she will. She is as anxious as I am to be married as soon as possible."

"Then I think you should consult Karin before reaching any decision," advised Papa. And Mama certainly agreed.

Nim lost no time in following Papa's suggestion. Karin was coming down for the week end. Mama refused to worry, although her heart was heavy over Nim's decision. She prayed and left the matter to the wisdom of God in His own time. She hadn't the slightest idea how Karin would react to Nim's proposal, but whatever developed she knew would be right.

When Nim came in Friday evening with Karin, Mama saw at once that Nim had told her about his plan, for both were quite solemn. But nothing was said until after

supper when the four of them were together in the
privacy of Papa's study.

"How do you feel about this, Karin?" Papa asked as
soon as he knew Nim had fully discussed the proposal
with her.

"Of course I love him very much, Pastor Franzon,"
Karin began. "But I think it is unfair to him to give up
the career he cherishes or have the responsibility of a
wife when he is so near his goal. It isn't that I'm afraid
of making sacrifices; marriage demands many sacrifices.
But I want our marriage to be a real marriage—one we
can build *together*. Somehow getting married and not
being together just doesn't seem like marriage."

She was sitting beside Nim as she talked, but her eyes
were on Papa. Now she slipped her arm around Nim's
shoulders and looked into his troubled face.

"Please understand, darling! I do want to marry you—
so very much. I'll wait forever if necessary. But I want
our marriage to be right all the way."

Nim said nothing for several seconds, then a reluctant
smile spread over his tense features. "All right, Karin.
But you won't have to wait forever—just two years."

"Darling, listen to me. I know how much you want to
be a surgeon. Why, you've talked about it ever since I
met you. You don't have to give it up for me. Don't you
know I'd wait ten years—or twenty—to make you happy.
It's *you* I want to marry, and only you."

"And marrying you right now would *make* me happy.
But if you won't do that, I certainly am not going to wait
seven years to call you my wife."

Karin looked at Mama and Papa, her eyes beginning to
twinkle. "You've a very stubborn man for a son," she
said, sighing deeply, "but I guess I love him anyway. All
right Nim, you win half the argument. I'll marry you
when you have finished medical school if that is what
you want. And, darling, I'll be *so* happy to be your wife."

What more was there to say? thought Mama as she
dipped coffee into the percolator a few minutes later.

After what they had all been through emotionally the past hour, they needed strong coffee and something to eat. But she couldn't help wondering what Papa felt about Karin now. That child certainly had both feet on the ground. She would make Nim a wonderful wife, and if Nim were going to give up being a surgeon for any reason, Karin was the best reason she could think of.

July melted into what promised to be a hotter August. Nim had been working late almost every night in spite of the heat, and had been spending his week ends in the mountains with Karin's family. He seemed completely happy about the grave decision he had reached, and Doctor Davis was equally pleased with the prospect of having him full time in a couple of years. Already he was saying, "When I retire and Nim takes over. . . ."

But as the humid days of August crept by, Mama noticed that Nim was looking a bit worn. At first she charged it to the heat, but gradually was forced to realize something was bothering him. He was unusually preoccupied, often not even hearing her when she spoke to him. But when she questioned him he insisted everything was fine; he loved his work and was happy. Mama tried to believe that, but her intuition told her differently. Watching him at times when he was unaware of her scrutiny, he seemed a man wrestling with inner torment. Had he begun to regret his decision? Had he quarreled with Karin? Whatever mental emotional battle was going on within him was beginning to show in his face. His cheeks were drawn and at times his eyes looked haunted. Mama's heart broke for him, but she could do nothing. She was sure now that all this stemmed from the conflict between his love for Karin and his desire to become a surgeon which had been part of him for so many years before he met her. She knew, too, that his sense of fairness and right would be sufficient to set up a battle with his conscience that would have destroyed the resolutions of a less determined man.

For two weeks Mama watched him in forced silence—
and prayed. This was something in which not even a
mother could help. Nim had to work it out for himself,
with God's help. And God would help him. She had no
doubt about that.

Papa always took the month of August for his vacation.
He planned this year, as always, to spend it on the farm
with the family; but Mama felt she had to stay in the
city and keep an eye on Nim. She did not like the way he
looked; if left to himself he might not eat regular meals,
and that to Mama was a serious crime. Papa did spend
the first week of August on the farm alone, but the second
week he was back in the parsonage again.

"If you won't go with me, Maria, I'll stay here, too,"
he informed Mama reluctantly. "If you insist on being
nursemaid to Nim, we'll just spend our vacation in the
parsonage garden."

Mama smiled, pleased that Papa did not like taking
second place with her, even for his oldest son. But toward
the middle of the month Doctor Davis telephoned Papa
with an invitation.

"Why don't you and Maria drive up with me to the
lake Friday night and plan to stay a couple of weeks?
Best fishing in the world, Pontus! And after the hot spell
we've been having, the cool mountain air will do you
both good."

Mama was reluctant to leave Nim to a bachelor life
for two whole weeks, but she knew Pontus wouldn't go
without her. She also knew that the prospect of mountains *and* fishing would be more than Papa could resist.
The oppressive heat had been like a heavy woollen blanket
for days. It *would* be good to breathe cool mountain air
once more.

Nim really settled the matter. He announced that evening that he had promised Steve to help with the crops
the last two weeks in August when Doctor Davis's office
was closed.

"So you have no excuse now, Mama. And anyway I'll

be spending the week ends at Karin's place. There will be no one for you to be home for."

"I suppose you are right, Nim, but——"

"No *buts* now. Tell you what, Mama. You go with Papa, and Karin and I will come up for the last week end and drive back with you."

Mama had to give in. "All right. Papa and I will drive up with Doctor Davis and you can bring the car to drive us back."

The Davises' summer home was a rustic lodge, high in the White Mountains. Mrs. Davis opened the place each year the first week in July and remained until the middle of September, and Doctor Davis drove up for week ends and his vacation the latter part of August.

Seeing it for the first time from the foot of the hillside, Mama thought it was like a brown rock which might break loose any moment and tumble down into the valley. But as the car moved slowly up the hill, she saw that it was a rambling structure of cedar logs, sheltered by great pines and elms which cast cooling shadows over the long front porch. Beyond the lodge, wide green lawns sloped down to a natural swimming pool fed by little mountain streams and warmed by the summer sun. And a mile or so away, the mountain itself, towering against the sky like a brooding giant, was reflected in the quiet silvery waters of the lake which lay at its feet. Here, according to Doctor Davis, "ran the best trout in the whole wide world."

Inside, she was amazed at the spaciousness. A huge fireplace stretched across one end of the big two-storeyed living room. At the other end a wide stairway led to a balcony, off which were several bedrooms.

"It's a wonderful place, Agnes," Mama exclaimed. "I can see why Doc enjoys the week ends so much."

"I don't know what we would do without this place in the summer. We both feel the city heat terribly. This lodge has been our sanctuary."

It had been years since Mama had had a real vacation

or had been away from the children so long a time at once. But after the first few days she began to relax and enjoy "being company." It was especially good to see Pontus so contented and happy. With the hills and his beloved fishing, it was the next best thing to being back in Lapland.

Nim and Karin arrived midafternoon the second Friday, as planned—an event for which Mama and Mrs. Davis had been busily preparing for days.

"Smells just like the parsonage on baking day," said Nim, sniffing hungrily as he came into the big kitchen with Karin. "Ummmm, hot coffee bread."

"And coffee to go with it," laughed Mrs. Davis, setting the cups and saucers on the table. "You children go on upstairs and freshen up. Take the two rooms at the east of the balcony. We'll have coffee on the front porch when you are ready."

She was pouring the coffee a few minutes later when Papa and Doctor Davis appeared around the corner of the lodge each with a string of perch.

"No *plättar* for supper tonight," whooped Nim. "That's some catch!"

"What do you mean, no *plättar*, Nim?" asked Karin.

And with much laughter, Nim told the family joke about Papa and his no-catch fishing.

After supper that evening—a delicious supper of perch with Mama's special Swedish sauce, and vegetables from Mrs. Davis's garden patch—plans were discussed for the week end's activities.

"The rest of you can make your own plans," Doctor Davis interjected. "As for me, I'm going to show Preacher Franzon I'm a better fisherman than he is."

"Don't forget," warned Nim, "Papa's prayers are pretty powerful. Remember Farmer Jones's potatoes, Papa?"

Mama told *that* story, to Papa's embarrassment. When the general laughter had died down so she could make herself heard, Mrs. Davis said, "Then I suppose you two are not interested in our picnic of fried chicken, home-made ice cream and apple pie? Just fishing!"

"Well . . ." demurred Doctor Davis. "When are you planning to *have* this picnic?"

"Saturday afternoon. But never mind. Maria, Karin, Nim and I will enjoy it. I wouldn't *think* of asking you to delay your fishing trip."

"Oh, that won't be necessary. We'll join you at the picnic and *then* go fishing. All right with you, Pontus?"

"With homemade ice cream and apple pie on the menu? I should say so."

Everyone was up early the next morning. By eleven o'clock the chicken was fried and the pies baked. Nim and Karin had been given the job of turning the old-fashioned ice-cream freezer. No ice cream could compare with what came out of an old-fashioned freezer, Mrs. Davis contended. Mama's homemade rolls, big bowls of potato salad, coleslaw and pickles completed the lunch.

The spot they had selected for the picnic was near the lake, where later Papa and Doctor Davis would fish. Nim and Karin took their bathing suits to have a dip in the lake before lunch.

When the last piece of chicken had been eaten and everyone swore he never wanted to see food again, Papa and Doctor Davis set off along the lake front for their favorite fishing spot—"away from the women."

"How about a little mountain climbing, Karin?" asked Nim, "to work off that full feeling?"

"Just what the doctor ordered. Want to come along, you two?"

"Not me," said Mrs. Davis hurriedly. "I couldn't take a step, let alone climb a mountain. I'm going to stretch out here on this robe and take a nap."

"How about you, Mama?" asked Nim.

"Please come, Mama Franzon," pleaded Karin. "I want to show you *our* mountains."

Mama hesitated, but Karin looked so crestfallen, she

finally agreed to go along. The three of them started out along the mountain path which, at first glance, seemed to go straight up, but strangely leveled off as they walked.

"Isn't it the strangest thing?" laughed Karin. "It *looks* too steep for anyone to climb, but somehow you never get to the steep part."

Karin linked her arm in Mama's and, with Nim on the other side, they pressed upward along the narrow trail.

"The view I want you to see is just around the next bend, Mama Franzon. Think you can make it?"

"Karin thinks there are no mountains in the world like the White Mountains," laughed Nim, breathing heavily himself despite his ruggedness.

Mama wanted to boast about the mountains around Lapland, but she was too short of breath to talk. And she was glad she hadn't talked when they reached the turn in the path and the view Karin had been so enthusiastic about burst full upon them. Mama caught her breath sharply. For a moment a sudden wave of homesickness swept through her. She took a deep breath of the cool mountain air.

"Oh, Karin, it *is* just as beautiful as you said it was."

"As beautiful as Lapland?" teased Karin.

"Well . . . I guess to us Franzons no place is quite as beautiful as Lapland. But I got to admit, Karin, it almost takes your breath away. I do love your mountains."

"You see! You see! Your mother admits our mountains are as beautiful as Lapland."

Nim caught her hands and pulled her to him. "All right, young lady. Just for that I'm going to take you to Lapland one of these days and make you eat your words. And when you see the miracle of the midnight sun from the top of Gellivara mountains, you will know what I mean."

Karin pretended to make a face at him, then drew herself up in mock dignity. "Well, of course I can't show you the midnight sun from the top of *our* mountains," she said, her eyes beginning to dance with mischief, "but how do you know what *other* miracles might happen? Especially to us?"

"Only one way to find out," challenged Nim. "We'll climb to the top."

Mama's eyes followed theirs along the narrow mountain trail which seemed endless. But if Nim thought to dampen Karin's enthusiasm, he had been mistaken. "I'm ready, Doctor Franzon," she said firmly, but the mischief was still in her eyes.

"I'll wait here," Mama hurried to say. "It's so beautiful and peaceful, I'd just like to sit on this mossy rock in the shade and enjoy the view."

Karin came over to her. "You sure you don't mind waiting here alone? It *is* a pretty steep climb, I'm afraid."

Mama smiled inwardly, understanding how much Karin wanted to be alone with Nim. "Of course not, Karin. You two just go along and don't worry about me. I'm going to sit here and dream about Lapland."

Mama watched them go, arm in arm, Karin measuring her steps to Nim's. Her own heartbeat quickened just seeing their happiness. How lucky Nim was to have fallen in love with Karin! She was sweet and gentle and fine—and so very beautiful. She would make Nim a wonderful wife. If only he didn't have to give up being a surgeon to marry her. She knew how difficult it was for a girl to wait years for the one man she loved, and she couldn't blame Nim for feeling it wasn't fair to Karin to ask her to wait that long. But the more she saw of Karin and came to know her, the surer Mama was that she was made of stern fiber and equal to any demands that might be made upon her—even sacrifices.

She tried to put herself in Nim's place and see his side of things, fairly and honestly. When he was with Karin, the restlessness, which seemed to possess him at other times, vanished, and he was like a different man. The hollows were still in his cheeks, and he looked tired, but there was laughter in his eyes and his whole manner was relaxed. If being separated from Karin affected him as it seemed to, perhaps it was God's will that Nim make the decision he had made. She had so wanted him to be a surgeon and she knew how deeply Pontus also wanted that now. But if God wanted Nim to be just a fine doctor, it certainly wasn't right to question His ways.

Mama dismissed her serious thoughts, chiding herself for being so gloomy on such a beautiful day, and especially when before her lay God's beautiful mountains and valleys. She should be "lifting up her eyes" to those hills instead of worrying about Nim and Karin. Life too had its hills, but somehow those hills also leveled off when you reached them, just as the road had done today as they climbed. She let her gaze reach out to the distant hills, now mantled with a silver-blue haze, and realized suddenly that the afternoon was waning. She glanced at her wrist watch and was surprised to find she had been sitting here dreaming for more than an hour. Karin and Nim should have been back by this time. But she must not be annoyed or worried. It was a beautiful day and they were so much in love. Time meant nothing to them. But Mrs. Davis was alone, unless Papa and Doctor Davis had returned from fishing, and it wasn't very considerate leaving her this long. Besides, they should be starting back to the lodge soon.

She looked upward along the trail, and suddenly Karin, alone, rounded the bend and ran toward her, weeping.

Something had happened to Nim! "Dear God, no," prayed Mama.

Karin stumbled toward her, blinded by her tears. "Come quickly, Mama Franzon. Something terrible has happened."

"What is it, Karin? Is Nim hurt?"

"Not Nim. But a man is badly hurt. His foot is caught between two boulders. He's still conscious, but he is in terrible pain. He's been there since yesterday praying help would come, he says. Nim was able to move the rocks and get his leg free, but it is awfully crushed. Nim says he must be gotten to the hospital at once."

Mama was on her feet, her arm around Karin. "Don't cry, child. We'll do the best we can. But how can we get him down the mountains by ourselves? Hadn't I better bring Papa and Doc?"

"I don't know, Mama Franzon. Nim says there is no time to lose if the man's life is to be saved. He's making a stretcher of branches and thinks the three of us can carry him."

"All right, Karin." Mama had thought the climb was too steep for her earlier, but now, with the renewed strength of emergency, she kept up with Karin. When they reached the spot where Nim waited with the half-conscious man and Mama saw the seriousness of the accident, it was difficult to keep from fainting. Nim had fashioned a stretcher of crossed branches and had lifted the suffering man onto it. Slowly and prayerfully they made their way down the mountain to the lake.

"If only Doctor Davis and Papa are there," panted Nim.

And fortunately they were. Their jokes about the day's fishing broke off abruptly as the grim procession reached the camp. Doctor Davis agreed with Nim that there was no time to lose getting the man to a hospital. There was little he could do, for it was pretty obvious amputation was the only way to save the man's life, *if* it could still be saved.

At the lodge, Doctor Davis stopped the car only long enough to let the women out, then started for the nearest hospital some fifteen miles away.

On the porch of the lodge there was silence. Karin stood looking out across the hills. Occasionally a dry sob broke from her, but she did not cry. Poor child! She was having her first taste of what it meant to be a doctor's wife. The anxious hours of waiting when a life depended upon the skill of the doctor; and the agony of spirit that doctor, her husband, must endure when the patient did not live. A wife could be aware of this agony, but power-less to ease it.

"Why don't you lie down for a while, Karin," Mama suggested. "All this has been a terrible shock for you. But there is nothing we can do now except wait until they return. It may be hours."

"That's right, Karin," said Mrs. Davis. "You lie down and I'll fix some hot coffee."

"I'll be all right. I'm sorry to act this way. But if you could have seen the suffering in that poor man's face when we found him. Oh, I'll never forget it."

Mama took her arm gently and led her to a chair. "Try to, dear. It does no good to remember things like that. You'll feel better after a cup of coffee."

It was almost midnight when the men finally returned. The injured man would live, but amputation had been necessary. They had stayed at the hospital long enough to know he was out of danger.

"You did all you could do, dear," Mrs. Davis consoled her husband.

"That's just it, Agnes. *All* I could do was too little—so inadequate."

"Now don't blame yourself. Just be thankful Karin and Nim found the man when they did. Come! Drink this hot coffee and try to eat something. You all look exhausted."

Whatever plans had been made for Sunday seemed to hold no interest the next morning. Mama knew that Nim was trying to rise above the experience as a soon-to-be practicing doctor should; to accept it as part of a doctor's life. But it was obvious he had been deeply affected by the tragedy. He would smile when Mama attempted a light remark to pull him out of his morbid thoughts, but the haunted look was back in his eyes almost before the smile had left his lips. Her heart ached for him, but there was nothing she could say or do.

As soon as seemed feasible after breakfast, Doctor Davis telephoned the hospital. The man was doing fine; he would probably have a good deal of pain when the anesthetic wore off, but that was to be expected. He was out of danger and was able to talk.

"How did it happen?" asked Doctor Davis. "Did you find out who he is?"

The hospital doctor explained that the man was a summer resident from Boston. He had started to climb to the top of the mountain, but had noticed a small cave off the main trail and decided to explore it. A rock near the entrance had slipped, starting a minor cave-in, in which he had been caught. He had called for help until he became unconscious. He had just revived when Nim and Karin passed on the trail, and his cries had attracted their attention.

"He would like to see the young man who found him," concluded the hospital doctor. "Do you think he would mind coming in?"

Doctor Davis assured him Nim would be very glad to drive over during the day. And immediately after lunch, Karin and Nim left for the hospital.

"Don't stay too long, Nim," advised Mama. "Papa wants to get an early start back this afternoon to avoid the heavy traffic."

But it was long past dark when they returned, and Papa had been reconciled to going home in the morning. Mama noticed at once that both Karin and Nim were more relaxed than when they left. What had the man wanted with them? To reward them? Nim would never accept a reward for saving a man's life. But her intuition told her something had happened. Something more than just relief that the man would live. However, she said nothing. Nim would tell her when he was ready, whatever it was.

So it was a quite normal group who sat down to Mrs. Davis's fine supper. Nim was in better spirits, as though a great load had been lifted from his shoulders. Mama was pleased he had adjusted himself so well to the accident. He would see a lot of this kind of thing, unfortunately, as a doctor.

Mama and Mrs. Davis cleared away the dishes after

supper, and Nim and Karin went out for "a breath of air." Doctor Davis made a fire in the fireplace and got out his favorite pipe. He and Papa were back on the subject of fishing when Mama and Mrs. Davis returned to the living room. Presently Nim and Karin came in.

To Mama's surprise, Nim seemed quite nervous—not at all relaxed as he had been at supper. Before she had time to wonder about it, he said abruptly, "Karin and I have something to tell you. That is, I do; Karin agrees."

Doctor Davis put down his pipe and Papa leaned forward attentively. A log broke in the fireplace, the bright blaze sharply outlining the questioning faces turned toward Nim and Karin.

"I don't know quite how to say this, Doctor Davis," Nim began, "but I have to. Would you mind very much if I changed my mind about accepting your offer? I just have to be a surgeon! And Karin has agreed to wait for me until I've finished all my training and interning and . . ." He broke off, confused and embarrassed.

Mama's heart was in her throat, and Papa was staring at Nim as though he couldn't possibly be hearing right. Doctor Davis spoke in a quiet voice.

"Why don't you both sit down and you, Nim—start from the beginning."

"Well, I guess I am muddling this pretty badly," said Nim. He brought a chair for Karin and placed it beside Mama, then sat down opposite Doctor Davis.

"It wasn't just the accident yesterday that made me change my mind, although that had a good deal to do with it. All of you know that I have wanted to be a surgeon since I was ten years old and cut up my first frog." He was completely composed now and continued in a low voice. "Until I met Karin, there wasn't anything in the world that meant so much to me as reaching that goal. But when you find the *one* girl in ten million, you can't let her get away from you. I couldn't ask her to wait seven years until I could marry her and support her as a wife has the right to expect. And *I* didn't want to wait that long either. I thought I could be happy being a very good doctor and working to be good enough to take over your practice, Doctor Davis, when you wanted to retire—just as we planned. At first I *was* happy. Then I began to feel like a quitter—a man who was running out on something because it was too difficult, because it required sacrifices. It bothered me. I've worried about it all summer. Then yesterday when I realized how helpless we both were in the face of the need for surgery, and you said what you did, Doctor, I knew I *had* to go on and complete my work. Yes, even if it meant losing Karin—the biggest sacrifice I could be asked to make."

He got up and crossed the room to put his arm around Karin. "But this most wonderful of all girls loves me enough to wait *seven* years for me. Think of it. A miracle right from the Hand of God."

Although there was only devoutness in his remark, the lightness of his tone and the happiness in his face broke the tension which had held even Mama in silence since his first abrupt announcement.

Now there was a buzz of voices, all speaking at once. Finally Doctor Davis's deep voice rose above the others. "Since I am the loser in this deal, I think I should have the floor," he laughed. Then he spoke with seriousness. "Nim, I'm proud of you. Today you have found your real strength as a man. You'll make a great surgeon. I couldn't be prouder of you if you were my own son."

He got up and took Karin's hand in his. "And you, Karin. A doctor—*or* a minister—needs a fine wife, and your decision today has proved how fine you are." A smile came into his eyes. "And this young man better prove worthy of *you*, or I'll personally take him over my knees, big as he is, and give him a darned good paddling."

He was drowned out for a moment by laughter. "And now, since this is a very momentous occasion, Agnes, I think there's a gallon of sweet cider in the icebox. A toast to Surgeon Franzon and his beautiful and *patient* bride-to-be."

Much later, when the others had gone to bed, Mama went out onto the porch alone. A gentle wind stirred the great branches of the elms above her. Soft darkness enveloped the distant hills, now dimly outlined against the starry sky. Crickets sang their night song and from the lake came the deep-throated call of the frogs.

She remembered suddenly what Karin had said yesterday about a miracle on *her* mountain. And a miracle had happened. *Two* wondrous miracles. A man's life had been saved, and another man had found peace of mind and heart and the way of life God intended for him.

"Thank you, God," she whispered, her heart ready to burst with gratitude.

CHAPTER 16

Papa Climbs the Mountain

Winter came early that year. The tangy bright days, glorious with color, too soon gave way to leaden skies and somber barren branches, whipped by sharp winter winds. A full week before Thanksgiving, Mama awoke to a white world. The parsonage itself seemed strangely quiet as she slipped into her warm robe and stole softly downstairs. Pontus was still sleeping soundly. She let him sleep. It was Saturday and he needed this extra hour of rest.

She set the coffee to perking and laid the breakfast tray with special care. Lately she had noticed Pontus seemed to tire more easily. How little the church people realized the demands they made upon the strength of their pastor. Yet it was not in his nature to shirk what to him were his duties. Mama wanted to remind him that he wasn't as young as he once was, but she couldn't do that; he might feel she was complaining for her own sake. How could he even think such a thing? He had given her the most wonderful life any woman could ask. Still, she couldn't help worrying a little, and she prayed a silent prayer as she prepared breakfast.

The ticking of the kitchen clock sounded loudly in the room, reminding her again of the silence of the house.

Calle and Torkel had gone to the farm for the week end, Greta was spending the day with Button, and Kerstin was at Pelle's for the Thanksgiving holiday.

This is how it will be, she thought, when the children are all married and Pontus and I are alone.

The thought saddened her a little. It wasn't easy to let your children go, even when you knew they were happy in homes of their own. Not that she wouldn't be content with Pontus alone. But she would miss the excitement of the children's coming and going, the sharing of joys and disappointments as a family.

She shook herself out of such morbid thoughts. Here she was borrowing trouble for no reason. It would be a long time before all the children were married. With Nim's decision to postpone his marriage, Mama was sure the others would wait a while. Greta went to parties occasionally with Gunnar Olson, but she was far more interested in taking her master's degree, than in marriage. Calle preferred sports to dates with girls, and Torkel was intent upon following the profession Pelle had abandoned—teaching. Kerstin, of course, was too young even to think of marriage.

Yes, they would be together as a family for many years yet. And while Papa hadn't said so, she was sure he was pleased too. Two weddings in so short a time had made heavy demands upon his bank account.

She picked up the breakfast tray and started upstairs. Then she remembered the mail. She ran through it quickly and stopped at one with a Swedish postmark. From Deacon Lund! She put it on the tray and hurried upstairs.

Papa read the letter through, between sips of black coffee, before he spoke. "We might do it, at that," he said irrelevantly.

"Do what, Pontus?" Mama laughed. "How do you think I know what is in your letter?"

"I'm sorry, Maria. It's from Deacon Lund. He writes—but here; you had better read it yourself."

" 'Dear Pastor Franzon,' " Mama read aloud, then

skimmed through the pages until she came to the part Papa was referring to. " 'Pastor Engwall is taking two months' vacation next summer to visit relatives in England. We wonder if it would be possible for you to take over your old pulpit during his absence? It has been a long time since you left us for America, and I'm sure a visit to your homeland would bring joy to your heart as it would to all of ours. The parsonage will be at your disposal, and it is our hope that Mrs. Franzon will be able to accompany you. I'm sure I do not need to tell you how much your coming would mean to all of us, and we shall do everything possible to make your stay here both pleasant and restful . . .' "

Mama was too excited to read more. "Oh, Pontus, how wonderful! Do you think we *could* go?"

"Well, after two weddings, it might take some planning. But we still have the 'Home-to-Lapland' fund—remember?"

Until that moment, Mama *had* forgotten it. But it was only five hundred dollars. Traveling was more expensive now than it was when she had planned the surprise for Pontus. He would need that much at least for his own passage and expenses. And it wouldn't be fair to expect him to cut deeper into his bank account when he had spent so much already for weddings. She would love to go with him, but now it was important that Pontus go. Doubly important. He badly needed a long rest. The ocean voyage and seeing his beloved Lapland again would be just the best medicine in the world for him.

"I remember, Pontus," Mama laughed. "It seemed like such a lot of money then. I guess that was because I baked so many thousand cookies to earn it. But it wouldn't take us very far now."

Papa didn't say anything, just went on drinking his coffee, and Mama wondered if he was remembering how unhappy those cookies had made him.

Presently he set down his coffee cup, and when Mama looked up there was a smile behind his eyes trying to break through. Why, even the *hope* of seeing Lapland again, she thought, was like a tonic.

"Maria," he began, "do you remember the night you and the children presented me with the money for the trip back to Lapland?"

"Why, of course, Pontus."

"And I told you we'd put it in a 'Home-to-Lapland' fund, and maybe it would grow, like the Franzon family?"

Mama nodded.

"Well, I guess I had better tell you that is what has happened. All the money Steve has paid me from the farm, I put into the fund. And by the time we are ready to leave for Sweden, it will be very well nourished indeed."

"Oh, Pontus! Then we *can* go."

"That, Maria, is what I have been trying to tell you."

And so it was that some six months later, on a bright June morning, Mama stood beside Papa on deck of the Swedish-American liner, both straining their eyes for the first glimpse of *Vinga Fyr*.

"Look, Maria," Papa exclaimed. "It's only a little after five and that sun is shining as brightly as noonday in America."

Mama looked, but mostly at Papa. His cheeks glowed and his eyes were alight with excitement. This was the day he had waited for so many years. She had thought she knew how much "coming home" would mean to him, but now she felt a little pang of guilt that she could not completely share his happiness. It was a feeling so deep no one really could share it. Pontus was a true Swede. All those years in America had not dimmed his loyalty to his homeland; whereas she had loved America, almost from her first day in the new country, quite as much as she loved Sweden. For America had given their children a chance at education—the chance to dream dreams and see them fulfilled.

"Today we are landing, Maria," Papa said with subdued excitement. There were tears in his eyes now, and his voice shook with emotion. "Soon we shall stand once more on Swedish soil. How good God has been to us!"

Mama's throat tightened, but the words she wanted to speak would not come. Now for the first time she fully realized the sacrifice he had made so many years ago. And never a word of complaint from him in all those years.

They had been alone on deck, having come up early to offer a prayer of thanks for the safe and wonderful journey. Now other excited, eager passengers began to line the rail and crowd the deck, each scanning the horizon for the first glimpse of their homeland.

Presently a shout went up and almost simultaneously hundreds of voices broke into the Swedish National Hymn. At first they sang softly, prayerfully, then the music swelled into a mighty chorus, echoing across the bright waters.

> "Du gamla du fria
> Du fjällhöga Nord
> Du tysta du glädjerika sköna. . . ."

Papa stood reverently, hat in hand, but with head held high. A shameless tear rolled down each cheek, while he sang with the vigor of youth. Mama could not help joining in with:

> "Ack jag vill leva
> Jag vill dö i Norden. . . ."

How true were the words—old pilgrims returning home! Mama was wiping her eyes now along with others. This was her homeland too, even if she was happy in America.

When the first exciting, hectic moments of landing were over, Mama finally stood beside Papa, confronted, across their opened trunks and suitcases, by a stern customs officer. She smiled her nicest smile.

"I assure you, Officer, we are not smugglers. My husband is a *minister*. We are very happy to be in Sweden again."

"Minister or not, the law is the law," he said gruffly. "Now let's see what you have here." He picked up one of Pontus's white shirts and started shaking it.

"I don't know what you expect to find hidden in that," Mama said sharply.

"You'd be surprised, lady. The couple ahead of you was a home-loving pair and *so happy* to be back in Sweden. And what do you think I found? Fifty packages of cigarettes wrapped in a nightgown! Now let me see what you have in that shirt."

Mama said no more, but Papa laughed. "You'd better not wrinkle that shirt, Officer. My wife is very particular about my appearance."

The officer glanced suspiciously at Papa before folding the shirt carefully. And then to Mama's surprise, he winked at Papa. Why, he wasn't as cross as he sounded, thought Mama. He must get awfully tired going through so many trunks and bags. Unfortunately, everyone *wasn't* as honest as Pontus.

With their luggage safely on the way to the central railroad station, Papa linked his arm in Mama's. "Let's walk, Maria. Just to get the feel of home soil under our feet."

Göteborg was a busy harbor city, but Mama couldn't help noticing how clean it was; not at all like American harbor towns she had seen. It seemed almost no time before they were comfortably seated in the train for Stockholm, where they would change trains for Lapland.

Mama settled back, watching the beautiful Swedish countryside rush by. She had really forgotten how green the forests were in summer and how blue and placid were the lakes. And the farms! As neat as pictures with their red-and-white barns surrounded by flower gardens. Cows grazed in the broad meadows and red-cheeked children, flaxen-haired and blue-eyed, hung on the fences, shouting and waving as the train rushed past.

"It hasn't changed at all, Maria," exclaimed Papa. "Praise God for that! It is as though time had been standing still right here in Sweden."

"It's true, Pontus. I guess I had forgotten just how beautiful it is. But America is beautiful, too; and she has been good to us and our children. We must not forget that either."

Papa laughed. "Always loyal to America, aren't you, Maria?"

When the train finally reached Stockholm, Papa discovered it was a few hours before the fast express left for Lapland. Time enough to visit the ancient capital and stroll along the banks of Lake Mälaren, lying like a great mirror in the golden light of the never-ending day.

"Such peace and contentment, Maria. Nowhere in the world is there so much."

"I know, Pontus. But you must remember we are in a country that has not known war for almost two hundred years. Contented, peaceful *people* live here."

"It could be like this everywhere, Maria, if human beings would only live by God's law and try to be kind to one another."

"Yes, Pontus. But countries are like children. They have to grow up. Sweden is old and wise. America is still young and lighthearted—and sometimes like a spoiled child too. But one day America will be old, like Sweden, and when that day comes, I think she will be wise also."

Early that afternoon they boarded the train for Lapland, their journey's end, and reunion with all their old and dear friends. This was the longest part of the trip. As the train rushed northward, new and different scenes swept into view. Tall straight pines and spruce, towering beside broad swift rivers, replaced the dense green forests seen earlier. Noisy waterfalls instead of placid blue lakes.

Here was a wild, savage beauty to challenge the physical strength of any man and woman. Perhaps, thought Mama, that was why Sweden did not have wars—its people were too busy living and enjoying their own country to want the countries of others.

The hours seemed to pass with the speed of the train. Presently Mama's attention was pulled away from the landscape by the sound of soft snoring. Dear Pontus! His tired body had finally won out over his excitement. His head rested easily against the back of the seat. His cheeks were flushed like a child with fever, but a smile still lingered about his mouth. His white hair, longer than he usually wore it, curled softly about his temples. But for the whiteness of his hair, Mama thought, he would look like a very young man. Sometimes it was difficult for her to believe he was actually seventy-one years old.

Even before the train had come to a full stop, Mama had spotted Tant Renberg in the crowd that waited to greet them.

"Maria, I think the whole church is here to welcome us."

"There's Tant, Pontus. Look how tiny she has become."

"And the Lunds, and the Ericksons, and . . ."

The train screeched to a stop, and in a moment Mama and Papa were surrounded by a happy, laughing crowd of old friends and neighbors, and many new faces.

Presently Deacon Lund clapped his hands for attention. Gradually the happy chatter died, then he lifted his hand, a signal for the singing of a hymn of welcome. What wonderful people they are, thought Mama. It seemed only yesterday that she had stood on this very station platform, with Pontus and the children, listening to speeches and songs of *farewell* and finally the strains of "God Be With You 'Til We Meet Again," fading into the distance as the train gathered speed, taking them away from Lapland.

Now Deacon Lund was speaking, a quiver in his voice which Mama decided was more from emotion than his advancing years.

"This is a happy moment for all of us. We bid you welcome, Pastor and Maria Franzon. Welcome to your homeland! We only hope your visit here will be so pleasant you will not want to return to America."

The applause drowned out his voice for a moment. Then:

"And now we know you must be tired from your long journey. And hungry! The ladies have prepared a delicious picnic-supper for everyone, which will be served on our lawn."

Mama was tired, and she knew how tired Pontus was. But it was a happy tiredness, and they could not disappoint their wonderful friends. How strange it was. A picnic at nine o'clock at night, and the sun shining brightly.

It was still shining, two hours later, when they stood on the parsonage steps, saying good night to Deacon Lund.

Inside the parsonage, time truly rolled back. Except that the furniture was worn, everything was the same. Silently they walked from room to room, all so filled with memories. The table in *salen*, with Button's tooth marks still visible, reminded them both of the spanking she had received. The footstool on which Mama had sat every Saturday night to shine the shoes. And Papa's beautiful mahogany desk with the high-backed chair, where he had prepared so many inspiring sermons. The *vardags*-room where they had spent many happy hours with the children.

It was when they reached the bedroom, where the picture of Mama's model still hung, that she broke down, weeping softly and smiling through her tears.

"Oh Pontus! It *was* a wonderful model, wasn't it? The children are so fine, so beautiful."

Papa put his arm about her shoulders. "It was indeed, Maria." Then he laughed softly. "But I don't think the boys would exactly appreciate being called beautiful."

Downstairs again, Papa found his old comfortable rocker, and for a while, tired as they were, they sat in silence, Mama's hand in his, while memories poured through their hearts and minds like a mountain stream flowing backward.

"You know, Maria," Papa finally said, "they were wonderful years here in the parsonage. But some of those times I'm glad we shall not have to live over."

"Like the nights you walked the floor with Button?" Mama laughed. "Or the Sunday Torkel painted his face with ink to look like a heathen, after he had heard the missionary from India?"

Papa chuckled softly. "Those too. But I was thinking particularly," he said soberly, "of the night Calle's temperature soared to a hundred and five degrees and we despaired of saving him. But God heard our prayers that night, as He has so many times since."

Mama sighed a happy sigh. "Yes, Pontus. We have so much to be thankful for. God has been very good to us."

She was remembering their conversation the next morning, as she let her eyes feast on the splendid view from the kitchen window. Life was made up of joy and sorrow —balanced measures of each—so that you appreciated the joy more because of the dark hours. Like dark strands woven with threads of gold in a fine tapestry, but to which, at the time of weaving, you were too close to understand its values.

The big homey kitchen was filled now with the aroma of herring sizzling in the frying pan. On the back of the stove, plump brown potatoes were bursting from their jackets.

"Just like old times," Mama said aloud to herself, as she sliced the loaf of fresh *limpa*-bread Tant Renberg had brought her, and spread each slice thickly with butter.

After breakfast, Papa went to the study to prepare his Sunday sermon.

So the days passed—peaceful happy days, bright pages from the past. Mama wondered about the children, how they were managing without her, but she said nothing, for Pontus must not think she was impatient to return to America. Or know how much she missed the children.

Midsummer Eve fell on Sunday that year. The church was beautifully decorated with newly cut tree branches which stood in great clusters about the altar, filling the whole chapel with spicy fragrance. And there wasn't an empty pew! Mama's heartbeat quickened with pride as Pontus took his place behind the high pulpit and slowly opened the big Bible. A shaft of sunlight from the small window behind him, fell over his white hair like a bright crown. The chapel was hushed, waiting.

"I shall read to you this morning from the seventh chapter of St. Matthew: 'Judge not, that ye be not judged. For with what judgment ye judge, ye shall be judged; and with what measure ye mete, it shall be measured to you again. . . .'"

How full and sure his voice was, Mama thought. Like the music of an organ. It was as though she were hearing him for the first time—that long-ago Sunday morning when she had lost her heart to him completely. For several moments she let her mind drift in treasured memory. Then the sound of her own name brought her back.

". . . . Maria and I, as most of you, will again climb the old mountain to behold the miracle of the never-setting sun, and to praise God for such mighty wonders. But let us remember that life is very much like the climbing of a mountain. We must reach the heights before we can behold the view. And in like manner do we all see the world from different levels, for we have not all come the same journey. How, therefore, can we afford to judge each other? Consider first the distance you have climbed. Has he, whom you would judge, reached the same pinnacle of wisdom and faith? For in the fullness of God's promise, the higher we climb, the smaller become the things of earth—doubts, envy, fear, selfishness. And the nearer your Heaven. . . ."

Later Mama stood beside Papa at the door of the church, her heart filled with thankfulness as she listened to the words of praise from these good people. "A wonderful sermon, Pastor Franzon. . . ." "I needed that ser-

mon. . . ." "It's like old times having you with us, Pastor
Franzon. . . ."

And finally all were gone, leaving Mama and Papa alone
in the quiet church.

"Come, Maria," Papa said fervently, "let us offer a special prayer of gratitude for this day."

As she knelt beside him at the little altar, Mama was
acutely aware of the long procession of weary, truth-
hungry souls that had found help and guidance in this
small white church; souls led from darkness into the light
of true spiritual love, as God had spoken to them through
Pontus's sermons.

Wordlessly they arose and walked down the narrow
aisle, closing the door softly, reverently, behind them.
Only when they were outside did Papa speak. "I hope no
one was hurt because we refused the many dinner invitations."

"I'm sure they understood, Pontus lilla, how many
memories we have to live over again. How wonderful it is
for us to be back in the old parsonage. And, besides, we
aren't as young as we once were, remember. We shall need
to rest before we climb that mountain tomorrow."

Papa brightened at the mention of the excursion. "I still
can't believe it, Maria. That we shall once again see the
midnight sun from the top of old Gellivara mountain!"

The morning of Midsummer Day was as perfect as a
dream. The sun shone from a forget-me-not sky, with not
a cloud in sight. Papa was in high spirits as they began the
ascent along the mountain trail.

"Have I ever told you how beautiful you are, Mrs.
Franzon?" he teased.

Mama looked up at him, the old mischievous twinkle
in her eyes. "I think you might have, Pontus lilla—once
or twice in about thirty years!"

But Papa did not laugh. "The worst of it is, Maria, it's
true. I wish now I had told you every time I thought it."

Mama blushed in embarrassment. "Why, Pontus, darling, you know you did not have to tell me; I always

knew." But she was remembering the early days of their marriage, before Papa got used to love, and how many times she had woven fanciful dreams, imagining that he spoke to her as he was speaking now.

"You have made my life so rich and happy, Maria. On this perfect day I think I should tell you how much I love you. Have you never wished you were not married to an old gray man?"

The tightness in Mama's throat lessened with laughter. "Oh, Pontus! How can you ever think such a thing? Love does not die when the body grows older."

As the path became steeper, Mama noticed how heavily Papa was breathing. But his step was firm, and his cheeks pink as a young boy's. He had taken off his cap, and the wind, more noticeable at this height, ruffled his white hair. He might have been a patriarch, stepped from the Bible.

"When we reach that rock," Papa panted, pointing upward, "we had better have some of that coffee. I guess I'm not used to mountain climbing any more. I feel a bit winded."

Coffee and *Vienerbröd* always seemed to taste better in the open, Mama imagined, filling Pontus's cup the second time. And it was good to rest a while. She hadn't realized how tired she was until she sat down. Pontus finished his cup of coffee, then leaned against the back-rock and closed his eyes. It was then she noticed the perspiration beading his forehead and how pale he had suddenly become.

"Why don't you take a little nap, darling? We'll still be able to reach the top in time."

"I think I will, Maria. I *am* tired. And a little dizzy. I guess the altitude—"

He stopped suddenly. Mama regarded him with alarm.

"Just rest, darling," she urged.

She should never have permitted him to attempt this climb. She should have pretended it would be too much for *her*. But he had so wanted to see the midnight sun from the top of the mountain; and she had forgotten he wasn't used to such strenuous exercise. She was deeply worried.

"Maria," Papa said weakly, "we cannot go on to the top. I'm sorry. I hope you won't be too disappointed." He paused, breathing with difficulty. "I think we had better start down again . . . slowly. . . ."

For a moment panic seized her. He would never make it back to the parsonage. She had to find help. But where? With an effort she controlled the fear that was smothering her reason. "Wait here, Pontus *lilla*. There will be others on the trail. I will bring help as quickly as I can."

She ran down the trail as fast as she could, praying that soon she would meet someone. An endless time later she heard voices, and rounded the bend to come face to face with two young men. Quickly, breathlessly, she told them what had happened and urged them to hurry.

Time stopped for her after that. But it must have been many hours later that she sat beside Pontus, lying pale and still in the big parsonage bed. He had not spoken since she had left him on the mountain trail to find help. Her own throat was choked with tears, but she could not cry. She must not. Through the long night hours she sat beside him, listening to his labored breathing. Dimly she was aware of Tant Renberg and Deacon Lund moving about downstairs. How good they were to wait with her— ready to help in any way they could.

Toward morning, Papa stirred and opened his eyes. He smiled weakly and lifted his hand. Mama took it, pressing it tightly in her own as though she could hold back the curtain of darkness she now knew was closing about him.

"Thank you, Maria," he whispered, ". . . for bringing me home."

It was her stifled cry of grief which brought Tant and Deacon Lund to the bedside. Gently Deacon Lund drew the sheet over Papa's face, now so white and peaceful. Tant Renberg's sobbing mingled with her own.

"Oh, why, Maria, *why?* How could God let this happen?"

Deacon Lund placed a comforting hand on their shoulders. "God never makes a mistake. Pastor Franzon taught us that. He will sleep now, where he would have wanted to sleep his last sleep—in Swedish soil."

Later, when they had taken him away, Mama asked to be left alone in the room for a while. And when they had gone, she dropped to her knees beside the bed and buried her face in her hands. "Dear God," she prayed from the very depth of her soul, "help me not to grieve—to willingly let him return to You and the Heaven he so well deserves."

In those moments, alone with her God, it seemed to Mama that a new strength and a deeper understanding poured into her mind and soul; as though God spoke to her with infinite compassion: *He could not climb the mountain with his tired earthly body. I have given him new life—life everlasting—that he may climb ever higher —upward—upward. . . .*

Without Pontus, Mama had no wish to remain in Lapland. Wonderfully kind and thoughtful as everyone had been to her, she was eager to return to the children. For now that the cable had reached them, bearing its saddening message, her place she felt was with them; to comfort them with the knowledge that Papa had said farewell to life as he would have wished to; that his last days had been gloriously happy.

She had spent the past week in Tant Renberg's neat little home. Deacon Lund had taken care of arranging an earlier passage back to America than she and Papa had originally planned. Then, alone, she had gone to the parsonage to bid farewell to the rich, dear memories it would always hold for her. Slowly she walked about each room, living over again every moment from that first day, as a young girl barely sixteen, when she had sat on the rose-

colored sofa and convinced Papa he should hire her as a
maid, to the last evening they had enjoyed together.

Now she stood alone on the deck of the big ship, waving a final farewell to *Vinga Fyr*. The wind, blowing in
from the North Sea, whipped the great waves into emerald
foam. Mama tied the scarf closer about her hair and lifted
her face to the wind. An unconscious gesture with which
she would face the future without Papa. But no! Papa
would never *leave* her. It was true that his body slept in
the little cemetery beside the big State Church; that loving
hands would plant flowers and the grass would grow
green each summer over his resting place; and the birds
would sing above him in the day-long sunshine. Snow
would cover him with a soft white blanket, and the years
would come and go. But always his spirit would walk beside her—close—so very close. Until one day she too would
walk into the golden sunset and find him waiting to greet
her.

Mama brushed the tears from her eyes—tears not of sorrow, but for renewed faith. Presently she went below to
her cabin for the long journey home.

Mama had been back in America a little more than a
month when Vickey brought her the news.

It had been a busy time, moving from the parsonage into
her own little home on the same tree-shaded street, to
make way for the new pastor who would arrive in September. A time of stirring old memories again and of finding new happiness. It seemed to Mama that suddenly all
her children were grown-up, each of them wanting to take
care of her, concealing their own deep feeling of loss so
that her own might be lessened. But it was Nim who had
taken Papa's place in material things—the way Papa himself had planned—and revealed to her for the first time
how thoughtfully and well Papa had provided for her and
the children when he no longer would be with them. He
had even arranged, before they left for Sweden, for Steve
to buy the farm. Could Papa have sensed, Mama won-

dered, that his time on earth was almost ended? Had he
known his heart was weakening, but kept the knowledge
from her, lest she worry about him? Dear Pontus!

Mama sighed deeply. A thankful, comforting sigh, feeling Papa's nearness as she had every moment since her
return to America.

After a while she picked up her sewing again—a new
dress for Kerstin to wear to the concert on Saturday. It
would be her very first date with a boy; a nice, tall, well-
mannered boy, whom Kerstin explained she had met at the
Fourth-of-July picnic.

"Oh, Kerstin," Mama had exclaimed when she learned
of it, "you're too young. You're my *baby!*"

Kerstin had drawn herself up to her full five-feet-two,
in utter disdain. "I'm *not* a baby, Mama. I'm almost sixteen. And besides, it's *just* a concert. Konrad loves music
as much as I do."

There was nothing more Mama could say. It was true.
Kerstin had somehow passed out of childhood in those few
weeks Mama had been in Sweden.

So as soon as the family was settled in their new home,
she had asked Kerstin to bring her friend to tea. He was
a quiet, serious-faced boy, whose father was an engineer
with the Telephone Company. Mama was sure Papa
would have approved of the boy, but she wasn't sure how
he would have regarded little Kerstin having dates. . . .

The music of chimes sounded through the house. It
was a second before Mama realized it was that newfangled
doorbell Pelle and Felicia had given her. She put aside her
sewing and hurried to the door.

"Vickey," she greeted her daughter. "What a lovely
surprise."

"*I'm* not the surprise, Mama." Vickey was so excited
she could hardly talk. "But I have a surprise for you. A
glorious surprise."

"Well, take off your hat and sit down and tell me about
it. Before you explode."

Suddenly Vickey threw her arms around Mama and

started to cry. "Oh, Mama, I can't wait to tell you. It's a baby—my very own baby at last."

"*Your* baby? What about John?" Mama chuckled. "And why are you crying?"

Vickey was laughing now through her tears. "You know I always cry when I'm happy. Isn't it wonderful, Mama?"

"The most wonderful thing in the whole world, darling." Mama held her in her arms for a moment while she got control of her own emotions. "Now sit down and I'll bring you a cup of coffee, and then you can tell me all about it."

Mama was almost as excited as Vickey. Her hand shook visibly as she poured the coffee. Her first grandchild! And she was especially glad that it was to be Vickey and John's child. Now their dream was to come true.

Long after Vickey had left to tell Button the happy news, Mama still sat in the quiet room, her sewing forgotten in her lap, her head bowed in silent prayer. God in His infinite wisdom—His perfect planning—was sending a new little life for her to love and cherish. Soon the house would echo again with children's laughter. A new generation would be growing up to replace the old. God's glorious plan of creation—an endless cycle of lives coming and going—timeless, eternal.

Suddenly Mama sat up, her eyes wide. Then she began to laugh.

"Oh, Pontus *lilla*," she said aloud. "I'll no longer be just Papa's wife. I'll be Grandma Franzon!"

But was there anything in the whole wide world more beautiful than a baby—your very own little grandchild?

ABOUT THE AUTHOR

THYRA FERRÉ BJORN was born in a small village in Swedish Lapland, the daughter of a Baptist minister, and one of eight children. The family came to America in 1924 when the father was called by a Swedish church in Springfield, Massachusetts.

Thyra met and married Robert John Bjorn, a native of Sweden. They live in Longmeadow, Massachusetts, where Mrs. Bjorn is prominent in church and civic affairs and has become popular as a lecturer.

In addition to *Papa's Wife*, which is based on the author's reminiscences of her early life, she has also written *Papa's Daughter* (1958), *Mama's Way* (1959), *Dear Papa* (1963), and *Once Upon a Christmastime* (1964).

Bantam Book Catalog

It lists over a thousand money-saving best-sellers originally priced from $3.75 to $15.00 —bestsellers that are yours now for as little as 60¢ to $2.95!

The catalog gives you a great opportunity to build your own private library at huge savings!

So don't delay any longer—send us your name and address and 25¢ (to help defray postage and handling costs).